Lincolnshire
COUNTY COUNCIL

COMMUNITIES, CULTURAL SERVICES
and ADULT EDUCATION
This book should be returned on or before
the last date shown below.

CM1

ONK 02|15

- 8 APR 2015

2 7 MAY

2 JUL

To renew or order library books please telephone 01522 782010
or visit www.lincolnshire.gov.uk
You will require a Personal Identification Number.
Ask any member of staff for this.

EC. 199 (LIBS): RS/L5/19

A FATHER'S REVENGE

Thirteen years ago Kevin Dolby was sent to prison for a violent robbery. Upon his release, he sets in motion a chilling plan to get what is owed to him. Kevin's ex-wife Pearl left her old life in Battersea and re-married, determined to protect her son John from knowing the truth about his real father. But when her friend Bessie dies, Pearl makes plans to take over Bessie's shop and look after Nora, the young woman who was in Bessie's care, while Kevin is swindling his parents for money. Once he gets what he wants, Kevin is going to find his son, whatever it takes...

A FATHER'S REVENGE

by

Kitty Neale

Magna Large Print Books
Long Preston, North Yorkshire,
BD23 4ND, England.

British Library Cataloguing in Publication Data.

Neale, Kitty
    A father's revenge.

A catalogue record of this book is
available from the British Library

  ISBN   978-0-7505-3683-7

First published in Great Britain in 2011 by
HarperCollins*Publishers*

Copyright © Kitty Neale 2011

Cover illustration © Mirrorpix

Kitty Neale asserts the moral right to be identified as the author of
this work

Published in Large Print 2013 by arrangement with
HarperCollins Publishers

Magna Large Print is an imprint of Library Magna Books Ltd.

Printed and bound in Great Britain by
T.J. (International) Ltd., Cornwall, PL28 8RW

For Nobby Dack who sadly died earlier this year; a husband, father and grandfather who is sorely missed. My love and thoughts are with his family.

Acknowledgements

To Georgina Baskerville, for kindly suggesting the character Adrianna, and sparking my imagination.

Also to Judith Broadbent, a journalist and kindred spirit whom I met when she travelled to Spain to join us in a charity event in aid of Help for Heroes.

And not forgetting my husband for his support while I'm writing, along with checking the manuscript; and my daughter, Samantha Hurren, who brings so much sunshine into my life.

Prologue

Wandsworth Prison, 1970

If he torched the place, how long would it take for their bodies to burn?

He wanted them to suffer a prolonged, painful death, and now, as Kevin Dolby imagined his parents' screams, he chuckled. While serving his sentence, he'd had years to brood, his hate festering until it had become an obsession. It was his mother's fault that he was serving time and to top that he'd been cut out of their will. Him, their only son and heir!

He would punish them. They'd suffer. He'd see to that.

In his dismal cell, Kevin had fantasised about the many ways he could end their lives, but twice so far the parole board had denied him early release. He'd been a mug, played the hard man, had time added on after attacking his cellmate, but at last he had begun playing the game. Now, after serving thirteen years of a fifteen-year sentence, Kevin had 'found' religion – or so they thought. He'd become a consummate actor with his meek and mild manner, a 'reformed' character.

He was sure that he'd be granted parole this time – that he'd soon be free and ready to exact his revenge. Another scenario began to form in Kevin's mind, this time taking into account that it couldn't reach its finale until his parents had changed their will in his favour again. To make that happen he'd have to lull them into a false sense of security ... play the part of a loving son.

A scowl marred his handsome face. *Love!* It wasn't love he felt for them. It was hate!

Chapter One

Dolly Dolby smiled at her secret. For so long she had been woolly-minded, medicated after her mental breakdown, but just lately she had surreptitiously stopped taking the pills that Bernie, her husband, fed her. She felt that her mind had come alive again, that she was in control and thinking clearly for the first time in years.

It was a lovely spring day in March and Dolly was looking forward to seeing John, her grandson. He was the image of his handsome and dark-haired father, so like Kevin that every time she saw him her heart jolted.

Kevin was in prison, serving a fifteen-year sentence for robbery with violence, and had refused to allow her to visit him. She had no idea why, but then, to her joy, he had at last replied to one of her letters. The first thing she'd noticed when she went to see him was that Kevin's eyes now burned with religious fervour and it was as though her son had been reborn. He wrote regularly now, his letters full of his plans to help others when he was released, and though until then she hadn't had much time for religion, Dolly had gone down on her knees and thanked God for her son's religious conversion.

At last Dolly heard the sound of a car pulling up outside their cottage which sat on a quiet lane on the outskirts of a village near Southsea in Hamp-

13

shire. They had no close neighbours, though that didn't bother Dolly. Nowadays she preferred seclusion. She had once owned a café in Battersea, London, and ruled the roost. No one had dared to cross her, but her world collapsed when Kevin had been arrested. There had been so much gossip, the story reaching the newspapers, and she'd been brought low with shame.

However, many long years had passed since then and pushing the memories to one side, Dolly flung open the street door. Her husband Bernie had taken to gardening with a passion and some of the daffodils were in bloom, but Dolly only had eyes for her grandson as he walked up the path.

'Hello, Gran,' John said, briefly accepting a cuddle before pulling away.

Dolly flinched, upset that he wasn't more affectionate with her. Kevin had once rejected her too, and now his son was doing the same. No, stop it, stop being silly, she told herself. John was nearly thirteen years old now, no longer a little boy who wanted hugs. She had to control herself, had to stop imagining slights where none was intended. Briefly touching John's shoulder, Dolly ushered him inside.

'You took your time,' she said huffily to Bernie.

Bernie frowned and for a moment he looked at her intently. 'You seem to forget it's a two-hour round trip to Winchester and back.'

Dolly didn't want Bernie to realise that she hadn't been taking her pills. 'Sorry, love,' she said meekly. 'It's just that I couldn't wait to see John and the time seemed to drag. I expect you could do with a cup of tea?'

'Yes please,' he said, 'and I might as well tell you now that Pearl wants John back by four. They're having a bit of a do.'

Dolly's lips pursed at the mention of Pearl. She had no time for John's mother, never had. It didn't matter how many years had passed, she refused to talk to her and even sacrificed calling John on the telephone in case it was Pearl who answered it.

Pearl had been a naive sixteen-year-old when Dolly first met her. She had been a thin, nervous, mousy little thing with huge brown eyes that seemed to take up much of her face. However she'd blossomed, ensnaring Kevin by becoming pregnant with his child. Dolly tried to prevent the marriage, to prove Pearl a tart, but then Kevin admitted she'd been a virgin. With no other choice, they had married, but Pearl then turned Kevin against her – his own mother. Dolly would never forgive her for that.

'Dolly, did you hear what I said?' Bernie asked.

'Yes,' she said, dragging her thoughts back to the present. 'Why is Pearl having a bit of a do?'

'It's her mother's fiftieth birthday.'

Nobody had made a fuss when it was *her* birthday, Dolly thought. Not only that Pearl's mother, Emily Harmsworth, got to see John every day, not just once a month, and now even this visit was being curtailed. It still rankled that when Pearl had divorced Kevin she'd been granted sole custody of John, and from the start she had laid down the rules. There was only one that Dolly agreed with: that John should be told only that his father was in prison for robbery and the rest kept from him.

Dolly forced a smile as she tousled John's hair. 'I'd planned to cook you a lovely dinner, but never mind,' she said, pretending acquiescence to Pearl's demand for his early return, 'I'll do us a nice lunch instead.'

'Smashing,' said John, grinning.

Dolly led him into their sitting-cum-dining room which was overstuffed with heavy, mahogany furniture. It had come from their previous home, but looked a bit out of place in this low-beamed cottage.

'Sit down, love,' she said to John, thinking that though Pearl held the upper hand now, things were set to change. Kevin had been turned down last year, but he'd written to say that he was sure to get parole this time. Yes, Dolly told herself, of course he would, and as soon as the prison gates opened for her son she'd be ready to act. If Bernie dared to stand in her way she'd show him who was boss again, and if Pearl and Derek Lewis, her second husband, tried to stop Kevin from seeing his son, they'd have her to deal with.

Bernie looked at Dolly as she went through to the small back kitchen. She was fifty-five years old now, her brown hair greying, yet even when she had been young there was no way that Dolly could've been described as pretty, or even attractive. Far from it. She was tall and big-boned, with a broad, plain face over wide shoulders.

Of course, Bernie thought, he was no oil painting either. He was shorter than Dolly, with a paunch, and at fifty-six years old, almost bald now.

16

Their marriage couldn't be described as a love match: it had been forced on them by their respective parents when Dolly had been three months pregnant. From the moment she'd given birth, Kevin had been the centre of Dolly's world, and Bernie had hardly been allowed a say in the boy's upbringing.

Bernie's lips tightened. He'd been unhappy with the situation, with the way Dolly ruled him, but too weak to do anything about it. He'd stuck it out, because though divorce was commonplace now, in his day it was unheard of. Not only that, Dolly had held the purse strings and kept him short with a paltry few quid a week. Of course, Bernie reflected, that had been in the distant past and things were a lot different now – he was the one in control of their finances.

'I saw a jay last week, Granddad.'

'Did you now?' Bernie said as he sat down opposite John. 'They're lovely birds.'

Dolly appeared in the kitchen doorway, saying, 'Do you both fancy macaroni cheese for lunch?'

'Sounds good to me,' Bernie said and John agreed with him.

Bernie was unwinding after the long drive, yet found himself thinking back to when Dolly had her breakdown. For the first time in their marriage she had turned to him. He had seen another side of her, her vulnerability, for a short time, but then she had lost it completely and had been sent to a psychiatric hospital. The electroconvulsive treatment Dolly had received seemed to shrink her, and she'd developed a stoop along with a shuffle when she walked. He had seen his once

17

formidable wife diminished, and after each session Dolly appeared disorientated. It had affected her memory too, sometimes temporarily, yet there were other things she'd forgotten permanently.

'Here you are,' Dolly said as she placed a cup of tea in front of him, along with a glass of orange juice for John. She then went back to the kitchen and returned with a plate of chocolate biscuits. 'Don't eat too many or you'll spoil your lunch.'

Bernie winked at his grandson. 'I've got a sweet tooth so dig in or I'll scoff the lot.'

They munched companionably while Bernie's thoughts drifted again. Dolly had forgotten that when Kevin had been sent to prison, the thought of losing her grandson too when Pearl left, had turned her mind. John had been just a baby when Dolly had run off with him, and it was only thanks to Pearl's largesse that she hadn't been charged. Instead Dolly had been admitted to the psychiatric hospital and when she finally came home, it was again thanks to Pearl's kindness that they saw their grandson regularly.

Bernie's ears pricked up when Dolly spoke to John.

'Did you know that we once had a café in Battersea?' she asked.

'Yes, Gran, you told me, and my dad used to live in Battersea too. He ran a boxing club.'

'You're talking about Derek Lewis and he's not your real father,' Dolly snapped. 'You seem to forget that your name isn't Lewis – it's Dolby.'

Bernie tensed. There was something different about Dolly lately. For one thing she was standing straighter and at times, like now, she seemed

18

almost argumentative. Of course it could be that she was stimulated by John's visit. That could explain it, and there was the added excitement of Kevin's letter to say that his parole was likely to be granted.

Or was it that her medication needed adjusting? Worried now that Dolly was becoming psychotic again, and remembering the woman she had once been, who had thought nothing of laying into him with her fists to get her own way, Bernie decided to keep a closer watch on her. If she didn't quieten down, he'd ask the doctor to increase her medication.

John was used to his gran being a bit unfocused, but today she appeared more alert than usual, her dark brown eyes brighter than he'd ever seen them before.

She'd been annoyed that he had called Derek his dad, but he was the only father he'd known. Derek was great, but despite that John was curious about his real father and said, 'Gran, can I look at your photograph album again?'

'Yes, of course,' she said, her tone milder as she took it from the sideboard drawer.

John turned the pages, struck as always by the similarities as he looked at the grainy black and white snaps of his real father. 'I look just like him, Gran.'

'You certainly do. You're a chip off the old block.'

John peered intently at his father's face and said, 'I wish I knew more about him.'

'Kevin was a good lad, and when he left school he became an apprentice engineer. When he got

19

his papers he worked in an engineering factory for a while, but then he got in with the wrong crowd. They led him astray and that's how he ended up in prison.'

'I'd like to see him, but I'm not allowed,' John muttered.

'I know and it's disgraceful! You should tell your mother that you have every right to visit your father if you want to.'

'That's enough, Dolly!' Bernie chipped in, sounding annoyed. 'You know Kevin gave instructions that he didn't want John to see him while he's in prison.'

'Did he? But I don't remember that!' she cried, pulling at her hair. 'Why can't I remember? What's wrong with me?'

'There's nothing wrong with you, Dolly. You get a bit confused now and then, that's all.'

John was nervous of his gran's behaviour, but as his granddad took a bottle of pills and shook one on to his palm, he said calmly, 'It's all right, John, don't look so worried. Your gran's a bit under the weather, but she'll be better soon.'

Dolly took the pill without argument, and shortly after John saw a familiar distance in his gran's manner.

'Why don't you come and give me a hand in the back garden?' his granddad suggested. 'Leave your gran to rest for a while.'

This was something John loved to do, and when his gran nodded, her smile sweet, he flung on his coat again. It was chilly outside, but soon the two of them were so absorbed that they hardly noticed, John learning more and more about the plants and fauna.

'See that?' his granddad said, pointing to the bird table. 'It's a chaffinch.'

'And there's a blue tit.' John shared his granddad's love of birds.

'I could hear a woodpecker in the woods yesterday, but though I got my binoculars, I couldn't spot it.'

'I remember the first time I saw one. It was bigger than I expected,' John said as he eyed the dense woods that started where the back garden ended. They stood quietly for a while, watching the various small birds that came to feast on the seeds and nuts his granddad put out, then they went back to work on the garden.

When they were called in to lunch, John saw that his gran had rallied a little. Later when it was time to leave, his gran hugged him and kissed him on the cheek, leaving him to wonder what was really wrong with her.

Chapter Two

Pearl was sitting beside Derek in the car as he drove her to see Bessie Penfold. She didn't like going to Battersea, and rarely went. It was a place that held so many bad memories, but Bessie was special to her, a woman who had taken her in when she had fled from her first husband, Kevin Dolby, and his terrifying mother.

She saw that nothing much had changed. The

21

stalls still lined the High Street with the coster-mongers shouting out their wares, and as Derek looked for somewhere to park he said, 'While you're visiting Bessie, I'll go to see my gran.'

'All right,' she agreed. Derek had lost his mother when he was still a child and it had been his gran, Connie Lewis, who raised him. Connie didn't like her, but Pearl felt she deserved the old woman's anger. She had been going out with Derek, had agreed to marry him, but then been mad enough to fall for Kevin Dolby. She'd been such an innocent at the time, unworldly, and had been helpless to stop what happened. When she had found that she was pregnant she had married Kevin and they had moved in with his parents, but Pearl had been so ashamed of herself for breaking Derek's heart.

When Kevin went to prison, it took several years before her divorce was granted, and during that time Derek came back into her life. Then, when he'd asked her to marry him, she had gladly agreed.

'I'll stop off to buy Gran some of her favourite sweets,' Derek said.

'I still can't believe she agreed to go into an old people's home.'

'Even my gran had the sense to see that with her hands and knees riddled with arthritis, she was no longer capable of looking after herself.'

'We've been married for nearly ten years, but she's never softened towards me. I don't suppose it helped that you gave up the tenancy on her house.'

'I knew you wouldn't agree to live in Battersea

again and, anyway, it's just as small as your mother's cottage.'

'I don't want John to hear the truth about Kevin, but he'd soon find out if we moved back here,' Pearl pointed out, thankful that Derek had been happy to move to Winchester.

'Here we are,' Derek said as he found a space and pulled into the kerb.

Pearl smiled at him fondly. Derek was nine years older than her, with fair hair, pale blue eyes and a face battered by years of boxing. The antithesis of Kevin, he couldn't be described as handsome, but with his innate kindness and the love he showered on both her and John, Pearl thanked God for the day she had become his wife.

With the engine still running, Derek said, 'Right, love, I'll see you later.'

'To give us time to prepare my mother's birthday treat, we've got to get back to Winchester by three at the latest,' Pearl pointed out.

'I know, but that gives us about an hour and a half.'

'Don't leave it any longer than that before you pick me up again,' Pearl urged, leaning across to kiss Derek on the cheek.

'I won't,' he replied.

As Derek drove off, Pearl walked the short distance to Bessie's shop, which was set in a tall, terraced building, the two floors above providing ample living accommodation.

When Pearl entered the shop she saw that it had hardly altered from when she had lived with Bessie and worked there, making improvements that had increased trade. There were racks of second-hand clothes, and a few long trestle tables almost buckling under the weight of old china and other stuff. There were a few pieces of battered furniture for sale too, and every spare surface was piled with old books. Pearl wrinkled her nose at the musty smell, but at least everything looked as tidy as possible.

Lucy Sanderson was standing behind the counter, a lovely young woman who had been through hell. She had lost both parents in a fire, but had somehow managed to get on with her life. Then more tragedy followed when her husband died in a traffic accident before Clive, their only child, was born. It had almost broken Lucy, but for her baby's sake she had somehow battled on. Clive was seven years old now, and as far as Pearl knew there had never been another man in Lucy's life. She took in sewing alterations to make ends meet, along with her earnings when working part time for Bessie.

'Hello, Lucy,' Pearl said. 'How is Bessie?'

'Her chest seems really bad and she insisted that I ring you.'

'She's probably got bronchitis again,' Pearl said, thinking that despite it looking a bit washed out and home made, Lucy looked nice in a floor-length, high-necked, Laura Ashley-style floral dress. Her hair was a halo of frizzy blonde Afro curls, the result of a home perm, yet they framed her pretty, delicate features and the style suited her.

'I sent Nora along to the chemist to pick up Bessie's medicine,' Lucy said. 'I think she can manage that.'

chair close to the bed.
on your own at nigh
won't let Nora sleep i

'Leave it out. She s
with the door shut, I'

'Oh, and *you* don't?
arranging the blank
doctor?'

'Yes, but a fat lot of g
croaked when anothe
think me number's up

'Don't be silly. You'r

Despite the reass
gripped Pearl's hand,
to promise that if I do
care of Nora. Don't
financially, I've seen t

'Of course I'll look a
other bout of bronch
sary.'

'Promise me, Pearl.
Bessie pleaded.

'All right, I promise
though Bessie was be
be best to placate her.

'Thanks, love,' Bes
hand and sinking bac
easy now.'

'Is this why you war

'Yes. I don't suppos
time I get to see him
chester.'

'You know why I do
'No matter how m

'You shouldn't be up here
t. I don't know why you
ı the room next door.'

ıores like a trooper. Even
hear her.'

Pearl said wryly while re-
:ts. 'Have you seen the

ɔod that's gonna do,' Bessie
fit of coughing ended. 'I
this time.'

: going to be fine.'

ırance, Bessie suddenly
aying urgently, 'I want you
ı't pull through, you'll take
vorry, you won't lose out
• that.'

fter her, but this is just an-
tis and it won't be neces-

'ou've got to promise me,'

,' Pearl said, thinking that
ng overdramatic, it might

;ie said, releasing Pearl's
: on her pillows. 'I can rest

ted to see me?'
John's with you? The only
is when we come to Win-

ı't bring him to Battersea.'
ch you try to hide it, the

truth has a way of coming out,' Bessie warned.

'John is too young to cope with it yet. Maybe when he's older, but even then it's going to be an awful shock.'

'I know you regret the day you married Kevin Dolby, and if you remember, I tried to warn you against him,' Bessie said, but then she doubled up in another fit of coughing.

'Your chest sounds terrible. If you'd stop smoking it would help.'

'After thirteen years of nagging me, you might as well give up. Anyway, I'm nearly eighty years old now and it's too late.'

'Don't be silly. Of course it isn't.'

'Bury your head in the sand if you must, but now you've promised to take care of Nora it's eased my mind. You're settled with Derek, and though you all live with your mother, which isn't ideal, it's plain to see how happy you are. Your son is a lovely boy and one of the few people who doesn't mock Nora.'

'He loves her, Bessie.'

'I know, and she adores him, which is another reason why I know Nora will be fine when you take her on. When I go, you'll find a box under the bed with my papers in, and when you sort my things out you'll find a nice little cache of stuff to help you out.'

'I wish you'd stop talking like this.'

'I'm just putting me affairs in order, that's all. Now enough said, so how about making me a cup of tea?'

'Yes, all right, and can I get you anything to eat?'

'No, thanks, a fag and a cuppa is all I want.'

'Oh, you and your cigarettes,' Pearl said wearily, sad that all her years of nagging Bessie to stop had come to nothing. She went down to the kitchen, pleased to see it sparkling with cleanliness. Bessie was hopeless when it came to housework, but it was one of the things Nora excelled at. Without even thinking about it Pearl had agreed to take Nora on if anything happened to Bessie, but now she realised that it would pose a rather large problem. They shared her mother's two bedroom cottage, and with her mother in one of them and John in the other, she and Derek already had to sleep in the front living room. That just left the kitchen, which fortunately was a large one, and a small conservatory which now served as a sitting room. As Pearl was pouring the boiling water into the teapot, Nora appeared. She was short, plump, with a round face and straight, light brown hair. Though her eyes often appeared vacant, Nora was usually cheerful; yet this wasn't the case now.

'Bessie really bad this time,' Nora said woefully.

'She'll be all right,' Pearl said kindly. 'You're doing a wonderful job of looking after her.'

Looking tearful, Nora shook her head. 'No, Bessie not get better.'

Nora's words sent a shiver along Pearl's spine, but despite that she managed to sound reassuring. 'Of course she will. Did the chemist give you her medicine?'

'Yes,' she said, holding it out.

'Good girl, and now you can take it up to her,' Pearl said as she regained control of her feelings. Like Bessie, Nora had the strange ability to predict the future – but surely she was mistaken

28

this time?

'All right, I give to Bessie,' Nora agreed.

As Pearl waited for the tea to brew, she decided that as always Nora was just being overly anxious, as she was every time Bessie got a bout of bronchitis. She wasn't predicting the future. Bessie would get over it. She always did. She was a tough old bird and would probably live long enough to get a telegram from the Queen.

Bessie dutifully swallowed her medicine, but she knew there was nothing now that could help. She smiled fondly at Nora, but it did nothing to soothe the girl's anxiety. Instead Nora looked as she had for the past week, pale and tearful.

Like her, Nora knew of course, sensed that the end was in sight and Bessie's heart went out to her. How long had it been since she'd taken the girl in? Girl, no, Nora wasn't a girl – she was forty-three now and they'd muddled along together for thirteen years.

With a sigh, Bessie closed her eyes as her mind drifted back to 1957. Both Pearl and Nora had been like waifs and strays then, both needing her sanctuary and help. When Pearl had to get away from the Dolbys she had nowhere else to go, and Bessie recalled how she'd felt compelled to take her in. However, she had also sensed that Pearl wouldn't be with her for long. On the other hand, as Nora's mother had been admitted to a home with senile dementia, she had known that taking Nora on would become a permanent arrangement.

Bessie opened her eyes again to look at Nora,

forcing a smile to alleviate her fears. It was odd that Nora could predict too, almost as if they were meant to be together, and over the years Nora had become like the daughter that Bessie had never had, a woman who remained like a child, capable of some tasks, yet so vulnerable. There was one thing that Nora feared, and that was change, but Bessie had now taken steps to ensure that all that was familiar to Nora would remain.

With a croak in her voice, Bessie said, 'Thanks for fetching my medicine, love.'

'I look after you,' Nora said gravely.

'You certainly do,' Bessie agreed as the door was pushed open and Pearl appeared carrying a tray. 'It's about time. I thought you'd gone to India to hand-pick the tea leaves.'

'Very funny,' said Pearl.

With a small, elfin face, Pearl had a delicate look about her, but Bessie knew she was stronger than she appeared. She was very fond of Pearl, and with no family of her own left Bessie felt there had been no choice – no other way to secure Nora's future. Even so, she felt a twinge of guilt at the burden she was going to lay on Pearl. Would she agree to the conditions of the will?

Bessie longed for reassurance, for a glimpse of the future, but her second sight failed her.

Derek left the old people's home, pleased to see that his gran was still happy there. At seventy-nine she had women of her own age to talk to and obviously enjoyed joining them in putting the world to rights.

His gran certainly hadn't been happy when he

married Pearl, and it hadn't helped that he'd moved to Winchester. Despite all the years that had passed and all his attempts to persuade her, she still stubbornly refused to have anything to do with Pearl, though it didn't stop her from complaining that she was the only one in the home who couldn't brag about having great-grandchildren. He'd tried over and over again to tell her that he saw John as his son, but his gran refused to recognise him as such. It saddened Derek that he and Pearl hadn't had children, but despite the pleasure of trying, it had never happened.

Battersea High Street was still busy, the market stalls doing a brisk trade, and for a moment Derek envied the costermongers their camaraderie. He had once had a pitch himself and there were a few men he'd known still working the stalls; one of them waved as he got out of the car, but mostly it was strange faces.

Pearl looked worried as they left Bessie's and after popping upstairs himself to say hello to the old girl, he understood why. 'She looked a bit rough, Pearl.'

'I know, and thank goodness for Lucy. She's been cooking meals for them both, and though Nora manages to do most things for Bessie when she's ill, she can't use the telephone. I've asked Lucy to ring me again if she thinks I'm needed.'

'Lucy's a nice girl,' Derek commented and as always as he drove off he felt a pang at leaving Battersea. He liked Winchester, but this area would always feel like home to him. He knew they would never come back, never live here again ... but a man could dream, couldn't he?

31

Chapter Three

'Granddad, what's really wrong with Gran?' John asked. 'I've never seen her like that before.'

Driving the lad back to Winchester, Bernie knew he had to be careful with his words. In the past it had been easy enough to tell John that his gran suffered from headaches for which she took pills, but the lad was growing up now and Bernie doubted he could fob him off with the same story. He decided to tell him the partial truth.

'Your gran had a nervous breakdown from which she never fully recovered,' he explained. Though of course there'd been more to it than that. Dolly had lost her mind, ranting and raving like a mad woman. It was only the treatment and the pills she had been taking since leaving hospital that kept her on an even keel.

'Was it because my real dad was sent to prison?' John asked.

'I'm afraid it was partly to blame. Your gran doted on Kevin and it knocked her for six.'

'Poor Gran,' John murmured.

'Don't worry. As long as she takes her medication, your gran is fine,' Bernie assured him. John might be like his father in looks, but he was nothing like him in character. The boy was gentle, caring and it had become clear from an early age that he hated any form of violence. Growing up in Winchester, John had a love of the surrounding countryside, along with animals, wild or tame, and it was something they shared. With this thought, Bernie smiled. He wasn't sure how Pearl would feel about it, but knew that John would love the gift he had planned. He was looking forward to the boy's birthday.

The drive back to Winchester had the same soporific effect it always had on John and Bernie saw that his head was soon nodding. While the boy slept, Bernie reflected on Kevin's letter and the news he would have to break to Pearl. He doubted she'd be pleased to hear that Kevin was up for parole again. When Pearl married Kevin, Bernie had hated the way that both his son and Dolly had treated her. At times he'd tried to intervene, to make things a little easier for Pearl, and the two of them had grown close.

'Are we nearly there?' John said sleepily.

'No, we've a fair way to go yet,' Bernie told him, yet a glance showed him that the lad had gone back to sleep already.

He wondered what effect Kevin's release would have on John, and doubted it would be a good one. As far as Bernie was concerned, he felt that Kevin should serve his full time: after all, the jeweller that he'd bludgeoned over and over again, leaving the poor sod brain-damaged, was going to suffer for the rest of his life. He also thought that Kevin's so-called religious conversion was unlikely to be genuine. Even before going to prison, Kevin had never done an honest day's work. Dolly had funded his idleness, but if his son thought that things were going to be the same when he got out, he was going to be very disappointed.

Bernie smiled with satisfaction. He handled their money now, but after buying the cottage he knew the rest wouldn't last forever. Though nervous at first, he'd discovered a talent when it came to investing in the stock market and had gradually quadrupled their savings. Fearful of his luck changing, he'd finally turned his shares into cash and with the interest it was earning, they were comfortably off.

'John, we're here,' Bernie now said, gently nudging his grandson.

John blinked his eyes, then slowly unfurled his limbs to climb out of the car. Bernie followed him to the front door of the small, flat-fronted, terraced house.

'Mum, Dad, we're back,' John called as they went into the house.

Pearl appeared, smiling when she saw them. 'Bernie, thanks for bringing him home earlier than usual. My mother has no idea that we're laying on a special tea for her fiftieth birthday and it wouldn't be the same without John being there.'

'Where is she, Mum?'

'Next door with Tim.'

'Tim?' Bernie asked, his eyebrows rising.

'Timothy Blake, our next-door neighbour. He hasn't been the same since his wife died last year and Mum often goes round to keep him company. We got Tim to ask her to pop round when we came back, but it's still been a mad dash to get everything ready and the table laid. Come and see the cake,' Pearl invited as she led them through to the kitchen.

'Derek, hello,' Bernie said and after his greeting was returned he duly admired Emily's birthday cake.

'I won't be a minute. I need the bathroom,' John said, hurrying off.

Bernie took the opportunity to talk to Pearl and Derek out of the boy's hearing. 'Dolly heard from Kevin. He's ... well ... he's up for parole again.'

'Do you think he'll get it this time?' Pearl asked worriedly.

'With his so-called religious conversion, Dolly seems to think so.'

Pearl frowned. 'What do you mean, *so-called* conversion?'

'When it comes to Kevin, I'm not as gullible as Dolly, yet she seems convinced it's genuine,' Bernie admitted. 'On her last visit Kevin was even spouting that if he's refused parole again it must be because God has work for him to do within the prison; that his calling might be to help the other inmates. He says if he does get out, he's going to start up some sort of refuge for alcoholics and homeless people – lost souls as he calls them.'

'Goodness!' Pearl exclaimed.

'I doubt there's any goodness involved,' Bernie said, 'especially as he was probably hinting for a substantial donation.'

'Do you think he'll want to see John?'

'I don't know, love. Dolly seems to think so, but she knows you've got sole custody. Mind you, John's curious about his father and said today that he'd like to see him.'

Pearl's face paled. 'But what if Kevin tries to take John away from me?'

'He'd better not,' Bernie growled. 'And anyway, if you tell John the truth about Kevin, he won't be so keen to see him.'

'No,' Pearl protested. 'He's far too young to cope with it yet.'

There was the sound of footsteps and John appeared in the doorway, bringing the conversation to an abrupt end.

'Well, lad,' Bernie said, 'I'd best be off, and Pearl, tell Emily I said happy birthday. I'm sure she's going to be thrilled with that cake.'

'Yes, she'll love it,' Pearl agreed, 'and we're taking her to the theatre tonight.'

'That sounds right up Emily's street,' Bernie commented, then said his goodbyes. He was thoughtful as he got into his car. They were a happy family and having lived in Emily's house since he was a baby, John had only ever known love and stability. If Kevin got out, all that could change, and Bernie found himself again hoping that his son would remain in prison.

At five thirty, Emily clapped her hands with delight. 'Oh, look, Tim, it's such a beautiful cake.'

'Yes, it is,' Tim agreed as he held out a chair ready for her to sit down.

The cake was in the centre of the table, and there were cucumber sandwiches, tiny rolls stuffed with tuna, some with egg, and lovely home-made biscuits. Emily smiled as she looked around the table. Her friends, Libby Moore and her husband, were smiling back, her gorgeous grandson too, and of course Derek and Pearl. From the day she had found her daughter again, Emily's life had been full of joy. They had lived together for thirteen years now and were very close, with Derek moving in too when he married Pearl. They had been happy years, yet it still hurt Emily that she had missed so much of Pearl's childhood.

Emily would never forget how furious her father had been when she had become pregnant out of wedlock. She had been kept a virtual prisoner in her parents' large house, out of sight of anyone, and when she had given birth she was heartbroken to be told her baby was stillborn. Many, many, years later, when her father was on his deathbed, he had taken great delight in telling her that she would inherit nothing. He had then confessed that her baby hadn't been stillborn after all, that she had lived, and he'd abandoned her on the steps of an orphanage. Her baby had been found clutching a tiny button, and with no other form of identification that was how she'd been named: Pearl Button, though of course she was now Pearl Lewis.

Derek laughed at something Pearl said, breaking Emily out of her reverie. She hadn't been sure about Derek at first. She had heard all about Pearl's first husband, Kevin Dolby, and Emily feared that as the two men had known each other, Derek would be cut from the same cloth. Thankfully she'd been wrong: Derek was a wonderful man and she'd become very fond of him.

'Happy birthday, Gran,' said John as he held out a package.

Emily unwrapped the gift, loving the pretty box of handkerchiefs with lace edging and her initials embroidered in one corner. 'Thank you, darling.

They're beautiful.'

'This is from us, Mum.'

In the small box, Emily was thrilled to find a delicate chain hung with a pretty pearl locket. 'I just love it,' she said, smiling with happiness.

'Emily, I'm so sorry,' Tim said softly, obviously embarrassed. 'I haven't got you a gift.'

'It really doesn't matter,' she told him, just glad to have him there. She had been friends with Delia, Tim's late wife, and had always been fond of them both. Tim had been lost when Delia died, but just recently Emily's platonic friendship with him had slowly begun to develop into something more. Of course he was still grieving and it was far too soon to take things any further, but maybe, in the future … just maybe...

Chapter Four

Derek awoke earlier than usual on Friday. Careful not to wake Pearl, he climbed out of bed, shivering as he threw on his dressing gown before making his way to the kitchen. It was still cold, but perhaps next month they'd see a decent rise in the temperature. He lit the fire, and then placed the kettle on the gas stove, unable to stop his thoughts turning to Kevin Dolby. There had been no news from Bernie about the parole hearing, and with any luck that meant he'd been turned down.

'I thought I'd be the first one up this morning.'

Derek turned to smile fondly at Emily. 'We're both early birds then,' he said, struck as always by her tiny, birdlike appearance. Some people assumed that Emily was frail, yet although she had angina, she hadn't had a bad attack for many years. He'd heard all the jokes about mothers-in-law, but none applied to his relationship with Emily. From the day he'd married Pearl and moved in, Emily had given them plenty of space, even using her bedroom as a sort of sitting room too, with a couple of chairs on each side of a small fireplace, along with a radio and television. They'd protested, but Emily insisted that she liked it that way and it meant that she could watch the TV programmes she preferred.

'I see you're making a pot of tea,' Emily said.

'Yes, it won't be long now.'

'I'll take over if you like,' she offered.

'Thanks. I'll go and get ready for work while it's brewing,' Derek said. As he went up to the bathroom his thoughts returned to their living arrangements.

Even now, when Emily wasn't next door with Tim, she spent most of her evenings in her room, watching programmes like *All Creatures Great and Small,* while Derek preferred *The Sweeney*. It was a good choice of title for the police series – Sweeney Todd, slang for the flying squad. Over the years Derek had suggested that they find a place of their own to rent, but somehow it never happened, both Pearl and her mother happy to keep things the way they were.

Derek hadn't found moving to Winchester easy. He'd managed a boxing gym in Battersea, but a similar role had been impossible to find here. With no other skills, or choice, he'd started out as a painter and decorator's labourer, but he'd learned quickly and his capabilities increased until he became proficient enough to start out on his own. He didn't make a fortune, his jobs only small ones, but he was working for himself and preferred it that way. Recently though, he'd quoted for a job on a housing development, a big one with a great profit margin, and now his shoulders straightened. If it came off they would have a deposit, a chance to buy a house. Surely Pearl would love that?

After taking Clive to school, Lucy was now at the shop. She switched on the lights and then went through the back to the bottom of the stairs. 'Nora, it's me,' she called. 'I'm just going to open up.'

All was quiet and, worried, Lucy shouted again, 'Nora! Nora, are you there?'

There was still no answer and, seriously concerned now, Lucy hurried upstairs. Nora was usually up by now and would have managed to prepare a simple breakfast of cereals for herself and Bessie.

Lucy looked in Nora's room, but the bed hadn't been slept in. She went up to the next floor and to her relief saw that Nora was there in Bessie's room, sitting in a chair, bent double with her head resting on the bed, fast asleep.

The bedside lamp was still lit, and as Lucy crept forward she gasped. Like Nora, Bessie was asleep but she looked awful, her breathing shallow and wheezing. Lucy floundered, unsure what to do, but just then Bessie's eyes fluttered open, and she struggled to sit up.

'Here, let me help you,' Lucy cried.

Nora awoke, her eyes cloudy with confusion for a moment, but when she saw Lucy trying to help Bessie, she joined in, plumping the pillows and putting them behind Bessie's back. It didn't seem to help and Bessie's breathing was still ragged.

'She really bad now,' Nora wailed, her eyes filling with tears.

'Don't worry. I'm going to call the doctor,' Lucy replied as calmly as she could.

'No... No...' Bessie managed to gasp. 'I ... I'll be all right.'

'You don't look all right.'

'Med ... medicine.'

Nora poured it. After swallowing a spoonful, Bessie seemed to start breathing a little easier and asked for a cup of tea. Lucy still wasn't sure, but as she stood looking down on her, Bessie said with more strength in her voice, 'I'm fine and don't you dare bother the doctor.'

Lucy knew better than to argue, but she wasn't happy as she went back downstairs to make the tea. Bessie refused food, but Nora ate her cornflakes, though she remained sitting by Bessie's side.

'We're fine,' the old woman said. 'Go and open the shop.'

Lucy thought Bessie looked a bit better, but decided she'd look in on her again in an hour or two. If there was no further improvement by then she was going to ring the doctor – whether the old woman liked it or not.

For Pearl, the weekday morning followed the usual routine. She made breakfast, Derek left for work and then John went to school. Her mother taught art in a local primary and had already left; the house now quiet as Pearl did a little housework before taking a break. While sipping a cup of coffee she let her gaze rest on one of her mother's paintings that hung on the wall above the fireplace. Her choice of pastels was restful to the eye, the scene a cottage window dressed with soft, blue, gingham curtains and a toning vase of cottage garden flowers on a windowsill.

Pearl had always loved painting. She had inherited her mother's talent but what with housework, cooking, and a part-time job in a chemist, her days were full. There had once been a time when Pearl had dreamed of being an artist, of her paintings being shown in an exhibition, but those dreams had long been put aside in favour of being a wife and mother.

Though she hadn't wanted to think about him, the news of Kevin's possible parole loomed heavy in her mind. The things he'd done, his violence, had sickened her, yet there was no denying that from the moment John had been born, Kevin had loved him. At his own insistence, Kevin hadn't seen John while he was in prison, but Pearl felt he would want to see him when he was released. Her stomach lurched as the same fears made her hands tremble. What if he tried to take John away from her? He was certainly capable of doing that.

Her thoughts were cut off by the ringing of the telephone. It was Lucy.

42

'Pearl, despite Bessie insisting that she's fine, she's getting worse. I know she'll do her nut, but I want to call the doctor. What do you think?'

Frowning worriedly, Pearl asked, 'Has she got a fever?'

'No, I don't think so and as I said, Bessie insists she's fine. It's just that her breathing is really bad.'

'In that case, call the doctor.'

'All right then. I just hope she doesn't have a go at me.'

'Bessie's bark has always been worse than her bite, but if you like, tell her it was my idea.'

'Thanks Pearl. I'll give that a try.'

'There's no need to thank me. I'm just glad you're there to keep an eye on her. I've got to go to work soon, but I'll give you a call as soon as I come home.'

'Right, I'll speak to you again then,' Lucy said, saying goodbye before hanging up.

Pearl could just imagine Bessie's reaction when the doctor walked in. Poor Lucy, she was right and fur would probably fly. She put on her white nylon overall, something the chemist insisted all the staff wear, and with Bessie on her mind, all thoughts of Kevin were put to one side. There was no news of his parole so perhaps it had been denied and she was worrying about nothing.

Pearl enjoyed her part-time job at the chemist's but today the hours seemed to drag. At last she was on her way again and on arriving home she immediately went to the telephone. The news was reassuring. Lucy told her that the doctor hadn't seemed overly worried, but he had put Bessie on a stronger dose of antibiotics.

Pearl at last relaxed, and after telling Lucy that they'd drive down to see Bessie on Sunday, she replaced the receiver, flooded with relief.

Chapter Five

Pearl liked Saturday mornings and she woke up at seven to stretch out leisurely. Now she knew that Bessie had seen the doctor there was no rush to get up, but she'd ring the shop when Lucy arrived soon after nine to make sure that all was still well. She snuggled close to Derek, enjoying the warmth of his body. She had expected him to go to work, but he had just finished a decorating job and was obviously in no hurry to get up either as he gathered her into his arms.

'Morning,' he said, kissing the tip of her nose.

'Good morning to you too,' she said.

'Does this mean what I think?' he said, aware of the signals after so many years of marriage.

She silenced him with a kiss, and for a while they took pleasure in each other's bodies, tenderly at first, but then with growing passion, until at last, pink with pleasure, Pearl lay satiated.

'I suppose you want me to make you a cup of tea now?' Derek said, smiling.

'That sounds nice, but I think I'll get up.'

They took it in turns to scoot up to the bathroom and when dressed they walked into the kitchen. Pearl wasn't surprised to see her mother. She was always an early riser and for the next

44

hour they sat over a leisurely breakfast, and the morning newspapers.

'Pearl, I'm going out to look for a pair of shoes,' Emily said. 'Do you fancy coming with me?'

'Yes, all right, but before we go out I want to ring Lucy to see how Bessie is this morning.'

'Fine, darling,' Emily said, smiling, 'and in the meantime I'll get ready.'

'Emily, didn't you buy a new pair of shoes a few weeks ago?' Derek asked.

'Yes, but they were brown. I need black ones this time.'

'What is it with women and shoes?'

'What is it with men and wood?' Pearl countered. 'The shed's full of odd bits and pieces.'

'You never know when they might come in handy.'

Emily chuckled as she left the room, saying, 'You can't win, Pearl.'

'I'll just clear up before calling Lucy,' Pearl told Derek as she took their cups and plates to the sink. 'I doubt John will surface before we leave.'

'I'll sort his breakfast out when he does,' Derek offered.

'Thanks, love,' Pearl said, her hands immersed in water when the telephone rang.

'I'll get it,' Derek said.

Pearl turned to look at Derek when he returned, and something in his expression stilled her. 'What is it? What's wrong?'

'Pearl, you'd better sit down.'

'Derek, just tell me.'

'It's Bessie, love. She ... she's passed away.'

'No! Oh no!' Pearl cried, her knees giving way.

45

She sank onto a chair then. 'How? When?'

'She died during the night. Lucy found her this morning.'

Pearl stared up at Derek in dismay. She couldn't take it in. Bessie! Bessie dead! No, it couldn't be true.

Derek knelt in front of her, his urgent tone penetrating her foggy mind. 'I know you're upset, but Lucy needs you. Nora's in a dreadful state and she can't cope with her.'

As Pearl stood up she was struggling to put her thoughts into coherent order and as her mother returned to the kitchen, she cried, 'Mum, Bessie's dead and I've got to go, but there's John and...'

'I'm here and he'll be fine,' Emily said reassuringly.

Derek's tone was urgent. 'Come on, Pearl. It'll take us well over an hour to get there and Lucy sounded a bit frantic.'

Pearl was still feeling utterly dazed and dejected when they arrived at the shop.

'Thank goodness you're here,' Lucy cried as soon as she saw them, holding her son close. 'Nora's howling has upset Clive and I ... I want to take him home.'

'Where is she now?'

'All that wailing must have worn her out and a short while ago she fell asleep in her room.'

'Lucy, what happened?' Pearl asked.

'I don't know!' she cried, but then as Clive flung his arms around her legs, Lucy took a deep breath as though to calm her emotions. Quietly, she continued, 'As I told you on the telephone yesterday, the doctor didn't seem worried about Bessie, but when ... when I arrived this morning she ... she was dead. Oh, Pearl, I can't believe it. I'm so sorry.'

'Lucy, it's all right. You have nothing to be sorry for.'

'I ... I panicked when I found her. I called the doctor, but of course it was too late. He ... he was very kind, and as I didn't know what to do, he suggested an undertaker.'

'Kind!' Pearl cried. 'He should have shown more concern when he saw Bessie yesterday. He should have had her hospitalised.'

'I don't think it would have made any difference. The doctor said that Bessie's heart had failed.'

'So it wasn't the bronchitis?'

'Not according to the doctor, and as Nora was in such a state, refusing to leave Bessie, he was good enough to ring the undertakers for me while I tried to comfort her. They came to take Bessie's body away. That's their address,' Lucy said, handing Pearl a card. 'I hope that's all right.'

Pearl had managed to hold herself together, but now guilt swamped her. She groaned loudly, 'Oh, Derek, I should have listened to Nora. She knew this was going to happen.'

'Leave it out, love,' Derek said gently. 'Bessie was no spring chicken and she had a good innings.'

'We're talking about someone's life, Bessie's life, not a game of cricket!'

'Mummy, I want to go home,' Clive wailed.

The plaintive cry stilled Pearl. Here she was, yelling in front of Lucy's son and the boy was

47

already upset. 'Lucy, I'm sorry.'

'It's all right, it's been a shock for you, for all of us, but I'd best take Clive home,' she said, though before ushering him out of the door, Lucy whispered to Pearl: 'Nora went hysterical when the undertaker took Bessie away and I was really worried about her. She might start up again when she wakes up.'

'Don't worry, we'll see to her,' Derek assured her.

Lucy nodded and seeing Lucy's small, sad wave as she left, Pearl blinked several times, yet nothing could stem the tide of tears as grief overwhelmed her. She sobbed, and as Derek's arms wrapped around her, she gave vent to her feelings.

Derek continued to hold Pearl until she was able to pull herself together, then, with a juddering sob, she said, 'I'd best wake Nora. We'll need to take her back to Winchester with us and sort out somewhere for her to sleep. I suppose it'll have to be a camp bed in the conservatory, but it's hardly ideal.'

'Pearl, what are you talking about? Nora isn't our responsibility.'

'There isn't anyone else and anyway, you told Lucy that we'd look after her.'

'Yes, but I didn't mean taking her home with us. We need to talk to someone, maybe the council welfare department. They'll need to find her a place in some sort of institution.'

'No, Derek. I promised Bessie I'd take her on.'

'*You did what!*' he gasped, appalled.

'All right, I know it was hasty, but when I made

48

that promise I had no idea that Bessie was going to ... to die. I thought she'd live to be a hundred.'

Derek was annoyed that Pearl had made such a promise without thinking of the ramifications. 'You don't seem to realise that looking after Nora isn't going to be easy. It'll be like having another child, but one who will never grow up. We'd be responsible for her financially too, but with less income because you'd have to pack in your part-time job to look after her. Not only that, you can't expect your mother to give up her conservatory indefinitely. We'll have to find somewhere else to live.'

'I'm sorry, Derek, you're right. I didn't think it through. But Bessie did say something about making sure I wouldn't lose out financially.'

'She never seemed to have two pennies to rub together so I don't see how,' Derek said, but then, seeing that Pearl's eyes were welling with tears again, he shut up. There was no way he'd agree to take Nora on permanently but Pearl's feelings were too raw to sort this out now.

'Derek, there's something else. What about Bessie's funeral? We'll have to arrange that too.'

'Blimey, do you know if she's got a life insurance policy to pay for it?'

'I'm not sure, but she told me that if anything happened to her, I'd find papers in a box under her bed.'

'Right, I'll go and get it while you sort Nora out.'

Pearl dabbed at the tears on her cheeks before going to wake Nora, while Derek went to Bessie's room. For a moment he stood on the threshold,

49

looking at the empty, unmade bed. Bessie had been a bit strange, odd at times, but he'd liked her. Though she was no longer there, no longer alive, it felt like an intrusion as he ferreted around under her bed, and at any moment he expected to hear Bessie's strident voice asking him what the hell he was doing. Blimey, Derek thought, he was getting as fanciful as Pearl in believing that both Bessie and Nora had some sort of strange powers. Nevertheless, once his hand touched a wooden box, he pulled it out and beat a hasty retreat.

As he passed Nora's room, Derek could hear her crying, but deciding that he'd be of no use he went to the living room. He felt a little cowardly in leaving Nora to Pearl, but consoled himself with the thought that women were always better at handling such things.

The box wasn't very big but it was handsome, made of mahogany and beautifully carved; however, Derek was more interested in the contents. If Bessie had life insurance it would help with the cost of the funeral, yet as he sat down and opened the lid, the first thing Derek saw was an envelope addressed to Pearl.

He turned it over, finding the flap sealed, but had he opened it, Derek would have been shocked at the contents – as shocked as Pearl was going to be.

Chapter Six

Lucy Sanderson sat in her tiny flat. Though deeply saddened by Bessie's death, she couldn't help but start to really worry about her wages. She'd been helping out in the shop on a part-time basis for three days a week. However, since Bessie went down with bronchitis, she'd been working every day, along with doing little extras, like cooking their hot meals. On the strength of extra money coming in she had splashed out on a new pair of trousers and shoes for Clive. Now though, she hadn't been paid and the rent was due.

I'm daft, she mused, I should've had a word with Pearl. But it hadn't seemed right to bring up the subject of money when they were all so upset about Bessie. Not only that, Lucy had no idea who was responsible for her wages now.

Though it was sad, at least Bessie had lived to a ripe old age, Lucy thought, unlike her husband, Paul, who had died before setting eyes on his son. She bit her bottom lip, fighting back tears. Clive had seen enough upset for one day without her crying too.

'I'm hungry, Mum.'

His voice roused Lucy. Clive had soon recovered from the upset at the shop, and though it was a bit early for lunch, she took a tin out of the cupboard. 'How about beans on toast?'

'Cor, smashing,' he said eagerly.

51

As Lucy prepared the meal, she couldn't help wondering what was going to happen to the shop now. She had no idea if Bessie owned or rented it, but one thing was certain, Nora wasn't up to running it.

Would it remain closed? Lucy suspected it would and she sighed, her financial future even more uncertain now.

Pearl was trying to persuade Nora to come home with them, but so far nothing was working.

'Bessie said I stay here.'

'Darling, we can't leave you on your own.'

Stubbornly, Nora repeated, 'Bessie said I stay here.'

With no other choice, Pearl had to use guile. 'But you haven't been to see us for a while and I know John would love to see you.'

'Johnny. Like Johnny.'

'Yes, I know,' she said. Nora was the only one who still called him Johnny, 'and he likes you.'

'Nice, Johnny nice.. But I stay here.'

Pearl sighed and deciding that it was doubtful Nora had eaten, she tried another tack. 'If you come home with us, we could buy fish and chips on the way.'

'Yes, I like fish and chips.'

'Right then, why don't you go and have a nice wash and I'll sort you out something pretty to wear?'

The ruse worked and while Nora was in the bathroom, Pearl hurriedly stuffed a few of her things into a bag. She then went to find Derek, puzzled when he handed her a bulky envelope. 'It was in this box,' he said.

Pearl saw that her name was written on it in Bessie's spidery hand and for a moment she just clutched it to her chest, still unable to believe that she would never see her again.

'Aren't you going to open it?'

'Yes,' she said and found that along with a letter, it contained Bessie's last will and testament. She sat down, read both and cried, 'Oh, no! How could Bessie do this to me?'

'What is it? What has she done?' Derek asked.

'Bessie has left me these entire premises, shop and flat.'

'But that's good, isn't it?' he said, looking confused.

'No it isn't. It's awful.'

'Pearl, you aren't making any sense. You've just been left this place and you should be over the moon.'

'Read the conditions and then you'll know why I'm not,' Pearl said, passing the document to Derek.

He quickly scanned it. 'All right, I can see now why you're upset, but it wouldn't be the end of the world, would it?'

'How can you say that? You know how I feel about living in Battersea. Bessie knew my feelings too, yet she's put in this provision that I can't inherit these premises unless I live in them.'

Derek rubbed his chin. 'I don't know why she's insisted on that.'

Pearl brandished the letter at him. 'I do. It's all in here. Bessie says that Nora can't cope with change, that moving away from here would confuse and upset her. This way, she says, if we agree to the provision, not only will Nora have continued stability, but we'll have a home large enough for all of us, with a business thrown in.'

'Well, she has got a point, love.'

'*No!* I won't move back to Battersea. Bessie may have been thinking about Nora, but I'm thinking of my son.'

'I suppose you could always sell the place.'

'Read the will again. If I don't take this place on it's to be sold, with the proceeds going to Battersea Dogs' Home.'

'*What!* Blimey, that's a bit harsh. So much for making sure we'd have the finances to look after Nora.'

Pearl's voice cracked as she ran a hand tiredly across her face. 'I still can't believe that Bessie has done this.'

'Come on, love, I think you've had enough for one day. You need time for it all to sink in and we can talk about it later. For now, let's go home,' Derek said, a tower of strength and support as ever.

Pearl didn't argue. Hoping that Nora was ready, she hurried back to her bedroom, feeling relieved when she didn't become difficult again.

Pearl and Derek agreed not to mention anything about Bessie in the car so as not to distress Nora, yet as they neared Winchester she began to cry again.

'Told you, Pearl,' she sobbed. 'I told you Bessie not get better.'

'I know you did, darling,' Pearl said, her mind

54

twisting and turning. They would have to arrange Bessie's funeral and perhaps consult the solicitor who had drawn up her will. Maybe he'd be able to tell them if there was a way around the conditions of the inheritance.

'Go home now.'

'But we haven't had our fish and chips yet,' Pearl said, hoping Nora's favourite meal would placate her again.

'What's it to be, Nora?' Derek asked. 'Cod and chips?'

'Yes, and can I have a pickled onion?' Nora asked.

'Yes, love. I fancy fish and chips too, but I think with a gherkin.'

Once again the thought of food quietened Nora and at last they were pulling up outside a chippie close to home. Pearl got out of the car, pleased to be served quickly, and then with packets of steaming fish and chips they arrived at the cottage.

Inside, Nora ran straight to John. 'Bessie dead, Johnny.'

'I know, but don't cry,' he said, hugging her short, bulky body to him. 'Bessie wouldn't want you to be unhappy.'

Pearl was impressed by her son's maturity, but when she looked at her mother it was to find her expression less than pleased. She drew Pearl into the conservatory to ask quietly, 'What is Nora doing here?'

'I couldn't leave her on her own, Mum.'

'But she can't stay with us. We've got nowhere to put her.'

'It won't be for long. We'll find somewhere else

55

to live as soon as we can, but in the meantime, I … I thought maybe a camp bed in here.'

'Well, yes, I suppose so, but–'

'Mum, can we talk about it later?' Pearl interrupted. 'I don't think Nora has eaten today and I need to dish out the fish and chips before they get cold. Would you like some?'

'No, thank you, darling.'

Pearl went back into the kitchen to find that Derek had already put the meal onto plates and Nora was already tucking into her portion.

'Are you all right?' he asked her softly.

Pearl nodded, but in truth she was far from all right. Their life had been chugging along nicely, without a care in the world really. She loved living here with her mother, loved the area, the cottage and her little part-time job.

Now, with the responsibility of Nora, they would have to make changes and Pearl felt as if her world was spiralling out of her control.

Chapter Seven

On Tuesday morning Kevin Dolby punched the air in triumph as the prison gates closed behind him. He was free, but to fulfil his immediate needs he had to have more than the funds he'd been given on release. Still, he had the means to get to Southsea; and once he'd twisted his mother around his little finger, his wallet would be stuffed with notes.

Mugs, that's what most people were in Kevin's opinion, including the parole board who had fallen for his pious act. His religious persona was one he'd continue to use – at least when it suited him, he thought, chuckling.

Despite his bravado, after thirteen years in prison, Kevin found the outside world intimidating as he walked to the train station. The sound of traffic was loud in his ears, the roads busier than he remembered, and there was space, so much space after the confines of prison walls.

On reaching the station, Kevin purchased a ticket and then stood on the platform, taking note of the people around him. Most of the fashion was unrecognisable to him and he was amazed when he spotted a bloke with hair flowing over his shoulders, wearing burgundy velvet trousers that flared at the bottom and a flowery top beneath an odd-looking fur-edged, suede coat. In his day poofs didn't flaunt themselves; but the bloke was good looking and for a moment Kevin felt a twinge of interest. However he got a shock when the girl standing next to the poof suddenly stood on tiptoe to give him a kiss, the pair becoming locked in an embrace. Kevin couldn't help staring and the bloke met his eye over his girlfriend's shoulder.

'What are you looking at?' he asked belligerently.

There was nothing girly about his manner and in no mood for a confrontation, Kevin said, 'Nothing,' before quickly looking away.

'Leave it, Pete,' he heard the girl say. 'Don't get into a fight.'

'Yeah, yeah, all right. Peace and love and all that.'

It clicked then and Kevin kicked himself for being stupid. They were hippies – but this was the first time he'd seen them in the flesh. Blimey, there was no way he was going to wear daft clothes like that, and now, as a girl passed him wearing a skirt that was little more than a belt, he feasted his eyes on her legs. Now that he was free and had the choice, Kevin found he much preferred the female form to the male, and licked his lips in anticipation of holding a woman in his arms again.

By the time Kevin reached the village he felt a little more confident, though his parents' cottage was on the outskirts and hadn't been easy to find. Before walking up the path, Kevin braced himself. His mother had ruined his life, had made him think from childhood that sex was a dirty word. If he so much as touched himself, she called him a filthy boy, saying she wouldn't love him if he dared to do it again. She had ruled his father too and his sickening weakness had made Kevin determined to be different, to show any woman he took out who was the boss. To keep them in line, he'd enjoyed giving them a few slaps, and then one day it had escalated into violent rape. He'd loved it, relished showing the woman that, unlike his father, he was a real man, and she was helpless to stop him.

Of course he hadn't had to rape Pearl. She'd been so innocent, so naive, a virgin, and it'd been easy to take her down. He'd been careless though and had been forced to marry her.

From their wedding night, it had all gone wrong, thanks to his mother. She'd walked into their bedroom and the disgust on her face at their nakedness had made him impotent. From then on, with his mother in such close proximity, he'd been unable to make love to Pearl. Kevin scowled. His mother had turned him into less than a man, weak like his father, and he would never forgive her for that.

Kevin knew he couldn't continue to stand outside, and shook off his thoughts, his hate veiled as he now walked up the path to knock on the door. 'Hello, Dad,' he said with a false smile when it was opened.

'What do you want, Kevin?' Bernie asked, his expression cold.

'To see you and Mum, and to show you I've changed, Dad.'

His mother appeared behind Bernie, her eyes lighting up when she saw him. 'Kevin! They've let you out?'

'Yes, and praise be to God,' he said piously.

'Oh, son,' Dolly cried as she shoved Bernie to one side. 'Come in. I'll make up a bed for you.'

'No, Mum, I didn't want to burden you so I've made other arrangements,' he said. The thought of sleeping under the same roof as his mother again made him shudder.

'You'll never be a burden to me,' Dolly said, drawing him inside.

The words almost choked him, but he managed to say, 'I once was, Mother, but never again.'

'We're about to have lunch. Would you like some of my home-made soup?' she asked eagerly.

'Yes, please. I must admit I'm rather hungry,' Kevin said as he looked around the room. He recognised a lot of the furniture from their old place in Battersea, along with the mahogany-cased clock in the centre of the mantelpiece and the silver candlesticks that stood at each end. A fire was burning in the hearth, but with his father's eyes fixed on him, Kevin hovered uncertainly.

'Kevin, come and talk to me in the kitchen while I'm heating the soup,' his mother said.

'Yes, all right.'

'How are you finding the outside world?' she asked as she lit the gas under a saucepan.

'A bit strange,' Kevin replied, which was actually the truth.

'Of course you are. You need time to adjust and you can forget those other arrangements. I'll get the bed in the spare room made up for you. It's nice and quiet here so you'll be able to take things slowly.'

Bernie marched into the kitchen. 'Hold on, Dolly. I haven't agreed to that.'

'It's all right, Dad. I can't stay. I feel I'm being called to London; that my mission is there.'

'So you're going back to Battersea?'

'No, Dad. I know I have much to repent for in that area, but I'm going to Ealing.'

'But why there?' Dolly asked. 'And where will you live?'

'I'm in God's hands, Mother, and He has been guiding me,' Kevin told her, 'so much so that while in prison I met a fellow inmate in the chapel, one who is like-minded. He was released six months ago, but we've been corresponding. He's interested in setting up a refuge in a needy area too

60

and to that end he's offered me a rent-free room in his house.'

'Humph,' Bernie grunted, a sceptical look on his face as he walked out of the kitchen.

Kevin wasn't worried. He knew his mother handled the purse strings and that she was a soft touch where he was concerned. He intended to get every penny out of her that he could. His father had disowned him, had refused to visit him in prison, and this was the first time he'd seen him in thirteen years. Despite that, it was his mother Kevin hated the most: it had been his desperation to get away from her that led him to robbery. Then when it all went wrong, something had snapped in his mind and while bludgeoning the jeweller over and over again it had been his mother's head he saw ... *her* blood flowing...

'What do think of our little cottage?' Dolly asked, breaking into his thoughts.

Worried that she'd see the hate in his eyes, Kevin fought to hide his feelings. 'It's very nice,' he said quietly.

'Your father chose it, and got it for a good price. He handles all our finances now.'

Flaming hell, Kevin thought, his dad had found some balls at last. That meant it wasn't his mother he had to work on, it was his father; and that wasn't going to be so easy. He'd need more time and now hoped his mother would ask him to stay again. Of course he'd put on an act, pretend that he couldn't, before giving in.

When Dolly put their lunch on the table, Bernie sat down opposite Kevin, taken aback when he

61

asked if they minded if he gave thanks for the food before they began to eat.

Bernie shrugged, but bent his head, and then afterwards he listened carefully as his son spoke of his plans. By the time the meal ended, Bernie had to admit that Kevin had mastered his act well. If he hadn't known his son of old, he might have fallen for it, but he wasn't as easily fooled as Dolly.

'Kevin, surely staying for one night won't hurt,' Dolly appealed. 'We've hardly seen you.'

'I'm sorry, but Rupert is expecting me.'

'With a name like that he sounds like a toff,' Bernie commented.

'I suppose he is,' Kevin mused. 'Rupert's certainly well off, but though he's offered me a rent-free room I'd prefer to pay my own way. To that end I must find work and the sooner I get started the better.'

'You're getting a job? That'll be a first,' Bernie said sarcastically.

'I've changed, Dad.'

Bernie didn't believe it for one moment, but before he could make a comment, Dolly said, 'Please, Kevin, surely it won't hurt to delay leaving for one night? You can travel to London in the morning.'

'Well, Dad, I can see how much it would mean to Mum. What do you think?'

'All right, but just one night,' Bernie said grudgingly.

'That's settled then,' Dolly said happily, 'though I don't like the thought of you living in one room when you go to Ealing.'

'Don't be daft, Dolly,' Bernie said scathingly. 'He's been sleeping in a prison cell for thirteen years.'

'Yes, you're right, Dad. After that anything will seem like luxury.'

'If you really are looking for work, what have you got in mind?' Bernie asked.

Kevin shrugged. 'With a prison record it won't be easy, but I'll try the building sites.'

'Kevin, I don't like the sound of this,' Dolly protested. 'First you say you'll be living in one room and now that you'll be labouring on a building site.'

'There's nothing wrong with good, honest labour, and as most of my earnings will go towards setting up a refuge I don't want to waste money on renting a flat.'

'But that could take you years.'

'Everything starts with one small step,' Kevin said piously. 'I'm hoping the mission Rupert's involved with will be interested enough to make a donation.'

Bernie had been expecting this and said derisively, 'I suppose you're hinting that we should chip in too?'

'No, Dad, in making John your heir, you've done enough.'

'So your mother told you about our wills?'

'Yes, she did, and as I'll be involved in charitable work I won't be earning a great deal, or buying property to leave my son. Though of course I hope you live for many, many more years, it's a huge weight off my mind knowing that you've taken care of John. I can't thank you enough.'

Bernie was surprised. He'd expected Kevin to be upset about being usurped, but instead he was thanking them. Maybe he really had changed, maybe his religious conversion was genuine. If that proved to be the case, perhaps it wouldn't hurt to help him out a bit – but not by way of a donation to this daft idea of a refuge. He'd give Kevin a few bob to tide him over until he found his feet, Bernie decided, but as he'd be leaving first thing in the morning, he'd have to get to the bank that afternoon before it closed.

He looked at his son again; still a little wary, he decided not to say where he was going. Instead Bernie found another excuse to go out. There was no need to give the money to Kevin yet, and it might be prudent to hang onto it until the morning. If this was all an act on Kevin's part, there was no way he could keep it up indefinitely and by morning it was sure to slip.

Pearl was back in Battersea once more, this time for an appointment with the solicitor. It was four thirty by the time she left his office and returned to Bessie's flat where Derek and Nora were waiting for her.

'Well, what did he say?' Derek asked as soon as she came in.

'There isn't any way around the conditions of the will,' Pearl said despondently. 'It's watertight.'

'So it's live here, or nothing.'

'Yes,' Pearl said shortly, flopping wearily onto Bessie's old sofa. It had been a long, fraught day and it hadn't got any better. First they'd had to get the death certificate to arrange the funeral,

64

which had been complicated as they weren't Bessie's blood relatives, but armed with her will they finally managed to get everything in place other than the flowers. At least the solicitor had said he'd sort out Bessie's life insurance policy, and that it should cover the cost of the funeral.

'So what are you going to do?' Derek asked.

Pearl sighed. 'I can't live in Battersea. You know that.'

'It isn't a case of can't. It's more that you won't.'

'If we move back here, John is bound to hear the truth about his father, and you're right, I *won't* have that.'

'Why not?' Derek said curtly. 'He isn't a child any more, and by keeping it from him it sounds more like you're protecting Kevin than him.'

'Don't be ridiculous.'

'All right, have it your own way, but if we don't move back here, we can't take Nora on.'

Appalled, Pearl cried, 'We'll have to. I can't break my promise to Bessie.'

'Have you given any thought to how I feel about all this? What if I don't want to take Nora on? What if I don't want the financial responsibility?' Derek said as he agitatedly ran his fingers through his hair.

Pearl leaned forward to place both hands across her face. Derek was right; she hadn't given him a thought. With the loss of her wage, he would be the one to bear the sole brunt of the financial burden.

She felt the sofa dip beside her and as Derek's arm wrapped around her shoulder, she leant against him. 'You're right. I'm sorry,' she told him.

'I'm sorry too. I shouldn't have got out of my pram, but you're asking a lot of me, love. Surely you can see that it makes more sense to find Nora a place in some sort of institution?'

Pearl felt as though she was being torn in two, with Derek tugging her one way and her promise to Bessie pulling her the other. 'Derek, I'm sorry, I just can't think straight at the moment. Let's go home and we'll talk about this later.'

'All right, but you might have a job to persuade Nora to leave with us again. She's done nothing but cry since you left and I can't get her to come out of her bedroom.'

'She's confused, upset, and it's probably where she feels safe,' Pearl said, heaving a sigh as she stood up. However, she was pleased when in the event it only took a little persuasion to coax Nora into the car.

'Peace at last. Nora's gone to sleep,' Derek said when they were half an hour into the journey.

Pearl closed her eyes too. She had so much thinking to do, but at last, as they reached the outskirts of Winchester, she came to a tentative decision.

Chapter Eight

'Other than thanking us for taking care of John in our will, you've hardly mentioned him,' Dolly said as Kevin prepared to leave on Wednesday morning. 'I know Pearl has sole custody, but she should let you see him.'

'I want to achieve something first, to show John, and everyone else, that I've changed,' Kevin replied.

'John has only been told that you went to prison for robbery,' Dolly pointed out. 'Just recently he said he'd like to see you and I think he's waited long enough, Kevin. It's about time he met his real father.'

Kevin knew his father was listening and that if he wanted money he still had to impress him. 'Mum, I've hardly been a father to be proud of, and I wouldn't blame Pearl if she refused.'

'It won't matter if she does. Your father goes to pick John up from Winchester once a month and he spends the day with us. When he's here, if you just happen to turn up, Pearl needn't know about it.'

'It would be wrong to deceive her. If I'm to see my son, it must be with his mother's permission.'

'But...'

'Dolly, you heard what Kevin said,' Bernie interrupted. 'I for one am pleased to hear that he wants to do things properly.'

'That's right, Dad. I don't want to cause any upset, to Pearl or to John.'

'Kevin, I want you to take this.'

He looked at the wad of notes his father held out, wanting nothing more than to grab them; but as he might need to come back for more, he kept up his act. 'No, Dad. I've caused you and Mum enough heartache as it is and I certainly can't take your money.'

'That's all in the past now and this is just a little

something to help you out.'

'There's no need. I trust in God to provide for my needs.'

'Kevin, please, it would ease my mind if you take it,' Dolly cajoled.

'You have no need to worry about me. I still have a little money and I'll be fine.'

'If you don't find a job straight away, it'll soon run out,' Bernie pointed out.

'Then as I said, Dad, God will provide.'

Bernie stuffed the money into Kevin's hand, saying firmly, 'Right then, you can call this a small donation towards the opening of your refuge.'

Kevin used a practised gentle smile. 'In that case, thank you. The money will be used for just that purpose, and God bless you. Now I must go, but I'll keep in touch.'

'Don't leave it too long before we see you again,' Dolly begged tearfully.

'I'll ring you as soon as I'm settled,' Kevin said, forcing himself to kiss his mother's cheek as he said his goodbyes. He wanted to get out of there, wanted to count the money. How much had his father given him? Would it fund what might be an expensive trip to Soho?

Bernie waited until Dolly was having an afternoon nap, and then rang Pearl in Winchester. 'Pearl, it's Bernie. Kevin's been released. You have nothing to worry about though. Kevin insists that he won't try to see John without your permission.'

'And you believe him? You didn't sound so sure the last time we spoke.'

'I must admit I was sceptical, and I still am – but think about it, Pearl. If Kevin was just using his religious conversion as a ploy to get parole, he has no need to keep it up now that he's been released.'

'Where is he? Is he staying with you?'

'No, he left this morning. He'll be staying with a friend of his in Ealing, but once he's on his feet again he may get in touch with you. If he does, what are you going to do? Will you allow him to see John?'

'I don't know. I don't want to, but maybe if I know he won't be alone with John...' Pearl's voice trailed off.

'From the way Kevin spoke, it won't be for a while yet.'

'Bernie, I've got a bit of news too.'

'Oh, yeah, what's that?'

'Bessie Penfold has passed away,' she said, her voice catching.

'I'm sorry to hear that, love. I know you were fond of her.'

'Yes, I was, but that's not all. She's left me her shop and the flat.'

'Has she? Now that was good of her.'

'There are strings attached,' Pearl told him, going on to explain about the provision in Bessie's will.

'If you ask me, it's a bit much,' Bernie said when she'd finished. 'Nora isn't your responsibility.'

'Derek says the same.'

'Yeah, well, he's right. So what are you going to do?'

There was silence on the line for a moment, but

69

then Pearl said, 'I'm not sure yet, but if I do as Bessie asks, it'll mean telling John the whole truth about Kevin.'

'I don't see why.'

'There are sure to be people in Battersea who remember what Kevin did. I'd rather tell him myself before John hears it from them.'

Just then Bernie heard Dolly stirring and had to end the call. He wondered how John would react when he heard the truth about Kevin. Would he still want to meet his father? Somehow, Bernie doubted it.

After dinner that evening, Pearl went over things in her mind once again. It was early days yet, but at the moment Nora was clinging to her like a limpet. The strangeness of staying here, away from Battersea and all that Nora knew wasn't helping, but Pearl knew if she didn't agree to the terms of Bessie's will, they would soon have to find somewhere else to live. That would not only exacerbate Nora's fears, it would put a huge strain on their marriage, both mentally and financially.

Taking everything into consideration there seemed only one choice, and if they returned to Battersea at least Kevin would be on the other side of the Thames in Ealing. Oh, she was tired – tired of trying to make the right decision. There was so much to consider: her son, her mother and of course her husband. She couldn't do it alone, it was too much, and turning to Derek she voiced one of her concerns. 'I know you think we should move back to Battersea, but it would disrupt John's education.'

'He's young and he'll adapt,' Derek reasoned. 'There's the financial side of things to consider too and as the shop and the premises are worth a good few bob it's a lot to give up.'

'What about your business?'

'Pearl, I'd hardly call it that. I do a bit of painting and decorating, that's all, and the new contract I was hoping to get has fallen through. With only the hope of small jobs coming in now, there's nothing to keep us here.'

'There's my mother.'

'Pearl, she won't be that far away, and we'll see her regularly, or we could ask her to come with us.'

'Come where?'

Startled, Pearl turned to see her mother standing in the doorway.

'To live with us in Battersea,' she explained.

'Oh, no. Surely you aren't going to agree to Bessie's terms?'

'Mum, I don't think we have any choice.'

'Well, I'm sorry, but I won't be coming with you, and what about John? He'd hate it in London. He loves the countryside – and what about his friends?'

'Derek, my mother's right,' Pearl cried as she turned to him. 'Oh, I just don't know what to do.'

'There are weekends, school holidays, and as you don't want to come with us, Emily, perhaps John could spend them with you,' Derek suggested. 'That's if you'd like that.'

'Well, yes, of course I would, but...'

'There you are, Pearl,' Derek cut in. 'Your mum would be pleased to have John and I'm sure he'd

71

be happy with that too.'

'Yes, maybe, I ... I'll go and talk to him,' Pearl said, and aware that she would have to tell her son about his father too there was a dull ache growing in her temples.

Steps faltering, Pearl walked upstairs.

Chapter Nine

'I still can't believe that Bessie Penfold has left Pearl everything, and there's my poor Kevin having to live in one room,' Dolly complained. 'It doesn't seem fair.'

'Leave it out,' Bernie complained. 'It's all you've been going on about and it's getting on me wick.'

Dolly's hands clenched into fists. She wanted nothing more than to lay into Bernie, but somehow, with gritted teeth, she managed to control herself. Bernie still had no idea that she wasn't taking her pills and she wasn't about to give the game away. With an even tone, she said, 'Unlike Pearl, our son is homeless and I'm just worried about him, that's all.'

'There's no need. He's got a room and a good few bob in his pocket on top of that.'

'How much did you give him?'

'A hundred quid.'

'That isn't much towards the refuge.'

'I only said that to get him to take it. If he runs out of money it'll be enough to tide him over.'

'I see. So when he comes to see us again we'll

give him a substantial donation.'

'No, we won't, Dolly.'

'Yes, we will! It's Kevin's dream to open a refuge and I intend to help him.'

Bernie's eyes narrowed. 'Have you taken your pill?'

'Yes, you saw me.'

'In that case, I think I need to make an appointment for you to see the doctor.'

'Whatever you say, Bernie,' she said, climbing into bed. It was so hard to keep up the act, to pretend mildness, but she'd have to be more careful. If she could keep her temper under control, Bernie wouldn't be so suspicious. Nonetheless, she wasn't really worried about the doctor increasing her medication. After all, she wasn't going to take it.

Dolly snuggled down in bed, aware of Bernie climbing into the twin one next to hers. He'd been in control for too long, in control of her pills and her purse. If he was daft enough to think he could stand in the way of her helping her son, then he had another think coming.

When the time was right she'd take over their finances again, and to do that the only one who'd be swallowing her pills would be Bernie.

While his parents slept, Kevin was in Soho. Thanks to one of the many cards displayed in a telephone box, he had found a tart, a tom, but she hadn't been willing to indulge his fantasies. Instead, at the first sign of violence she had threatened him with her pimp and he'd been forced to do things her way. While his immediate needs had been met he'd been left dissatisfied and now

73

drifted into one of the many clubs, finding it surprisingly busy, despite being midweek.

Though thirteen years had passed, Kevin found that nothing had changed, the bar prices astronomical, but there was a stripper gyrating on a small stage who held his attention for a while until her act came to an end.

Kevin looked at his empty glass, unwilling to pay for another drink and about to leave when there was a drum roll. Like those of every other man in the room his eyes were riveted to the stage as the next performer appeared. She was stunning, though it wasn't her long dark hair or perfect features that held his attention: it was her haughty attitude. She stood with her legs slightly apart in a tight black skirt with a side slit, hands on hips as she looked loftily down at them.

What felt like minutes passed, yet probably was only seconds, and Kevin found he was waiting, holding his breath until at last her shoulders and upper body began to sway to the rhythm of drums. Gradually the tempo increased and tauntingly she began to strip, the skirt flung off to reveal long, shapely legs encased in black net stockings and suspenders. She paused for a moment, posing, her smile mocking as though totally aware of her extraordinary sensuality.

Tantalisingly, she took off her top and then knelt on the stage, leaning towards her audience with her breasts oozing out of a tight, black basque. Slowly she ran the tip of her tongue over her lips and then flipped over onto her back, one long leg raised as she peeled off one stocking, then the other.

74

Though he was longing to see more of her stunning body, Kevin found he didn't want her act to end, but then she was on her feet, the basque flung off and all that was left was a tiny thong. With a smile she swung around, bending at the waist to wriggle her magnificent rear end before she turned back, and with a final flourish left the stage, waving like a queen to her subjects.

Kevin was hardly aware of the whistles, the shouts for more as the breath left his body in a rush, his voice a rasp as he leaned over the bar. 'That stripper, I'd like to meet her. What's her name?'

'Adrianna, but forget it, mate, you haven't got a chance.'

'I'd like to buy her a drink.'

'I told you to forget it. She never mixes with the punters.'

Kevin wasn't about to give up and moving to a table, he waited, knowing that shortly a hostess would sidle up. Sure enough, he didn't have to wait long before a brassy, scantily dressed blonde appeared to sit by his side.

'Hello, handsome,' she said as her hand found his thigh. 'Would you like a bit of company?'

'Sure, and I expect you'd like me to buy you a drink?'

'Yes, please.'

'What would you like?'

'Champagne would be lovely.'

Kevin smiled wryly. It was no more than he expected and of course the price would be exorbitant, but as long as he got what he wanted it would be worth it. 'Champagne it is.'

75

She introduced herself as Yvette, but Kevin guessed that the name was fake, just like her hair. Not that he cared. He wasn't interested in her. She was just a means to an end.

'That last stripper was good,' he said casually. 'It explains why this place is so busy.'

'Yeah, Adrianna always pulls them in.'

'If she likes champagne too, perhaps you could invite her to join us and I'll buy another bottle.'

'Take my advice and stay well away from Adrianna. She's the exclusive property of someone you wouldn't want to upset.'

Kevin scowled. He didn't know how he was going to do it yet, but he was going to find a way to get close to Adrianna, exclusive property or not. 'Will she be on again?' he asked.

'No, Adrianna only does one turn a night.'

Did that mean she'd be leaving soon, Kevin wondered. He stood up abruptly, leaving Yvette to the cheap plonk that was supposed to pass for champagne as he drawled, 'See you,' before heading for the door.

It was past two in the morning as Kevin stepped out of the club. There was an alley to one side and glancing down it he saw a side exit. As though the gods were smiling on him, Kevin saw that Adrianna was just coming out, her fantastic body now hidden by a fur coat, her slanted, cat-like eyes becoming wary when she saw him.

Kevin's mind worked quickly, searching for a way to stop her from walking straight past him. 'Excuse me, I'm sorry to bother you but I'm afraid I'm lost. Can you direct me to the nearest Underground station?' he asked appealingly, with what he hoped was a charming and unthreatening manner.

'Go away,' she hissed urgently, her eyes wide with fear as a large, dark car pulled into the kerb.

The door was flung open and a voice ordered, 'Adrianna, get in.'

As she bent to get into the car, Kevin heard the menacing question from the man inside. 'Who's that geezer, Adrianna? Do you know him?'

'No, it's just a bloke asking for directions.'

Taking a chance before the car door closed, Kevin leaned in and though many, many years had passed, he instantly recognised the face that looked back at him. He quickly recovered, saying, 'Sorry, but do you by any chance know where the nearest tube station is?'

'Sod off!' the voice growled.

Kevin did just that, his face sombre as he headed for Ealing. That hostess, Yvette, was right – he didn't want to mess with Vincent Chase.

But he still wanted to mess with his bird.

Chapter Ten

'Thank goodness Nora's still asleep,' Derek said on Sunday morning. 'She hardly leaves your side and we don't get a minute to ourselves nowadays.'

'I know, but it's because she's still unsettled. She'll be a lot better when we move to Battersea,' Pearl said, feeling awful that she couldn't say the same for John. He'd taken the news that they were moving badly, though he had seemed somewhat mollified when Pearl had told him that he could spend every weekend with his grandmother in Winchester. As he'd been upset enough, Pearl hadn't told him the truth about Kevin, but she knew it was something she had to face.

John came downstairs only moments later, mumbling a reply to their greetings. He sat at the table and poured himself a bowl of cornflakes, then paused. 'Mum, I know you said that when we move to Battersea I can spend every weekend here, but you seem to have forgotten something.'

'Have I?'

'I spend one Saturday a month with my grandparents in Southsea.'

'We'll work something out,' Pearl said. She hadn't forgotten. It was another thing that lay heavily on her mind. One complication seemed to follow another and Pearl was at a loss to know what to do.

'Well, Dad, if you ask me, it sounds like you'll be spending hours every weekend driving me around,' John commented, his eyes on Derek.

'Yeah, but I don't mind,' he replied.

Pearl smiled at Derek and knowing that she had to get it over with, she took courage from his presence as she said, 'John, I have something to tell you. It ... it's about Kevin ... your real father. He's been released from prison.'

She watched her son's eyes light up, heard the excitement in his voice. 'He has? Where is he now? Can I see him?'

'Before we get into that, I'm afraid I have to tell you something about your father that I had

78

hoped to keep from you...'

John's brow creased as Pearl hesitated and he urged, 'What is it, Mum?'

'When I felt you were old enough to understand, I told you that your father was sent to prison for robbery, but I'm afraid there was more to it than that. You see ... he ... he tried to steal jewels from a shop, but the old man who owned it tried to stop him and your father, well, he...' Once again, Pearl floundered to a halt.

Pearl saw the bewilderment on her son's face, confusion instead of excitement now clouding his eyes. 'He what, Mum?'

Her eyes went to Derek and he must have seen an appeal in them as he took over, saying bluntly, 'He smashed the poor old sod's head in and left him brain-damaged.'

John just gawked at Derek for a moment, the colour draining from his face. He then stood up, flung back his chair and without a word, he dashed out of the room.

'Did you have to put it like that?' Pearl said angrily. 'Couldn't you have softened it a bit?'

'I don't see how. It's what Kevin did and, as you pointed out, someone in Battersea is sure to bring it up, and I doubt they'll do it delicately.'

Though Pearl acknowledged the truth of Derek's words, she was still angry. 'I'll go after John, tell him that Kevin's changed, that he's a different person, a good man who wants to set up a refuge for the homeless.'

'You can make Kevin sound like a saint, but I ain't so easily fooled,' Derek called after her as she left the room.

In Battersea, Lucy cleared the table. She hoped that Clive would be happy playing with his toy soldiers for a while as she began to take up the sleeves on a jacket. The alteration wasn't going to make her much money, but at least it was something. She needed more sewing, more clients, but with a sinking heart Lucy knew that even if she spent all day stitching, it was never going to make her a fortune.

What she still needed at the moment, and desperately, was the money she was owed from working in Bessie's shop. Take today for instance. Instead of a bit of cheap meat, like belly of pork for their Sunday dinner, all she could make was a pot of vegetable stew.

Unable to concentrate on the sewing, Lucy threw it down. The trouble was that even if she somehow got her pay, once spent there'd be nothing to replace it now that the shop was closed and her job gone.

After shedding so many tears when Paul died, Lucy wasn't one for crying nowadays, but still her eyes welled up at the thought of attending another funeral, this time Bessie's. She had no idea what arrangements had been made and so far Pearl hadn't been in touch to let her know. She'd have to ring Pearl in Winchester, but that meant going to the telephone box and paying for a long distance call. With a heavy sigh, Lucy ran her hands through her hair. She just couldn't afford it ... but then it struck her that she still had the keys to Bessie's shop. She'd go there to use the telephone, and under the circumstances, surely there was nobody who would mind.

Lucy finished the jacket and put it to one side ready for collection. 'Come on, Clive,' she called. 'Get your coat on. We're going out.'

Derek didn't like the way he was feeling, the direction his mind was taking him, but now that Kevin had been released the past was coming back to haunt him. He could remember the day that Pearl had married Kevin Dolby, her belly already rounded in pregnancy. She had been besotted by him, madly in love, only to have her illusions shattered when Kevin had been convicted of robbery with violence.

If it hadn't been for the fact that they were moving back to Battersea, he doubted Pearl would have told John the truth about Kevin, but for the life of him Derek couldn't understand why. Was it because she was still in love with Kevin? Was that it? Had she been hanging on to some sort of long-held dream – a dream that when Kevin was released they'd get back together, with John in ignorance of what his father had done?

No, no, of course Pearl didn't want that, Derek told himself. He was being stupid, his fears arising out of his own stupid insecurities. Instead of worrying about the past, he should be thinking about the future: though Pearl had inherited Bessie's shop and flat, he still had to find work.

The telephone was ringing and with everyone but Nora upstairs, Derek went to answer it. It was Lucy Sanderson asking about Bessie's funeral arrangements. He told her it was to be held on Friday, where and when, said they'd see

81

her there and then ended the call.

As Derek replaced the receiver, Pearl came downstairs, her face pale and drawn. He held out his arms and she walked into them to lay her head on his chest as she spoke. 'I didn't make Kevin sound like a saint. I just told him what Bernie said – that he thinks Kevin has changed – but John doesn't want to know. He said from now on, he's only got one father, and that's you.'

'Are you happy with that?' he asked.

'Of course.'

To Derek her reply sounded terse, and his irrational fear of losing Pearl rose again as he blurted out, 'Do you love me?'

She leaned back to look up at him. 'You know I do.'

'Say it then.'

She looked puzzled. 'What's brought this on?'

'Just say it, Pearl.'

'For goodness' sake, I love you, Derek Lewis. There, are you satisfied?'

'I would be if it sounded like you meant it.'

'This is ridiculous and after seeing the state John was in I'm not in the mood for this,' Pearl said as she pushed his arms away. 'Now I've told you I love you, and maybe after all these years of marriage I don't say it enough, but neither do you.'

Derek hung his head. 'Yeah, you're right and I'm sorry. It's just that with Kevin being released and all this talk of him turning over a new leaf, I thought you might want to go back to him.'

Pearl's eyes widened, her voice high as she cried, 'Are you mad? Not only did he almost kill a defenceless old man, while awaiting trial he was

82

also accused of raping a young woman. She had no proof so the charge was dropped, but as I'd once had a taste of Kevin's perverted idea of love-making, I knew she was telling the truth.'

There was a gasp of horror and they both turned to see John standing behind them on the stairs. He stood frozen for a moment, a look of sheer horror on his face and then, as he had done earlier, he fled.

'Oh no!' Pearl cried. 'Derek, he must have heard everything.'

Nora appeared, her face creased with confusion as she asked, 'What matter, Pearl?'

'You see to Nora and leave John to me,' Derek said. 'I'll go and speak to him.'

Pearl nodded, looking sick with worry, while Derek was inwardly raging. So it was true – Kevin was a rapist, and thinking of his sick, evil hands on Pearl, Derek wished that he was standing in front of him now.

His huge fists clenched – fists he hadn't used since his days as a boxer, fists he had never used outside of the ring, yet all he wanted now was to use Kevin Dolby as a punchbag.

Chapter Eleven

It was Friday and Dolly was growing impatient. Eleven days had passed since Kevin's release but he hadn't been to see them again. She had no idea how to contact him and cursed herself for not thinking to ask for his friend's address and telephone number in Ealing.

'I still feel a bit odd,' Bernie complained. 'I hope I'm not losing it like my father when he was around my age. Maybe I should see the doctor.'

'I suppose it wouldn't hurt,' Dolly agreed. She'd been crushing a half of one of her pills to mix into Bernie's tea in the mornings, but wasn't worried about him seeing the doctor. In fact she could just imagine how the consultation would go. The doctor would ask Bernie what the problem was and he'd voice his worries, list vague symptoms: that he lacked energy, felt tired, and that his head felt sort of muzzy. It was hardly enough for the doctor to diagnose anything, let alone the onset of early senility.

'My head feels a bit clearer so I think I'll leave it for now.'

'Suit yourself,' Dolly told him, already planning her next move. The last few days had been a trial run, one with unexpected results. Bernie thought that he was going senile and she could play on that to gain control of him – and the purse strings again.

Kevin would be so grateful when she gave him a large donation for the refuge, and he wouldn't have to live in one room. They'd both live in a nice house or flat, and though Dolly had no intention of living in Battersea again, there were other boroughs. There was John too. Once he saw how much his father had changed, the lad was sure to want to live with them and that would be one in the eye for Pearl.

84

Pearl sat through Bessie's funeral service, Derek on one side of her and John on the other. Nora was beside John, weeping gently. There were few people behind them: most of Bessie's old acquaintances had died or moved away.

Pearl was in tears too, though she was still reeling from all the changes Bessie's death had wrought. She could understand why Bessie had put those conditions in her will, but knew that if she had just walked away from it all, from the shop and the premises, it wouldn't have been necessary to tell John about his father. Nor would he have overhead her spouting her mouth off to Derek about the rape. It had been an awful week since then, John quiet, withdrawn and unwilling to talk about his feelings.

Pearl lowered her head while a prayer was read. She felt sick inside and now feared that their lives would never be the same again.

A hymn was sung, a few words spoken by the vicar about a woman he had never met, and for Pearl it felt so little to mark the passing of someone who had lived on this earth for seventy-nine years. The curtains had drawn in front of the coffin, but there was a pause, as though they were all waiting for something else to happen, for something else to be said.

Pearl rose to her feet, dabbing her cheeks as she began to leave the pew, but then saw that Nora was still seated, blocking both John's and her mother's path. John bent over Nora speaking so softly that Pearl couldn't hear what he said, but Nora at last stood up, her face wet with tears.

Once outside, Pearl saw that her mother had

led Nora to the scant display of floral tributes, while John held back. She knew it wouldn't be long before Nora would start looking for her, so took the opportunity to hurry to his side. 'John, thank you for taking care of Nora. She's still finding it hard to cope.'

He just shrugged then walked away, while Pearl felt a tug on her arm and turned to see Lucy Sanderson. 'Oh, Lucy, Derek told me that you'd called to ask about the funeral arrangements. I'm so sorry, I should have let you know, but it completely slipped my mind.'

'Don't worry about it,' she said, biting her lip before adding, 'Pearl, can I have a quick word with you?'

'Yes, of course you can. We're going to the Nag's Head for a bite to eat and a drink if you'd like to join us?'

'I'm afraid I can't come and that's why I need to talk to you before you leave. I know this isn't really the time, or place, and I feel awful for bringing this up, but I'm desperate, Pearl. Do you by any chance know who I should talk to about my wages?'

The penny dropped and Pearl felt awful. She knew how hard things were for Lucy, but in the light of all that had happened she hadn't given her a thought. 'How much did Bessie owe you?'

'Ten quid and without it I don't know how I'm gonna pay my rent. I fobbed the landlord off last week with half, but I don't think he'll stand for it again.'

Pearl took her purse out of her bag, thankful to see that she had enough as she pulled out two five-pound notes. 'Here,' she said, holding them out.

Lucy shook her head vigorously. 'No, no, Pearl, I can't take your money.'

'Yes you can.' Pearl said as she stuffed the notes into Lucy's hand. 'Bessie has left me her shop, in fact the whole premises. I'm so sorry, I should have realised that you hadn't been paid.'

'That's all right. I'm just relieved to get my wages.'

'Pearl, it's time we made our way to the Nag's Head,' Derek said as he came to their side. 'Will you be joining us, Lucy?'

'No, I'm afraid not, but Pearl, will you be opening the shop any time soon? If you are, and there's a job going, will you keep me in mind?'

'Yes, of course I will, but we can't do anything until probate has been granted. As soon as I have any news, I'll let you know.'

'Thanks, Pearl. I'll just have a quick word with Nora before I leave.'

Pearl had no idea how long it would be before she could open the shop, but as she watched Nora flinging her arms around Lucy, an idea began to form. One that as she thought about it, became more and more compelling.

John found that nothing about Battersea attracted him as he sat in the pub next to Derek, drinking a glass of lemonade. This was where he'd been born, yet he felt nothing but a desire to go back to Winchester.

'Are you all right, son?'

John nodded and as he looked at Derek he wished he was his real father instead of Kevin

Dolby. He hated that he'd been lied to, told that his real father had been sent to prison for robbery, when it had been so much more than that. He hated looking in the mirror now too, seeing a face that was almost identical to the one he'd seen in his gran's photograph album. 'Dad, can I ask you something?'

'Of course you can.'

'I know I look like him – Kevin – and we've got the same blood too. Does ... does that mean that I'm capable of doing the things he did ... terrible things?'

'Other than looking a bit like him, believe me, you're cut from a totally different cloth. You're more like your mother, with a little of your Gran Emily thrown into the mix.'

'Are you sure?'

'John, I've known you since you were a baby and I've watched you grow up. You haven't got a bad bone in your body and though I'm only your stepfather, I'm proud of you, son.'

John felt a well of emotions and if he hadn't been nearly a teenager, he'd have reached out to grasp Derek's hand. Instead he fought to choke back his feelings, his voice sounding gruff to his ears as he said, 'Thanks, Dad, but there's something else. I don't want to see him. I never want to see him and I'm not going to Southsea again. He might turn up there.'

'That's going to upset Dolly and Bernie,' Derek pointed out.

'I know, and I'm sorry about that,' John said, then blurted out, 'I wish we could stay in Winchester.'

'I know you do, son, but there really isn't room for all of us in your gran's house. Don't worry though, she'll have my guts for garters if I don't drive you down there every weekend.'

'I suppose you're looking forward to moving back here.'

'I can't deny that. This is my home turf and the boxing club I used to manage isn't far from here,' Derek said with a hint of pride in his voice. 'I know it's nothing like Winchester, but it isn't so bad. It's not all built up, you know. There are lots of open spaces, walks by the Thames, and Battersea Park is close by, with a boating lake and lots of other things to explore. It's also just a hop to Wimbledon Common. When I was a nipper we used to fish in the ponds, though I mostly netted newts. I used to bring them home in a jam jar, but my gran used to go potty and wouldn't let me keep them. Blimey,' he mused, 'those were the days.'

John didn't think a park or common could compete with living in the country, but at least it was something. Maybe it wouldn't be too bad, and at least Derek was going to take him home every weekend. John knew that Winchester would always be that to him – home. And when he was grown up, he'd go back there permanently.

John sipped his lemonade again, finding a measure of comfort in that thought.

That night, unable to get Adrianna out of his mind, Kevin was getting ready to go out. From the way she'd reacted when he tried to talk to her, he suspected that Adrianna was terrified of

Vince, and that meant she might want to get away from him.

As he looked in the mirror, Kevin turned this way and that. He was pleased with his appearance, but now he'd bought new togs the money his father had given him was disappearing fast. Still, he thought, there was always Rupert.

Kevin had told his mother that he and Rupert were like-minded, inferred a religious connection, but that was far from the truth. Rupert had in fact been Kevin's cellmate, an old poof who was inside for having sex with a fifteen-year-old boy.

Of course Rupert protested that he was innocent, that the boy had told him he was older, and that like others before him he was just after his money. It was a comment that had piqued Kevin's interest. He decided that if his mother didn't cough up some dosh when he got out, it would be handy to add another string to his bow until he was able to carry out his plan.

Unlike most of the other inmates, Kevin had found that when he was desperate with frustration, any port in a storm was better than nothing. Of course he preferred women, but some of the pretty, effeminate types of men that passed through had been passable substitutes.

Kevin couldn't call Rupert pretty, or effeminate, but he'd managed to perform and soon the soppy, soft old sod was blabbing about his inherited wealth, begging him to move into his home when he got out. Rupert had also thought Kevin's religious act was hilarious, but he'd helped him to tweak the role, something that proved invaluable in getting his parole.

What he hadn't bargained for was Rupert's sulks when he hadn't gone straight to Ealing when he got out, but he'd managed to placate him. The problem was that Rupert had been fleeced so many times in the past that he was distrustful and wary, his purse firmly shut, but it was time to change that, Kevin decided as he went downstairs. He had always got what he wanted from his mother, and he'd do the same with Rupert. It was just a matter of knowing how to handle him.

As he walked into the drawing room, Kevin asked, 'How do I look?'

'Gorgeous, darling,' Rupert said, licking his lips. 'I don't know why you won't let me come out with you tonight.'

'I told you, it isn't a social outing,' Kevin lied, thinking that the last thing he wanted was to be seen with such an obvious poof. 'I'm meeting an old friend who may be able to offer me a job.'

'Is this a male friend?' Rupert asked sulkily.

'Yes, but don't worry, if I'm late home I'll try not to wake you. In fact, if this job comes up I'll be able to find my own place.'

'Don't be silly,' Rupert said quickly. 'I don't want you to do that. You can stay here as long as you like.'

'It's good of you to offer, but I'll only stay if I get this job. If I don't get it and can't pay my own way, I'll move back in with my parents.'

'But–'

'Right, I'm off. I'll see you later,' Kevin interrupted as he walked out, leaving Rupert to stew on his words, sure that they'd have the desired effect...

Chapter Twelve

Adrianna had finished her act and was now taking off the heavy stage make-up before redoing her eyes with a lighter touch. Vince would be here in half an hour to pick her up and she didn't want to keep him waiting. He'd get annoyed if she did. Adrianna remembered the slap he'd given her just for talking to a bloke outside the club who'd asked for directions, and shivered. Her father had been a violent man too, and her childhood an unhappy one. She had been dragged from borough to borough as her parents dodged one rent man after another. Or sometimes it had been the police – her father preferred petty thieving to an honest day's work.

'If I had your looks,' said Lola, one of the other strippers, as she stroked Adrianna's fur coat, 'I'd get myself a sugar daddy too.'

'If you're talking about the boss, you're welcome to him.'

'Is that right? Well, maybe I should tell him you said that.'

'I'd deny it, and if you think he'll believe *you*, over *me*, then go ahead,' Adrianna said with a show of bravado. 'He'll be here soon to pick me up.'

'If I wasn't due on stage I would,' Lola spat before quickly leaving the poky dressing room.

Adrianna knew from Lola's hasty departure that it was an idle threat and got on with removing her make-up, thinking that she had to learn to keep her mouth shut. She knew the other girls thought she had it made, that Vince gave her everything, such as the fur coat, but little did they know that she longed for him to find someone else – another girl to take her place.

Adrianna knew she wasn't anything like the confident, haughty stripper who performed on stage. She was far from being in control: instead Vince controlled her and she was too afraid of him to break away.

Her mind shied away from Vince and drifted back to her childhood. Her parents had moved so many times, and she had been to so many different schools, that friendships had been hard to form, let alone sustain. She had been an only child, a lonely child, one who lived inside her head with dreams of one day becoming a dancer. Adrianna could remember to this day where that dream had come from, but not the place. It had been one of the many boroughs they had lived in, their flat cramped, but it had been close to a school of dance.

Like a magnet she had been drawn to the sound of a piano playing and had sneaked inside to peep round the door that led into a hall. A class was in progress, or perhaps some sort of rehearsal, young girls dressed in white tutu skirts and ballet pumps. Adrianna smiled. To her it had looked magical as they danced in a circle, their arms raised in pretty arches. The circle then opened to reveal another girl who appeared so delicate, almost ethereal as she performed a series of pirouettes and arabesques.

Adrianna could recall being so enthralled that she had hurried home and begged to go to the school of dance, but that night they had crept out of the flat in the early hours, dodging the rent and yet another landlord.

With a sigh, Adrianna now applied her lipstick. Becoming a dancer had been an impossible dream, and by the age of fourteen all she had longed for was the chance to get away from the life her parents led. Her chance had come when she was fifteen. She had seen a live-in job advertised and she'd been taken on, but by the time she was sixteen she hated being a skivvy. It was then that the offer of a job in a shop with a room above it had come up and she had jumped at the chance.

Once again her thoughts were interrupted when one of the hostesses walked in, a note in her hand. 'One of the blokes out front asked me to give you this.'

Without reading it, Adrianna screwed the note into a ball and threw it into the bin. 'You know I don't mix with the punters.'

'I told him that, but he offered me a good few bob to give that to you and I wasn't about to turn it down.'

'More fool him.'

'Yeah, there's a mug born every minute, but I'd best get back out front.'

Adrianna's smile was tight. It was still impossible to form friendships, Vince kept her too close to him for that, but even if she had the opportunity she knew that other women were jealous of her looks. The other girls in the club were proof of that and as Adrianna looked at her reflection in

94

the mirror, she wished that she had never met the woman who had tempted her into becoming what she had called an exotic dancer. She'd been Ruth Canning then, a name she refused to use now and nearly nineteen years old. She'd been hard up, sick of working in shops or factories and it was the magical word *dancing* that had drawn her in.

It hadn't been easy, but she'd managed to pay the woman for lessons. She'd learned the craft and learned it well, but it was a craft she now hated. It wasn't because of the leering punters. She'd grown used to them and could blank them out. She hated being an exotic dancer, a stripper, because it had eventually brought her to the attention of Vincent Chase.

Ready to leave now, Adrianna flung her fur coat around her shoulders, thinking that just as she had longed to get away from her parents, she was now desperate to get away from Vince. Of course any chance of achieving that seemed impossible – another impossible dream.

After being inside for so long without sight of a beautiful woman, Kevin had began to wonder if he'd exaggerated Adrianna's attractions in his mind. He hadn't, and once again he'd been riveted by her performance. Sultry, sexy, catlike, he relished the thought of taming her. However, paying a hostess to take her a note had been a waste of time. What he needed was a chance to be alone with Adrianna, a chance to turn on the charm, and with any luck when she left the club this time, Vince wouldn't be around to pick her up.

Kevin swallowed the last of his drink and walked

outside. Cars were parked along the road, but none of them looked occupied, the coast clear as he hung around.

Just fifteen minutes later Kevin's patience was rewarded when Adrianna left by the side exit. Stepping forward with a smile on his face, he said, 'Hello there, remember me?'

Kevin was only aware of her eyes rounding in panic before arms locked around him from behind. He struggled, but found himself spun around to face a man moving out of the shadows, his face contorted with anger.

'Get back inside,' Vince yelled at Adrianna. 'I'll deal with you later.'

Another of Vince's heavies moved to the kerb, beckoned, and as a car pulled up, Vince climbed in the back, the heavy in the front. Kevin was then shoved from behind, forced inside to find himself trapped between Vince and the mountain of a bloke who'd held him.

'Drive!' Vince ordered.

Kevin thought quickly. 'What's going on, Vince? We go back a long way so why have you snatched me?'

Vince's head snapped round, his hard, gimlet eyes studying Kevin for a moment before he said, 'Nah, I don't know you.'

'Yes, you do, Vince, though I must admit you didn't see me very often. Before I went inside I used to knock around with a couple of blokes and we fenced the stuff we nicked through you. My name is Kevin – Kevin Dolby.'

There was silence for a moment as Vince pursed his lips, but then he nodded. 'Dolby, yeah, that name rings a distant bell. Are you the bloke who beat the shit out of a jeweller?'

'Yes, that's me. I've just got out after doing thirteen years.'

'So what are you doing sniffing around my bird?'

'If you mean that stripper who was leaving the club, sorry, mate, I've only just got out of the nick and I didn't know she was your property.'

The blow to Kevin's stomach was swift and unexpected, leaving him doubled over in agony as Vince growled, 'Don't take me for a mug. You're the bloke who was hanging around last week. You saw Adrianna get into my car and you clocked me when you had nerve to stick your head inside me motor.'

'Vince ... mate...'

Kevin's apology was cut off. 'I ain't your mate!' Vince snarled. 'If I was you'd know that I'm a reasonable man who's prepared to overlook a genuine mistake. Yours wasn't. You knew she was my property all right, and you should have kept away, but instead you turned up again tonight.'

'I wasn't there to chat her up. We just happened to be leaving the club at the same time, and I just said hello, that's all.'

'Nice try,' Vince said, 'but I was in the club tonight, watching you from my manager's office and my girls know better than to cross me. I was shown the note you paid good money to send to Adrianna.'

'But...'

'Shut up! Stan, Bert, we're going to pull up here and then he's all yours.'

When the car drew into the kerb, Kevin was

97

yanked out. He tried to fight back, but up against two giant thugs he didn't stand a chance as they laid into him with fists, and when he hit the floor, their boots.

Pain shot through him with each kick, agonising pain, but finally when Vince called them they backed off, like dogs obeying their master. With one final kick each they returned to the car, leaving Kevin bruised, bloodied, and barely conscious as it sped away.

Kevin didn't know how long he lay there, drifting in and out of consciousness, and he had only vague memories of someone coming to his aid. The man helped him up and was good enough to drive him home when he refused to go to hospital.

The time had passed in a blur, though Kevin had flashes of memory: Rupert crying, being tended to by skilled hands, but only finding out days later that it had been Rupert's private doctor.

With broken ribs, his body in agony, and his face a swollen mass of cuts and bruises, it was Rupert who looked after him – Rupert who over the next few weeks nursed Kevin back to health.

Chapter Thirteen

It was Saturday morning, a special one in May, and as probate had been granted earlier than expected Pearl, Derek, John and Nora were moving to Battersea the next day.

To Pearl's relief, Kevin hadn't been in touch and John had become a little more communicative.

'Happy birthday, darling,' she said as he walked into the kitchen.

'Happy birthday, Johnny,' Nora said as she ran forward to give him a hug. 'You all right?'

'Yes, I'm fine.'

Pearl knew that Nora was sensitive to John's feelings, and it was obvious his words had failed to reassure her as she looked at him sadly.

Hoping to lift the mood, Pearl was about to give John his present when the doorbell rang. 'I'll get it,' she said, thinking that it might be the postman.

'Hello, Pearl.'

'Bernie! I wasn't expecting you.'

'It's all right. I know John won't come to Southsea with me, but as this is a present I couldn't put in the post, I left early to deliver it myself. It'll be nice to see the lad, but I can't stay long. I've got to get back to Dolly. She hasn't heard from Kevin again and despite her medication she's getting herself in a right old state.'

'Come in, but please, don't mention Kevin in John's hearing.'

'Now look here, Pearl, this can't go on,' Bernie protested. 'I know you felt you had to tell John the whole truth about Kevin, but we haven't seen the boy in ages and it isn't fair that we're suffering for it too.'

'I know and I'm sorry, but John won't visit you while there's a chance he'll bump into Kevin.'

'Let me talk to him. I might be able to persuade

him to change his mind.'

'No, Bernie, it isn't the right time. John's upset enough about us moving to Battersea tomorrow and I don't want anything else to ruin his birthday.'

After a pause, he agreed, 'Yeah, all right.'

Relieved, Pearl ushered Bernie into the kitchen. Derek looked surprised to see him too, while John's face was a picture as he looked at his grandfather, part pleasure, part panic.

'Happy birthday, lad,' Bernie said, placing the box on the table. 'Now don't hang about – open it.'

As he lifted the lid, John gasped with wonder. He reached inside to lift the tiny ginger kitten into his arms. 'Oh, Granddad...'

'There's a farm up the road and I knew that one of the cats was having kittens. The farmer was happy for me to have one, and thankfully it worked out the right time to take it away from the mother. Sorry, Pearl, I hope you don't mind.'

Even if she had minded, Pearl wouldn't have had the heart to burst John's bubble. Her son looked happier than he had in weeks. 'I'm fine with it, Bernie, but it's just as well we're moving out tomorrow. My mother isn't keen on cats.'

'Granddad, is it a boy or a girl?' John asked.

'It's a ginger tom, lad, a boy.'

'Has he got a name?'

'Not yet. It's up to you to choose one.'

John lifted the kitten onto the palm of his hand, gazing at it, and Nora came to his side, obviously enchanted too. 'Look, Johnny, he got stripes.'

'Yes, like a tiger. How's that for a name?'

100

Nora shook her head vigorously. 'No. Don't like tigers.'

'There's no hurry, John, think about it for a while,' Pearl suggested.

'My goodness,' Emily said as she walked in, 'what have you got there?'

'It's a kitten, Gran,' John said, holding it aloft. 'Bernie gave it to me for my birthday.'

'Yes, happy birthday, darling. Though I'm not a lover of cats, I must admit it's rather cute,' she said, then turned to Bernie. 'Has anyone offered you a cup of tea yet?'

'I suppose by anyone, you mean me,' Pearl said, smiling.

'I'll make it,' Derek offered.

Pearl persuaded John to open his other presents, but none could compete with the kitten. Not that she minded. It was just lovely to see her son's delight.

Only twenty minutes later, after Bernie finished his drink, he asked for their new telephone number and then rose to leave. 'I'd best get back to Dolly, but good luck with the move. I hope you settle in all right.'

'We'll be fine,' Derek said.

'John, say goodbye to your grandfather,' Pearl urged.

'Bye, lad, and I hope you'll come to see me and your gran soon.'

John's head went down. 'I ... I don't know ... maybe.'

'I suppose *maybe is* something to work on. Just remember that you mean a lot to your gran and she's missing you.'

101

John didn't respond to that, saying only, 'Thanks again for the kitten, Granddad.'

'You're welcome.'

As Pearl saw him out, Bernie paused at the door. 'If you can talk John into visiting us again, I don't mind driving to Battersea to pick him up.'

'I'll let you know,' Pearl told him. But in truth, as long as John didn't want to see his father, she knew he wouldn't go to Southsea.

Kevin had made so many plans while in prison, but now, when he'd been in agony every time he moved, it wasn't his parents or his son on his mind. It was Vincent Chase. His hate festered, taking over his every thought, and every time he looked at his face in the mirror, the thin scar that now cut through his eyebrow made Kevin's teeth grind with fury.

He was determined on revenge, to make Vince pay for ordering his henchmen to lay into him with their fists and boots. The beating had served to show him one thing; that Vince placed a very high value on Adrianna and she must be really special for the man to keep her so close.

Kevin smiled sardonically. Vince probably thought the beating had frightened him off, but he would learn differently. When the time was right he'd strike, and to rub salt into the wound, he'd also take Adrianna from under Vince's nose.

He'd been laid up for a long time, April passing into May, but now Kevin was on his feet again. With his suit ruined, Rupert had just surprised him with two new ones, along with some very expensive-looking shirts. There were casual

102

clothes too, and Kevin had feigned suitable gratitude.

'Time for elevenses,' Rupert said as he walked in with a tray. 'Coffee and cake.'

'I'm not hungry.'

'Now then, if you want to build up your strength, you must eat.'

'You gave me a huge breakfast, and I'm still full. In fact I've been inactive for too long and I'm going out for a walk.'

'Oh dear,' Rupert said anxiously. 'Do you really think you should?'

'Rupert, I'm sick of being cooped up.'

'All right, but I think I should join you.'

'No thanks.' Kevin said firmly. 'I'd prefer a nice quiet stroll on my own.'

'Why? Is it because you're sick of the sight of me?'

'I didn't say that,' Kevin said as he pulled on a pair of new jeans. 'It's just that walking alone helps me to think.'

'Think about what?'

'About getting a job,' he lied, 'and earning enough to repay the money you spent on my new clothes. Along with that I want to find my own place – something I was planning to do before those bastards put a stop to it.'

'It's awful that you were picked on by those drunken thugs, but those clothes are a gift, Kevin. I also don't think you're well enough to think about getting a job, and as for finding your own place, there's no need for that. I'd love you to stay here.'

'I can't go on living off you and I've got to find

work,' Kevin said, grunting in pain as he bent to tie his shoelaces.

'See,' Rupert tutted. 'You're not fit to work yet.'

'I'll have to manage. I should go to see my parents, but I can't even afford the train fare. I'm broke, Rupert.'

'I can soon sort that out,' Rupert said. 'If you really feel up to it you can go to see them today. Wait there. I won't be a minute.'

Kevin smiled. Rupert was about to open his wallet again. Of course when the money was offered, he'd protest, say he couldn't possibly take it, but then he'd give in.

He just hoped that Rupert wasn't going to be stingy. If he was ... well, there was more than one way to skin a cat, and if he played up his injuries his father might cough up some money again.

Chapter Fourteen

Dolly couldn't stand the way she was feeling, the anxiety about Kevin and the hurt that John wouldn't come to see them. To make sure that Bernie was fit to drive, she hadn't given him a half pill that morning, but he'd returned without John. She blamed Pearl, hated Pearl, wanting nothing more than to wring her neck, to see the life squeezed out of her.

'You should have talked to John,' Dolly said, trying to stay calm when Bernie returned alone from Winchester. 'You should have told him

104

yourself that Kevin really has changed.'

'Pearl didn't want him mentioned. It wasn't the right time.'

'You fool. Can't you see what she's up to?'

'She's only doing what she thinks is best for John.'

'And that's keeping him away from us.'

'Don't be daft, woman.'

Dolly's temper flared. 'Who do you think you're talking to! Woman! I'll give you woman,' she yelled, waving her fist in his face.

Bernie reared back, shocked. 'Now I know you haven't taken your pills.'

'When you dish them out, I take them, but you're getting more and more forgetful lately,' Dolly said, glad that her mind had quickly given her a way to use Bernie's fears against him.

'Forgetful?' Bernie said, blanching.

'Did you give me my pills before you left this morning?' she asked slyly.

'Yes, I think so ... but maybe I didn't,' he said. 'Can't *you* remember?'

'I can't recall taking them.'

'Bloody hell, I'll get them now.'

Dolly didn't care. She'd become adept at pretending to take them, sometimes palming them in her hand, or secreting the pills under her tongue until she was able to spit them out.

'This explains a lot,' Bernie said as he handed them to her, 'and I'm beginning to wonder how many times I've forgotten your medication.'

Dolly said nothing, leaving him to stew, and as usual she feigned taking the pills. She would shortly have to appear calm, even-tempered, yet with her mind filled with hate, it wouldn't be easy.

It was two thirty in the afternoon when there was a knock on the door. When Bernie went to open it, he called out, 'Look who's here, Dolly.'

Kevin walked into the room, and Dolly surged to her feet, 'Kevin, thank goodness. I was so worried about you.'

'Mum, there's no need. I'm a grown man now, though I'm sorry if I've caused you any concern.'

'I expected you to keep in touch,' she said, but then looking at Kevin closely she exclaimed, 'Your face! Have you been in some sort of accident?'

'Yes, I'm afraid so. I was doing a bit of driving work for an agency, but that came to a swift end when someone slammed into the back of me and my face had an argument with the windshield.'

Dolly's stomach lurched. Kevin could have been killed! 'Oh, my poor boy. No wonder you haven't been to see us.'

'I must admit I wasn't a pretty sight for a while.'

'Why didn't you ring us?' Dolly asked. 'We'd have come to see you.'

'I'm afraid I wasn't in any fit state to do that. I was laid up with concussion.'

'Oh, Kevin, you'd better sit down,' Dolly cried. 'How long were you in hospital?'

'I wasn't. Rupert's been taking care of me and I saw his private doctor. Now that I'm on my feet again I'm looking for a job, a permanent one this time.'

Worried, Dolly asked, 'Are you sure you're fully recovered?'

'Ready or not, I must find work. Rupert has refused to take a penny off me while I've been ill, and I want to repay his generosity.'

'What about the money your father gave you?'

'I can't touch that. It was a donation.'

'But he just said that to encourage you to take it,' Dolly protested.

'Thanks, Dad,' Kevin said, turning to his father, 'it was good of you, but I've put the money into the refuge fund.'

Bernie just acknowledged Kevin's thanks with a nod, and Dolly asked, 'Kevin, how much have you got in this fund?'

'So far there's just your donation, but I hope to get the mission I told you about on board.'

'I thought this chap you're staying with was going to help?'

'When I find the right premises, he will.'

'How much will it cost to get the place up and running?' she asked.

Kevin's lips pursed in thought. 'It's hard to name an exact figure. There'd be the lease, but Rupert will pay for that. We'll need beds, bedding, clothing, kitchen equipment, along with ongoing costs such as food for those we take in. I could go on, but that should give you an idea.'

'Bernie, we should help,' Dolly said.

'What?' he said, startled. 'Sorry, I was miles away.'

'I said we should give Kevin another, larger, donation.'

'I don't know. I'll think about it,' he replied.

Dolly wasn't worried. Bernie was welcome to think about it, but soon she'd be in control. She was going to help her son, and Bernie wouldn't be able to stand in her way.

Dolly was asking Kevin for his telephone number and as they continued to chat, Bernie's thoughts drifted. His mind was sometimes so foggy that he was unable to think straight, but at the moment he felt all right. It wouldn't last though. He'd seen it before, had watched his father's gradual deterioration, only small signs at first, but then he'd become more and more forgetful.

Bernie shuddered, remembering how his father had sunk further into senility until his mother had to tend to him as though he was a child, feeding him, cleaning up his bodily functions, until it had almost broken her.

'Are you all right, Dad?'

'What?'

'I asked you if you're all right.'

'Sorry, Kevin, I was miles away,' Bernie said. Yes, he was miles away, travelling the same route as his father. He was losing it. He was going senile.

'Bernie, you're always drifting off into a world of your own,' Dolly complained.

'Am I?'

'Yes. Sometimes it's like talking to a brick wall.'

Bernie's stomach churned as he wondered how long it would be before he couldn't look after himself, let alone Dolly. His mind felt clear at the moment, yet as he'd forgotten to give Dolly her pills that morning, maybe that was just an illusion.

'Dad, I can see you're worried about something. Is there anything I can do to help?' Kevin offered.

Bernie knew that he had no choice. There was nobody else, only Kevin and before he lost it completely, he'd have to put his affairs in order. 'I ... I'm getting forgetful and I think I might be going senile.'

'I doubt that, Dad. You're only around your mid-fifties, aren't you?'

'I'm fifty-six, and my father was about that age when he started showing the early signs of senile dementia.'

'That doesn't mean you are too. You seem fine to me, maybe a little tired, but that's all.'

'That's because your father drove to Winchester and back this morning,' Dolly said. 'It's your son's birthday today, Kevin, something *you* seem to have forgotten.'

'Of course I haven't. Even though I'm still on the mend it's another reason why I made the journey. I was hoping to see John.'

'He isn't here,' Bernie told him, 'and it's just as well. You said you wouldn't try to see him without Pearl's permission.'

'Whose side are you on, Bernie?' snapped Dolly. 'And you're forgetting that John doesn't want to see Kevin now. Pearl's seen to that.'

'What do you mean?' Kevin asked.

'She's turned him against you.'

'Now then, Dolly, that wasn't Pearl's intention,' Bernie said, quickly going on to explain things to Kevin, impressed when he didn't react angrily.

'I see,' Kevin said quietly. 'So because they're moving back to Battersea, Pearl felt she had to tell John the truth. I can understand why she felt it was necessary, though I'm sad that my son doesn't want to see me.'

'I blame Pearl. She's a vindictive cow,' Dolly snapped. 'She didn't have to tell John about the rape charge too. It was dropped, but she conveniently forgot that.'

'Now then, Dolly, you know it wasn't intentional,' Bernie reminded her. 'Pearl said John overheard them talking about it, and it was the last thing she wanted.'

'It doesn't matter, I'm just glad that the truth is out,' Kevin said. 'God forgave my sins and I can only pray that John will too.'

Bernie still found it strange to hear Kevin talking about prayers and God, but he also drew a little comfort from it. If it was genuine, then when the time came Kevin would take care of his mother. Of course he would need the means to do it, but what if Kevin was making a mug out of them? What if this was all just an act to get money out of them? He rose to his feet, deep in thought as he stood looking out of the window. Maybe he could test Kevin, suggest something to see how he responded. He had just come up with an idea when Dolly broke into his thoughts.

'Bernie, you're off in a world of your own again.'

'I've been thinking, that's all,' he said, deciding that this was as good a time as any, 'about giving Kevin a bit of money to help him out. Not only that, now that Pearl has inherited Bessie's place, we should change our wills.'

'What has Pearl's inheritance got to do with changing our wills?' Dolly asked.

'Because the shop and flat must be worth a

good few bob and one day it'll go to John. He'll be nicely set up then, so I think we should leave what we have to Kevin.'

'No, Dad, I'd rather it went to John. And as for giving me money, there's no need. You haven't got a regular income now and with many years ahead of you, I wouldn't want you to break into your capital.'

'I invested well and we can afford it, son.'

'Maybe you can now, but things can change. Interest rates can fall, and there may come a time when you need to do things to this cottage, a new roof for instance, and your car won't last forever.'

Bernie was impressed. Kevin had not only refused to take any money, he also talked a lot of sense. 'All right, son, as long as you're sure, but as for our wills my mind is made up and we'll change them in your favour.'

'I'd rather you didn't. As I've said before, I trust in God to provide all I need.'

Bernie just smiled. It didn't matter how much Kevin protested. He was now determined to make his son his heir.

Though Kevin had managed to sound pious, even calm, when told that his son didn't want to see him, his stomach had been churning with anger until his dad had brought up the subject of inheritance.

John had been a baby when Kevin had been sent to prison, and he hadn't wanted him to grow up seeing his father behind bars. He'd told Pearl to get John away from his mother and then stepped away, agreeing to a divorce and not contesting it

111

when Pearl was given full custody. After all, he could hardly be a father to his son while in jail; but he'd been sure that when released he'd have no trouble becoming part of John's life again. Pearl knew that he would never harm his son so there was no reason for her to object. He might have missed the boy's childhood, yet he would see him grow into a man.

But now Pearl was trying to put a stop to that and Kevin began to inwardly fume again. It didn't matter that he'd hardly spared his son a thought since his release, not even realising it was John's birthday, although he had covered the fact well in front of his parents. What mattered was that Pearl had turned his son against him. He'd make her sorry, he'd sort her out, but not now, he had other things on his mind now.

Dolly's voice broke into his musing. 'Kevin, you haven't touched your sandwich.'

'I was just about to,' he said, hardly tasting a thing as he bit into it. He'd been tempted when his father had talked about giving him some money, but something, a sort of sixth sense that it might be some sort of test, had made him turn it down. Their wills were more important, and he'd expected to use months of subtle persuasion to get his parents to change them, but that wasn't necessary now.

Of course it was too soon to carry out the rest of his plan. If it came to light that they'd died just after changing their wills in his favour, he'd be the obvious suspect, and after just getting out after serving thirteen years, there was no way he was going back inside again.

112

For now he'd have to be patient, but at the thought of the rewards in store, Kevin knew it wouldn't be easy. What he needed was a diversion – and as he still had to deal with Vincent Chase, working out a way to get his revenge would keep him happily occupied.

Chapter Fifteen

Lucy had spent most of the same day trying her hand at tie-dyeing some plain white T-shirts that she'd got for next to nothing from Eddie White, a stallholder who couldn't shift them. She had used money that she could ill afford, earned from a complicated alteration, but desperate times called for desperate measures, and she hoped to make a decent profit.

With a deft hand, Lucy took the centre of the fabric and twisted it into a spiral, securing it with elastic bands before immersing the garment in red dye. If they turned out all right, Lucy knew that she would need an outlet, somewhere to display them, but as she had known Eddie White since her childhood, she was hoping to persuade him to either buy them back, or to sell them for her with a share of the profit. Eddie was all right, though he was a bit of a womaniser who flirted with every female customer. Mind you, he was funny, she had to give him that, and nobody left his stall without a smile on their face.

'Mummy, you look like you've got red gloves

on,' said Clive.

'Oh dear, you're right,' she said, holding them up. 'I should have worn rubber ones, but it's too late now.'

'Will you help me with this jigsaw puzzle?'

'Not now, pet,' she said. 'It's nearly time to make dinner, but I'll rinse this batch out first.'

It was less then half an hour later, and Lucy was pleased as she held up the T-shirts. They looked great, each one a little different and good enough to sell, she was sure. She'd done enough for today, but tomorrow she'd try the blue dye. 'I'll just hang these up to dry,' she said to Clive, but then the doorbell rang.

Her eyes widened when she saw who it was.

'The landlord asked me to give you this,' the agent said without preamble.

'What is it?'

'Two weeks' notice to leave the flat.'

'But I paid the arrears and I'm up to date with the rent!'

'I know, but he's selling this place and he wants you out. You'll have to find another flat, or try the borough council.'

'I have. I've been on their housing list for years.'

The man just shrugged and walked away, while Lucy stood frozen on the doorstep.

'Mum, what's wrong?'

At the sound of Clive's voice, Lucy fixed a smile on her face. 'Nothing, darling,' she said, turning to face him. Somehow she had to hide her worries from Clive, but finding somewhere else to live in just two weeks seemed an impossible task.

Vincent Chase didn't have to worry about money. He'd come a long way and his clubs were highly profitable, but one thing he'd learned was to never take chances. He wasn't really worried, but just in case Dolby had connections, he'd sent one of his boys to check him out.

'He may have been inside for thirteen years, boss, but there are plenty of people in Battersea who remember him and were willing to dish the dirt. He hasn't got any back-up. He's just a small-time thief who got done for robbery with violence.'

'What about his family? Any connections there?'

'None,' Stan replied. 'He was married with a kid, but they're well out of the picture now, and apparently his mother went into a nut house.'

'Did you hear that, Adrianna? No wonder your fancy man had the nerve to take me on. Insanity must run in his family.'

'He isn't my fancy man.'

Vince chuckled. 'He was pretty, I'll give you that – at least he was before the boys got hold of him. I doubt they did his face any favours.'

'Can I go now?' Adrianna asked, appearing disinterested.

Vince agreed and as the door closed behind her, he said, 'I was a bit heavy-handed with her, but I don't think she knew Dolby. Still, it served as a warning in case she gets any ideas in the future.'

'Yeah,' Stan agreed, 'and for Dolby too. I don't think we'll be seeing his face again.'

'We'd better not,' he said. Adrianna was his star stripper, her performances guaranteed to pull in the punters, and he'd groomed her to his tastes in bed too. Nobody, connected or not, was getting their hands on his property.

Adrianna sat in Vince's room, one she was forced to share, hating it; the plush red velvet decor, the mirror above the bed, but most of all, hating the man who owned it – who owned her.

She didn't care that the bloke who'd hung about outside the club had been given a hiding. Because of him she'd got a slap too. All she cared about was finding a way to escape from Vince, but he hardly let her out of his sight and she didn't have any money. He had eyes and ears everywhere, and her only hope would be to get well away from here, but without funds it was impossible. Vince bought all her clothes, make-up and anything else she needed, giving her just a paltry few bob as pocket money. Any jewellery he had given her he insisted on keeping in his safe, and it was only brought out when he decided she should wear it.

Vince walked into the room and, seething with hate, Adrianna avoided looking at him. When they first met she had known that he was a powerful man, and though old enough to be her father, his age didn't seem to matter. He'd been so charismatic, so caring, and had showered her with gifts. Within a month she was working the top spot in one of his clubs and within three she had agreed to move into his house. The luxurious lifestyle he led had stunned her, blinding her to the early clues – the way he controlled her, his jealousy, but once the scales had dropped from her eyes, she had seen that she was living with a monster.

'Still sulking I see,' he said.

'I'm not sulking.'

'Prove it.'

Bile rose in Adrianna's throat. She knew what that meant and, feeling sick, she began to undress. Vince watched her, his eyes dark with lust, and when he began to slobber all over her body she willed her mind to another place. Thankfully, it was over quickly, it always was, and rolling away, Vince put his clothes back on. He then took a box from his jacket pocket and threw it onto the bed. 'Just a little something I thought you might like. You've earned it.'

Adrianna opened the box, and as she looked at the diamond-encrusted bracelet she felt nothing but self-loathing. She was an exotic dancer, not a tart, but this felt more like a payment.

Soho was far from Winchester and while Adrianna was just finishing her act, Pearl was tossing and turning, unable to sleep. This was the last night they would spend in her mother's house, and though they would still see lots of her, it was going to be so hard to say goodbye in the morning.

Pearl plumped up her pillows, but sleep was still impossible and irritably she got out of bed. Maybe a mug of hot milk would help. It was her own fault she was feeling like this. She had made the decision to return to Battersea, but nevertheless it felt forced upon her.

'What's the matter?' Derek mumbled.

'Nothing. Go back to sleep,' she said. Pearl knew it was unreasonable, but she was irritable with him too. He was happy that they were returning to

117

Battersea, whereas she just couldn't feel the same.

Quietly she left the room and padded softly to the kitchen, only to find a light on when she opened the door.

'Mum, I didn't expect to find you up.'

'It seems that neither of us could sleep. I can't say the same for Nora. The door to the conservatory is closed, yet I can still hear her snoring like a trooper.'

'At least you'll have your conservatory back tomorrow.'

'It's already tomorrow,' Emily said, nodding towards the kitchen clock.

Tears gathered and Pearl blinked rapidly. 'Mum, you could change your mind. Come with us. With four bedrooms there's plenty of room.'

'Darling, at my age I don't think I'd find another teaching job, and to be honest, I love the one I have. We'll still see each other regularly, and during school holidays I could come to stay.'

'That's something, but it won't be the same. Oh, why did I make that promise to Bessie? If it wasn't for Nora ... if I could just bring myself to put her in an institution, but...'

'Pearl, I know you,' Emily interrupted. 'If you did that you'd never forgive yourself.'

'If only we didn't have to live in Battersea ... and what am I doing to John, dragging him away from Winchester, his school, his friends?'

'Pearl, we've been through this. He's young, he'll adapt to a new school and when he comes to stay with me he'll see his friends.'

'Mum, I thought you were against us moving, but now you sound like Derek.'

118

'I was being selfish in thinking of myself instead of you. It was wrong of me to expect you to give up the chance of your own home and a business which I'm sure you can improve.'

'But I'm going to miss you so much,' Pearl choked, her heart heavy at the thought of leaving her mother, and Winchester, a town she loved so much.

'Come here,' Emily said as she stood up and opened her arms.

Pearl clung to her as though she were a life raft. 'I don't think I can bear to leave you.'

'Darling, I'll only be a drive away and I'll always be here if you need me.'

'Oh, Mum,' Pearl choked, a little comforted by her words.

'Now, come on, chin up,' Emily said, gently drawing away. 'You've got an early start and I think it might be a good idea if you try to get some sleep.'

Pearl saw the sense of her mother's words. 'Yes, all right. Good night, Mum.'

'Good night, darling.'

When Pearl climbed into bed again, she doubted that sleep would be possible. She was wrong. For a while she lay listening to the sound of Derek's rhythmic breathing, but then her eyes closed.

Yet Pearl's last thought before sleep overtook her was that her life was never going to be the same again.

Chapter Sixteen

It was quiet in Battersea High Street, the shops and market stalls closed. This was just what Pearl wanted and why she had chosen a Sunday to move. There were no prying eyes as she opened the door of the shop, though a musty smell greeted them as they trooped inside.

John was the first to complain. 'It stinks, Mum.'

'The shop just needs a good airing, but it can wait for now,' Pearl told him as they walked through to the back stairs. There was an entirely different aroma as they went up to the flat and Pearl frowned, wondering how it could possibly smell of fresh paint.

'Derek,' she gasped when they reached the first landing to see that new wallpaper had been hung, and the yellowing paintwork caused by years of accumulated nicotine was now sparkling white.

Derek grinned. 'I know I told you I had a job on, a bit of decorating for an old couple, but I was really coming here. I thought it would be a nice surprise.'

Pearl flung open the living room door, her eyes wide as she scanned the room. It was beautifully decorated too, with no sign of Bessie's old, worn furniture or sagging sofa. Everything was new — the cream three-piece suite, the cabinet, side tables, and picking up a peach cushion that matched the curtains, she said, 'Oh, Derek, this is just the style and colour I'd have chosen. How did you know?'

'I can't take the credit. I took sample swatches to your mother and she chose everything. I've decorated the whole flat, Pearl, but the colour scheme is your mother's. If you don't like anything,' he said with a smile, 'blame her, not me.'

'I go see my room,' Nora said, looking worried as she bustled off.

Nora's room was on this floor and Pearl said, 'She doesn't like change, Derek. I hope she isn't going to be upset.'

'Don't worry, I haven't done anything major, just enough to freshen it up. It's the same with the other rooms. Other than Nora's, I got rid of the beds, but for now we'll have to put up with Bessie's old bedroom furniture.'

'I'll get Ginger out of his box,' John said.

'He's can't go out yet, so make sure you set up his litter box,' Derek advised.

John opened the carrier and Ginger slunk out nervously, body low as his eyes scanned the room. John murmured reassurances, and it wasn't long before Ginger couldn't resist the urge to explore.

'He'll soon settle,' Pearl said.

'Where's my room?' John asked.

'It's on the top floor, next to ours,' Derek told him. 'Now that sounds like Tommy Harris with the van. I know you didn't get much of a chance to chat to him while we were loading, but he used to have a stall close to mine on the market and he's still a good mate. Come on, he'll need a hand.'

121

When they both left, Pearl stood alone in the living room, touched by Derek's thoughtfulness. Though it looked entirely different, she felt that the essence of Bessie would always remain, that echoes of the past were impregnated in the walls.

'I likes my room,' Nora said, looking happier than Pearl had seen her in ages. 'We stay here, Pearl?'

'Yes, we'll all be living here,' she said, thinking that they were divided into pairs: Derek and Nora happy to be back in Battersea, while she and John would have preferred to stay in Winchester.

'Not go away again?'

'No, this is our home now.'

'Bessie pleased,' Nora said smiling.

Pearl felt a shiver of goose bumps and rubbed her arms, but then heard the thump of footsteps on the stairs, the funny feeling leaving her as she said, 'No doubt Derek and Tommy will be looking for cups of tea.'

'I make it,' Nora offered.

'Take this then,' Pearl said, handing her the shopping bag containing tea, sugar and milk that she'd had the forethought to keep separate from their other things.

As Pearl stood alone in her new home, she was suddenly overwhelmed with emotion. This might all be hers now, this flat, the shop, a wonderful inheritance people would say, but with the conditions of Bessie's will, Pearl felt that she would be trapped in Battersea for many, many years.

It won't be that bad. Pull yourself together, girl, and get on with it.

Pearl spun around, but saw only an empty

room. She was sure that someone had spoken to her, yet she must have imagined it, the voice in her mind. Nora had spooked her, that was all, and she had to pull herself together.

It was five minutes later when Derek called from upstairs, 'Pearl, where do you want our bed?'

She took a deep breath, straightened her shoulders, and with renewed determination she strode up to the next landing. It was going to be strange sleeping in what had been Bessie's bedroom, but with the furniture moved around a bit, surely she'd get used to it. 'Put it over there,' she said, 'and would you mind shifting that wardrobe?'

'It's a big double, but I'm game,' said Tommy.

'Pearl, it's still full of Bessie's clothes and I wasn't sure what you wanted to do with them. I managed to shuffle it forward to wallpaper behind it, but it's heavy. It might help if you empty it.'

'Yes, all right.'

'While you're doing that, we'll bring John's bed up.'

As they left the room, Pearl opened the wardrobe door. Derek was right, it was full of clothes from a bygone era, but Bessie had been a hoarder so she wasn't surprised. There were hats and handbags on the top shelf, but as the wardrobe was so tall, she couldn't reach them.

Pearl lifted out as many clothes as she could and took them across to the stockroom, but as she walked in, her eyes widened. Derek had cleared it and it was now a spare bedroom, decorated in lemon and blue, her mother's favourite colour combination. It had obviously been designated

123

for her when she came to stay, and Pearl's eyes moistened with gratitude at Derek's thoughtfulness. Thankfully there were still a couple of racks, and Pearl was able to hang Bessie's clothes on them for now.

It took several more trips, but at last the wardrobe was empty other than the top shelf. Pearl pulled a chair over to stand on, but Derek came back in, immediately saying, 'Don't go climbing on that, it doesn't look safe. I'll clear the shelf.'

One by one he handed her hats that Pearl could never imagine Bessie wearing, and then came handbag after handbag until he paused. 'There's a long box of some sort tucked into the corner at the back.'

Pearl could guess the contents. 'No doubt it's full of gloves,' she said, taking it from him.

But she gasped with shock when she opened it.

'Bloody hell!' Derek exclaimed as he looked at the contents.

Pearl took out a few rings, puzzled. One was a diamond solitaire, though she wasn't sure if the stone was real, another a cluster of what looked like sapphires and the third a red stone, perhaps a ruby, set among more diamonds. 'They're all different sizes,' she said, 'and I don't remember Bessie wearing any of them.'

'She bought second-hand clothes and stuff; maybe she did the same with jewellery.'

'Yes, that must be it, but look, it's full to the brim with more rings, necklaces, brooches and a lot of watches.'

'I've heard of treasure chests, Pearl, but I never expected to find one. What are you going to do

124

with it?'

'Do with it?' Pearl parroted. 'I don't know what I'm supposed to do with it.'

'Well, love, if you don't want to keep it, how do you feel about selling it?'

'I can't do that. It isn't mine,' Pearl protested.

'Don't be daft, of course it is. Bessie left you everything, this place and all the contents.'

'There was no mention of jewellery in her will.'

'It doesn't matter. That lot still comes under the contents.'

As Pearl thought back to her last conversation with Bessie, tears threatened. Bessie had said something about finding a cache of stuff when she sorted her things out, but this box of jewellery was the last thing Pearl had expected. 'It just doesn't seem right to sell it.'

'It's up to you, but to be honest I've got to admit I was a bit hasty in spending most of what we had saved on doing this place up. I wanted to make it nice, thought it might help you to see it as a fresh start, but until I get hold of some work things are going to be a bit tight.'

Pearl was touched by Derek's thoughtfulness again and said, 'Don't worry, there's the shop.'

'Yes, but will it make enough to tide us over until some decorating jobs come in?'

'I don't know. I'll have to look at the stock,' she replied.

'Pearl ... Pearl ... where is you?' Nora wailed.

'Listen to her,' Derek said, shaking his head ruefully. 'It looks like she still isn't going to give you a moment's peace. I don't know how you're going to run the shop with Nora under your feet all the time.'

'Bessie managed, but I must admit I wouldn't mind a bit of a break now and then. I've got a bit of an idea, but it depends how much income the shop will generate.'

Before Derek could question her, Tommy walked into the room, Nora behind him. 'That's everything unloaded,' he said, 'and I've had a cuppa. Are you ready to move that wardrobe now?'

'Yes, but where do you want it, Pearl?'

She told them and then urged Nora out of the way while the two men heaved it into place. 'Thanks, Tommy.'

'You're welcome, missus, and unless you need me for anything else, I'll be off.'

'We're fine now,' Derek said, 'and I owe you one. Do you fancy a pint later?'

'You're on. Oh, and by the way, there's a market stall up for grabs if you're interested.'

'I'd love it, but how much is the backhander?'

'I dunno, but it's a good pitch so probably a fair few bob.'

'That leaves me out of the bidding then.'

'That's a shame,' Tommy said. 'It would've been nice to see you back on the market.'

'Yeah, I'm with you there,' Derek agreed, 'but if you hear of anyone looking for a painter and decorator, point them in my direction.'

Pearl could sense Derek's disappointment, and as Tommy said goodbye she looked down at the box still clutched in her hands.

'This Bessie's room,' Nora said.

'Yes, I know, but Derek and I will be be

sleeping in here now.'

'Bessie likes that.'

Pearl only smiled, her mind on other things. With Nora following, she went downstairs, and as Derek returned from seeing Tommy out she held out the box. 'Here, sell the lot and hopefully it'll be enough to get that stall.'

His eyes lit up. 'Are you sure?'

'Of course I am,' Pearl said, grinning. 'Mind you, if you're going to sell china again, I'll expect a discount on a nice new tea set.'

'Come here,' Derek said, putting the box down and holding out his arms. 'You can have anything you want from the stall. After all, we're partners, ain't we?'

'Always,' Pearl said as she was enfolded.

'Once we've got our stuff sorted, if you can manage without me for an hour or so, I'll pop down to the old folks' home to see my gran.'

'What did she say about us moving back to Battersea when you last saw her?' Pearl asked.

'She was over the moon, said she'd expect to see more of me, and I don't think she was far off suggesting that she'd like to see you too.'

'Derek, don't tell me that she's softening after all these years?'

'If she is, how do you feel about paying her a visit?'

'When your gran is ready to see me, of course I'll visit her.'

Derek hugged her again. 'Thanks, love. I know she's a stubborn old woman, but she's my gran and I think the world of her.'

'Of course you do,' Pearl said. It was obvious

how happy Derek was to be back in Battersea, and maybe, just maybe, she thought, there'd come a time when she could be happy here too.

Chapter Seventeen

Rupert was still fretting. When Kevin had returned from seeing his parents again, he'd looked self-satisfied and happy, but there had been no explanation. He knew that Kevin was a very private person; that he hated anyone prying into his business, but it had been so hard not to probe.

Rupert groaned, wondering if Kevin's parents were persuading him to move in with them. He couldn't bear the thought of losing him, yet how could he convince him to stay? Unlike the others, Kevin wasn't just after his money, but Rupert wasn't naive enough to think that Kevin returned his feelings either. He knew that Kevin swung both ways; that he saw this as a temporary arrangement, but Rupert felt that there had to be something he could do to keep Kevin under his roof.

With his mind still on the problem, Rupert boiled Kevin's egg just the way he liked it, and toasted the bread to perfection. 'Kevin,' he called, 'breakfast is ready.'

They always ate the first meal of the day in the kitchen, and when Kevin walked in, Rupert blurted out, 'Are you going to move in with your parents?'

128

'I don't know yet.'

'I'd rather you stayed here.'

'I've told you. I'll only do that if I can pay my own way.'

Rupert knew he had to come up with something and fast. The seed of an idea struck him and he said, 'Kevin, I'm a wealthy man and I don't need your money. However, what I do need is someone with a bit of expertise. You see, I'd like to invest some of my capital in a business.'

'What sort of business?'

'I'm not sure yet,' Rupert, mused, 'but one that would give me a good return on my investment. The problem is I'm not getting any younger and I would need someone to run it for me. That's where you would come in.'

Kevin just looked at him for a moment, his eyes unreadable, but then he said, 'Rupert, you're off your rocker and it's no wonder you've been taken for a mug in the past. I'm not a businessman, and I know nothing about running one.'

'You must have expertise in something.'

'I trained to be an engineer, but hated it. My parents had a café, but that was many years ago, and for the last thirteen years I've been in prison. That hardly qualifies me to run a business.'

'You would only have to manage things,' Rupert said quickly, 'act as an overseer, with staff employed to do the work.'

Once again there was a pause, Kevin frowning in thought, but then he said, 'I don't know, Rupert. I suppose with good bar staff I could run a pub or a club.'

'See, I knew you'd come up with something.'

'Hold on, buying a profitable and established one won't come cheap, or setting up a new one. Just how much money are you thinking of investing?'

Rupert had inherited his wealth and had no idea about commerce. His stockbroker handled his portfolio, and he knew the dividends paid well. He found anything to do with stocks, shares and bank interest rates tiresome, but they provided him with all the money he needed while his capital remained untouched. He shrugged and said nonchalantly, 'Oh, I don't know, Kevin, forty to fifty thousand. More if necessary.'

'You can get your hands on that sort of money?'

'Dear boy, of course I can.'

'In that case, I suppose I could look around,' Kevin said, though his voice lacked any real enthusiasm, 'make some enquiries with commercial agents, that sort of thing.'

'Does this mean you agree? That you'll find a business and run it for me?'

'If I think I could make a go of it, then yes.'

'Wonderful, and as you'll be spending your time searching for the perfect pub or club, it's only fair that I start paying you a salary straight away,' Rupert cried, thrilled that he had found a way to keep Kevin close.

In Battersea, Pearl was relieved to discover that a local school had a place for John, and that he could attend the next day. She was now on her way back to the flat with John and Nora, and knew she would have to think about opening the shop soon. Hopefully though, once Derek sold the jewellery, money wouldn't be so tight.

The musty smell still greeted them when they went in, and once again John wrinkled his nose. 'If I was a customer and walked into this stink, I'd turn round and walk out again. Come to that, yuk, you wouldn't catch me wearing someone else's castoffs.'

'Not everyone is as fortunate as you, John. There was a time when I didn't have the money for new clothes and I had to buy second-hand ones from this very shop. It's how I met Bessie.'

'I didn't know that. But surely there isn't a call for second-hand clothes now. Can't you sell something else?'

'I'd love to, but new stock would cost a lot of money. Perhaps as this sells, I can gradually replace it with something else. We'll just have to wait and see,' Pearl said, unwilling to voice her ideas yet. Derek had gone to Hatton Garden hoping to get a better price for the jewellery there, and surely, even after he had bid for the stall there'd be some left. Enough to at least get her plans off the ground.

Kevin kept his composure until he left Rupert's house, but then he couldn't suppress a huge grin. He'd feigned a lack of interest in Rupert's suggestions, but in reality he was over the moon.

Rupert was going to invest forty grand, maybe even more, and Kevin knew he had two choices. He could run a pub or club, skimming a good living off the top, but it would probably mean he'd still have to live with Rupert and he didn't fancy that.

131

On the other hand, Kevin thought, there might be a way for Rupert's investment to land in his own coffers. He was driven by his lust for money and with that sort of cash Kevin knew he'd be in clover. Of course it would take a lot of careful planning to set Rupert up and though he might be a mug, he wouldn't be stupid enough to just hand over a cheque for that sort of money... Or would he?

If he had a pot like that, Kevin thought, licking his lips, he could put his parents on the back burner for a good few years, and in the meantime he could go anywhere, live anywhere. The idea of living abroad appealed, perhaps in Spain, but with no idea of how long it took to get a passport, he'd need to apply for one straight away.

That just left Vince and the payback for the scar that made his guts churn with anger every time he looked in the mirror, but he'd already worked out a quick and easy revenge. All he had to do was find out where Vince lived, take Adrianna from him, and then torch his place with the bastard inside. Kevin smiled, relishing the thought.

For now though, he'd get hold of details of a few commercial properties to lull Rupert into a false sense of security, and then tonight he'd head for Battersea where he hoped to get the information about Vince that he needed.

Chapter Eighteen

Derek was staggered by the amount he'd been paid for the jewellery. Bessie must have had a keen eye, and though some of the watches weren't up to much, the other stuff along with the gold chains fetched a good price. Bessie had never looked as if she had two bob to her name and he couldn't understand why she hadn't sold it herself instead of salting it away for years.

He'd now made an offer for the stall, and as some of the other costermongers remembered him, they backed his bid. With plenty of money left over, Pearl had decided to completely re-furbish the shop, and Derek just hoped she knew what she was doing. It wasn't that he was worried about the money she'd be spending. What concerned him was how unhappy Pearl would be if her grand ideas for the shop didn't work out.

'Nora's gone to bed early,' Pearl said, 'so I'm going to take the opportunity to pop round to see Lucy. I'm thinking of offering her a job.'

'Shouldn't you wait to see if you're going to need help in the shop?' Derek asked, but Pearl just gave him a swift kiss on the cheek before she hurried out.

Derek frowned. He just hoped that Pearl didn't bump into anyone who would tell her that just a short while ago Kevin Dolby had been sniffing around. It was Tommy who had passed on the news and Derek had been furious. He'd calmed down when Tom said that Kevin hadn't been interested in them, just some bloke called Vincent Chase, and that he hadn't been seen in the area since. Derek just hoped it would stay that way. If there was one thing guaranteed to make Pearl want to leave Battersea, it was hearing that Kevin was back.

Lucy was busily ironing one T-shirt after another when someone knocked on the door. She opened it, smiling when she saw who it was.

'Pearl, come on in. It's lovely to see you.'

'I'm sorry to call so late, but it's the first chance I've had,' Pearl said, her eyes scanning the living room. 'This is nice.'

'It's not bad,' Lucy nodded. 'But I've got to move out.'

'Have you? Why?'

'The landlord is going to sell this place.'

'Where will you go?'

'I don't know yet. I went to the council today, but they fobbed me off by telling me to apply to a housing association that's doing up a lot of property around here. They said they'd support my application, that with a kid I stand a good chance, but as I've got to be out of here in two weeks I'm not banking on anything,' Lucy said, then remembering her manners she added, 'Sit down, Pearl, and can I get you anything? A cup of tea?'

'No thanks, I've not long had one.'

'Excuse the mess. You caught me in the middle of ironing this lot.'

Pearl looked puzzled as she noticed the rows of

134

T-shirts suspended by hangers on a door frame.

'I've had a go at tie-dyeing and now hope to sell them,' Lucy explained. 'I could do with the money.'

'They're lovely and I'm sure they will,' Pearl said.

Encouraged, Lucy smiled. 'Fingers crossed.'

'Lucy, I'm going to make alterations to the shop,' Pearl said as she took a seat, 'and it's going to cause a bit of disruption. Nora hates change and she might find it a bit stressful. Not only that, since Bessie died she constantly clings to me.'

'Her world has been turned upside down, but once she settles you'll see a big difference. Bessie mostly kept Nora in the shop with her, or she let her go upstairs to do some housework. The two of them seemed to chug along nicely.'

'Yes, I know,' Pearl agreed, 'but I'll have a lot to reorganise and until Nora settles I really could do without having her under my feet all the time. With that in mind I wondered if you'd be interested in a part-time job?'

'Oh yes, I'd love to work in the shop again,' Lucy said eagerly.

'I'm sorry. The shop won't be opening until all the alterations are done and in the meantime I need someone to look after Nora, to keep her occupied. It could turn into a permanent position, and as Nora knows you, you're the first person I thought of.'

'Do you mean a sort of carer?'

'Yes, that's it.'

Lucy was disappointed. She had hoped for a job in the shop, but at least it was work. There

135

was still a problem though, and she hoped Pearl would understand. 'I'd like the job, but I'm afraid I won't be able to start straight away. Until the housing association comes up with something I've got to find somewhere to live.'

'If it would help, I've got a spare room. You and Clive would have to share it, but it's not a bad size.'

'What about my furniture?'

'You could put it in storage for now,' Pearl suggested.

Lucy calculated what it would cost for a deposit on another flat against putting her furniture in storage, and asked, 'How much would you want for the room?'

'I wouldn't want anything.'

'I can't expect to stay with you for nothing.'

'Well then, let's call the room a perk of the job and it's yours for as long as you need it.'

Lucy wasn't sure how she felt about living in someone else's home, but there was no getting away from the fact that Pearl's offer would solve her immediate problems. 'All right, Pearl. I'd love the job and the room.'

'Great. When can you start?'

'As soon as I've arranged to have my furniture and things picked up for storage. Then it's just a matter of packing our clothes.'

Pearl looked happy as she rose to leave, pausing to look at the T-shirts again. 'You said you're selling them. Have you got an outlet?'

'I'm going to offer them to a stallholder, Eddie White.'

'If he turns them down, hang on to them. I

136

think they'd be just right for the shop.'

'Pearl, they aren't second-hand.'

'I know, but you see I'm going to turn the shop into an arts and craft outlet. I think those T-shirts would fit in really well, and may act as an inspiration for other people to have a go at tie-dyeing.'

Lucy wasn't sure how well that sort of business would go down in the area and hoped Pearl knew what she was doing. It sounded interesting though, and maybe when Nora settled down there might be an opening as a sales assistant.

For now she walked Pearl to the door, and as she closed it behind her it felt as though a huge financial burden had been lifted from her shoulders. She'd be earning a wage, living rent-free, and at the moment, that seemed perfect.

Chapter Nineteen

Two weeks had now passed and Derek was painting the shop, but he'd just been given the news he was hoping for. The pitch was his. He wasn't going to keep it as a fruit and vegetable stall – there were a good few of those already. Even if a bit rusty, he'd go back to what he knew, and that was selling china and glass. He might even add a few other bits for kitchens that could sell well, small things that would be simple to display.

Derek stretched his back. Pearl was checking out a few wholesalers and needing a break he went upstairs, where Lucy immediately offered to make him a cup of tea. He liked Lucy, and her son was a nice lad, but he wasn't too happy that Pearl had invited them to move in without consulting him. The flat had seemed large when they moved in, but in just a short time it seemed to be bursting at the seams. Still, at least it kept Nora from trailing after Pearl, who was busy with the refurbishments, along with sourcing stock, and thankfully seemed a bit happier in Battersea now.

'Is there anything else I can get you before I go to collect Clive from school?' Lucy asked as she placed the drink beside him.

'Lucy, I don't expect you to wait on me hand and foot.'

'I don't mind, and as Nora isn't any trouble it gives me something to do.'

'I've got a bit of news,' he said grinning. 'I got the stall.'

'You did? That's smashing! I bet you're dead chuffed.'

'Yes, I am,' he said, still smiling as Lucy left the room. He'd been unwilling to acknowledge it, but since Pearl had inherited this lot, along with the jewellery, he'd felt like a kept man and it didn't sit well with him. Now, at last, he'd be the breadwinner again, and as Pearl's ideas for the shop might not take off, he should be able to make enough money to support them.

Derek found his mind turning to his gran. She had at last agreed to see Pearl and he was taking her to the retirement home on Sunday. It was something he had wanted for so long, and was

138

looking forward to seeing Pearl and his gran reconciled.

For Lucy it had been so hard to leave her flat and to watch her furniture being loaded into a van for storage, but for Clive's sake, she had managed to appear cheerful. It helped that she found Pearl and Derek so easy to live with, but the lack of privacy, of having her own sitting room, with her own things around her, was already making her wonder if she had made the right decision.

Thankfully there was a light at the end of the tunnel. She'd had another interview with the housing association, explained that she and Clive only had temporary accommodation, both sharing one room, and had been thrilled to be put on the top of their list. They were modernising terraced houses in nearby streets, and from what Lucy had seen, some were nearing completion.

'Come on, Nora, leave that now and get your coat. We've got to collect Clive from school.'

'All right,' she said, reluctantly putting her duster down.

Lucy had never known anyone who loved housework so much and the flat sparkled with cleanliness. With Pearl busy sorting the shop out, Lucy was happy to do the cooking for all of them and she had taken over the laundry too.

'I'm ready,' Nora said. 'Get Clive and we do a jigsaw.'

Lucy had to smile. Since they had moved in, Nora seemed to love having Clive around. When he came home from school she would sit drawing or painting with him, and she liked simple jigsaw puzzles too. Thankfully Clive didn't mind and he treated Nora like a big kid who liked to play with him. 'I'm ready too,' she said, and with Nora beside her they were soon walking through the market.

As they drew close to Eddie White's stall she saw that he wasn't busy, and as Pearl said she'd display the tie-dyed T-shirts in the shop when the refurbishments were finished, she hadn't needed to approach him.

'Watcha, Lucy, have you got a minute?' he called.

'Yes, but that's about all,' she said as he came to her side.

'Lucy, I've wanted to ask you this for some time now ... but, well, I wasn't sure what you'd say. I ... I err ... err...' he floundered.

'Eddie, I can't hang about. I've got to fetch Clive from school.'

'Do ... do you fancy going to the flicks or something?' he asked in a rush.

Lucy gawked at Eddie, unable to believe her ears. She'd known him for years, since childhood, and he'd never shown the slightest interest in her before. 'You want to take me out? But why?'

'Ain't it obvious? I've always fancied you, but as soon as you started going out with Paul Sanderson you didn't have eyes for anyone else.'

Lucy bit on her lower lip. Yes, there had only been Paul, her first and only love. There wasn't a man on earth who could take his place. 'Leave it out, Eddie. I've seen what you're like around the women and I'm sure you've got a string of girlfriends.'

'You're the girl of my dreams and I'd rather have you.'

'Eddie, I know you and that's all flannel. Forget it. I've got no intention of going out with you.'

'You're breaking my heart.'

'Lucy, go out with him,' Nora said. 'It's good. You be happy.'

Embarrassed, Lucy flushed pink. 'Shhhh, Nora.'

'It's nice to hear she's on my side,' Eddie grinned.

'Look, Eddie, I'm sorry, but I haven't got time for this. Come on, Nora, we've got to go.'

'Will you at least think about it?' Eddie called as they hurried off.

She didn't reply, and her eyes narrowed as she looked at Nora, wondering if this was one of her strange predictions. 'Why did you say that, Nora?'

'What did I say?'

'That I'd be happy with Eddie.'

'You will.'

'How do you know?'

'Just do.'

Lucy gave up. What did it matter anyway? Eddie might be nice-looking, tall and slim with blond hair and blue eyes, but she wouldn't be going out with him. He was a terrible flirt and she'd just be another string on his bow.

When Emily arrived home from work that evening, she still found it hard to walk into an empty house. It had only been a short while since they left, yet she missed Pearl so much, Derek too; and though John would be coming to stay at the weekend, it wasn't the same as having him in the house every day.

It wasn't just that she missed seeing them; she missed the interaction, asking each other how their day went, exchanging views, discussing a radio or television programme, and so much more. She now ate solitary meals, and the kitchen, though it looked the same, felt so empty.

After eating her dinner, Emily sadly washed up just one plate, wondering if instead of remaining in Winchester she should have gone with her family to Battersea. As she was drying her hands there was a knock on her door.

It was Tim, her next-door neighbour. 'Come in,' Emily invited.

He followed her through to the kitchen. 'The amateur dramatic group are performing a play on Saturday night and I'd like to see it. Would you join me?'

'I've got John for the weekend.'

'He can come with us.'

'In that case I'd love to see it. Now if you have time, do sit down. I've been chewing something over in my mind and could do with a bit of feed-back.'

He pulled out a chair. 'Fire away then. I'm all ears.'

Emily smiled. Tim was such a lovely chap, and though in his late fifties he carried his age well. Just under six feet tall, with grey hair and eyes, he had a distinguished look about him that she found attractive. 'You know that I love my job,' she said, pulling out the opposite chair to sit down, 'and that I would find it hard to leave

142

Winchester, but I miss my family. I've been wondering if I should move to Battersea to live with them.'

The smile left Tim's face, his tone urgent. 'No, Emily, I don't think you should do that.'

'But I hate coming home to an empty house, and surely you understand. It must have been like this for you, worse, when you lost Delia.'

'Yes, it was, but I have a lot to thank you for, Emily. Without your support and company, many evenings would have been unbearable.'

'I was glad to help, but you don't really need me now.'

'It isn't a case of need, Emily. It's more that I've grown very fond of you and I would miss you terribly if you left.'

'I've grown fond of you too, but...'

Tim leaned across the table to grip her hand, interrupting her as he appealed, 'I know this is rather sudden, but don't leave, Emily. Marry me.'

Emily just stared at him, too surprised to speak.

'I can see how shocked you are, and I know I'm no spring chicken, but we have so much in common and I'm sure I could make you happy.'

'I ... I don't know what to say.'

'Please, Emily, say yes.'

She wanted to, but found that doubts flooded in. 'You ... you were so happy with Delia and I don't feel I could ever replace her.'

'I don't want a replacement. I want you: sweet, gentle, kind, lovely you. We've seen a lot of each other this past year, shared so many things, and I've fallen in love with you.'

'You have?'

'Yes, but I must confess I didn't realise how much until you said you were thinking of leaving.' Tim stood to walk around the table where he held out his hands. Emily took them and was pulled gently to her feet and into his arms. 'Stay, Emily, please stay. Say you'll marry me.'

She pulled back to look up at him and at that moment their lips met. Emily found herself melting, her reply when she was able to give it a breathless whisper. 'Yes, Tim. I'd love to marry you.'

Chapter Twenty

After giving Rupert the details of a pub, Kevin watched him reading the agent's blurb before saying, 'I don't think it's any better than the others, but if you're interested we can go to view it.'

'The ones we've been to look at so far have been dreadful and this doesn't look any better.'

'I can't find anything else and we may have to widen the field. An agent told me about a private club that might be coming up for sale, but it's in South London.'

'A private club sounds interesting.'

'That depends on the price. It isn't on the market yet, but it might be worth a look.'

'We can do that now.'

'It isn't open during the day.'

'Tonight then.'

'All right, but we'll have to be careful. If the owner's on the premises and thinks there's interest in the place before he's put it on the market, it might encourage him to up the price.'

'Don't worry, I won't say a word.'

Kevin hid a smile, thankful that his ruse had worked. The club he'd chosen wasn't going up for sale, but of course Rupert didn't know that. He still had another pressing problem, but hopefully the distance to the club held the key so he said, 'As the club's on the other side of the river it's going to take us quite a while to get there. We may have to change trains and then hop on a bus.'

'There's no need for that. We'll get a cab.'

'That'll cost a bomb and what about the return journey?'

'I hate public transport. It'll be a cab again and I don't care what it costs.'

'Since those thugs set on me, I'm not keen on hanging around late at night looking for a taxi. It's a shame you haven't got a car.'

'I used to have one, but I was such a nervous driver and didn't enjoy it. In the end I hardly used it so I let it go.'

'It would have made things so much easier, especially if we end up buying the club. With the distance involved it wouldn't be practical to come home every night. I'd have to live on the premises or close by,' Kevin murmured sadly.

'Can you drive?'

'Yes, I passed my test many years ago.'

'Then you must have a car, and this proves how useful it will be.'

'No, Rupert, I can't let you buy me a car.'

Kevin then found that Rupert wasn't without guile as he said, 'I'm not buying it for *you*. It'll be our company vehicle.'

'That's all right then,' he said, pleased that Rupert had taken the bait. This was still panning out perfectly, but he wasn't going to risk rushing things. He wanted it all to come together at the same time, needing to be sure that he had Rupert's money in his pocket when he torched Vince's place. That done he planned to leave the country straight away, to live the good life abroad, but he still had to get to Adrianna. He had Vince's address now, but he could hardly knock on the door. His only chance to speak to her would be when she left the house alone, and that meant watching the place.

The problem had been that Vince's house was in an upmarket street, and on foot he hadn't seen anywhere to keep out of sight. What he'd have now was a car to sit in and that would be just perfect.

'We'll be there in about ten minutes now,' Derek told John on the drive to Winchester. 'I expect your grandmother is already on the lookout for us.'

'Great,' John said, looking happier than he had all week. 'I'm glad Ginger turned up before we left. I thought he might have run off.'

'He was only under our bed and cats know where their grub is,' Derek told him.

'Will you keep an eye on him while I'm away?'

'Of course I will,' he said, knowing that John worried that Clive would tease his cat. He knew

146

that John was still finding it hard to settle in Battersea, but he was beginning to make new friends at school and that was sure to help. Derek's mind turned to other things. Next week he'd be taking over the stall, and on Monday he'd have to go to the wholesalers for stock.

'There's Winchester Cathedral,' John said as it came into view.

It was a familiar landmark that served to show them that they had almost arrived, and shortly after Derek pulled up outside Emily's house. He smiled when he saw that the door was flung open before they had got out of the car, Emily's face pink with pleasure. 'Oh, it's lovely to see you.'

She was soon ushering them inside, and Derek was greeted by the familiar aroma of lavender furniture polish, mingled with fresh baking. 'You've been making a cake,' he said, licking his lips.

'Yes, a Victoria sponge.'

As they walked into the kitchen Derek saw the cake resplendent in the middle of the table and soon Emily was placing a cup of coffee in front of him before cutting into it.

She gave a huge slice to Derek and then said, 'Here's one for you too, John.'

'Thanks, Gran.'

'Well, Derek, have you finished painting the shop?' Emily asked as she sat down.

'I couldn't start until all the second-hand stuff was taken away, but yes, it's all done, with cream walls and the white woodwork that Pearl wanted. It's just as well it's finished because I'll be opening my stall on Monday.'

'Now that Mum's got rid of all that junk, the

147

shop looks huge,' commented John.

'It'll need to be,' Derek said. 'No doubt Pearl's told you what she's going to sell now, Emily?'

'She has and I think it's a wonderful idea. I can just imagine it. Easels to display paintings on, others to sell, along with stocks of watercolour and oil paints, not to mention all the other paraphernalia that both budding and experienced artists might need. And Pearl said that's just one craft that she intends to cater for.'

'It's a far cry from selling second-hand stuff, that's for sure,' Derek said, hoping that Pearl knew what she was doing. Buying china for his stall would cost peanuts compared to stocking the shop. With that and the refurbishments it would probably use up most of the money they had left, but as long as Pearl was happy, it was fine with him.

'I can't wait to see the shop,' Emily said. 'When it's stocked and ready to open I'll come down for the weekend. I have something to tell you all, but it can wait until then.'

Curious, Derek asked, 'Can't you tell me now?'

Emily smiled, her eyes sparkling as she said, 'No, and I don't want to hear another word about it.'

'Fine, if you can keep it to yourself it can't be that important,' Derek joked, thinking that with Lucy and Clive using the spare room, Emily would have to sleep on the sofa.

'I'll work on her, Dad,' John whispered conspiratorially when he thought his gran was out of earshot. 'She'll tell me.'

'I heard that and I won't,' she chirped.

148

Derek rose to his feet. 'As much as I'd like to join you in persuading your grandmother to spill the beans, I'd best be off. Your mother has a list of things still waiting to be done so I'd best get a move on.'

John and Emily said their goodbyes and as Derek drove back to Battersea his thoughts turned to Kevin Dolby again. Derek hadn't been happy when his old pal, Tommy Harris, told him that Kevin had been in the area and sniffing around for information on Vincent Chase.

Derek couldn't work out why. Vincent Chase had once lived in the borough and had been a fence, but according to Tommy, the man had moved on to bigger things now.

He frowned, wondering what Kevin was up to – but if he was involved with Vincent Chase, so much for his religious conversion, Derek decided.

It was Sunday morning, and Pearl was feeling nervous as she went with Derek to see his gran. She hadn't seen Connie for years and as they approached the old lady sitting in a high-back chair, fingers twisted with arthritis, and her face lined with deep wrinkles, Pearl hardly recognised her.

'You're here then,' Connie said. 'Sit down. I'm not craning my neck to look up at the pair of you.'

'How are you, Gran?' Derek asked.

'The same as I was the last time you came to see me.'

Pearl took a deep breath and then said, 'It's nice to see you, Connie.'

'You ain't changed much,' she said shortly before focusing on Derek to ask, 'Did you bring me some Turkish delight?'

'Yes, here you are,' he said, taking a paper bag out of his pocket.

'Thanks, love,' Connie said, stowing it in her cardigan pocket.

'It looks nice here,' Pearl commented.

'It's not too bad,' Connie agreed, 'but there's nothing like yer own home. You've done all right though. By persuading Bessie to leave you her place, you've fallen on your feet. She was a silly old woman who never could see through you, but I sussed you out from the start.'

Pearl looked sharply at Derek, and it was he who answered. 'Gran, Pearl had no idea that she was going to inherit Bessie's place. As I told you it came as a complete shock, especially when there were strings attached.'

'One string, Nora, and now you're lumbered with her, Derek.'

'She's no trouble, Gran.'

'I'd have thought with bringing up another man's kid you've got enough on yer plate. The apple doesn't fall far from the tree and no doubt the son will turn out as rotten as his father. More fool you for taking him and *her* on, but no doubt she'll dump you now that Kevin Dolby is back on the scene.'

Pearl rose to her feet. 'Derek, I'm going home.'

'Sit down, you silly mare,' Connie said. 'I'm only speaking the truth and there's no need to be so touchy.'

'The truth is I don't want anything to do with

Kevin, and you know *nothing* about my son. He's a fine young man and I'm very proud of him.'

'I am too, Gran. You should meet John, he's a smashing lad.'

'Yeah, yeah, so you've told me before, but he's still Kevin Dolby's kid, not yours, and I don't want anything to do with him, or her,' Connie spat, nodding in Pearl's direction.

Pearl had heard enough and fled. Connie hadn't wanted reconciliation; she had just wanted to attack her verbally; to see her face to face after all these years and make her feelings clear.

Derek had caught up with Pearl and said, 'I'm sorry, love. I had no idea she was going to come out with all that rubbish.'

'It isn't your fault.'

'She had no right to talk to you like that.'

'Derek, I once hurt you and she can't forgive me. I understand how she feels. If anyone hurt John, I'd find it hard to forgive them too. But despite what your gran thinks, there's no way I want to go anywhere near Kevin.'

'I know that, love,' Derek said as he took her arm. 'Come on, let's get out of here.'

'No, I'll go home, but you go back to see your gran,' Pearl insisted. 'You're all she's got and she's just trying to protect you.'

'My gran should hear you now and then she'd realise what a wonderful woman you are.'

Pearl was touched, hugged Derek, and then urged him again to go back to his gran. He had only just disappeared out of sight when someone tapped her gently on the arm.

'Hello, Pearl, how are you?'

151

'Err ... I'm fine.'

'I don't think you recognise me. It's Ann, Ann Haynes. I used to live in the same street as Connie Lewis.'

'Mrs Haynes, of course. How are you?'

'I'm not too bad, love. I know we only met once or twice, but I've heard that Bessie left you her shop. I'm ever so pleased for you.'

'Thanks. Bessie was a lovely woman and I miss her so much.'

Ann smiled sympathetically then said, 'I know I shouldn't have been listening, but I overheard what Connie said to you. Don't take any notice, love.'

'I'll do my best not to,' Pearl said, but knew it would take some doing to forget the things that Connie had said. 'Bye, Mrs Haynes. It was nice to see you again.'

'Bye, and take care.'

Pearl thought it was nice of Mrs Haynes to come and speak to her, but she still felt so sad as she walked home alone. She was disappointed that Connie still felt the same about her, and doubted that her opinion would ever change.

Grim-faced, Derek sat down opposite his gran. 'I can't believe you spoke to Pearl like that. You said you wanted to put the past behind us, but instead you dragged it up.'

'You're blind when it comes to Pearl, but I'm not. Now that Kevin Dolby's around again, I know what's going to happen and I wanted to let her see that I'm well aware of what she'll be up to. Mark my words, you'll be out of Bessie's place

152

soon and Kevin will be in.'

'That's rubbish, and let me tell you, if it wasn't for Pearl I wouldn't be sitting here now.'

'What's that supposed to mean?'

'I was leaving, and after that performance I had no intention of coming back. Pearl has been through enough. The last thing I wanted was for her to be hurt again.'

'It's *you* I'm worried about, not her.'

'Yes, that's what Pearl said. Despite all the venom you threw at her, she said she understands how you feel and persuaded me to come back to see you.'

'Huh, that's probably because she knows you'll need a shoulder to cry on soon.'

'You're wrong, Gran. The last thing Pearl wants is to have Kevin Dolby back in her life,' he protested. Yet he was unable to help recalling that not long before they left Winchester, he'd had the same fears.

'You've always been a mug when it comes to Pearl, but you'll see that I'm right.'

'Stop trying to protect me. I'm a grown man, not a child, and I'm just about sick of this. I've had enough for one day and I'm going now.'

'Bring me some more Turkish delight when you come again.'

Derek couldn't believe his ears. She had taken it for granted that he would visit her again ... yet when all was said and done she was still his gran. 'All right,' he said, 'but I don't want to hear another word against Pearl.'

'Fine, but don't come crying to me when she lets you down again.'

Derek didn't want to hear any more and just said goodbye. He knew that Pearl didn't want Kevin back in her life, and he'd been daft to think she would. Yet as he'd had his doubts, was it any wonder that his gran did too?

Chapter Twenty-One

June had passed and it was now a glorious Tuesday in early July. On occasions, Dolly slipped half a pill to Bernie by crushing it into his tea, and it continued to convince him that he was in the early stages of senility. He had become preoccupied, too worried about himself to keep a close eye on her, and that suited Dolly just fine. Soon she hoped to get her hands on the purse strings again and when that was achieved she'd be off to find a place for both her and Kevin, with room for John of course, leaving Bernie here to stew in his own juice.

With her son on her mind, Dolly said, 'I rang Kevin yesterday, but that odd chap he's staying with said he was out.'

'What do you mean by odd?'

'It's difficult to describe. Rupert sounds very well spoken, but he's also breathy, like a woman if you know what I mean.'

'So you're saying he's a queer?'

'Don't be silly. Kevin would never live in the same house as one of those.'

'They aren't infectious, Dolly.'

'If you say so, but like me, our son has no time

for that sort of thing. Anyway, Rupert may speak strangely, but he's a lovely man. In fact he was very sympathetic when I told him that we're missing Kevin and would like him to come to see us. He gave me their address and said we're welcome to pay them a visit, but at the moment they're very busy and Kevin is hardly at home.'

'Busy doing what?'

'I didn't like to ask, but no doubt it's to do with the refuge. I'll tell you something else, Bernie. I miss John too.'

'So do I, but we'll just have to be patient. In the meantime there's nothing to stop you from ringing him.'

'Yes there is. *She* might answer the telephone. You should speak to John. He should hear it from you that Kevin's a different person now.'

'It hasn't been that long since John found out that his father nearly killed a man,' Bernie pointed out, 'and that he was accused of raping a young woman. On top of that, he's adjusting to a totally different environment in Battersea, along with a new school.'

'They moved to Battersea in May and I think that's time enough for John to adjust.'

'All right,' Bernie sighed, 'anything for a quiet life. I'll ring Pearl to see if I can pop down there on Sunday. But just in case John won't come back with me, why don't you come too? It's about time you buried the hatchet with Pearl.'

'*What!* You must be joking! There was a time when Pearl had nothing and it was only thanks to me that she didn't starve. I gave her a job, but what a mistake that was. The bitch trapped Kevin

155

into marriage and look what that led to.'

'Yes, Dolly, a lovely grandson.'

'That's about all, but now she's doing her best to keep John away from us. I want to see him, but I'm not going to Battersea. Oh, I can just imagine it: Pearl lording it up, showing off now that she's got Bessie's place.'

'Pearl isn't one to show off and I'm not listening to any more of this,' Bernie said as he stood up. 'I'll ring Pearl to make arrangements for Sunday, but then I'm off into the garden to tackle some weeds.'

Dolly was left fuming. Bernie was too fond of taking Pearl's side, but she'd make him pay for it. Her time would come, and soon, but in the meantime Bernie would need his wits about him when he drove to Battersea on Sunday. She wouldn't give him any more pills for now, but if John refused to visit them again she wouldn't wait any longer and would up the dose.

Bernie would be very amenable then, Dolly mused, so out of it that he'd sign anything that was put in front of him...

Despite all her misgivings, Pearl found that she was happy in Battersea. Derek had been so upset about the way his gran had spoken to her, but Pearl found that as Connie hadn't been in her life for so many years, it didn't really matter. What mattered were the people she saw daily, the stall-holders who remembered Derek, along with the new ones who had all welcomed him into the fold. They were all nice to her too, always with a cheery wave when they saw her, and so far it

156

seemed that nobody had said a word to John about Kevin.

When school broke up for the summer, her mother would be coming to stay with them for a week. No doubt all the talk would be of her wedding; though it had initially been a shock to hear that she was going to marry Tim, Emily's happiness was plain to see. They had decided on a small, Christmas wedding and already her mother was planning what she should wear, with a cream wool suit top of her list so far. Of course Tim would look immaculate, Pearl thought, he always did. He was a nice man, a gentleman, and somehow he seemed just right for her mother.

Pearl's mind turned to other things as she looked around the shop. The cream paint she had chosen gave a neutral background for the modern, pop art posters she had on display, and the glass shelving gave the place a light and trendy feel. She had spent money on advertising, along with letting local colleges and night schools know she was there, and it had paid off. Her stock of watercolour and oil paints had sold really well, along with brushes. She hadn't sold any easels yet and canvases weren't moving very well, but it was early days yet. Lucy's T-shirts were selling, along with craft kits, and the children's section was growing in popularity. Pearl knew it was fanciful, but on odd occasions she felt that Bessie was watching over them, that she approved, and the thought comforted her.

The only problem they'd encountered had been with John. When Derek opened his stall, it had meant working on Saturdays, and though it was unlike John, he had sulked because he had to wait until the end of the day before Derek could drive him to Winchester.

Derek had been the one to placate John, offering him a Saturday job on the stall which not only considerably increased his pocket money, but served another purpose too. Tired after a day's work on the busy stall, John realised that Derek must be too and he had cut down his visits to Winchester, happy to go with them on a Sunday once a fortnight when it also gave Pearl a chance to see her mother.

'Do you stock needles and cotton?' a customer asked.

Pearl had soon found there was a demand for sewing materials and had quickly added some to her stock; smiling, she said, 'Yes, there's some on a stand over there.'

The door opened again, and another customer came in with a different request. 'Do you sell macramé kits?'

'Yes, I do,' Pearl said, showing her one for making plant pot hangers.

'This is just what I'm looking for. I'll take it,' the woman said, but then she saw the children's section and wandered over to it.

The shop was getting busy and Pearl left her to it while she served another customer. Later the woman returned to the counter. 'My niece would love this jewellery making kit. The beads are so pretty. I think I'll buy it for her.'

Pearl rang both items up, but as she put the kits in a bag she noticed that the woman was looking at her intently.

'I've got it,' the woman said. 'I thought I recognised you from somewhere. It was years ago, but didn't you once live around here?'

'Err ... yes ... that's right,' Pearl said, feeling her stomach churn.

'I thought so. You're the poor cow who married Kevin Dolby. When I heard what he did and what you went through with his nutty mother, I felt so sorry for you, and a lot of others around here felt the same. Yeah, and you left the area after that I heard – married Derek Lewis, didn't you?'

'Yes, I did.'

'Is this *your* shop now?'

'Yes, it is,' Pearl replied.

'Well, love, I'm pleased to see you're doing well for yourself.'

'Thanks,' she said, handing the woman her items.

'You're well rid of Kevin Dolby. He was a nasty piece of work.'

Thankfully as another customer approached the counter, Pearl didn't have to make any comment, and the woman then said, 'I can see you're busy so I'd best be off.'

Pearl hid her feelings behind a pleasant smile as she said goodbye. She didn't want to think, or talk about Kevin, and though glad of her custom she was relieved when the woman left the shop.

Kevin wasn't thinking about Pearl as he sat in his car surveying Vince's house from a decent distance. He loved his new wheels, a black Ford Cortina, but though he had sat here many times before, and on different days, so far the only

159

times Adrianna left the house was when she was with Vince or one of his heavies.

Every time Kevin saw Vince, he felt a surge of anger, and was growing impatient to move forward with his plans. Rupert was ripe for picking now, and Kevin was ready for the last stage of his scam, but he didn't want to torch Vince's place with Adrianna inside.

He glanced at his watch. For the last few days he'd been watching the house in the morning, hoping that it was a time when Adrianna was let off her leash; that she at least might go shopping without an escort.

His patience at last paid off – there she was, leaving the house, and there wasn't anyone with her. *Walk this way,* towards me, Kevin willed, and was gratified when she did just that. He waited until she was almost alongside the car then he leaned across the passenger seat to swing open the door.

'Adrianna,' he called. 'Hello.'

She bent to look at him, and it was a few seconds before he saw recognition dawning in her eyes. 'Are you mad?' she said, glancing behind her. 'Go away.'

'Look, if you want to get away from Vince, I can offer you a way out.'

'I can't get away from him, he'd kill me, and if he thought you had a hand in it, he'd kill you too.'

'With what I've got planned there'd be no chance of that. Get in the car and we can talk.'

'He might see me.'

'I parked too far away for that.'

After another quick glance over her shoulder,

Adrianna scrambled into the passenger seat. 'Quick, drive further away.'

With a smile on his face, Kevin did just that. He'd done it. He'd got Adrianna on her own, and now all he had to do was convince her that his plan would work.

Adrianna was shaking with nerves. She had got into a car with a man she had only glimpsed twice, but if he really could offer her a chance to get away from Vince, surely it was worth the risk? She looked at him and as though aware of her scrutiny, his eyes left the road as he turned to smile at her. 'In case you don't know, my name is Kevin – Kevin Dolby.'

He was good-looking, very good-looking, and Adrianna asked, 'What's this about a way out?'

'I'll find somewhere to park up and then we'll talk.'

'There's no time for that. I had a bit of an emergency and Vince only let me out to go to the chemist's. If I'm not back soon he'll send Stan to look for me.'

'Stan, yes, I remember him well. I've got the scar to prove it,' Kevin said bitterly.

'Then you know what he's capable of. Look, there's the chemist,' she said urgently. 'As we drove here it's saved me a bit of time, so park up outside and it'll give us a few minutes to talk.'

To her relief, Kevin did as she asked, and after switching off the engine he turned in his seat to face her. 'You'll probably think I'm mad, but from the instant I saw you in the club I knew you were the woman for me.'

161

Adrianna felt sick. They were the same words Vince had used and she wasn't about to jump from the frying pan into the fire. She'd been so sure of herself at first, sure that she had Vince just where she wanted him, drooling, but her assumptions had proved wrong. Vince had begun to rule her, to watch her every move, and when she'd tried to stand up to him, she'd suffered for it. Now she lived in fear of him; of what he was capable of doing to her – and she wasn't about to make the same mistake again. 'Let's get one thing straight,' she said. 'I might hate Vince and want to get away from him, but that doesn't mean I'm prepared to run off with a bloke I hardly know. You could be as bad as Vince, another nutcase who wants to own me, and I'm not having that.'

'I'm nothing like Vince. Give me a chance and I'll prove it.'

'What's this plan then?'

'I'll have money soon, lots of it, enough to get us out of the country and to sunnier climates. I just hope you've got a passport.'

Adrianna's laugh was sardonic. 'Leave it out. Vince had you checked out and I heard him talking about you. You're a small-time thief who's just got out of prison.'

'Things have changed since then and I'm in for a windfall. I'll have plenty of money soon. You needn't worry about that.'

'Even if what you say is true, you don't know Vince. Yes, I've got a passport, thanks to the one time he took me on a trip to Paris, but he'd find me before I got out of the country.'

'I don't think he'll be in any fit state to do that.'

'I should have known this would be a waste of time,' Adrianna said derisively. 'You can't get to Vince. He's always surrounded by his heavies.'

'I know a way, but if I tell you what I've got in mind can I trust you to keep your mouth shut?'

'I'm not about to tell him,' Adrianna said. 'If I did, Vince would know I've been talking to you and believe me, he'd make me suffer for that.'

'Right then, if this is going to work we'll just have to trust each other. You said that Vince is always surrounded by his heavies, but not when he's asleep,' Kevin said, going on to lay out his plan.

Adrianna had thought of sneaking off when Vince was asleep, but without money she wouldn't be able to get far. With his contacts, the eyes and ears everywhere, Vince would soon find her. Now though, with what this bloke had in mind, she really could have a chance to get away. She wanted to trust him, wanted to believe that it really was going to happen, but she knew so little about Kevin Dolby. 'Are you really going to do it, or is this some sort of sick joke?'

'It's no joke, Adrianna. When you sneak out, all you'll have to do is to leave the door open and that will make it easy for me.'

She looked into his eyes, thought she saw sincerity there, but how could she be sure? 'I dunno. Vince said your mother was sent to a nuthouse. For all I know you're like her, delusional or something and this is all pie in the sky.'

'I'm nothing like my mother and I can assure you this is real. It's going to happen, and then we'll have all the time in the world to get to know each other.'

Adrianna just gave a small smile. If she agreed to this, she'd only use Kevin for as long as it suited her. He had the money to get them out of the country, and once safe she'd dump him and make it on her own. It was that thought that sealed her decision. 'Right then. If you're telling the truth, how will I know when you're gonna do it?'

'I'll get word to you.'

'How? Vince hardly lets me out of his sight, and you mustn't risk coming to see me again. If Vince spots you we're both dead, and you can't ring me because Vince or one of his heavies always answers the telephone.'

'I could leave you some sort of sign,' Kevin suggested. 'When I'm ready to make my move I could chalk something on a wall where you'd be sure to spot it.'

'I suppose that could work, but what wall?'

'Is the club closed during the day?' he asked.

'Yes, and there won't be many people around.'

'I could chalk a small cross low on the wall just before the exit door in the alley. I doubt it'd be noticed unless you're looking for it, and just in case you miss it. I'll do another one just above the door.'

'That sounds all right,' Adrianna told him.

'When you spot the signs, you'll know I'm going to do it that night and all you've got to do is to get out of the house while Vince is asleep.'

'What if he takes ages to go off? It could be the early hours of the morning before I can sneak out.'

'Don't worry. I won't do anything until I see you

leave,' Kevin assured.

'When should I start looking for the chalk marks?'

'With any luck in a week or two, but if it's longer, don't give up. I won't let you down, I promise.'

'I'll have to trust you. If I want to get away from Vince it's my only choice,' Adrianna said, but then began to panic about how long she'd been sitting in the car. 'I must go.'

'Just look for my sign,' Kevin murmured as he leaned towards her.

She tensed, but as he only kissed her cheek she allowed it. He was going to torch Vince's house and at the thought of flames licking up to the bed, Adrianna smiled wickedly.

Yes, it was apt. Vince was so evil that he deserved to burn in hell.

Chapter Twenty-Two

Bernie drove to Battersea, hoping he'd be making the return journey with his grandson. His eyes shied away from the café on the corner of the High Street that Dolly had once owned, one that held only bad memories.

He pulled up as close as he could to what was now Pearl's shop; it was Derek who let him in. 'Hello, Bernie. You made good time.'

'I left at eight thirty and the roads were fairly clear.'

It was Sunday and the shop was closed, but

Bernie looked around in amazement. 'Pearl told me on the telephone that she had made changes, but I didn't expect this.'

'It's doing surprisingly well.'

'I'm glad to hear it.'

'Bernie, before we go upstairs, I've got something to tell you. It was a while ago now, but Kevin was around here, sniffing for information on Vincent Chase.'

'That name sounds familiar, but I can't place him.'

'He's a fence and used to virtually run the borough, though from what I've heard he's moved on to other things. He owns a good few gambling joints and strip clubs.'

'Why would Kevin be interested in him?'

'I've no idea, but if he's mixing with the likes of Vincent Chase I doubt it's got anything to do with religion. I'm only telling you because it seems a bit fishy to me, but please, don't say anything to Pearl. She doesn't know that Kevin was in the area and I'd rather keep it that way.'

'So he didn't try to see John?'

'No. He was only interested in Vincent Chase.'

Bernie was frowning as he followed Derek upstairs. He too found it suspicious. If John wouldn't come home with him, he'd change his plans. Thanks to Rupert giving them his address, he would be able to drive to Ealing where he'd have a word with Kevin. For now, unsure of what direction he'd be taking when he left, Bernie planted a smile on his face as he walked into the living room. 'Hello, everyone.'

'Hello, Granddad,' John said, being the first to

166

answer as he rose to his feet.

'Come on, Clive, let's go out for a walk,' Lucy Sanderson said.

'Me come too,' begged Nora.

'Yes, all right,' she agreed.

'You don't have to leave because I'm here,' Bernie protested to no avail as Lucy left the room with Nora scuttling after her.

'Sit down, Bernie,' Pearl urged. 'I expect you could do with a drink.'

'I won't say no. A cold one would be nice.'

As Pearl left the room, Bernie said warmly, 'It's good to see you, John, and it looks like you've grown a few inches.'

'I don't think it's that much. My uniform trousers still fit me.'

'How do you like your new school?'

'I didn't at first, but it's all right now though.'

'He's made friends with a few lads in his class and that made a difference,' Derek said as Pearl returned with glasses of orange juice.

'Well, John, have you told your granddad that you've got a Saturday job on Derek's stall?' Pearl asked.

'Give me a chance, Mum, he's only just arrived.'

'So, John, you're a budding costermonger,' Bernie said, smiling.

'He is *not*,' Pearl protested. 'I want better things for John when he leaves school.'

'Well, thanks very much,' Derek said. 'And what does that say about me?'

'No, no, I didn't mean it like that. It's just that I want John to have some sort of career.'

Derek grinned. 'I'm pulling your leg, Pearl.'

167

'Oh, you...'

'I like my Saturday job,' John said, 'but I fancy going into horticulture, or forestry.'

Bernie smiled. 'Now why doesn't that surprise me? Though I had thought you might want some sort of job with animals.'

'I wouldn't mind that either and you should see my cat, Granddad. He's big now. I'll go and find him and you can see for yourself.'

Bernie waited until the boy was out of earshot and then said, 'Have you spoken to John about coming back with me?'

'Yes, but I'm afraid he still feels the same.'

'Maybe if I ask him he'll agree.'

There was a pause before Pearl said, 'I suppose you could try.'

When John came back with a huge ginger cat in his arms, Bernie was indeed surprised by his size. 'He's a whopper.'

'He's put on weight since he's been spayed,' Derek explained.

'And he's a bit lazy now,' John said as he fondly stroked Ginger.

'John, your gran would love to see you. Won't you change your mind and come home with me?'

John lowered his head, his voice little more than a murmur. 'I can't. I'm meeting my friends.'

'If you're worried about seeing your father, you needn't be. He's a different man now, a good man and...'

'I don't want to talk about him,' John blurted before Bernie had finished what he was going to say, and with the cat still in his arms he hastily left the room.

'That's blown it. I shouldn't have mentioned Kevin, but I thought he just might listen to me.'

'Maybe he will one day,' Pearl said, 'but at the moment I think he needs a little more time.'

'Yes, I can see that,' Bernie agreed, though he knew that Dolly was going to be disappointed. 'I won't press John, but can I see a bit more of him before I go?'

Pearl nodded. 'Of course you can.'

Derek offered to find him, and when he and John returned together, Bernie didn't mention a visit or Kevin. He stayed for another hour, but then decided it was time to head for Ealing.

He was determined to find out what Kevin was up to and to do that he had to see his son face to face.

While getting ready to go out, Kevin was thinking back to the first time he and Rupert had been to look at the club. Rupert had dressed in his usual outlandish style, his hair curled and high like a woman's as he had minced in. Though Kevin hadn't been expecting it, the owner's attitude had played right into his hands; the man's feelings about poofs clear. They'd managed to look around, to take note that the club was busy, the bar tills ringing regularly, but then, fearful of the hostile looks he was getting, Rupert had insisted on leaving.

After that incident it had taken a bit of persuading to convince Rupert that buying the club was still a viable option, but with a bit of sulking on Kevin's part, the soppy old sod had finally agreed. Shortly after that he told Rupert that he'd been

169

tipped the wink that it was going on the market, and that it might be a good idea to get in first.

Rupert had agreed and Kevin was now ready for his next move. 'Right, I'm off,' he said, throwing on his jacket.

'I've never heard of doing business on a Sunday,' Rupert said petulantly.

'It's the only time the owner could spare, and as the club looks like a goldmine I wasn't going to split hairs over an appointment.'

'I'm not sure I want to deal with that bigoted homophobe.'

'You won't have to,' Kevin pointed out. 'That's why I'm going on my own.'

'If he finds me so distasteful, I'm not sure I want to buy his club.'

'That's up to you, but I doubt another opportunity like this will come up. You've seen what else is on offer and there's no way I'd want to run one of those dumps,' Kevin said, feigning a fit of pique as he slumped onto a chair. 'In fact we might as well forget the whole thing. I'll go back to looking for a job and as I won't be working for you, somewhere else to live.'

'There's no need for that,' Rupert said hastily. 'Go and meet the man and if you can negotiate a reasonable price, we'll go ahead.'

'All right then,' Kevin said, hiding a smile of satisfaction as he stood up again. 'I'll see what I can do.'

'I have every faith in you,' Rupert said and after putting up with a hug Kevin left with a spring in his step.

It was all coming together nicely, and he'd even

had the foresight to tell Rupert that he'd taken his other suits to the cleaners when in reality, they were in the boot of the car, along with some of his casual gear. It would give the game away when he left if he walked out with a suitcase, but now he was well prepared.

There was just one more hurdle to overcome.

Kevin had been gone for under an hour when Rupert heard a ring on his doorbell, but when he went to open it, he didn't recognise the man who stood there. 'Yes, can I help you?'

'I'm Bernie, Bernie Dolby, I've come to see my son.'

'You're Kevin's father!' Rupert exclaimed, seeing no resemblance.

'Yes, that's right.'

'I'm afraid Kevin isn't here at the moment, but I'm Rupert and it's lovely to meet you. Please, do come in.'

'Will he be home soon?' Bernie asked as he stepped inside.

'I rather doubt it, though I suppose it depends on how well his meeting goes.'

'Meeting?'

'Yes, he's gone to see a chap who's selling a nightclub that I'm interested in buying. If Kevin can get it for a decent price he'll run it for me. But come on through,' Rupert said, leading Bernie to the drawing room.

'I'm sorry, but I'm not sure I understand – unless of course you're going to use the premises for the refuge?'

'Now *I'm* confused. What refuge?' Rupert asked.

171

'The one Kevin wants to set up for homeless people, alcoholics and such – lost souls he calls them.'

It sounded ridiculous now to Rupert and he giggled. 'He must have told you that while he was in prison, but of course with ears everywhere he would have kept up his act.'

Bernie's face paled. 'Do you mind if I sit down?'

The man looked grey and worriedly Rupert said, 'Of course not. Can I get you anything? A whisky, or perhaps brandy?'

'Whisky please.'

After downing his drink a little colour returned to Bernie's face and Rupert asked, 'Are you feeling better now?'

'Yes, thanks, but let me get this straight. Are you telling me that Kevin's religious conversion is all a load of tosh?'

'Well … yes, but surely you know that?'

'You'd think so,' Bernie said, 'but when Kevin has been to see us he still acts as though he's found God.'

'Really. How odd.'

'He's up to something, he must be, and you can bet your life it's to do with money. He was always a sponger, living off his mother and as I first thought, all this talk of a refuge is a scam to get a donation out of us.'

'No, no, I'm sure that isn't true,' Rupert protested.

'Then why the pretence, tell me that!'

'I can't, but I'm sure there's a perfectly reasonable explanation.'

'Huh, no doubt the git will find one, but it'll be

a pack of lies. Kevin is trying to fleece us, and he's probably doing the same to you.'

'Of course he isn't. He would never do that,' Rupert cried. 'I love Kevin and I trust him.'

'You love him!' Bernie said, his eyes wide with shock. 'Bloody hell!'

'Yes, and Kevin loves me too.'

'You're a pervert,' Bernie said in disgust as he surged to his feet, 'and a fool too. I can see by this house that you've probably got a few bob and Kevin is taking you for a mug. He isn't going to get a penny out of me though, and when you see my son you can tell him that I never want to set eyes on him again!'

With that, Kevin's father marched from the room and shortly after, the front door slammed. Rupert remained seated, his mind reeling.

Chapter Twenty-Three

Bernie was still pale with shock and found it hard to concentrate on the roads as he drove home. At last he made it, but when he walked in, Dolly looked none too happy.

'I see that John isn't with you,' she complained. 'You were supposed to talk to him, to put him straight about Kevin.'

Bernie was in no mood to placate her. 'I did, but he didn't want to know, and after finding out a few things about your precious son, it's just as well.'

'If you've been listening to Pearl, you're mad. She'd say anything to turn John against Kevin, and us too.'

'No, Dolly, I didn't get it from Pearl. I went to Ealing and had a very enlightening chat with Rupert, a nice bloke – or should I say woman.'

'What are you talking about?'

'I should have noticed it from the start, especially as Rupert was wearing some sort of flowery caftan. He's a queer, Dolly, and mad enough to be in love with Kevin. I should have taken more notice when you said Rupert sounded odd on the telephone. The poor sod. I actually felt sorry for him.'

'Don't talk rot. Kevin isn't like that and this proves that you really are going senile. You've gone as daft as your father.'

'I'm not that far gone yet, and it's just as well because I've found out that Kevin has been lying to us. He isn't religious and all that talk of setting up a refuge is just a scam to get money out of us. I'm on to him now though and he'd better not show his face at my door again.'

'*Your door!* This is *my* house, bought with *my* money from the sale of *my* café. And if you think you can stop Kevin from coming to see me, you've got another think coming! It'll be you who gets chucked out, not my son!'

Bernie eyes narrowed with suspicion as Dolly ranted and raved. He'd been worried about forgetting Dolly's pills and now marked the calendar each time he doled them out. He also counted them, making note of the amount left each day. She'd had them that morning, he was

174

sure of it.

'Are you listening to me, you daft sod,' she yelled, 'or are you off in a world of your own again?'

'I'm listening,' he said, thinking back to when he'd first noticed a change in Dolly's emotional stability. He had thought then that her dosage might need a bit of adjusting, but now it seemed the pills were having little or no effect. That couldn't be right. Something didn't add up, and as she continued to berate him the penny at last dropped. He'd been giving Dolly her pills. She just hadn't been taking them. 'All this ranting and raving proves you haven't been taking your pills.'

'That's your fault, not mine!'

'No, Dolly, I'm not falling for that again. You're as bad as Kevin, liars the pair of you.'

Dolly strode forward, and before Bernie had time to react, she punched him in the face. He reeled back, but she was moving towards him ready to land another blow.

'Dolly,' he shouted, 'if you hit me again I'll call the doctor out. He'll take one look at the state you're in and have you sectioned.'

That knocked the wind out of Dolly. 'You wouldn't do that,' she cried.

'If you carry on like this, I won't have any choice.'

She glared at him as though considering her options. 'All right, I won't hit you again,' she said at last.

Bernie's face was throbbing, but he hurried to shake her pills onto his palm. 'Take them, or else, Dolly.'

'Mark my words, Bernard Dolby. One day I'll make you pay for this,' she threatened before tipping the pills into her mouth.

'Swallow them, Dolly,' he ordered, handing her a glass of water.

'There,' she said after gulping them down. 'Satisfied?'

Bernie said nothing and went to get a cold flannel to put on his cheek. Without her medication, Dolly could be capable of anything, but she'd be calm again soon.

When he returned from his fake meeting, Kevin had his story ready. He walked into the drawing room, but as soon as Rupert saw him, he said, 'Kevin, your father called here to see you.'

'My father? But how? I've never given him my address.'

'When I spoke to your mother, I passed it on and told her that they were welcome to visit us.'

'You did *what?*' Kevin said, annoyed.

'What's the harm, dear boy – unless of course you're ashamed of me?'

Kevin fought to keep his composure. 'Of course I'm not, but what did my father want?'

'I don't really know, but we had a very interesting chat.'

'About what?'

'Oh, I think you know,' Rupert said sarcastically. 'The refuge you supposedly want to set up, along with your religious beliefs. Why have you been lying to your parents, Kevin? You're no more religious than I am, and there was no need to keep up the façade once you were released from prison.'

Kevin walked over to the sideboard and poured a glass of whisky while his mind worked overtime. He had to find answers, and quickly. Holding up the bottle, he asked, 'Do you want one?'

'No, thank you.'

Kevin took a sip of his drink, relieved when an explanation came to mind. He did his best to look unruffled as he sat down and said, 'It's simple enough to explain. My mother had a bit of a nervous breakdown when I was sent to prison and I know she was fretting that I'd get into trouble again when I came out. For her sake I kept up the pretence and it seems to have worked. She's much happier now.'

'That's nice, and it all sounds very commendable, but why keep the truth from your father?'

Kevin took another sip of his drink, deciding then to try for sympathy. 'We never really got on, and of course I let him down when I went to prison, so much so that he never came to visit me. I suppose I kept up the act because I wanted him to be proud of me.'

'Darling, I can understand that, but as I had no idea that your parents thought your religious conversion was genuine, I'm afraid I rather put my foot in it. Your father was very upset.'

'Yes, I can imagine. What did he say?'

Rupert hesitated, but then said, 'He said some very nasty things, but I'm sure he only spoke in anger. He seems to think that you're after his money, and he warned me against you too.'

Kevin reared to his feet. 'That's bullshit. I've never asked him for a penny. Whatever he said, it's all lies, but no doubt you believe him!'

'Of course I don't. I told your father that I love you, trust you, and I do, but he was so angry that he stormed out saying he never wants to see you again.'

Sod it, Kevin thought. His dad now knew he was living with a queer and he doubted it had gone down well. It was just as well that it didn't really matter. Rupert was his target now, and as he was leaving the country he wouldn't be seeing his parents again. It was Rupert he had to keep on side and it was time to change tactics, to go for dejection now instead of anger.

He flopped onto a chair again. 'I suppose I deserve that. I wanted to ease my mother's mind, but I should have told my dad the truth. Instead I wanted to impress him and now I've well and truly blown it.'

'I'm sure if you explain he'll understand.'

'It's too late. He won't believe me now and I can't say I blame him.'

Rupert's eyes were soft with sympathy. 'Maybe not at the moment, but once he's had time to calm down...'

'He's too unforgiving for that,' Kevin broke in. 'When I came out of prison, if it wasn't for my mother he wouldn't have let me over their doorstep, and he only softened when I kept up my religious act. I'm just glad that I was able to move in with you, but I suppose you want me to leave now, and stop working for you.'

'No, no, of course I don't,' Rupert protested.

'But after the things my father said...'

'Kevin, I understand why you lied to him, and as

for you being what he called a sponger, I know that isn't true. You've been the reverse – for instance you insisted on getting a job to pay your own way when you weren't really up to it after that awful beating. I know I've been a fool in the past, that I've let people use me, but you're different. As I told your father, I trust you.'

'Thanks, you don't know how much that means to me,' Kevin told him. He was relieved but nonetheless, just in case his father had put a shadow of doubt in Rupert's mind, he knew that he'd have to tread very carefully. It would mean a change of tactics and possibly a small delay to his plans, but better that than losing the chance of getting what he wanted. With that thought he continued, 'And now I wish I had better news to tell you about the meeting.'

'Oh dear, didn't it go well?'

'The bloke only agreed to meet me because he was looking for a quick sale. I think we should forget it and hope that something else turns up.'

'Surely we can accommodate him with a quick sale?'

'It isn't as simple as that. His marriage is on the rocks, his wife has filed for divorce and she's after everything she can get. Before that happens he wants to sell the club to bugger off abroad with his young and tasty new girlfriend.'

'I don't see what difference that makes. If you can get it for a good price, we can still buy it.'

'He's willing to drop ten grand to forty, and though it's still a lot, I think the club is worth it. The problem is he wants a cash sale, and just in case the wife gets wind of it he only wants twenty-five grand to show on the books. I told him to forget it, and now, if you don't mind, it's been one of those mornings and I've just about had enough. First of all I lost the chance of getting us the ideal club, and to top it all, my father doesn't want to see me again,' Kevin said, swiftly leaving the room before Rupert could respond.

Kevin's hands balled into fists as he cursed his father for turning up and probably putting doubts in Rupert's mind. He hoped he'd allayed them, that he'd done enough; but the last thing Kevin wanted was any further contact from his parents to add fuel to the fire.

With this in mind he decided to put the telephone out of action for now. He'd been an engineer and knew how to do it, though of course it could already be too late and his plans already scuppered.

If they were he'd make his father suffer. It wouldn't only be Vincent Chase's house that would burn to the ground – it would be his parents' place too. With both of them inside.

Chapter Twenty-Four

'Here's one for you,' Pearl said on Monday morning as she handed Lucy a letter.

The envelope was brown and looked official. Lucy tore it open to read the contents and squealed with excitement. 'Pearl, it's from the housing association. They've offered me a flat in

Bullen Street!'

'That's nice,' Pearl said, though there wasn't a trace of enthusiasm in her voice.

Lucy could guess why and worried about losing her job, she said hurriedly, 'It's only a hop and a skip away so it won't make a lot of difference. Once I've taken Clive to school I can come here.'

'Yes, of course you can and when Nora gets used to the new arrangements, I'm sure she'll be fine.'

Relieved, Lucy said, 'I'd best get Clive to school now. When I come back, do you mind if I ring the housing association to arrange a viewing?'

'You don't have to ask permission to use the telephone.'

'I don't want you to think I'm taking liberties.'

Pearl smiled. 'I know you'd never do that. In fact, in the short time you've been living with us you've become like a part of the family.'

Lucy was touched. Like Pearl, she was an only child and it was like having a big sister. She liked Derek, John too, but though it hadn't been bad staying with them, she couldn't wait to have her own home again.

'Thanks, Pearl,' she said, then going to the door she called, 'Clive, Nora, come on, we've got to go.'

With lightness in her step, Lucy set off to take Clive to school, Nora on one side as she walked along and her son on the other. As she passed Eddie White's stall, he stepped forward, a friendly grin on his face.

'Hello, sunshine. It must be seeing me that's brought that smile to your face!'

'Don't kid yourself,' Lucy quipped.

'Gawd, you know how to crush a man, but I'd still like to take you out.'

Lucy was unable to wipe the smile from her face. It was a lovely morning, the sun was shining, and she'd just had the smashing news that she was getting a flat. 'I'll think about it,' she said, but then her face flamed. It was as though the words had left her mouth of their own volition.

'Really? That's great.'

'I've got to go,' she spluttered. 'Come on, you two, get a move on.'

'Don't think about it for too long,' Eddie called after her. 'After all, you don't want someone else to come along and snap me up, do you?'

Nora giggled. 'He funny ... nice.'

Lucy just shook her head and as they hurried away she wondered what had made her blurt that out to Eddie. As they passed Derek's china stall he waved at them and she waved back, but her mind was still on Eddie. Had she unconsciously been considering going out with him? No, that was silly, of course she hadn't. Or had she?

The question remained unanswered as Lucy watched Clive run into the school playground, and on her way back she ignored Eddie as she hurried past on the other side of the road, the telephone call she had to make to the housing association now uppermost in her mind.

Dolly was anxious to speak to Kevin – and of course to give Rupert a piece of her mind – but though she had tried several times to ring them when Bernie was out of the way, she hadn't been able to get through.

She'd try again later, but for now Dolly was glad that she could set the clock by Bernie's morning routine. At the moment he was upstairs having a shave and in just a few more minutes he'd be down for his breakfast.

She poured herself a cup of tea and then upped Bernie's dose by tipping a whole crushed pill into the pot. She stirred the tea vigorously and popped the cosy back on, knowing from previous occasions that the taste would be smothered by the amount of sugar Bernie spooned in, two teaspoons at least, sometimes three.

When Dolly heard his footsteps on the stairs she composed her face to one of calm, yet inside she was still seething. Yesterday Bernie had threatened her with the doctor, forced her to take pills, but she'd pushed them into her cheek with her tongue until able to dispose of them. She pretended they had calmed her, and as usual it had fooled Bernie; though it had been hard to sit still when all she had wanted to do was lay into him with her fists over and over again.

Never again, Dolly thought. She wasn't going to let the little runt rule her ever again. It was time to act, and as Bernie walked into the room she asked quietly, 'What do you want for your breakfast?'

'I'm not hungry. I'll just have a cup of tea, but I'll get your pills first.'

As always now, Dolly didn't swallow them and as Bernie looked a bit distracted it was easy enough to surreptitiously spit them out while he poured himself a cup of tea.

She smiled inwardly. From now on she wouldn't

183

have any trouble from Bernie. He'd be as docile as she had been for far too many years.

In Ealing, Kevin found that he was so uptight that he wasn't able to eat his breakfast. Rupert hadn't mentioned the club since he'd told him to forget about buying it yesterday, and though he'd had the chance to sleep on it, so far Rupert hadn't raised the subject this morning either.

Kevin's stomach knotted with anxiety. He'd promised Adrianna that it wouldn't be too long before he'd be able to leave the chalk sign and he could just imagine her looking for it every night when she went to perform at Vince's club.

'You're rather quiet this morning, Kevin. Are you feeling all right?' Rupert asked.

Kevin decided that he'd have to risk bringing up the subject and said despondently, 'I must admit I'm gutted about the club, especially as he was willing to knock ten grand off the price. I'll have to go out this morning to check a few more areas, a few more commercial agents, but I'll only give it another month. If nothing turns up I think paying me to carry on searching is just wasting your money and I'll refuse to take it any more. There must be a job out there for me, something I can do, though it won't be the same as working for you.'

'Hold on, Kevin. I know you said we should forget about buying the club, but I'm not sure I agree with you.'

'Rupert, I told you, he wants cash *and* he wants to fiddle the books. Surely that could cause a problem with the Inland Revenue?'

'I suppose there's a slight possibility, but it's hardly the crime of the century. There are lots of people who are less than honest, especially when it comes to taxes – for instance those who salt their money away in offshore accounts.'

Kevin had never heard of offshore accounts, but he didn't want to show his ignorance. 'So are you telling me that you're willing to go along with it?'

'Yes, I am, so now all you have to do is finalise the deal.'

Kevin hid his delight, only feigning concern as he said, 'Rupert, are you sure? I still think it's a bit dodgy and I'd hate you to come a cropper with the Inland Revenue.'

'It's lovely to hear that you're worried about me, but I'm sure there's no need.'

'All right, then, I'll ring him now to arrange another meeting,' Kevin said, and on the off chance that Rupert would hear, he'd pretend to do just that, though of course Rupert still had no idea that the phone was out of action. Luckily Rupert hardly used the telephone, and if by any chance he did, he'd think it was out of order and suggest getting in an engineer to fix it.

Once out of sight, Kevin allowed himself a huge smile. He'd done it, covered every base, and very shortly he'd have a cheque made out to cash in his hands.

Bernie felt ill, muzzy-headed, and had spent most of the morning and early afternoon sitting in a chair before his mind began to clear. He'd had bouts of this before, but never as bad as this.

185

At last, he stood up, drinking a glass of water before going out to the garden for a bit of fresh air. Dolly was outside too, sitting on the garden bench, but she rose to her feet when she saw him.

'It's about time you bucked yourself up. I've been sitting here thinking, and I can't believe you listened to anything that Rupert had to say. For one thing, *if* you remember, Kevin refused to take money from you and at the same time he even protested about changing our wills. The only money he accepted went into the fund for the refuge.'

'There is no refuge,' Bernie said tiredly, but he couldn't find the energy to argue.

'Don't talk rubbish,' she snapped, and with that final parting shot she went inside.

Dolly had sounded a bit sharp and Bernie wondered if he'd forgotten her medication again. He was still woolly-minded, however, and the thought didn't remain in his head for long as he flopped onto the vacant bench.

It was four o'clock before Bernie felt fully alert again. He didn't know how long he'd been sitting, but his bottom felt numb and his back was aching as he stood up to stretch. He knew he was going senile, but it seemed odd that after feeling like a zombie for most of the day, he now felt that his mind was clear. If anything, his pattern of behaviour was more like Dolly's than his father's: her pills kept her quiet for long periods until they wore off and she had to have another dose.

An awful thought crossed Bernie's mind and, sickened, he flopped down again. He already knew that Dolly hadn't been taking her pills, but now he suspected that she'd been giving them to him instead.

'Bernie, you've been out there long enough,' Dolly called. 'Come inside. I've made a pot of tea.'

Tea ... yes, he'd started to feel muzzy-headed after drinking a couple of cups that morning. Despite this, Bernie didn't want to believe that Dolly was giving him her drugs, but there was only one sure way to find out.

'All right, I'm on my way,' he called in reply, and soon after drinking the brew Bernie's anxieties disappeared as his mind floated, cushioned, as though resting on a cloud of cotton wool.

Chapter Twenty-Five

Before getting dressed early on Tuesday morning, Emily stared with distaste at her reflection in the mirror. She was thin, bony, her breasts tiny, whereas Tim's late wife Delia had been curvaceous with long, shapely legs.

Though Emily had agreed to marry Tim and the wedding was planned for Christmas, she was plagued with doubts. It wasn't just that she felt Tim would find her body unattractive; it was fear of the intimate side of marriage. She hadn't been with a man for many, many years and the thought of that side of things made her nerves jangle.

Emily threw on her clothes, wishing there was someone she could talk to. She felt uncomfortable at the thought of discussing it with a friend and it was at times like this when Emily wished she had a sister. It would have been lovely to be able to share confidences with someone she could truly trust, safe in the knowledge that anything they talked about wouldn't be repeated or gossiped about.

When her doorbell rang moments later at almost seven o'clock, Emily knew it would be Tim. They had taken to sharing breakfast before leaving for work. She quickly brushed her hair and then hurried downstairs to let him in.

'Good morning,' Emily said, forcing a smile.

'Hello, darling,' he said, kissing her cheek.

Soon they were sharing a pot of tea and a rack of toast, but as Tim spread marmalade on a slice he said, 'You're very quiet this morning.'

'Am I? I didn't realize.'

'Emily, I know I'm not the most perceptive man, but even I've been aware that there's something on your mind.'

'No, there isn't. I'm fine.'

'I know you too well to believe that. Please, darling, tell me what the problem is and maybe I can help.'

Emily just shook her head, but as though struck by a thought, Tim asked worriedly, 'Is it me? Is that it? Have I done something to upset you?'

She saw the concern in his eyes, and blurted out, 'It isn't you, Tim. *I'm* the problem.'

Tim reached out to clutch her hand as he said, 'Darling, I love you, and though I don't know what the problem is, there's nothing you need to hide from me ... nothing you can tell me that will change that.'

Emily so badly wanted to unburden her fears. This was the man she had agreed to marry, one she trusted, and if she could talk to anyone, it should be Tim. At last she said, 'If we get married, I know I'm going to disappoint you.'

'You couldn't possibly do that, but what do you mean by *if* we get married? Surely you're not telling me that you want to call it off?'

'I ... I ... just don't feel that I can compete with Delia. She was beautiful, and she had a lovely figure, but me ... well ... I'm tiny, thin, and I haven't got any of her ... her attributes.'

'Emily, I don't care that you're thin – in fact I prefer slim women.'

'You do?'

'Yes, and if you must know Delia was very slender when I married her.'

Now that she had started, Emily found that she wanted to carry on, to bring all her fears into the open. 'Tim, there's something else. You ... you see I've only been intimate with one man, and that just once with Pearl's father. I've so little experience and ... well, the thought of that side of marriage makes me very nervous.'

'You're not the only one. I'm nervous too.'

'You! But why?'

Tim was quiet for a moment, but then he said, 'This is a bit difficult for me to talk about, especially as Delia is no longer with us, but you see she wasn't exactly a warm woman, well, not in that way. She was very warm and welcoming to our friends, and of course you knew that, but I'm afraid in our bedroom it was a very different story.'

'But you seemed so happy.'

'I suppose in all other ways we were. I had come to accept it, you see, though I often used to wonder if it was me; that I failed to, well, please her.'

Emily found herself lost for words, but she at last managed to say, 'Oh, I'm sure that isn't true.'

'Isn't it? I don't know, Emily, and now you know why I too am nervous.'

Emily squeezed Tim's hand. He was nervous too, and somehow that wiped away her fears. For the first time her smile was genuine as she said, 'We're as bad as each other, but don't worry, with a bit of practice I'm sure we'll be fine.'

'Practice sounds perfect to me.'

Emily smiled. Now that her fears had all but dissipated, she was looking forward to becoming Tim's wife, and to the many happy years they'd hopefully share together.

Bernie was usually an early riser, but his mood was so low that he'd remained in bed until at last, with his mind set on what he was going to do, he finally got up. Despair swamped him, his movements slow, but he washed, shaved and then put on his best suit. It was nearly time now.

At first Bernie had tried to find excuses for Dolly's behaviour, one being the fact that she hadn't been taking her medication which made her unstable. Yet she must have planned to stop taking her pills, and he was sure it coincided with Kevin's release from prison.

Bernie had worked it out that the pair of them were up to something, his wife and son devious liars, and until now he'd been the idiot they'd taken in. He'd let Dolly fool him into thinking she was taking her pills, and though he'd been suspicious at first, he'd finally fallen for Kevin's so-called religious conversion.

On top of that, when Dolly's drugs had affected his thinking, she had convinced him that he was going senile. Her cruelty and her lies sickened him, Kevin's too.

Bernie had been over and over it in his mind, and realised that with Kevin involved, whatever they were up to had to do with money. He of course stood in their way, and with Dolly already sedating him, Bernie guessed there was worse to come.

The thought of being drugged and helpless in their hands was more than Bernie could bear. They could even be planning to get rid of him, to kill him! Though it might sound extreme to anyone else, Bernie knew they were both capable of such an act.

What they didn't know was that the bulk of his money was hidden away in a secret account and when he died, they'd never be able to get their hands on it. That was the only thought that gave Bernie any comfort, and rather than wait for them to kill him, he'd decided to save them the job.

He just couldn't stand it any more, couldn't live like this... It was time to put an end to it all.

'I've never known you to lie in bed for so long,' Dolly complained when he went downstairs. 'I've just made a fresh pot of tea and I was about to call you.'

'I don't want it,' Bernie said. 'I'm going out.'

'Wait! Where are you going?'

He ignored Dolly's shout as he hurried down the path. All his affairs were in order, and as he hadn't yet changed his will in favour of Kevin, John still stood to inherit his house. Yes, *his* house – it was in *his* name only, and there wasn't a thing Dolly could do about it.

Bernie knew he would miss his grandson, but he hardly saw the lad now and at least by doing this, John would shortly have his inheritance. It gave him great comfort to know that John's future would be financially secure, and though the lad might miss him for a while, he would still have the most important people in his life; his mother, Derek and Emily.

With everything clear in his mind now, Bernie got into his car. He was ready ... ready for the final act. He had the means, after all – he was driving it – and he'd enjoy this last journey in a vehicle he was fond of. It would take him out of Hampshire and into Sussex. When he got to the top of the cliff Bernie intended to make sure that there was nobody around to see, or stop him.

It was strange really, Bernie thought. Now that he'd made the decision, he felt strangely calm. His only regret was that he wouldn't be around to see Dolly's face when she found out she was going to be penniless.

Chapter Twenty-Six

Both bewildered and annoyed, Dolly stared at the untouched pot of tea. If Bernie had drunk at least one cup he wouldn't have been in any fit state to drive off without telling her where he was going. He'd said he had things to sort out, but what did that mean? Was he going to see Kevin again, was that it?

She hurried to the telephone, but again she was unable to get through. She tried the operator, her voice reflecting her impatience. Only a short while later, Dolly huffily replaced the receiver. The line would be checked, but there had been no indication of how long it would take.

It was only when she sat and thought about it that Dolly came to the conclusion that Bernie wouldn't have gone to Ealing. He'd made his feelings about Kevin clear, had said that he never wanted to see him again – but how dare he speak for her? There was no way she'd allow Bernie to turn Kevin away from their door, and to that end she would make sure that soon he'd be incapable of protesting against anything.

With no idea where Bernie was, or how long he'd be out, Dolly had to get rid of the tea, but she had already decided to make sure that this didn't happen again. When Bernie came back she'd add two pills to the next pot and then the soppy old sod would be completely under her control.

It was time to get things moving, to get poor Kevin away from that awful Rupert. No matter what it took, Dolly wasn't going to let anything stand in her way.

In Battersea, Lucy had taken Clive to school and then she was going straight to Bullen Street to view the flat. Pearl had convinced Nora to stay with her and as soon as she asked her if she'd like to dust the shop, a smile appeared on Nora's face as she set to work.

Like Lucy, Nora's love of housework always amazed Pearl, and at first she had felt guilty at seeing her do so much. They were tasks that Pearl felt she should be doing, but when she had tried to help it had upset Nora. She had retreated to her room and it had taken hours to persuade her to come out, with only the promise of letting her do the housework finally doing the trick.

'Lucy back soon?' Nora asked.

'Yes, I should think so.'

'I don't want her to go.'

'I know, sweetheart, but she won't be far away and you'll see her nearly every day,' Pearl consoled.

'Clive too?'

Pearl smiled. 'Yes, of course.'

Nora seemed placated and shortly after that Lucy returned, entering the shop flushed with happiness. 'Pearl, the flat is lovely. I was hoping for the ground floor, but that only had one bedroom so I'm upstairs. It's smashing though, with a brand new modern kitchen and a newly fitted bathroom. You'd never believe it was once an old scruffy terraced house. Everything is brand spanking new: the paintwork, the wallpaper, and even the doors and windows.'

'It sounds lovely. When can you move in?' Pearl asked.

'Now if I want to,' Lucy replied, flourishing the keys, 'but of course I'll have to get my furniture out of storage first.'

'Then you'd better give them a ring to sort it out.'

'Thanks, Pearl,' she said, hurrying towards the telephone.

Pearl found it lovely to see Lucy so happy. After all she had been through she deserved it, and now Pearl started thinking about what she would buy her as a house-warming gift.

'Talk about luck,' Lucy said as she replaced the receiver. 'They can deliver it tomorrow.'

'That's good. And as you'll need a couple of days to sort yourself out, the last thing you need to worry about is Nora. She seems happy enough in the shop and I'm sure I can find enough to keep her occupied.'

'Pearl, are you sure?'

'Bessie managed without any help, and I'm sure that I can too.'

The smile disappeared from Lucy's face. 'I ... I know that Nora is settled now, and I suppose you don't really need me.'

'Of course I do,' Pearl said hastily. 'I just wanted to put your mind at rest by saying that I could manage.'

Lucy looked relieved. 'Thanks, Pearl, that was thoughtful of you, but for a moment there I thought ... well ... that I was out of a job.'

'There's no chance of that,' Pearl said and meant it. She had grown very fond of Lucy, and as she did a lot – the laundry, the cooking – she really didn't think she could manage without her.

It was after midday when Kevin returned to Ealing. He found Rupert sitting in the drawing room, legs crossed and a glass of whisky in his hand. 'Do you want one?' Rupert offered.

'No, thanks,' Kevin said, going into his act. 'Sorry, Rupert, I tried, but it was forty grand or nothing. I still think it's a bargain so if you want to go ahead he's already had a bill of sale drawn up by his solicitor.'

Rupert frowned, 'Goodness, he really is in a hurry.'

'Yes, he is, but if we delay we run the risk of someone else coming along with a better offer. I got a tip from one of the bar staff that another man has been taking a lot of interest in the club, taking note of how many customers turn up, and clocking what goes into the till. He must have worked out, as we did, that the place is a goldmine.'

'I don't mind moving quickly, but I'd prefer my own solicitor to look at the books and such, let alone this bill of sale.'

'Fine,' Kevin bluffed, 'do that, and as I hoped you'd agree to the conditions I've got it with me. I suppose I can get hold of the books too, but if your solicitor can't look at the lot today, and this other bloke makes a better offer, I think we can kiss goodbye to the club.'

'Oh dear, I don't want that to happen, but I don't know what else to suggest.'

Kevin kept his cool and spoke persuasively. 'Look, I've seen his yearly accounts and the profit margins look impressive. Not only that, as a solicitor has drawn up the paperwork, it's bound to be kosher. After all, these legal bods aren't going to chance anything coming back on them. Now if it were me, I'd go ahead and seal the deal rather than risk losing the club, but if you want to act like a cautious old man, it's up to you.'

Kevin knew his barb had hit the mark when Rupert bristled, 'I'm not *that* old.'

'Sorry, I shouldn't have said that, but you don't seem to realise how much the club means to me. I can run it for you, and increase the profits, I'm sure. I could then go on living here with you, knowing that I'm paying my own way, whereas if the sale falls through...' Kevin choked, the sentence deliberately left unfinished.

'Oh, please, don't get upset,' Rupert cried. 'Nothing is going to fall through. Give me that paperwork. I'll sign it now and you can take it back to him.'

Rupert had reacted just as Kevin had hoped, but still with a subdued voice he asked, 'What about the money?'

'I'll write him a cheque, made out to cash, and you can take that along too.'

Rupert scrutinised the document, reading every line. To make it look legitimate, an old contact had told Kevin about a less than honest solicitor's clerk who would draw it up for the right price. It had cost Kevin more than he'd expected, and now

197

he just hoped it was good enough to fool Rupert.

'It all looks fine to me,' Rupert said at last, signing the document with a flourish.

'Brilliant.' Kevin enthused.

'It still rankles that I can't be there with you to complete the deal, but as the idiot is so totally homophobic I suppose at this stage it's better not to rock the boat. However, once everything is finalised and he can't back out, we're going to my club in style.'

'What are you going to do? Hire a Rolls-Royce?'

'Yes, good idea,' Rupert said. 'I'm also going to reward you for everything you've done for me.'

'Reward me? How?'

With a small smile, Rupert said, 'It's going to be a surprise, dear boy.'

There was something in his eyes that worried Kevin, but he couldn't put his finger on it. No, he decided, he was imagining things, and shaking his head, said, 'You've done enough for me already, and now I just want to prove that I've got what it takes to make the club a success.'

'You've already proved yourself to me,' Rupert said as he held out the cheque.

Once again, Kevin tensed, worried by something in Rupert's tone, but as the cheque was flourished, greed took over and he wanted to snatch it from his hand. With a quick intake of breath, Kevin managed to remain composed as he said, 'I'll get over there straight away, and I'll insist that his solicitor is present when we finalise the deal. I'm not sure how long that will take, but I'll be back as soon as I can.'

'I can't wait, and as we'll have something to

198

celebrate I'll put a bottle of champers on ice.'

'Sounds good to me,' Kevin said as he forced himself to give Rupert a hug, thankful that it would be for the last time. He wouldn't be coming back, but of course at the moment Rupert didn't know that. By the time he worked it out the cheque would be cashed and it would be too late for him to do anything about it.

Chapter Twenty-Seven

When Pearl answered the telephone that afternoon she was shocked to hear Dolly's voice asking abruptly, 'Is Bernie there?'

'No, he isn't. Is he on his way, then?' Pearl asked, wondering why Bernie would be coming to see them at this time of day.

'How do I know if he's on his way or not? He went out before ten this morning and I haven't seen him since.'

'That's odd. Didn't he say where he was going?'

'Would I be ringing you if he had?' Dolly snapped.

Pearl gripped the receiver tightly. It was only her concern for Bernie that kept her from slamming it down. 'If he left at ten, that's five hours ago and it doesn't take that long to drive here. I hate to say this, but maybe he's been involved in an accident or something. Have you tried ringing the police?'

'What's the point of doing that? If anything had happened to him they'd be knocking on my door.

Now listen, if he turns up there, tell him to get back here or else,' and with that she slammed the phone down.

Pearl hadn't spoken to Dolly for many, many years, but her voice had sounded the same: cold, unfeeling and demanding. Nevertheless, concern about Bernie was uppermost in Pearl's mind. She went to the back stairs and called, 'Lucy, I want to pop out for a few minutes to have a word with Derek. Do you mind keeping an eye on the shop?'

'Of course not,' Lucy replied brightly as she appeared at the top of the stairs. 'Come on, Nora, we're going downstairs and when Pearl comes back it won't be long before we fetch Clive home from school.'

Pearl hurried to Derek's stall, finding him busy with a customer, but as soon as he'd completed the sale he came to her side. 'What's wrong, love?'

'Dolly rang. Bernie went out this morning without telling her where he was going and he hasn't come back.'

'Why did she ring you?'

'She wanted to know if he'd turned up here, but of course he hasn't. I'm worried about him, Derek.'

'Did he have a suitcase with him when he went out?'

'I don't know. I didn't think to ask,' Pearl said, but then realised the implication behind Derek's question. 'Surely you don't think he's left Dolly?'

'If he has I wouldn't blame him,' Derek said, 'and if Dolly doesn't know where he is, it sounds likely.'

'No, I can't believe he's walked out on Dolly.'

200

'Pearl, whatever Bernie's up to, he's a grown man and I'm sure he'll be fine.'

'How much is this coffee set?' a potential customer called.

'I'll leave you to it,' Pearl said. However, returning to the shop, she found that despite Derek's reassurance, she was still concerned. She still couldn't believe that Bernie had left Dolly. So where was he?

Kevin had been to the bank and left it smiling, congratulating himself for thinking of everything. He had opened an account when Rupert began to pay him a salary, and there was enough money in it for now. He drew out what he needed and then paid in Rupert's cheque. It was made out to cash, but despite that Kevin felt it might raise a few eyebrows if he tried to draw on it straight away.

Tomorrow, before he left the country with Adrianna, he'd take out a nice chunk and once abroad transfer the rest to a Spanish bank, or he might even enquire about one of those offshore accounts that Rupert had spoken about.

Kevin then went to Soho to leave the signs for Adrianna, but afterwards, with time to kill and needing a distraction, he decided to drive to Battersea. His mother had said that John was a chip off the old block and he wanted to take a look for himself.

At one time Kevin had wanted his son back in his life, but that all changed when he'd found a way to fleece Rupert. He had money now, lots of it, and he was leaving the country. It still rankled that Pearl had turned the boy against him, but at least he could take this opportunity to put the boy straight.

There was a school close to the High Street that seemed the most likely, and as he didn't have time to check any others, Kevin decided to hang around to see if John came out.

After sitting outside for ten minutes there was a sudden surge of boys coming out of the school gates. There were so many and Kevin tried to scan their faces, but found it impossible. It was hopeless, but then his eyes became riveted on one lad. It was like looking in the mirror, at his own face when younger, and Kevin knew without a shadow of doubt it was John.

He watched as his son walked towards the car and when he was almost level, Kevin jumped out.

'Hello, John,' he said with a soft smile.

The lad was startled, but there was instant recognition and his face screwed up with anger. 'Go away,' he said belligerently.

'John, please, I've cleared this with your mother and I just want to talk to you.'

'No, just go away and leave me alone.'

Kevin walked calmly around the back of the car and as he stood in front of John, he went into his act. 'I know you've been told about my past, but I'm a different man now,' he said softly, adding a look of contrition as he continued. 'I did some terrible things, but God forgave me and as I'm leaving the country in the morning, this will be my last chance to speak to you.'

'You're leaving?' John parroted. 'Where are you going?'

'Why don't you come with me for a short drive?' Kevin gently urged. 'We'll find somewhere to have an ice cream or something and I'll tell you all about it.'

John hesitated for a moment, but then said, 'All right.'

'Thank you, son, this means a lot to me,' Kevin said, hiding his triumph. It wasn't much in the way of payback, but if John was late home it would put the wind up Pearl.

At that thought, Kevin smiled sardonically.

'Watcha, Lucy, you're looking very chirpy,' Eddie said as she passed his stall. 'It's nice to see you smiling, but of course it's perfectly understandable. I seem to have that effect on the ladies.'

'I think you'll find they're laughing *at* you, not *with* you,' she said.

'Now that hurts,' Eddie said, but his eyes were sparkling with mischief.

'If you must know, I'm happy because when I picked up Clive from school I took him and Nora to see my lovely new flat in Bullen Street.'

'It's nice,' Nora said.

'Yeah, it's smashing,' Clive agreed, 'and Mum said we're moving in tomorrow.'

'In that case, young man, I hope I'm invited to the house-warming party.'

'He can come, can't he, Mum?'

'I hadn't planned on throwing a party.'

'Now that's a shame,' Eddie said, 'but seriously, if you need a hand with anything, let me know.'

'Go to shop!' Nora suddenly cried as she grabbed Lucy's hand and tried to pull her along.

'What's the matter, Nora?'

'Go see Pearl! Go to shop!'

'Sorry, Eddie, I'll have to go, but thanks for the offer,' Lucy called out as she was tugged away with Clive holding her other hand.

Only minutes later they arrived, Nora crying as soon as she saw Pearl behind the counter, 'He's coming! Pearl, he's coming!'

'Who's coming?'

'The bad man!'

'Nora, who do you mean?'

'Bad man! Bad man,' she cried frantically.

'Who are you talking about and where did you see him?' Pearl asked worriedly.

Nora looked confused as she cried, 'I not know!'

'Mum, I'm scared,' Clive said, clutching at Lucy's skirt.

'It's all right, darling, there's nothing to worry about. Nora's just having a funny turn, that's all. Isn't that right, Pearl?'

'Yes, yes, of course it is,' she replied as a customer walked into the shop.

'Right,' Lucy said, 'come on you two, we're going upstairs. Pearl is busy.'

'Tell Derek! Pearl, you tell Derek!' Nora appealed urgently.

'Yes, don't worry,' she said as the customer came to the counter.

For Clive's sake, Lucy did her utmost to hide her concern as they went upstairs, where almost immediately Nora calmed as if she'd already forgotten her strange warning.

Pearl tried to serve the customer, but found it

hard to focus on what she was doing. Nora had said a bad man was coming. Questions tumbled one after the other in her mind. *Bad man*. It was something Nora had once called Kevin. Had she seen him? Is that why she'd said that he was coming? Was he going to walk into the shop at any minute?

'You've given me the wrong change.'

'I'm sorry, what did you say,' Pearl asked.

'This is two bob short,' the woman said, holding it out.

'Is it? I'm so sorry,' Pearl said as she quickly took the money from the till.

'I should think so too,' the customer huffed before marching out of the shop.

Pearl stared at the door, expecting it to open again at any moment and for Kevin to walk in. As the minutes ticked by, Pearl's imagination leapt to the thought of Kevin lurking around somewhere to intercept John as he walked home from school.

When the door opened, it was just another customer, one who took ages to select what she wanted. By the time she left, Pearl was growing increasingly concerned. John should be home by now, but when she stepped outside to scan the High Street, there was no sign of him.

She went back inside and when another fifteen minutes passed, Pearl began to panic. Surely Kevin wouldn't take John somewhere without her permission ... would he? Worse, what if he didn't bring him back?

Fear froze her mind and she dashed out of the shop, running, and she didn't stop until she reached the school gates.

Her chest heaving, Pearl saw that the playground was empty, and there wasn't a single pupil in sight. Ineffectually she shouted, 'John! John!'

Silence greeted Pearl's cry, dread knotting her stomach as she began to run again, this time heading for Derek's stall. When she reached him he must have seen her distress and said anxiously, 'What is it, love?'

'John,' she gasped. 'I think Kevin has ... has taken him.'

'What? When?'

'He must have been waiting for John when ... when he came out of school.'

'Are you sure?'

'Yes ... yes ... Nora warned me. I ... I ran to his school but John wasn't there. Derek, please, we've got to find him!'

'Harry,' Derek called to the neighbouring stallholder. 'I've got a bit of an emergency and I'll have to shoot off. I haven't got time to close up so can you keep an eye on my stall?'

'Yeah, no problem.'

With that, Derek headed for where his car was parked, his money pouch jingling. As soon they got in he gunned the engine to life. 'Right, where do we start?'

'I don't know,' Pearl groaned.

'If Kevin's got a car they could be anywhere by now.'

'Oh, don't say that. Please don't say that,' Pearl begged. 'We've got to find John, we've just got to.'

They didn't find John, and an hour later they returned to the flat, Pearl almost in a state of collapse.

Lucy jumped to her feet when she saw them. 'Pearl, you went out without locking the shop! I only found out because a customer shouted up the stairs.'

It was Derek who answered. 'Pearl was in a bit of a panic.'

'It's John, isn't it?' gasped Lucy. 'I guessed something must have happened when he didn't come home from school. Please, Derek, please tell me he's all right.'

'Pearl thinks he's with Kevin. We've been out looking for them.'

'Oh, Derek, what if Kevin doesn't bring him back?' Pearl cried, voicing her fears again as she sank onto the sofa.

'John isn't a little kid, and he wouldn't stand for that. He'd get away from him.'

'You should ring the police,' Lucy said. 'Tell them that John's been kidnapped.'

'If he's with his father I'm not sure they'd take it seriously, but yes, I'll ring them,' Pearl said. But just as she stood up to go to the telephone, John walked into the room. Tears spurted, running down her cheeks as she ran to put her arms around him. 'John, thank God you've come home! I've been worried sick.'

'But why? You know I've been with him … Kevin. He took me to a café, got me a glass of lemonade and we talked for ages. He said he was sorry for the things he'd done, that he was different now and went on about God a bit. He was all right, really, nice. He said he was sorry too for not being around to be a proper father, but once he's settled abroad I'll be able to spend holidays with him.'

'Abroad? What do you mean?' Pearl asked as she dashed the tears from her eyes.

'I thought you knew, thought he'd spoken to you. He's leaving the country in the morning.'

'John, I had no idea where you were. Derek's been driving me around looking for you and I was just about to ring the police.'

'But Kevin said he'd cleared it with you!'

'That isn't true,' Pearl said. 'He didn't.'

John's face paled. 'He lied to me?'

'Yes, I'm afraid so.'

'But why?' John asked, looking bewildered.

'I don't know. Perhaps he thought I wouldn't agree to let him see you,' Pearl offered.

'Do you think he's really leaving the country in the morning or it that another lie?'

'I don't know, darling,' Pearl said.

'I don't care if he goes or not,' John said bitterly. 'I'm never going to talk to him again.'

'I'm sorry, John, this must be hard for you. You and I can have a chat later,' offered Derek, 'but for now I've got to get the stall packed up and closed.'

'I'll give you a hand, Dad.'

'Thanks, son.'

Pearl knew how hurt John was, how Kevin's lies must have shattered his fledgling feelings for his father. She didn't know if Kevin was leaving the country or not, but deep down she suspected that he only said that as a ploy to get John into his car.

208

She flopped onto a chair, reliving her terror that Kevin had taken John away. At least that hadn't happened, her son had returned home, but what if Kevin tried to see him again?

Chapter Twenty-Eight

Adrianna had spotted the chalk marks, and she was so excited that she didn't know how she got through her act.

When she left the club, Vince had his heavies, Stan and Bert, in the car with him as usual. The door was flung open and she got in, her nerves on edge, but thankfully none of them seemed to notice.

As they drove down the street towards Vince's house, Adrianna forced herself to stare straight ahead. If she looked for Kevin's car, Vince might notice and the last thing she wanted was to give the game away.

As though he was a gentleman – which knowing Stan was a joke – he held open the door as they climbed out. Vince walked ahead of her and once again Adrianna had to resist the urge to throw a look over her shoulder before they went inside. The chalk mark had been there, and that meant Kevin would be out there somewhere waiting for her, and at least that thought was reassuring.

'You can knock off now, Stan,' said Vince. 'You too, Bert.'

'Thanks, boss,' they said, before heading for

their rooms at the back of the house.

Vince turned to Adrianna. 'I'm going to have a nightcap. Do you want one?'

'No, thanks,' she said. 'I think I'll go straight to bed.'

'All right, I won't be long.'

When Vince came upstairs shortly after her, he wasn't wearing his jacket and as he undressed Adrianna didn't hear the jangle of the door keys in his trouser pockets. His smile was a leer as he climbed into bed, and Adrianna knew she would have to endure his sexual demands. She hated the stench of whisky on his breath, and wanted to turn her face away, to avoid his slobbering kisses, but could only console herself with the knowledge that this would be the last time he laid his hands on her body.

When it was over he rolled onto his side, his back towards her, and she tried to keep her breathing steady as she listened for his snores. Yet even when she heard them, she was so nervous of waking him that she didn't move.

An hour passed, and it was only the thought of Kevin giving up that forced Adrianna to gently push back the blankets. Slowly, oh so slowly, she got out of bed, her legs shaking so much that she had to pause for a moment. She moved carefully to pick up her discarded clothes, a skirt and silk blouse from the back of a chair, along with her handbag, and crept onto the landing to dress.

The bed creaked and Adrianna froze. She heard a snort, a rustling, and for a few moments was terrified that Vince was getting up. She remained rigid, her heart thumping with fear.

When there were no further sounds of movement, Adrianna quickly threw on her clothes and tiptoed downstairs holding her shoes. She crept into the drawing room, relieved to see that Vince's jacket had been thrown carelessly onto the sofa.

She had never been given any house keys: the locks served both to keep intruders out and her in. With her ears pricked for any sound of movement, Adrianna rifled through Vince's pockets and with relief her hand closed on his keys.

Stan and Bert were on this floor, and at the front door Adrianna prayed they wouldn't hear as she carefully inserted one into a lock and turned it. It hadn't made a lot of noise, but there was still the other one and then the bolts. With no idea if they were heavy sleepers or not, Adrianna put on her shoes before tackling the other lock and bolts.

To Adrianna's ears, the noise she made was deafening, but at last she wrenched the door open and ran down the steps, her eyes searching frantically for Kevin's car. Headlights flashed momentarily and she fled towards them.

As she scrambled into the car, Kevin hissed, 'Did you leave the door open?'

'Yes, but I'm scared. What if you get caught?' she cried, her own safety paramount. 'That means I'll be done for too. Can't we just go?'

'I'm not leaving that bastard to come after us,' Kevin said. He reached for a can in the well of the car and then dived out.

Adrianna would never know how she managed to just sit there, while all the time her mind was screaming at her to run, but at last Kevin returned and they were driving away.

211

'Did ... did you do it?'

'Yeah, and I poured so much petrol around that there's no chance of him, or anyone else, getting out. The hall was blazing nicely when I left and the flames were heading for the stairs.'

Adrianna looked back over her shoulder, but so far nothing was visible from the outside. She hated Vince, and his heavies, but even so, the thought of them burning to death made her shudder.

'They deserve it,' Kevin said, reading her expression.

She forced the images from her mind. 'Where are we going now?'

'Down to Dover. After an overnight stop we'll be on a ferry to France and from there we'll drive to Spain where I intend to buy a nice villa.'

'You've got the money?'

'Of course I have.'

'That's good, because I've only got the clothes on my back and a handbag with a bit of make-up and my passport inside.'

'Don't worry, I'll buy you everything you need before we head for France in the morning.'

Adrianna was glad to get away from Vince, but she would still be dependent on a man, this time Kevin Dolby. What she really wanted was to be independent, to run her own life. Surely there'd be work abroad for an exotic dancer? In the meantime she'd stick with Kevin – but only for as long as necessary.

Just before turning the corner, Adrianna looked over her shoulder again, but they were too far away to see anything. What if Vince survived?

What if he came after her? The thought made her feel sick with fear, and she longed to get out of the country as soon as possible.

When darkness had fallen in Hampshire, Dolly, though still peeved, decided to take up Pearl's suggestion. She had rung the police, but after checking they had called back to say none of the hospitals had admitted Bernie and that there were no reports of any traffic accidents. If he still hadn't returned in twenty-four hours, they would list him as missing, but in the meantime there was nothing further they could do.

Dolly didn't know what Bernie was up to, but as he hadn't taken any of his clothes with him, she was sure he'd turn up. When he did she'd give him a piece of her mind, but finally, fed up with waiting up for him, she had gone to bed.

However, when Dolly woke up on Wednesday morning, she saw that Bernie's bed hadn't been slept in, and at last she felt a tinge of concern. He hadn't been in an accident, he wasn't in hospital, so where was he? She still couldn't believe that he'd left her, but what if he had? What if he'd sussed out what she'd been up to? He had control of all their money, and other than the house, Dolly knew she'd be left with nothing. There was no way she was going to stand for that. She had to find him!

Dolly heard the doorbell ring and after throwing on her dressing gown she hurried downstairs.

'Mrs Dolby?'

'Yes,' she said, finding herself looking at a policeman and woman.

'Can we have a word with Mr Dolby?'

'He isn't here. I rang the station yesterday to say that he's missing, and as he didn't come home last night, I was going to ring again this morning.'

'I see. May we come in?'

'Yes, all right.'

As they stepped inside, the constable took a notebook from his pocket and after looking at it for a moment, he said, 'Does your husband drive a green Morris Minor Traveller?'

'Yes, yes he does.'

'I think you should sit down, Mrs Dolby,' the policewoman said.

'I don't want to sit down,' Dolly snapped. 'I just want to know why he's asking me about Bernie's car.'

'Mrs Dolby, we've had a report from the Sussex constabulary that a green Morris Minor Traveller, registered in your husband's name, has been found at the bottom of the cliffs at Beachy Head.'

'*What?* Never! Bernie loved that car,' she protested, but then the full implication of his words sank in and she gasped, 'You're ... you're not telling me he was in it?'

'At this point your husband's body hasn't been recovered, but there are indications that he was in the vehicle.'

'What do you mean? What indications?'

The constable hesitated, but then said, 'I'm afraid there were traces of blood, and indications that he may have been washed out to sea.'

Dolly at last staggered to a chair. They were telling her that Bernie was dead, and probably ex-

214

pected hysterical tears, yet in reality all she could feel was shock mingled with relief that Bernie hadn't left her, or run off with their money. She placed both hands over her face and forced a groan. 'Oh, Bernie, Bernie.'

'Mrs Dolby,' the policewoman said as she crouched down in front of her. 'Is there anyone we can contact to stay with you, a relative?'

'My son. I want my son.'

'Do you have his telephone number?'

'Yes, it's on that pad over there, but it's been out of order.'

She stood up, asked the constable to try the number and then said, 'Would you like me to make you a cup of tea?'

'Yes, yes, please.'

When the constable couldn't get through, he asked for Kevin's address and then said that he'd arrange for a local station to send someone round to the house.

Dolly just nodded. She was still dry-eyed, but hoped they'd think it was because she was in shock, and this proved to be the case for they then rang her doctor. He knew her history and Dolly knew she would have to be careful, but at least she didn't have to worry about fooling Bernie any more.

He was dead, and soon she'd have all the money she needed to help Kevin.

Chapter Twenty-Nine

Rupert knew that Kevin wasn't going to return. Though he hadn't wanted to believe Kevin's father, Bernie had planted a seed of suspicion that Rupert couldn't ignore. He wasn't a businessman, but there had been so many clues: the necessity of a cash payment, as well as the sales contract that Kevin had with him so conveniently. He had played along with it, but inwardly Rupert's heart had been breaking.

He'd been made a fool of so many times in the past, and though this time at least he'd been prepared, it was little consolation for Rupert. He had got up that morning, his emotions still in tatters and his eyes soon filling with tears. He still loved Kevin, despite everything, and the future now stretched out bleak and lonely without him.

When there was a ring on the doorbell, Rupert went to answer it, his red-rimmed eyes widening when he saw the police constable.

'Mr Dolby?'

'No, and he isn't here. He left yesterday and I don't expect to see him again.'

'I need to speak to him urgently. Have you a forwarding address or any other means of contacting him?'

'I'm afraid not,' Rupert said, curious to know why the police were looking for Kevin. 'Can you tell me what this is about?'

'We were asked by the Hampshire constabulary to contact Mr Dolby as the telephone number they were given for this address is out of order.'

'Yes, I found out yesterday and an engineer is coming today to fix it. However, as the Hampshire police are involved, I would guess that this has something to do with Kevin's – sorry, Mr Dolby's – parents?'

'Do you know the family, sir?'

'Yes, very well,' Rupert said, exaggerating. 'Dolly, his mother, is a lovely woman and I saw his father recently.'

'In that case, when your telephone is repaired and if Mr Dolby rings you, would you tell him to get in touch with his mother urgently?'

'Oh dear, is she all right?'

'It's his father, sir. I don't know the details, but it seems he died in some sort of accident.'

'Goodness, that's dreadful. Yes, yes, of course I'll pass on the message.'

'Thank you, sir.'

Rupert waved his thanks away before closing the door. Of course he wasn't expecting a call from Kevin, but as an awful thought crossed his mind, he shivered with fear.

He'd been so hurt – then incensed, and so intent on making sure that Kevin didn't get his hands on his money, that until now Rupert hadn't thought of the consequences. He'd made a fool of Kevin and he must be seething with anger. What if Kevin wanted revenge? What if he came back to punish him?

Rupert began to feel very alone and frightened. If he told the police that Kevin had tried to rob

217

him, perhaps they'd help, offer him protection... But then he shook his head, realising it was a foolish hope. Kevin might have tried to rob him, but he hadn't succeeded, and he doubted the police would show an interest in what they'd see as a minor offence.

Though far too early, Rupert went into the drawing room and poured himself a large whisky, and then another, deciding after a third that if Kevin was going to come back he'd have done so by now.

Surely he was worrying about nothing?

In Hampshire, Dolly had seen the doctor. She had feigned grief, though hadn't gone over the top, and when she told him that she was taking her medication, he had looked reassured. The doctor then had a word with the constables before he left, and Dolly gladly closed her eyes, tired of all the acting.

She heard the telephone ring, but before she could get to her feet the policewoman answered it. 'Mrs Dolby,' she said, replacing the receiver, 'a constable has been round to the address you gave us, but your son no longer lives there.'

'He moved out? But if he isn't there, where is he?'

'I'm afraid we don't know. He didn't leave a forwarding address or any means of contacting him. Is there any other way you can get in touch with him?'

'No ... but he might be coming here,' Dolly said hopefully.

'Mrs Dolby, I'm sorry, but the doctor told us

218

that you shouldn't be left on your own. Is there anyone else who can stay with you?'

'Yes, of course there is,' Dolly lied. 'I'll ring them now, but you don't have to wait until they arrive.'

'That isn't a problem, Mrs Dolby.'

Dolly held her temper, her voice calm and reasonable as she said, 'I don't mean to sound rude, but I'd rather you left. This has been such a shock and I really would like a little time to myself before all my relatives turn up.'

The policewoman looked at her colleague and when he shrugged his shoulders, she said, 'All right, we'll leave now, but if we have any more information about the ... err ... accident, we'll let you know immediately.'

'Thank you,' Dolly said, relieved when they left. She *would* make a telephone call. She had to tell John about his grandfather, but for now her mind dwelt on her son. As though he could hear her she whispered, 'Please, Kevin, where are you? I need you.'

Kevin had problems of his own and his parents were the last thing on his mind as he stood in the bank, arguing with the manager.

'Now look, I know I've got the funds so don't muck me about.'

'I'm afraid the amount you're requesting exceeds the monies in your account.'

'Leave it out. I paid a cheque made out for cash into my local branch yesterday, and now I want to draw on it.'

'I'm sorry, sir, but that cheque was invalid.'

'How can it be invalid?'

'Because the bank it was supposed to be drawn from went out of business many years ago and all the accounts were closed. I'm afraid the teller didn't notice this until after you left, but your branch has been trying to contact you, though obviously without success.'

'I'm not going to stand for this. That cheque was made out to cash and there must be something I can do.'

'The error was noted before the money was paid into your account, and therefore I can only suggest that you take it up with the signatory.'

'Oh, I will, you can be sure of that, but I'm not happy with you lot. I want to clear my account and then you can close it.'

'Very well, sir,' the manager said.

Kevin waited impatiently and when the small amount of money was given to him he stormed out of the bank. He had thought there was something strange in Rupert's expression when he'd handed over the cheque, but had disregarded it. Now he knew that Rupert had deliberately made a fool of him.

'What's wrong?' Adrianna asked as he flung open the door and climbed into the car. 'You've got a face like thunder.'

'The money isn't in my account,' Kevin snapped.

'What are you talking about? You said you've got it!'

'I thought it was in the bag, but he's made a mug out of me and there's no way he's getting away with it. We're going back to London and

220

this time I'm not leaving until I've got the money in my hands.'

'Are you mad?' Adrianna said, her tone high with what sounded like panic. 'I don't know who you're talking about, but we can't be sure that Vince died in that fire. There's no way I'm going back to London.'

Kevin's head was thudding and he couldn't think straight. He needed time to calm down, to work out a plan. 'We haven't got any choice, but for now we'll go back to the hotel.'

'I'm *not* going back to London,' Adrianna repeated.

'Fine,' he snapped, thankful that she was in a sulk and didn't open her mouth again until they were in their room.

He lay on the bed, his temples still throbbing and the sunlight pouring through the window burning his eyes.

'Adrianna, I've got a pounding headache. Do me a favour and close the curtains.'

'I've got a couple of painkillers in my bag. Do you want them?'

'Yeah, all right,' he said, and after taking them he closed his eyes, soon drifting off into fitful sleep.

Adrianna watched Kevin until his face relaxed in sleep. They had spent one night together and she'd been tense, expecting him to try it on, but he hadn't. Kevin had been a proper gent, telling her that he was prepared to wait until she was ready, and despite the fact that she was just using him, it had impressed her.

221

She wasn't impressed now though and her mind was racing. Kevin said he could still get his hands on the money, but it would mean going back to London and, as she'd told him, there was no way she was going to do that.

Adrianna knew that if she had money of her own she could just bugger off, then, struck by a thought, her eyes went to Kevin's jacket. He'd paid for the hotel in cash, and maybe he had more in his pockets.

It felt like *déjà vu* as she searched his jacket, but this time Adrianna didn't pull out any keys, finding instead a small wad of notes. She swiftly counted them, disappointed at the measly amount. She only had the clothes she stood up in and though she'd rinsed out her knickers in the sink, they were her only pair. She wanted to get as far away as possible, and if this was at least enough to get her to France, she'd have to sacrifice buying any new clothes.

Adrianna's eyes narrowed in thought. Maybe she'd be able to nick a few bits, and now she quickly stuffed the money into her handbag. With her hand on the doorknob, she was about to open it when Kevin woke up.

'Adrianna, wait!' he cried out croakily.

'I thought you were asleep,' she said nervously.

'I've got too much on my mind for that. I know what you're up to, and I don't blame you, but you won't get far on that paltry amount of money.'

'I know I shouldn't have taken it, but I don't want to go back to London.'

'You won't have to. I've been thinking and there's no reason why you can't wait here. I won't be that long, and though it's a delay, it's only a short one.'

'It'll have to be, Kevin. Unlike you, I haven't got any spare clothes.'

'You can keep some of that money to buy yourself a few bits and pieces, and then tonight we'll be on our way.'

'What if you're seen?' she asked worriedly. 'If Vince survived the fire and you're followed, it would lead him to me.'

'I won't go anywhere near Vince's territory.'

With her hand still on the doorknob, Adrianna considered her options. If Vince had survived the fire, he'd be looking for her, putting out the word, and she wouldn't be safe anywhere in England. She needed to go abroad to be safely out of his reach.

At last she came to a decision. 'All right, I'll wait, but if you aren't back by nightfall, I'm leaving.'

'I will be,' he assured her.

And with that, for now, Adrianna had to be content.

Chapter Thirty

John had been upset about Kevin's lies, subdued that morning, but he had gone to school. Pearl hadn't mentioned Dolly's call. She didn't want John to worry, and as Dolly hadn't rung again, it probably meant that Bernie had turned up.

Lucy had taken Clive to school before going to

her flat to wait for her furniture to be delivered. So far Nora was happy to be in the shop, and Pearl found herself thinking about her warning. She had said that a bad man was coming, yet if Kevin had been waiting for John outside his school, how could she have seen him? Maybe she hadn't. Maybe it was another one of her strange foresights – though Derek always dismissed them, Pearl couldn't do the same.

The shop was quiet and Pearl carefully wrapped the lovely dinner set that she'd seen on Derek's stall. It would make a nice house-warming present for Lucy, along with a lovely pair of lace-edged sheets she'd found in the linen shop on the corner.

Nora was happily occupied too and when the telephone rang, Pearl went to answer it, her grip on the receiver tightening when she heard Dolly's voice.

'I've got a bit of bad news,' she said. 'You'll need to tell John that his grandfather has ... has passed away.'

'What? Oh no! What happened?'

'He had an accident.'

'I'm so sorry,' Pearl said. Though she had no time for Dolly, she felt overcome by a flood of compassion. 'Is there anything you need, anything I can do?'

'No,' Dolly said abruptly. 'I'm hoping Kevin will turn up, but at the moment it seems he's moved from his current address and I'm not sure where he is. I don't suppose you've heard from him?'

Pearl hesitated, but then said, 'I haven't spoken to him, but he was outside John's school yesterday. He told John that he'd come to say goodbye as he's leaving the country.'

'Don't be ridiculous!' Dolly thundered. 'Of course he isn't!'

'So you're saying he lied to John?'

'Kevin wouldn't do that. The boy must have misunderstood.'

'I don't think so.'

'I want to talk to John,' Dolly demanded.

'He's in school.'

'Tell him to ring me when he comes home,' she ordered and then hung up without another word.

Pearl was annoyed, but she was also close to tears. Poor Bernie had died in an accident, and somehow she would have to tell John.

'Have you heard the rumours, Derek?' Harry asked as he walked over to Derek's stall.

'What rumours?'

'There's talk that Vincent Chase's house was torched last night.'

'Blimey,' Derek whistled. 'He must have upset the wrong person.'

'Yeah,' Harry agreed, 'and gossip has it that Chase might have been inside.'

'Did he survive?'

'I dunno,' Harry said, shrugging, 'but no doubt we'll hear more shortly. Sorry, mate, I've got a customer.'

Derek frowned in thought as Harry went back to his stall. It hadn't been that long ago when Tommy had told him that Kevin had been nosing for information on Vince. Then, yesterday, Kevin had told John that he was leaving the country. Was Kevin mixed up in this? Had he torched

Vince's place or was it all just coincidence?

Before Derek could think it through any further, he saw Pearl hurrying towards him, her face strained and pale.

'What is it, love?' he asked urgently.

'Dolly just rang me. Bernie ... he ... he died in an accident.'

'No!' said Derek, horrified. 'I can't believe it. How did it happen?'

'I don't know. Dolly didn't say.'

'The poor sod. I hope he didn't suffer.'

'I'll have to tell John, but I don't know what to do,' Pearl said, trying to blink away tears. 'Do you think I should fetch him home from school?'

'It's up to you, love, but I reckon it can wait for now. When you do tell him he's going to be very upset and I doubt he'll be fit for school again for a good few days.'

'Yes, you're probably right. Oh – and though Dolly insisted that Kevin isn't leaving the country, she did say that she can't get hold of him as he isn't at his current address.'

'Then how can she be so sure that he hasn't gone abroad?'

'I don't know,' Pearl said, still fighting tears. 'I ... I'd best get back to the shop. I'll close up early when John comes home from school.'

'Yeah, do that,' Derek said, giving her a swift kiss on the cheek before she walked away. He hadn't believed for one minute that Kevin was leaving the country, suspecting that the story was just a ploy to get John to talk to him. But now he wondered if Kevin had actually been telling the truth.

Either way, Kevin had managed to worry the life out of Pearl when John didn't come home from school, and now Derek's hands balled into fists. He hoped Kevin really had gone abroad, because if he hadn't and he came face to face with the twisted little shit, it would be hard to keep his hands off him.

Eddie White was trying to coax his sister, but so far without success. 'Come on, I'm only asking you to look after my stall for a couple of hours.'

'I've got better things to do.'

'Like what? You're not working and I'm not expecting you to do it for nothing. I'll pay you.'

'Yeah, yeah, all right then,' she finally agreed.

'Thanks, love,' he said, grinning as he headed for Bullen Street. It had been a stroke of good luck that he'd known the van driver who had delivered Lucy's furniture, a good omen, and he'd been tipped the wink that she'd moved into the top flat at number twelve.

'I thought you could do with a hand,' he said, noting the look of surprise on Lucy's face when she opened the door.

'Well, you thought wrong,' she said.

'So all your furniture has been put where you want it?'

'Well ... no. But I'm sure I can manage.'

'Now why struggle when I'm offering to help?'

She hesitated, but then said, 'I must admit I'm finding it a bit of a job to put our beds together.'

'Lead me to them,' he said, pleased when she moved aside to let him pass. He'd always had his eye on Lucy. Though he played the part of a cheeky chappy who loved the ladies, it had taken all his nerve to ask her out. So far she had only agreed to think about it, but Eddie was sure that he was at last breaking through her reserve.

Half an hour later, with the beds put together and a cup of tea put in his hand, Eddie sat on the edge of Lucy's bed and asked, 'Right, what next?'

'I can't expect you to do anything else.'

'I don't see why not. I'm here, I've offered, so why not make use of me?' he said, but then to his chagrin there was a loud thump and his tea spilled as the bed tilted. 'Sod it! I think one of the legs has fallen off.'

Lucy giggled, but then she began to laugh and laugh, until gasping, she said, 'Oh, you should have seen your face.'

He put his cup on the floor to stand up, laughing too, and somehow they fell into each other's arms. Instantly they sobered, and as Lucy looked up at him, Eddie was unable to resist lowering his head to kiss her.

From that moment on Eddie would never be able to recall how they ended up on the wonky bed. All he remembered afterwards was the miracle that Lucy had welcomed him, her body moulding to his, and for Eddie it was just perfect.

Things weren't at all perfect for Rupert as he drunkenly lifted his head to look up at Kevin. He thought blearily that he should have had the locks changed, but it was too late for that now. All he could do was bluff, and somehow managed to slur, 'Kevin, the police are looking for you.'

'Is that so? Well, as you can see, they haven't

found me.'

'So you don't know?'

'Know what?'

'That ... that your father died in an accident.'

There was only a slight hesitation before Kevin spat, 'Good, it'll save me a job.'

'You can't mean that!'

'I can and I do, and as my father is out of the way that just leaves you,' Kevin said, moving swiftly. When the punch landed, Rupert's head thumped into the back of the chair, but his cry of pain didn't drown out Kevin's voice. 'I want money, and if I don't get it, that's just a start.'

'My wallet, there's cash in my wallet,' Rupert cried, cowering.

There was a snort of disgust. 'I'm not here for peanuts.'

'I ... I could write you a cheque.'

'Don't insult me. You fooled me with an old and out of date account once, but you won't be doing it a second time. We're going to your bank and I'll be right beside you when you draw out the money I want in cash.'

The doorbell rang, and though Rupert didn't know who it was, self-preservation kicked in as he managed to croak a lie, 'That'll be the police looking for you again. If ... if you don't go, I'll tell them that you tried to rob me.'

'Do that and I'll be back to kill you,' Kevin hissed before he ran from the room, heading for the back door. It slammed just as the bell rang again, and rising unsteadily to his feet, Rupert went to open it.

The engineer frowned as he looked at him, and

said, 'I'm here to repair your telephone, sir, but are you all right?'

'Yes. I walked into a cupboard door, but I'm fine now. Come in,' he invited.

Despite the throbbing pain in his head, Rupert was rather pleased with himself. He'd told Kevin it was the police again, and though he knew it unlikely, Rupert was pleased that his bluff had worked. Maybe he wasn't such an old fool after all. Of course there was still the risk that Kevin might return, so it might be prudent to disappear for a while. He knew of a lovely hotel in the West Country, and he would spend the rest of the summer there. Rupert left the engineer to it and went upstairs to pack, hurriedly stuffing clothes into a suitcase.

When he returned downstairs, the engineer said, 'I've managed to find the fault, a disconnected wire. Your telephone is in working order now.'

'Thank you,' Rupert said, and showed him out. He wondered if he dared risk taking the time to ring a local locksmith. He didn't care what it would cost to get the main lock changed; he just wanted them to send someone immediately. If Kevin came back he'd find that his key didn't work, and even if he still managed to get in, the house would be empty.

Rupert then had a stupendous idea to put Kevin off the scent and he smiled at his own cleverness. Once away he'd find an estate agent who would be happy to accept a nice payment to put a false 'House Sold' sign on display.

Chapter Thirty-One

After speaking with his grandmother, John replaced the receiver and turned to Pearl, his eyes brimming with tears again. 'Gran can't get hold of Kevin, and she's in a terrible state. She ... she's all on her own and it doesn't seem right. Do you think Dad would run me down to see her?' he asked anxiously.

'Yes, on Sunday,' Pearl nodded. 'Though she may have got hold of Kevin by then.'

'He might have been telling the truth about going abroad and I don't want to wait until Sunday. If Dad will take me I'd like to go to Gran's now. If not, I could go by train. She needs me and perhaps I could stay with her for a while.'

'Oh, I don't know about that, darling.'

'Please, Mum. School breaks up in about ten days so it's not as if I'll miss much.'

'I ... I'm not sure,' Pearl stammered as she desperately sought the right words. 'Your gran can be a little unstable and I'm not sure you'd cope.'

'I know she takes pills, but Gran has always been nice and kind to me when I'm there. It's never worried you before when I went to see her.'

Pearl floundered, still unsure, and said, 'Darling, you'd be alone with her.'

'What difference does that make?' John cried, and then tears began to flow in earnest. 'Please,

231

Mum, I haven't seen Gran for ages and I feel rotten about it. The last time Gr ... Granddad was here he wanted me to go back with him, but ... but I wouldn't.'

Pearl could see how guilty John felt, and was torn in two. 'Let me talk to Derek,' she said. 'I'll ask him to run you down to your gran's and if he thinks she's stable, that you'll be fine with her, you can stay for a couple of nights, but no more.'

'Thanks, Mum.'

'If you stay, I want you to promise that you'll ring me immediately if ... if your gran becomes difficult.'

'I'm sure she won't, but yes, I promise.'

Pearl went to have a word with Derek, and when he said he'd make sure that Dolly was stable, she felt reassured.

To begin with, Kevin had his foot down on the accelerator, but then, realising that he might be pulled for speeding, he slowed down. He didn't think Rupert would dob him in – sure his parting threat had been enough to ensure his silence – but he'd had to run off empty-handed and Kevin was beginning to panic.

If he went back to Adrianna without any money, she'd bugger off, and he didn't want that. He'd played the gent, kept his hands off her, and it had been a bit of a shock to his system to realise that the feelings he'd had in the past, the need to dominate, to punish women, hadn't arisen with Adrianna. It was different this time – he wanted her willing, and when he finally took her it would be with triumph. He'd have taken

Vincent Chase's property, without forcing her, and though the bastard might not be around to see it, he would still savour that sweet taste of revenge.

Kevin made a swift decision. He would have to take a chance, go back to Rupert's, and he swung the wheel to change his direction. It didn't take long to get there and he pulled into a quiet road, deciding to give it an hour to make sure the coast was clear.

With the engine off, Kevin's thoughts turned to his father. So he was dead. It was just a shame that it hadn't happened earlier, before the old git had been to see Rupert. His father had ruined everything, putting doubts in Rupert's mind and scuppering all his carefully laid plans. Kevin's only regret was that his father had died before he could punish him.

He found his head beginning to ache again, so he slumped low in the seat and closed his eyes, deciding to pass the time by having a little nap, but the nap turned into a long one and it was nearly two hours later before he woke up again. Kevin rubbed his eyes, his mouth dry, but then saw the time. He had to get Rupert to the bank before it closed, so gunning the engine to life, he put his foot down hard on the accelerator and sped off.

When Kevin arrived at Rupert's, he found he couldn't get in. He rang the bell, thumped on the door with his fist, and then looked through the letterbox. There was no sign of Rupert and startled by a voice, Kevin turned.

'Rupert isn't there. He's gone away.'

It was the elderly lady who lived next door, her equally elderly poodle on a pink, leather lead studded with diamantes. 'How do you know?'

'Because, young man, I saw him leaving with a suitcase and he told me.'

'Where has he gone?'

'I have no idea and I'm not one to pry. Now if you'll excuse me, Fifi has had her walk and now she'll be expecting her dinner.'

Kevin's jaws locked in anger as he watched her walk away. Rupert had done a runner, and with no idea where he'd gone it would be impossible to find him. He'd failed, and seething, Kevin got into his car and drove off, his mind desperately trying to think of an alternative way to get his hands on some money.

He drove aimlessly, but then his hands tightened on the steering wheel. His mother! With the old man out of the way she'd have control of their money – but how long would it take before she could get her hands on it?

For now, Kevin knew he had to get back to Dover before dark. If he didn't Adrianna would leave. He drove steadily, and as he reached the hotel, it at last hit him. He'd get some money out of his mother, but that wasn't all. His father had said he'd make him his heir, and that meant he'd inherit the house.

Kevin was smiling as he got out of his car. He'd flog the house of course, and though it might take a little time, he'd find somewhere secluded to lie low with Adrianna, a place well out of the way, where he'd at last be able to explore the delights of her body.

Derek drove to Dolly's place, and though he didn't have any time for the woman, he'd promised Pearl that he'd stay long enough to make sure it was safe to leave John with her. There were times when Derek felt Pearl should loosen the apron strings on John, but recent events had made her tighten them. He understood and didn't blame her. When it came to Kevin and his mother, he too was wary.

John had rung Dolly to say they were coming and when they arrived Derek pulled John's suitcase from the boot, and then stood behind him as he knocked on the door. When Dolly opened it, she not only greeted John warmly, she welcomed Derek in too. When they stepped inside Derek saw a middle-aged man sitting at her table.

'Here they are, doctor,' she said to him. 'I told you my family were coming. This is Derek, and this young man is my grandson.'

The man eyed the suitcase in Derek's hand and then rose to his feet, smiling. 'It's nice to meet you.'

'Nice to meet you too, doc,' Derek returned.

'I'm sure you're busy, and as you can see, I won't be alone now,' Dolly said, ushering the man to the door.

'Yes, I had an unusually packed surgery and then several house calls to make, hence the lateness of the hour,' he said, stepping outside.

'Good night, doctor,' Dolly said and swiftly closed the door.

Derek's eyebrows rose, but she turned to him to say, 'Derek, it was good of you to drive John here. You must have something to drink before you leave. What can I get you?'

'A coffee would be nice if you've got any. I'm uh ... really sorry for your loss,' Derek said awkwardly.

'Thank you for your condolences,' Dolly said, then headed for the kitchen.

'Your gran doesn't seem to be in a state,' he said quietly to John. 'She seems calm enough now.'

'I might know why,' John said and when Dolly returned, he asked, 'Gran, when I rang you, had you taken your pills?'

'No, I'm afraid not, but I have now.'

'That's good, but you mustn't forget them again,' John said firmly.

'I know, dear,' Dolly acquiesced.

Derek was impressed by John's maturity. The lad had also promised to ring if there were any problems, and if he did, Derek would drop everything to drive down here like a shot.

When Dolly handed him a cup of coffee, he thanked her, and then watched as she fussed over John. It was obvious that she was very fond of him. Derek felt reassured, and left twenty minutes later, after telling John that he'd pick him up on Sunday.

As he was driving home to Battersea, Derek had no idea that someone else was on their way to Dolly's place. If he had, he would have done a swift U-turn and driven straight back.

Chapter Thirty-Two

Driving steadily towards Southsea, Kevin said to Adrianna, 'Don't expect a palace. My mother's place isn't very big.'

'I'm turning up in these cheap, tacky clothes, so it's just as well.'

'I left you all the money I could,' Kevin told her, 'but don't worry, once I get my inheritance, I'll dress you like a princess.'

'I don't care about that. I just want to get out of the country.'

'When my father's will is sorted out we'll be able to go, and in style too.'

'Yes, but how long is that going to take?' Adrianna asked.

'I don't know, but in the meantime we'll lie low.'

'If we knew for sure that Vince died in the fire, we wouldn't have to hide,' Adrianna said. 'There hasn't been anything in the newspapers.'

'I doubt it was big enough news for the nationals, though it might have been reported locally. I could put out feelers, but it would mean driving to London again.'

'Definitely not!' Adrianna said sharply. 'Once was bad enough, and now you're talking about going to where Vince is known. It's too risky. One of his narks might spot you and...'

'It might lead him back to you,' Kevin finished for her.

'Yes, it might,' she said, her tone rising. 'I don't want you to go!'

'All right, calm down. It was only a suggestion,' Kevin said soothingly. With the possibility of Vince on their tail, Adrianna was looking out for herself and he didn't blame her. He was interested in self-preservation too, but he'd seen the flames roaring towards the stairs and doubted that Vince, or his heavies, had got out alive.

'Are we nearly there yet?' Adrianna asked like a sulky child.

'Another couple of miles and we'll be at my mother's place,' Kevin told her as his headlights pierced the inky darkness of the unlit country road.

'What's she like?'

It was now or never, Kevin thought, ready to use the story again as he said, 'My mother was once a very strong woman, but she had a nervous breakdown when I was sent to prison.'

'Oh, dear... But surely she's all right now?'

'Not really. She's still a bit fragile, on medication, and of course I knew she'd worry that I'd get into trouble again when I was released. To prevent that, and to protect her of course, I felt I had to pretend to be something I'm not.'

'And what is that?' Adrianna asked.

'Religious.'

Adrianna laughed, but then quickly apologised. 'Sorry, it's so sweet that you want to protect her, but surely she didn't believe you?'

'She did and I don't want to shatter her illusions so while we're there I'll have to keep it up.'

'Won't she think it's funny when you turn up

with me?'

'I didn't say I'd become a Catholic priest, but I'll think of something. Just don't tell her that you're a stripper.'

'I am not!' Adrianna said indignantly. 'I'm an exotic dancer.'

'Yeah, if you say so – but don't tell her that either!' Kevin said as he drove through the outskirts of the village.

It was past ten and John had gone to bed. Dolly was pleased. He and Derek had turned up at a fortuitous moment, and the doctor had surmised that Derek was her son. In any other circumstances she'd have been annoyed, but it had worked perfectly in getting rid of the doctor.

Now though, Dolly was in two minds about having John here. It had been bad enough when Bernie tried to make sure she took her pills and now it seemed that John was going to do the same, with eyes keener than his grandfather's. With so much to sort out the last thing she wanted was a foggy mind; even with a clear head she didn't know where to start.

Her ears pricked when she heard the sound of a car pulling up outside and shortly after it was followed by a knock on the door. Who would be calling at this time of night? Could it possibly be Kevin? She rushed to the front door, her eyes lighting up with delight.

'Kevin! Oh, Kevin, thank goodness.'

'Hello, Mum.'

Dolly threw her arms around him, but then saw that he wasn't alone. She moved back, saying tersely, 'Who is that?'

'It's Adrianna, a friend of mine,' he said, completing the introduction as they both came inside. 'Adrianna, this is my mother.'

'Hello,' the young woman said.

Dolly saw that she was striking, with long, dark, sleek hair and almond-shaped eyes. She wanted to shove Adrianna outside again, to slam the door in her face, but somehow she returned the greeting with an abrupt nod, before saying, 'Kevin, I've been desperate to get hold of you. Why didn't you tell me you were moving out of Rupert's house?'

'We fell out and it was all a bit sudden.'

'You ... you've heard about your father?'

'Yes, as soon as I was told that he'd died in an accident I got here as fast as I could.'

'I'm sorry, but may I use your bathroom?' Adrianna asked.

'It's upstairs, the first door on the left,' Dolly told her and as soon as Adrianna was out of sight she snapped, 'Why have you brought her here?'

'She's broke, homeless, and God guided me to help her. I was trying to find somewhere for her to live, and for myself too when I was told about Dad. I couldn't just leave her to live rough on the streets so felt it best to bring her along.'

'She isn't my problem and I've got enough to deal with as it is. Your father's death wasn't an accident and it's something I'd rather not discuss in front of strangers.'

'What do you mean?' Kevin asked, frowning. 'If it wasn't an accident, how did he die?'

Dolly knew what people would think, that they'd blame her and say she must have driven

240

him to it, but it would all be supposition. She would never tell anyone that she'd been giving Bernie her pills, or that they had caused him to think he was going senile, but Kevin could be told part of the truth. 'Your father drove off a cliff at Beachy Head.'

'What? No! You're not telling me it was suicide!'

'It's what the police think.'

'I don't believe it. Why would Dad take his own life?'

'I don't know, but maybe he couldn't face it that he was becoming senile.'

'I suppose it's a possibility, but he didn't seem that bad the last time I saw him.'

'Kevin, it's late and we can talk about this again tomorrow. There's so much to arrange and I'm so relieved that you'll be here to help me. You'll have to find somewhere for Adrianna to sleep, a guest house or something.'

'I was hoping we could both stay here.'

'No, that's impossible.'

'I don't see why. Adrianna could have the spare room and I don't mind sleeping on the sofa.'

'John's in the spare room.'

'He's here?' Kevin asked, surprised.

'He arrived earlier this evening and he's staying for a couple of days. I'm sorry, but though you can have the sofa, there isn't room for Adrianna.'

'I can't afford to put her in a guest house or anywhere else. I'm broke, Mum. I spent the last of my money on petrol to get here. I knew you'd need me and I couldn't let you down.'

Dolly was gratified and said, 'Don't worry, I'll be able to help you, but I can't do anything until

I can get to the bank tomorrow.'

'I suppose I could bunk down in my car, and Adrianna can have the sofa.'

'Kevin, you can't sleep in your car,' Dolly protested, thinking rapidly. 'Adrianna will have to share my room, while you take the couch for now.'

'Thanks, Mum,' Kevin said, kissing her cheek.

Dolly smiled, but then Adrianna returned and her face straightened. Even dressed in a cheap cotton skirt and top she was a stunning young woman, a temptation for any man, but she wasn't going to get her claws into Kevin. Dolly wanted her son and her grandson to herself, and there was no room for another woman.

She'd find a way to get rid of Adrianna – and the sooner the better.

Chapter Thirty-Three

'John, wake up,' Kevin urged.

'Wh ... what?'

'Come on, wake up. I want to talk to you.'

John cranked open one eye to look blearily at the figure standing over him. When he realised who it was, he shot up in bed. 'What are you doing here? You said you were going abroad.'

'When I heard about my father I postponed my departure and got here as soon as I could.'

'I'll go home then,' John said. 'I don't want to stay now you've turned up.'

'John, why are you in such a hurry to leave?'

'Because you lied to me. When you were waiting for me outside my school, you said you'd cleared it with my mum.'

'I'm sorry about that, but your mother might have refused to let me see you and as I was leaving the country, I didn't have a lot of time. I pray that God will understand my desperation to talk to you and forgive my deceit.'

John recalled how worried his mother had been and threw back the blankets, saying bullishly, 'I'll ring my dad to come and fetch me.'

'Your gran needs her family around her right now and it might upset her if you leave. For her sake, at least stay for one more night,' Kevin urged.

John paused in thought, but then decided to talk to his gran. She wasn't alone now and maybe she wouldn't mind if he left. 'I want to get dressed,' he said pointedly.

'All right, I'll see you downstairs... And, John, though it isn't the best of times, it's nice to see you again.'

John went to the bathroom to have a wash, and then got dressed. He hadn't been to see his grandparents because of Kevin, and now he felt that he was being driven away again.

Adrianna was up soon after Dolly. She was none too happy. She hated sharing a room with Kevin's mother, albeit in separate beds. Kevin had spun his mother some sort of story that she was broke and homeless, but the woman was making it obvious that she didn't want her here. It was humiliating, but Kevin seemed oblivious

243

to his mother's snide comments.

'John, there you are,' Dolly said, smiling at the lad who had entered the room.

Adrianna found herself staring at him, thinking that he was a young double of Kevin, and then saw that he was staring at her too, his expression puzzled.

'John, this is Adrianna, a friend of mine,' Kevin said. 'Adrianna, this is my son.'

Adrianna remembered then. There'd been mention of a wife and kid when Vince had Kevin checked out, but she'd been sure it had been said that they were out of the picture. Her smile forced, she said, 'Hello, John.'

'Hello, Adrianna,' he replied, smiling back shyly.

'Adrianna my foot,' Dolly said derisively. 'Why aren't you using your real name? Ruth, isn't it? Ruth Canning.'

'How do you know that?' Adrianna gasped.

'I saw your passport.'

'You've been snooping in my handbag! You had no right to do that!'

'When my son brings a so-called waif and stray into my home, one who's been lying to him, I have every right!' Dolly snapped.

'Mum, there's no need for this,' Kevin said, placing a placatory arm around his mother's shoulder. 'It's just a name Adrianna uses as she prefers it to Ruth, that's all.'

John went to her side too, asking, 'Gran, have you taken your pills?'

'Yes, of course I have.'

'That's good, and would ... would you mind if I go home today?'

'Go home! But I haven't seen you for ages and you've only been here overnight.'

'Kevin is here now, and Adrianna too, and there isn't really room for all of us,' John pointed out.

Dolly heaved a sigh. 'I suppose you're right, but will you come to see me again soon?'

'Yes, of course I will,' John said, but Adrianna felt she saw a trace of doubt in his expression.

'Right then, Mum, if you feel up to it I think you'd better feed us before we fade away to nothing,' Kevin joked, introducing lightness into the atmosphere.

'Oh you, but you're right, we can't have that,' Dolly said, managing a smile. 'I'll make breakfast, and then you can run me to the bank.'

Adrianna wasn't smiling. She was still seething that Kevin's mother had been nosing in her handbag. No matter what the woman said, she had no right to do that.

Breakfast had been eaten by eight thirty, and Dolly was clearing the things away, annoyed that Adrianna hadn't offered to help. She wanted to get to the bank as soon as it opened and to be back before John left.

There was a knock on the door and quickly drying her hands, Dolly went to answer it. She saw it was the same police constables who had broken the news of Bernie's death.

'We're sorry to disturb you, Mrs Dolby,' said the policeman. 'But we need to ask you a few questions concerning the details surrounding your husband's death.'

Dolly saw John pale. He still believed his

granddad had died in an accident and she wasn't ready for him to hear the truth.

'John, these police officers need to talk to me in private,' she said quickly. 'Go upstairs or into the back garden. You too, Adrianna.'

Tight-lipped, Adrianna marched upstairs, and thankfully Kevin urged John to do the same, though the lad didn't look happy. Only then did Dolly stand aside to let the constables in.

'I'm sorry,' she said quietly, 'but my grandson has only been told that my husband died in an accident.'

'We understand,' the policewoman said. She removed her hat and the policeman took off his helmet as they stepped inside.

'This is my son,' Dolly said, and both officers nodded at Kevin. 'Is there any news? Have ... have you found my husband's body?'

'I'm afraid not. We're checking the shoreline, but so far there's no sign of him.'

'He's sure to wash up eventually,' the male constable said.

The policewoman glared at her colleague as though to admonish his insensitivity, and then asked, 'Can we all sit down?'

'Yes, I suppose so.'

'I'm sorry, Mrs Dolby,' she said when they were seated, 'I know that these questions may be difficult, but can you tell us what state of mind your husband was in the last time you saw him?'

Dolly closed her eyes as if searching her memory. 'He was down in the dumps, but as he's been like that for some time it didn't seem unusual.'

'What was causing him to feel like that?'

'He'd become forgetful, and as his father had senile dementia, Bernie was frightened that he was going the same way.'

'Was he on any medication?'

'No. He may have been worried but he hadn't been to see the doctor.'

'Did he seem any worse that morning?'

'I don't think so.'

'Are you sure?'

'Look, I told you,' Dolly said, 'he was a bit down in the dumps, but how could I have known he'd do something like that? You're blaming me! You think it's my fault! I bet everyone will think it's my fault!'

'Of course they don't, Mum. Come on now, calm down,' Kevin said as he came to crouch in front of her.

Dolly clung to Kevin, while he said to the constables, 'I think my mother has had enough for now. If you have any more questions, they'll have to wait.'

They rose to their feet. 'I think we've covered everything, but if we have any news at all we'll be in touch.'

Dolly kept her head buried until they left, then she pulled away from Kevin to say, 'I dread telling John the truth ... that his grandfather drove off the top of a cliff.'

'I don't think you'll need to,' he said.

She looked up to see John in the doorway. He must have heard everything, but as Dolly held out her arms he turned away from her and fled back upstairs. 'See, I was right. John blames me

247

and everyone else will too!'

'I doubt he does, but I'll talk to him,' Kevin said reassuringly.

Dolly was once again overwhelmed with relief that her son was there. She still had to go to the bank and could imagine Kevin's reaction when she gave him some money. He'd be so grateful, especially when she would then offer to fund his dream of a refuge. That would definitely keep him by her side.

Chapter Thirty-Four

After Lucy had taken Clive to school on Thursday, she passed through the High Street on the opposite side of the road to Eddie's stall in an attempt to avoid him. She didn't want to see him but to her annoyance he spotted her and was rushing over.

It had been so long, Lucy thought, so many years since she had been held in a man's arms and somehow her pent-up frustration had overwhelmed her. It didn't matter that she'd known Eddie since childhood, that he was so familiar to her; it didn't excuse her behaviour. What had happened between them had been a mistake, a terrible mistake, and she still felt sick inside that she had betrayed Paul's memory.

'Hello, gorgeous,' Eddie said softly. 'Can I take you out tonight?'

She was aware of the heat rising to her face, of the twinkle in his eyes, his amazing smile, but somehow managed to harden her heart. 'No, you can't, now please leave me alone.'

'Lucy, what's wrong?' he asked looking mortified.

'I don't know how you've got the nerve to ask me that. You came round to my flat on Wednesday, uninvited, offering so-called help, when ... when all the time you just wanted to get me in ... into bed.'

'No, Lucy, it wasn't like that. I didn't expect it to happen, really I didn't.'

'I don't believe you and in future, just stay away from me,' she snapped, marching off and heading for Pearl's shop.

'Good morning,' Pearl greeted. 'It's nice to have you back, and how's the flat?'

Lucy felt so ashamed of herself and fought to hide her feelings. 'It... It's lovely.'

Nora ambled over to hug her, then said, 'Johnny gone, Lucy.'

'Gone! What does she mean, Pearl?'

'It's a long story, but Bernie died in a car accident and John has gone to stay with his gran for a couple of days.'

'Oh, that's awful,' Lucy said. 'Poor John, he must be dreadfully upset.'

'Yes, I'm afraid he is,' Pearl said.

They spoke a little more about it, but then Lucy took Nora upstairs and as she happily began to dust, Lucy set up the ironing board. Though born in Battersea, her parents' house hadn't been near the High Street and as a child she had never heard of the Dolbys. Lucy thought back. When had she first heard the name? Yes, she'd been around

249

fourteen when the local papers had been full of Kevin Dolby and the robbery. There'd been a lot of talk about it, but not much of it had registered with her. At that age all she'd been interested in was fashion, music, and of course, boys.

So much time had passed since then, with so many unhappy memories of her own. Her mind shied away from them, and instead Lucy found her thoughts dwelling on Eddie again.

Pearl was finding it hard to concentrate as she put out stock. She couldn't stop thinking about John and the fact that he was alone with Dolly. If Kevin really had left the country, would it send Dolly over the edge again? Unable to stop worrying, she went to the telephone.

It was John who answered, and she could tell immediately by his voice that something was wrong. 'John, are you all right?'

'I was just going to ring you. I ... I've just found out that Granddad didn't die in a car accident. He ... he killed himself.'

'No!' Pearl exclaimed. 'I can't believe it. Are you sure?'

'Yes, the police were here earlier to ask Gran some questions and I overheard them talking about it.'

'Oh, John, no wonder you sound so upset.'

'I felt so guilty, thought it was my fault, but I hadn't overheard everything and Kevin told me that Granddad was very depressed because he was going funny, senile, or something like that.'

'Kevin's there?' Pearl asked sharply.

'He turned up last night, but I was already in

250

bed so I didn't see him, or Adrianna, until this morning.'

'Adrianna? Who on earth is Adrianna?'

'She's Kevin's friend.'

'John, I want you to come home,' she said quickly. 'Derek will have to sort out someone to cover his stall, but then I'll send him down to fetch you.'

'Kevin's taken Gran to the bank, but I've already told her that I'll be leaving,' he said, but then his voice cracked. 'I ... I can't stop thinking about Granddad.'

Pearl desperately wanted to hold him in her arms, to comfort him, and said, 'Derek should be there in two, or maybe three hours, and when you come home we'll talk it through.'

'All ... all right,' John croaked. 'I ... I'll see you soon, Mum.'

Pearl said goodbye, close to tears too. Poor Bernie. She hadn't seen any signs that that he was going senile, or that he was depressed, and it was incomprehensible to her that he'd taken his own life. What had driven him to do such a thing?

It was only a short drive to the village and Kevin had gone to buy a newspaper. Alone in the bank Dolly was livid, red-faced with anger as she faced the manager.

'I don't care what you say, you stupid man! The account may not be a joint one, but my husband is dead and as his wife I'm his next of kin.'

'That may be true, Mrs Dolby, but as I've already told you, we will need to see his death certificate, and that probate has been granted.'

251

'Are you calling me a liar?'

'No, Mrs Dolby,' the man said, a picture of resigned patience. 'I am very sorry to hear that your husband has passed away and you have my deepest sympathy, but unfortunately we are unable to assist you without the aforementioned documents.'

'I'll get them, but in the meantime I want to draw money from the account.'

'I'm afraid that isn't possible.'

Dolly glared at the small, weedy-looking man, her anger reaching boiling point. To get Adrianna out of her house she needed money urgently and had no idea how long it would take to get the documents. She reared to her feet and leaning over his desk she yelled, 'It's *my* money, you pretentious pig!'

'Please, Mrs Dolby, calm yourself,' he said, taking out a handkerchief and distastefully wiping her spittle from his face.

Rage gripped Dolly's mind. In fury she began to hit out, sending everything flying off the desk with one sweep of her arm, and then she went for the man.

When Kevin walked into the bank he couldn't see his mother, but he could hear her yelling and screaming. He hurried towards the sound, and in an office saw two men trying to pull her off another. He dashed forward, trying to help her. 'Let go of my mother!'

'Can't you see what she's doing?' one yelled. 'She's a bloody mad woman!'

'I said get off her,' Kevin shouted, fighting to

252

remove their hands, but then he caught a glimpse of his mother's face, the foaming mouth, and the man who was cowering away from her.

'The police are on their way,' a young woman called from the doorway.

'Mum! Mum, that's enough!' he shouted, he too now joining in the attempts to pull her away from the man. 'Stop it!'

She didn't seem to hear him, but at least with three of them holding her, the man she'd been attacking managed to scramble away. Kevin caught a glimpse of his bloodied face, but it took all their combined strength to stop his mother from going after him again.

At last, abruptly, she stopped fighting and when they finally let her go, she slumped onto the floor, rocking back and forth, wailing, 'He wouldn't give me my money.'

'What's she talking about?'

Kevin was told, and he too felt a surge of anger that his mother hadn't been able to draw out any money. Kevin looked at her, still rocking, and didn't know what to do. Moments later the decision was taken out of his hands as the police arrived. They spoke to the staff, came to look at his mother who seemed unaware of anything going on around her, and then asked him, 'Do you think she'll fight us if we try to get her into our car?'

'I don't know,' Kevin told them, and it was true. He had no idea.

'I think we'll get a doctor to take a look at her. The manager's all right, it's mostly scratches, but the doc can take a look at him too.'

A call was made, and during the next half hour while they waited for a doctor to turn up his mother remained unresponsive, as though in a world of her own. When he arrived, Kevin did his best to answer the man's questions, telling him that she had once been in psychiatric care but that he couldn't tell him what medication she took.

'I'll need to consult with my partner, your mother's doctor, but in my opinion she needs to be sectioned. I'll ring him as soon as I've taken a look at the manager.'

After cleaning what were superficial scratches, the doctor asked to use the telephone, and while making calls, the police interviewed the manager. They returned to tell Kevin that due to Dolly's mental condition, he wasn't going to press charges.

'Can I take her home, then?'

'No, Mr Dolby,' the doctor said. 'Your mother has a history of mental illness and as she's become unstable, I've made arrangements for her to be admitted for psychiatric care and assessment.'

'How long is that going to take?'

'At this stage, it's impossible to say.'

Kevin was left alone with his thoughts until the ambulance arrived. His mother offered no resistance when led away, and told he couldn't accompany her, the doctor wrote down the name and telephone number of the psychiatric unit.

As the vehicle drove away, Kevin felt nothing for his mother, no love, no pity, just annoyance that she hadn't been able to get her hands on any money. She could be in the loony bin for ages, and that left him skint.

There was the house of course, and as it had been left to him he would sell it. It would take a bit of time, but first he had to find his father's will to prove his inheritance. In the meantime he was broke, and though he hated the thought of doing it, Kevin knew the only solution was to sell his car.

Chapter Thirty-Five

'Where's Gran?' John asked when Kevin came back without her.

'She had a funny turn and they had to take her away.'

'What do you mean? Who took her away?'

'It would have been the police, but luckily for her the bank manager didn't press charges.'

'The police!' exclaimed John. 'What did she do?'

'She lost it, went for the bank manager and got her claws into his face.'

'But why?'

'I don't know, something to do with money,' Kevin said impatiently.

John couldn't make sense of the answer, but he continued to ask questions, concerned about his gran. 'Where did they take her?'

'To a funny farm.'

John frowned. 'What's a funny farm?'

'All right then, a psychiatric hospital.'

'When will they let her come home?'

'I don't know, John. It may not be for some time.'

'Can't you find out?' he begged.

'Yes, I suppose so, but not now. I've got more important things on my mind,' Kevin said as he began to pull out drawers, throwing the contents aside as he rifled through them.

'What are you looking for?' Adrianna asked.

'My father's will.'

John watched as another drawer was emptied, wondering why finding a will was so important. Deeply upset he walked out of the room and into the garden. The sun was blazing down from a clear blue sky, yet it failed to cheer him. His neck drooped, and the limp blooms of roses on bent stems seemed to echo his feelings. John knew that a simple dousing of water would perk them up, but it couldn't do the same for him.

For a moment John sat on a bench, but he knew how much the garden had meant to his grandfather and went to find the hosepipe. He watered the plants, finding it soothing as he recalled the many happy times he'd spent in the garden with his grandfather. He'd learned so much from him and the memories brought unshed tears to his eyes.

At that moment John saw a blue tit landing on the bird feeder, but it only settled for a while before flying away. Tears flowed in earnest then and he found himself praying that wherever his grandfather was now, he was like the bird, able to fly, to soar, free of the unhappiness that drove him to his death.

Adrianna wasn't sorry that Dolly had been taken away and hoped she and Kevin would be gone by the time she was let out. 'Kevin, when can we get out of here?'

'As soon as I've sold this house.'

'Leave it out!' Adrianna protested. 'You said you'd find somewhere remote to lay low. You didn't say anything about staying here until you sell the house.'

'Yeah, well, I've changed my mind. With woods behind this place and a small lane out front, it's well secluded and safe enough.'

'I don't want to be here when your mother comes home.'

'I think it'll be ages before they let her out, and this place is sure to be sold by then.'

'You said her funny turn had to do with money. What did you mean?' Adrianna asked.

'Without proof of my father's death she wasn't allowed to draw money from his account. It may mean there's no cash available until I sell this place, but not to worry, I'll flog my car. I can buy another one once this place is sold.'

Adrianna was getting sick of Kevin and his promises. So far none of the big money he'd talked about had materialised and now he was down to selling his motor.

'Sod it, I can't find the will,' he complained. 'Maybe it's in his bedroom.'

Adrianna didn't comment and when Kevin went upstairs she was left with her thoughts. She had wanted to get away from Vince, and though Kevin had served his purpose, maybe it was time to move on. She'd have to wait until he'd sold his car, but then she'd somehow get her hands on the money. It would be more than enough to get her out of the country, and there'd be a nice amount left over to live on for a while.

'I still can't find it,' Kevin complained when he marched back into the room.

'Maybe he left it with a solicitor or something?' Adrianna suggested.

'Yeah, you could be right. In this dead and alive hole there's probably only one, maybe two. I'll take a drive around later to see if I spot them.'

'When are you going to sell your car?'

'I'll see if there's anywhere in the village while I'm out.'

'You'd better make it quick. I had a look in the cupboards and there isn't much in the way of food.'

'All right, I'll do my best. Where's John?'

'He's in the garden.'

'I'll go and have a word with him,' Kevin said. 'Then once he's been picked up I'll drive to the village.'

'Do what you like,' Adrianna snapped, wanting nothing more than to get away from this dump. 'It's like a bloody oven in here and I'm going to have a cool bath.'

Kevin saw that John was turning off the hose-pipe, his expression hopeful when their eyes met. 'Did you ring the hospital?' he asked.

'Yes,' he lied, 'but they couldn't tell me much. They're still assessing your gran.'

'Will I be able to go to see her?'

'John, I know it's difficult for you to understand,

258

but your gran is unstable, both mentally and emotionally. She'll receive treatment, but it could be some before she's stable enough for visitors.'

'Will you be staying here?'

'I can't leave until I can arrange your grand-father's funeral. Even then, I can't go until I know your gran's going to be all right,' Kevin told him, yet in truth he couldn't give a shit about her and he was only going to stay until he could sell the house.

'Will ... will you let me know about ... about the funeral?'

'Of course I will.'

'And ... and Gran?' John asked.

'As soon as there's any news, I'll be in touch.'

John began to roll up the hose. 'My dad should be here to pick me up soon.'

Kevin's lips tightened. John referred to Derek as his father when the title should be his. It annoyed him, but he kept his feelings to himself. He'd do the same when Derek turned up, keep up the front, but it wasn't going to be easy.

They had only just gone inside when there was a knock on the door and John hurried to open it and said, 'Come in, Dad.'

'No, I'll wait here,' Derek said tersely. 'Just get your stuff and we can go.'

'My ... my gran has been taken away.'

'Taken away! What do you mean?'

'She had a funny turn and they took her to hospital.'

Kevin got into character as he walked to the door, his expression one of sadness. 'Hello,

Derek, I heard John telling you about my mother.'

Derek's expression hardened. 'She was all right when I dropped John off yesterday. When did this happen?'

'Earlier this morning. I wasn't there at the time, but she was in the bank and the manager upset her. I'm praying for her and hope she'll be home again soon.'

Derek's eyebrows rose sceptically, but he looked at John and said, 'I'm sorry about your gran, son, and your granddad, but get your things now.'

John nodded and as soon as he was out of sight, Derek leaned forward menacingly, his voice a soft growl. 'I could wring your bloody neck for that stunt you pulled. Pearl was frantic when John didn't come home from school.'

'I know,' Kevin said meekly. 'John told me and I'm so sorry. I was leaving the country and acted on impulse, but I've prayed for forgiveness and it won't happen again.'

'It better not,' snarled Derek. 'And you can forget all this talk about prayers. You're not fooling me, Kevin. You're no more religious than I am, and I know you were sniffing around a while ago for information on Vince Chase.'

Kevin managed to keep his composure. This might be his opportunity to find out if Vince had died in the fire. Keeping his voice soft, he said, 'I was looking for Mr Chase as I'd found out he has a large, derelict house that would be ideal to turn into a refuge for the homeless. I was hoping to persuade him to donate it to us.'

Derek's eyes narrowed. 'Who do you think you're kidding? Especially as since you came

260

back on the scene his house has been torched.'

'But that hasn't got anything to do with me,' Kevin protested. 'Why would I want to harm the man? I hardly knew him and hope he got out alive.'

'He may have, but nobody seems to know yet. There wasn't any news about it until the local paper came out this morning, and they say the fire service are still searching for bodies.'

John appeared with a bag in his hand. 'I'm ready to go now,' he said. 'Adrianna's in the bathroom, but I called goodbye to her.'

Kevin ruffled John's hair, said goodbye, and got only a grunt from Derek. He remained at the door, a fixed, soft smile on his face, yet inside annoyed that he still didn't know if Vince was alive or dead.

Derek didn't know how he'd managed to keep his hands off Kevin, but for John's sake he'd fought to keep a lid on his feelings. Pearl had told him how upset John was about his grandfather and the last thing he needed was to see him at Kevin's throat.

Now Dolly had been put away again and no doubt John was reeling from that too. 'Are you all right, son? he asked.

There was a moment of silence, but then John blurted out, 'I still can't take it in that my grand-dad drove off a cliff...'

Derek fought for words. 'I know, and it's hard to believe, but if his mind had gone...'

'Ke ... Kevin talked to me about it,' John croaked, as Derek's voice trailed off, 'and I understand that. It ... it's just that I'll never see my granddad again.'

'I'm sorry, son, I really am,' Derek murmured, feeling totally inadequate as he took one hand from the steering wheel to gently touch John's arm. 'I liked your granddad. He was a good man.'

'Ke ... Kevin said he'll ring me if there's any news about my gran,' John said as if unable to bear talking about his grandfather any more.

'I'm sure she'll be home again soon,' Derek said encouragingly, yet remembering how long Dolly had been in psychiatric care the last time, he knew it could be ages before she could be released.

John became quiet then and Derek drove steadily. He'd found a lad of fifteen to look after the stall but he was inexperienced and so he was anxious to get back.

When they arrived, Pearl pulled John into her arms, and as the lad began to cry, Derek quietly left to go back to his stall. He'd been hopeless, but at least Pearl would be able to comfort John, though he felt it would be some time before the boy would be able to come to terms with the loss of his grandfather.

Chapter Thirty-Six

Kevin drove to the village, his mind for a short while on his son. It might have been nice to spend a bit more time with the boy, and if he hadn't been leaving the country, he'd have enjoyed usurping

Derek. The ugly git had threatened him, and Kevin would have liked to make him suffer for it, but he had more important things to sort out right now. Money was currently his main priority.

Kevin parked up and soon spotted a sign for a solicitor's office on the wall next to a small shop, the offices above it. He went upstairs to find an elderly woman sitting at a desk, in front of a row of filing cabinets. 'Excuse me, but I'm looking for my father's solicitor. His name was Bernard Dolby.'

'Oh dear, I see you've used the past tense. Has Mr Dolby passed away?'

'Yes, he has.'

'I'm so sorry to hear that. He was such a lovely man. You'll want to see Mr Marchmont and fortunately he's free at the moment. If you'll excuse me, I'll tell him you're here.'

Talk about a bit of luck, Kevin thought, he'd found his father's solicitor at his first port of call. He only had a few minutes to wait before the elderly woman was back again, this time with an equally elderly man by her side.

Introductions were made before Kevin was led into the solicitor's office, the man saying as soon as they were seated, 'I'm sorry to hear about your father and offer my condolences.'

'Thanks.' Kevin nodded in acknowledgement. 'Did he leave his will with you?'

'Yes, he did, but I'm sure he has a copy.'

'I can't find it. Can I have the original?'

'I'm sorry, but may I see some form of identification, along with your father's death certificate?'

'I haven't got a death certificate.'

'I'll need to see it, I'm afraid.'

'How do I get hold of it?' Kevin asked.

'When did your father die?'

'On Wednesday.'

'If he died at home, you must first register his death and this must be done within five days. You'll need to take with you the medical certificate that states the cause of death, signed by a doctor.'

'He didn't die at home, and how can I get hold of this medical certificate if there isn't a body?'

'I'm not sure I understand,' Mr Marchmont said, frowning. 'There must be a body.'

'From what the police told us, my father drove off the top of a cliff and his body was washed out to sea.'

'Oh dear, that makes things very difficult. Unfortunately, in these circumstances, the coroner won't be able to issue a death certificate until there can be proof of death.'

'The cops seem to think he'll eventually wash up somewhere,' Kevin said. 'In the meantime that just leaves my father's will to prove that I'm his heir. I need it because I want to get the house on the market.'

'I'm afraid you won't be able to do that. As the law stands, until your father's body is found his assets will be frozen. If he remains unfound, it can be seven years before a presumption of death can be granted, and even then there has to be sufficient evidence to support the claim.'

Kevin couldn't take it in and asked the solicitor question after question until at last, understanding what it all meant, he left the office. With his father expected to wash up, he wasn't worried about his assets being frozen for seven years, but there would still be a delay until the body was recovered. If he wanted to hold onto Adrianna he'd have to keep that information to himself, but with the money from the sale of his car and no rent to pay, he'd be able to indulge her a bit to keep her sweet.

Unable to find a dealership in the village, Kevin had to drive to Southsea. He found one there, but wasn't about to take the ridiculously low price he was offered. The car was almost new, in perfect nick, and when he found another dealer the bloke had more sense and offered him the going rate. Kevin asked for cash, and the dealer was happy to oblige, no doubt pleased he could keep the sale off his books. Then, with a wad of notes in his pocket, Kevin did some shopping before he took a bus back to the village.

Kevin hated lugging the bags around, being without wheels, and it was already late afternoon by the time he got back to the house. He was consoled by the thought that with his mother out of the way he and Adrianna would have the cottage to themselves.

Kevin licked his lips in anticipation of at last tempting Adrianna into his bed.

Pearl had spent many hours comforting John, and on Friday she kept him home from school. They had spoken about Bernie again, and though John was still upset, he was calmer.

When she woke up on Saturday it was to see the sun shining through the bedroom window and an empty space beside her. Derek was already up and Pearl was yawning as she went downstairs. Derek always left early to set up the stall, and she found he'd already seen to his own breakfast, his kiss on her cheek swift before he hurried off.

Nora appeared and Pearl made them both toast, unsurprised that John wasn't up yet. Lucy arrived with Clive at eight thirty, and as she looked a bit flustered, Pearl asked, 'Lucy, are you all right?'

Before Lucy could respond, Nora urged, 'Clive, do jigsaw?'

'Yes, all right,' he agreed.

'I got good one in my bedroom. We get it,' Nora said, and with Clive behind her, she bustled off.

'What's wrong, Lucy?' Pearl asked as soon as they were out of sight.

'I ... I'm all right, it's just that Eddie White keeps pestering me to go out with him again.'

'Again! I didn't know you were seeing him.'

'I'm not, and ... and I haven't exactly been out with him,' Lucy said, her cheeks pink but then she blurted out, 'Oh, Pearl, I feel sick with guilt. I shouldn't have done it.'

'Lucy, I don't want to pry, and you don't have to tell me if you don't want to, but what have you done that makes you feel so guilty?'

For a moment Lucy stood motionless, biting on her bottom lip, but then said, 'If I don't talk about this ... if I don't get it off my chest, it's going to drive me mad and I know I can trust you to keep it to yourself.'

'Of course you can,' Pearl assured her.

'When I moved into my flat, Eddie called round

266

to help me with my furniture. Honestly, Pearl, I didn't want it to happen, but somehow it did, and ... and ... we ended up making love. How could I have let it happen? I've betrayed Paul and I can't live with myself.'

'Lucy,' said Pearl as gently as she could. 'If it had been you who died instead of Paul, would you have wanted him to spend the rest of his life alone?'

'No, of course I wouldn't.'

'Well then, don't you think he'd feel the same? He'd want you to move on, to let him go and find happiness with someone else.'

'Do you really think so?'

'Yes, I do,' Pearl said, and as Lucy's eyes filled with tears, she moved forward to put her arms around her small, shaking frame.

'Since ... since it happened, I've been horrible to Eddie.'

'Talk to him, tell him why. I'm sure he'll understand.'

'Yeah, maybe,' Lucy murmured, sniffing now as she pulled away. 'Thanks, Pearl. You've got enough on your plate and I shouldn't have laid this on you too. John's in a state about his gran and granddad and there's me going on about Eddie.'

'I don't mind,' Pearl said and meant it. She wanted Lucy to be happy and hoped she'd helped. It was almost time to open the shop, but then the telephone rang and she hurried to answer it.

'Hello, darling,' Emily said. 'I know I spoke to you yesterday, but how is John?'

'He's still upset, Mum, and of course he's

worried about Dolly too.'

'I still find it hard to comprehend that Bernie took his own life.'

'Yes ... me too.'

'I was thinking of coming to stay next weekend. Is that all right?'

'Mum, you know it is. It'll be lovely to have you here.'

'Good, I'm looking forward to it.'

They chatted for a few more minutes, but then Pearl went downstairs to open the shop. She missed living with her mother and at times she felt such a longing to return to Winchester.

You've got to make the best of it here, girl.

Pearl spun around, sure she had heard Bessie's voice, but then berated herself for being silly. Yet was she? Was Bessie somehow watching over them? It might be a bit fanciful, yet despite that, Pearl found the thought comforting.

'Emily, that was delicious,' Timothy said, as he finished his dinner that evening.

'I told Pearl I'd spend next weekend with her.'

'I'm going to miss you,' Timothy said, 'but I know you're anxious to spend time with your family.'

'I'm very concerned about John. Pearl said that he's still taking Bernie's death badly.'

'The poor lad. I wish I could do something to help.'

Timothy had been living next door since before Pearl had moved in with John as a baby and had watched him growing up. He wasn't a terribly demonstrative man, but Emily knew he was fond

268

of John, along with Pearl and Derek. 'When I come home, maybe I could persuade John to join me. A change of scene might help.'

'A complete change would be better,' Tim said. 'I could book us a holiday, take John to somewhere that would capture his interest, at least enough to take his mind off his grief for a while.'

Emily was touched and reached across to hold Tim's hand. 'I think that would be lovely, and thank you.'

'There's no need for thanks, but we'll have to put our heads together to think of somewhere that fits the bill.'

'John loves the countryside and wildlife,' Emily offered.

'It would have to be a place with completely different scenery, and wildlife that he hasn't seen before. I know,' Tim said, suddenly inspired, 'what about Scotland? I'm sure he'd love to see the red deer, and we might even spot some Scottish wildcats.'

'That sounds perfect,' Emily said smiling, 'but don't book anything yet. There'll be the funeral, and I'm not sure when it will take place.'

'Will you go?'

'I don't know. If John wants me to, I suppose I'll have to attend.'

'What about Pearl?' Tim asked.

'With Kevin there it's sure to be difficult for her, but again, I don't know. Everything is so up in the air at the moment.'

'I don't suppose it's easy for Derek. He's been the only father John has known for all these years, but now Kevin is on the scene and I

269

wonder how he feels about it.'

'I doubt he's happy but I haven't had a chance to speak to him yet.' Emily sighed. 'Oh, Tim, there's so much unhappiness around and it all seems to have stemmed from when Pearl moved to Battersea, along with Kevin's release from prison. It's like the place, and the man, brings nothing but misery.'

'Unhappiness can strike wherever you live, darling,' Tim said, 'and as Pearl told you that Kevin is still going to leave the country, that's one problem solved.'

'Yes, I suppose so,' Emily agreed. All she wanted was her family to be happy, and though Kevin might be leaving, she now wished with all her heart that she had persuaded Pearl not to move back to Battersea.

Chapter Thirty-Seven

When her mother arrived on the following Saturday, Pearl could see that John was pleased to see her, but his mood was often distant and unreachable. The two days passed all too quickly for Pearl and when her mother returned to Winchester, things didn't get any better.

One of the worst moments for her had been when Kevin rang to speak to John and she was the one who answered the phone. The sound of his voice jolted her, but she felt nothing for him now. She found herself barely able to speak to

270

him and had passed the phone to John, able to judge by the one-sided conversation that Bernie's body still hadn't been found, and that Dolly was no better.

More weeks had passed since then, nearly five now since Bernie had taken his own life and at five thirty Pearl locked the shop before going upstairs. 'Lucy, you can go now and thanks for all you've done today.'

'It was only a bit of ironing.'

'I still appreciate it,' she said as Lucy chided Clive to put his crayons and drawing books away.

'Nora is still using them,' he said.

'Yes, I is,' Nora agreed. 'Look, Pearl.'

Pearl smiled at the childish drawing of flowers. 'That's lovely.'

'See you tomorrow,' Lucy said, once she'd got Clive ready.

They exchanged goodbyes, and then, seeing that Nora was still absorbed, Pearl went to find John. He was in his room, sitting up on his bed, a pillow propped behind his head and reading a book on British trees. Though Ginger the cat was stretched out beside him, it seemed such a solitary and unlikely pursuit for someone of John's age, and she was saddened that he wasn't out with friends, kicking a football around.

Her mother had rung half an hour ago, and now she hoped John would agree to what she had suggested. 'John, I've had a call from your gran.'

His eyes lit up. 'They've let her out? Is she all right? What did she say?'

'Darling, I'm sorry,' Pearl said, aghast that she'd misled him. 'I meant your Gran Emily.'

271

'Oh, right,' he said, the pleasure in his eyes dimming.

'Tim and your gran are booking a holiday in Scotland and they wondered if you'd like to go with them.'

'No, I can't. What if they find Granddad? What if Gran gets better and they let her go home?'

'You'll only be away for a week, and as you'll be in a hotel I can ring you if there's any news, or you can ring Kevin yourself from there. I think it would do you good to go away for a little while. From what your gran said about it I'm sure you'll love Scotland.'

'I don't know, Mum. It just doesn't seem right to go off on holiday as though nothing has happened.'

'John, we're not talking about fairgrounds, or frolicking on a beach somewhere. It'll probably be somewhere remote and you'll mostly be out walking. Your gran said you might see red deer and even Scottish wildcats.'

Pearl saw a spark of interest in John's eyes, and crossed her fingers. She was pleased when eventually he said, 'All right then, I'll go, but if anything happens, will they bring me straight back?'

'Of course they will.'

'I think I've got a book on wildlife found in Scotland,' John said with a touch of enthusiasm as he scrambled off his bed to search his shelves.

Pearl left him to it and went to ring her mother, grateful that she and Tim had been so thoughtful. Like them, she was sure it would do John good to have a change of scenery.

Lucy was deep in thought as she left the shop. Nora was touched by the atmosphere, sad for John and unusually quiet, but on occasions Lucy had heard her murmur something about a bad man again. When questioned, Nora just clammed up and as Pearl had been through enough lately, Lucy had decided not to mention it. Yet it was playing on her mind and before Lucy knew it, she was alongside Eddie's stall.

'Are we still on for tonight?' he asked quietly, as he packed up his stall for the day.

Lucy was glad she had taken Pearl's advice and her lonely evenings were a thing of the past now. 'Yes, but don't come round until *you know who* is tucked up for the night,' she said as Clive went to take a proffered apple from the costermonger on the next stall.

'Clive must know that something is going on between us,' Eddie said.

'Only that we're friends. I don't think he's ready to accept more than that yet.'

'Lucy, I'm sure he likes me so why don't we all spend the day together on Sunday? We could go out somewhere, perhaps take a drive to Brighton. Clive would love it at the seaside.'

'I don't know. I'll think about it,' she said. Clive had been chatting to the costermonger, but now after thanking him for the apple he was trotting back. Lucy quickly said goodbye to Eddie, her mind on him as she headed home.

She liked Eddie, really liked him, but she didn't want Clive getting too close to him until she was sure their relationship was going to last. Eddie came round at least three times a week now, and invariably they ended up in bed. Their love-making was passionate and fulfilling, but was that all Eddie wanted her for? Had she been too willing? Did he see her as easy, a lonely widow ripe for the picking?

Lucy hated the thought, and resolved to find out. If Eddie only wanted her for sex, he'd soon break things off if she turned cold on him.

Adrianna had discovered that Kevin was no fool and she hadn't been able to get her hands on the money from the sale of the car. He had hidden it somewhere, almost as if he expected her to nick it, and her search for it remained fruitless.

During the long days and nights spent alone with Kevin, there had been a change in their relationship. They had grown close, but something else was bothering her and she said, 'Kevin, it's been about five weeks since you put this place on the market and it seems funny that there hasn't been a single viewing.'

'The estate agent said it's always quiet during the school summer holidays.'

'He's just making excuses. Tell him if he doesn't get his finger out you'll find another agent.'

Kevin pursed his lips. 'I'll give it another week and then if he doesn't drum up some interest I'll take it off his books.'

Adrianna sighed, sick of being stuck in the cottage for so long now with only the little games she played with Kevin to break the boredom. She'd enjoyed acting hard to get, secretly smiling at his every move to get her into bed, until at last, with nothing else in the way of distraction to pass the time, she had given in.

Adrianna had been determined that this time she'd be the one in control, and it had been fun to treat Kevin like her slave. It had been a laugh, but after a while she had become bored with that too. They now played other games, and at least their imaginative sex lives served to occasionally break the monotonous days and nights. With Kevin, she found sex enjoyable, even fun, and titillated by her thoughts, she said, 'I'm bored.'

'And I'm hungry,' he said.

'Is that for me?' she asked huskily.

'No, it's for food,' he said grinning as he stood and stretched his back. 'What's for dinner?'

'I've told you before, I'm neither your cook nor your cleaner,' Adrianna said indignantly, 'but I suppose I could rustle up a ham salad.'

'Not again. I'm fed up with rabbit food.'

'Other than me, it's the only thing on the menu.'

'In that case,' he said, pulling her up and into his arms, 'I'll take you.'

He was hot, pungent with sweat, and her nose wrinkled. 'Not until you've had a bath.'

'Will you wash my back?'

'Now you want a cook, cleaner *and* a hand-maiden.'

'No, Adrianna, I just want you.'

Adrianna knew that Kevin had fallen for her, but hardened her heart. After being made to feel like a piece of Vince's property, she was still determined that no man would ever hold that power over her mind and body again.

Once abroad, the rest of her life stretched ahead of her and Adrianna was already making plans.

She didn't fancy doing some sort of mundane work that paid peanuts, but felt confident about getting a job as an exotic dancer, and with her skills, a well-paid one. All the money she earned would be hers and she'd be frugal, save every penny, her ambition to eventually open her own club.

Adrianna smiled. She wouldn't be performing then. She'd be the boss, in charge, and everyone would dance to *her* tune.

Chapter Thirty-Eight

John didn't care about the misty rain falling in the Highlands as he and Tim walked the glen on the lookout for red deer. So far they had only been able to admire the wonderful photographs of them displayed in the hotel lobby, but suddenly, in the near distance, a stag appeared. They both froze, John awestruck by the creature's proud stance and magnificent antlers.

'How about that, young man?' Tim said quietly. 'The Monarch of the Glen.'

'He's magnificent. It's been great to spot a pine marten, a wild cat, and all the other birds – the buzzards, the eagle – but this ... well...' John's voice trailed off.

'Do you want to take a shot?'

Still with his eyes riveted on the stag, John held out his hand for Tim's camera, praying the deer wouldn't move as he held the viewfinder to his eye and zoomed in. His granddad would have loved this, John thought, and for a moment his vision was blurred by tears. He blinked them away and focused again, just as the rain magically stopped. The strange sight of a single ray of sunshine bursting between dark clouds was enthralling as John took a shot, hoping he could do justice to this wild and wonderful animal.

'Got him,' he said to Tim as he handed back the camera. Tim had been showing him how to take photographs and he enjoyed it, though the rolls of film would have to be developed before he found out if they were any good.

'As it would have been our last chance, I'm glad we caught sight of one today,' Tim said. 'I've arranged to do something different tomorrow.'

'Have you?' John asked, though he didn't turn to look at Tim. His eyes were still riveted on the stag until, as though aware of them, it bounded out of sight.

'The hotel manager told me that if we drive to Gruinard Bay, which is about ten minutes from Camusnagaul, we might be lucky enough to spot whales, dolphins or porpoises.'

John's head now snapped around. 'You're kidding?'

'That's what he said. We'll start out early and if the weather is kind to us, we could take a picnic.'

'I doubt Gran will agree to that. She hates the midges and it's a job to get her to venture outdoors.'

Tim nodded in agreement. 'I know, but it's our last day tomorrow and we'll just have to do our best to persuade her.'

John doubted they'd be successful and this proved to be true when Tim put the suggestion to Emily over dinner that evening.

'No,' she said firmly. 'I can't stand the midges. You two go, but I'm happy to remain here.'

'I'm sorry, but I couldn't help but overhear. May I make a suggestion?' the waiter asked as he put the starters on the table.

'Please do,' Emily said, smiling sweetly up at him.

'You'd have a greater chance of seeing whales or dolphins by boat. You can pick up a trip from Ullapool and at sea I doubt if the wee midges would pester you.'

'Oh, yes, that sounds wonderful,' Emily enthused. 'What do you think, Tim?'

'Well, I'm game and thank you for your suggestion,' he said to the waiter before he moved away from their table.

His gran looked so excited, but John's grip on his spoon was tight as he picked it up to start on his soup. When he'd rang Kevin there hadn't been any news and the thought that he hadn't had a chance to make things up to his grandfather, or even to say goodbye, still tortured his mind. He'd found some solace in Scotland, absorbed when they went out to search for wildlife, but at night, alone in his bed, he was tormented by nightmares of his grandfather's body still drifting somewhere in the sea, picked at by fish and other sea life. It haunted John so much that the thought of going on a boat trip horrified him.

'I'm really looking forward to tomorrow,' Emily said. 'It'll be nice to go out without being eaten alive by midges. I bet you're going to love it, John.'

He looked into his gran's shining eyes. She'd been cooped up for so long in the hotel, he didn't have the heart to tell her how he really felt.

'Yes, I'm sure I will,' he said, hiding his feelings.

'Lucy, it's been a while now, but if you don't want to sleep with me, that's fine. I'm not going to force you,' Eddie said, 'though it would be nice to know why you've gone cold on me.'

'I've got my reasons.'

'You're not ill, are you?' he asked, his expression showing his concern.

'No, I'm fine,' Lucy told him.

'So what's the problem then?'

'I just don't want to sleep with you, and now I suppose you're going to tell me that you don't want to see me any more. Please yourself, I don't care,' she said with a show of bravado.

'Well, I care, Lucy. I think the world of you and the last thing I want is for us to break up.'

'You'd soon find someone else.'

'I don't want anyone else. It's you I want to marry.'

'M ... marry!'

'Sod it, I didn't mean to blurt that out.'

'No, I'm sure you didn't,' Lucy said bitterly. 'I suppose it's one of the ruses you use to get a girl into bed, but of course you didn't have to use it on me. I was easy, a willing widow, one who would sleep with you without any strings attached.'

Eddie sprang to his feet, his face suffused with colour. 'What sort of bloke do you take me for? I

279

don't use tricks to get a girl into bed, and though I might play Jack the lad it's just a front for the customers.'

'So you say, but if that's the case why mention marriage?'

'We've only been seeing each other for a few months and I didn't intend to. It's too soon for you and I know that, but I love you, Lucy, and one day I'd hoped to marry you. Now though, seeing that you've got such a low opinion of me, I might as well go,' he said dejectedly.

Lucy didn't have a chance to respond as Eddie quickly left the room. He loved her! He wanted to marry her!

Oh, God, what have I done, she thought, yet even as it occurred to her to run after him, Lucy found that she couldn't. She liked Eddie, liked him a lot, but love? Marriage?

No, no, she wasn't ready for that, and slumping, with her head resting on the back of the sofa, Lucy let him go.

Chapter Thirty-Nine

When John returned from Scotland, Pearl was disappointed to see that he looked tired, strained, and she was worried. In another week the summer holidays would be over and John would have to return to school.

She watched her son closely as the days passed and saw that he was developing dark circles around his eyes, yet he insisted he was all right, until on Saturday, his cries in the night awoke her.

When she went to his room, Pearl found John thrashing in bed, shouting, 'It's got him! No! No!'

'John, wake up, darling,' Pearl said, gently shaking him. 'You're just having a nightmare, that's all.'

'No! Let him go! No!'

'John, John,' she urged.

His eyes opened, for a moment unfocused, but then he sat up and Pearl wrapped her arms around him as she had when nightmares frightened him as a child.

'It's all right, darling,' she murmured. 'It was just a bad dream.'

Though no longer a small child John began to cry and she hugged him tightly as he said, 'It ... it was awful. A ... a whale got Granddad and it ... it was eating him.'

Pearl had to swallow a lump in her throat. 'It was just a bad dream, that ... that's all,' she repeated, her voice breaking.

'But they haven't found his ... his body?'

'I don't know, darling.'

Fully awake, John pulled himself from her arms and said, 'Since we went out on a boat in Scotland to look for whales and dolphins, I've been having the same horrible nightmare night after night.'

'John, why didn't you tell me?'

'I'm not a kid now, Mum, and I know that they're not real.'

'Did you spot any whales?'

'My nightmare would make some sort of sense if we had, but no, we didn't.'

281

'Are you all right now?' Pearl asked as she stroked his hair.

'Yes,' he said, lying down again.

'Try to go back to sleep.'

'All right. Good night, Mum.'

Pearl kissed his cheek, stroked his hair again and then returned to her own bed, hoping that talking about his nightmares would bring an end to them. She nestled into Derek's back. She too had been wondering why they hadn't recovered Bernie's body. Yet surely they would soon and when they did his funeral would help to bring some closure for John.

Tim glanced at Emily as they drove to Battersea on Sunday morning, a week after returning from Scotland. This was her last day off before the new term began, but she was so excited and the journey would be worth it.

Emily was looking at the photographs again and he said, 'Don't you think they're amazing?'

'In almost every one John has captured something, some sort of essence. The backgrounds are wonderful too, and the light in this one is superb.'

'Yes, the red stag, the dark skies, with just one ray of sunshine that seems to reach down to touch the animal.'

'It's so artistic, and would make a stunning painting.'

'He must have inherited your talents – though he doesn't paint, it's a fabulous photograph. It's as good as, no even better, than the ones on show in the hotel. I'm going to get it enlarged and framed.'

'I can't wait to show them to John.'

'We're nearly there,' Tim said and only ten minutes later they pulled up outside the shop. As did Emily, he felt that John had a talent, and one that could be nurtured. When they got out of the car he took the parcel from the back seat, happy to give the lad a start.

Pearl welcomed them in and Emily hugged her daughter before they went upstairs. Nora remained seated at the table as she attempted to thread a string of coloured plastic beads.

'Hello, darling,' Emily said, hugging John.

Tim shook Derek's hand, and said, 'I hope you don't mind the invasion.'

'You're welcome any time, you know that.'

Pearl went off to make a pot of tea while Emily urged John to sit beside her on the sofa. She handed him the wallet of photographs and said excitedly, 'Take a look at these, darling.'

'They're good,' John said after looking at them. 'I think I took the one of the stag.'

'You took *all* of them and we think they're wonderful, don't we, Tim?'

'We certainly do. These are my efforts,' Tim said as he held out another wallet.

'They're good too,' John said after going through them.

'Nice of you to say so, but they aren't a patch on yours.'

'Can I have a look?' Derek asked and after handing out the drinks, Pearl did the same.

They admired both sets of photographs, but Tim could see how Pearl's eyes lingered on John's. 'You can see it, can't you?' he said. 'There's something about the perspective and the way John has captured the light that makes them special.'

'Yes, they're marvellous,' Pearl agreed.

Tim turned to John and asked, 'Did you enjoy taking those photographs?'

'Yes, but I don't think they'd have turned out like that if you hadn't taught me how to use your camera.'

'Well, you've got one of your own now,' he said, holding out the parcel.

'Wow, thanks, Tim!' John said, animated, as he tore open the parcel to find not only an identical camera, but four rolls of film too, one of which he deftly threaded from spool to spool. 'I can't wait to take some shots.'

'If you're that keen, off you go then,' Derek urged, 'but be back in an hour.'

'Tim, thank you,' Pearl said as soon as John had left the room. 'I think you've given him a new interest and it's just what he needs.'

'If he takes to photography and continues to learn, with talent like that he could end up taking our wedding photographs.'

'Tim, I think you're expecting too much of him,' Emily said, smiling. 'Our wedding is only a few months away.'

'Is it that soon?' he said, acting surprised yet knowing it was true. 'Did you hear that, Derek? I've only got a few months of freedom left.'

'In that case, you'd better make the most of them. Once they get that ring on their finger, we get one through our nose.'

Pearl laughed. 'Derek, having a ring through your nose sounds like a good idea.'

Tim joined in the merriment, pleased everyone

284

was smiling again. He was happy to be marrying into this family. In fact, December couldn't come quickly enough for him, but he just hoped that nothing else would come along to mar Pearl, Derek and John's happiness.

What upset them, touched Emily, of course, but no matter what, he would do his utmost to make her happy.

Chapter Forty

Lucy was on her way to work on Monday. She missed Eddie – the way he made her laugh, the feel of his arms around her – but now, when she walked past his stall, he didn't even look at her.

She had misjudged him and wanted to apologise, but every time she plucked up the courage it deserted her. She had driven him away, knew it was her fault, but how could she explain her complicated feelings to Eddie?

'Did you speak to him this time?' Pearl asked as soon as she walked into the shop.

She shook her head. 'No, he was busy.'

'Lucy, it's been nearly two weeks now and the longer you leave it, the harder it will be.'

'What if he won't accept my apology? I ... I don't think I could face it if he's nasty to me.'

'Lucy, if you really want him back, it's a chance you'll have to take. Go and talk to him.'

'What about Nora?'

'Look at her, she's busy dusting and she'll be

285

fine for a while.'

Lucy knew she had run out of excuses and biting her lower lip nervously she headed back to Eddie's stall.

When Eddie saw Lucy walking towards him, he quickly went over to another stall and engaged the costermonger in an inane conversation about the weather. He still loved Lucy, felt he always would, and it tore his guts out that she thought so badly of him. All right, he might enjoy a bit of flirtation, liked to make his customers laugh, but that was as far as it went. As for girlfriends, yes, he'd had quite a few, some that had been willing to indulge in a bit of slap and tickle, and others that hadn't, but never before had he found one that he wanted to marry.

Lucy had probably passed by now, so bringing the pointless conversation to an end he turned to go back. His stomach lurched. Lucy was still there, standing at the corner of his stall.

'Eddie, can I talk to you?'

'What for?' he asked bluntly.

'I ... I want to apologise. It wasn't you. It was me.'

'I don't get it. What do you mean?' he asked.

'I was ashamed of myself for being so ... so easy, and because I was I started to think that you only wanted me for ... for sex,' Lucy said, hurriedly glancing around as though to make sure that nobody had overheard before continuing, 'I wanted to test you, to see if you'd stop seeing me when I started to turn you down.'

Eddie frowned, wondering why women had to be so complicated. It sounded daft to him, but he

286

sort of got it. 'I think I understand, at least partly, but if it was some sort of test you seemed to be goading me to fail. I had no intention of breaking up with you, but as you made your opinion of me clear, I didn't have much choice.'

'I don't have a low opinion of you, really I don't. It was me. I ... I was afraid of my growing feelings for you, afraid of being hurt, and so I pushed you away.'

Eddie moved closer to her and said softly, 'What feelings, Lucy?'

She shook her head, refusing to answer, but Eddie didn't mind. He understood now and pulled her into his arms. 'Lucy, I'll never hurt you. I just want to be with you, to take care of you, and Clive too if you'll let me.'

He felt her stiffen slightly, but said softly, 'It's all right, I'm not talking marriage. I know you're not ready for that yet.'

She looked up at him then, her eyes shining. 'I might consider a long engagement.'

'Lucy Sanderson, I love you,' he said, lifting her to swing her around, laughing when he heard some of the other stallholders whistling in appreciation.

Eddie was happy again. He had Lucy back and this time he wasn't going to let her go.

Pearl took the telephone call and her stomach lurched as she listened to what Kevin had to tell her.

'As there are only partial remains,' Kevin went on, 'mainly my dad's torso, which I'm told has been got at by either fish or crabs, identification could take some time. I'd like of course to arrange his funeral, but that won't be possible until the coroner releases what's left of his body.'

'Will you let ... let us know when you do arrange it?' Pearl said. It was as if John's nightmare had come true, and heaving badly now she quickly ended the call as soon as Kevin agreed. She dashed to the bathroom and was violently sick, afterwards standing at the sink to splash cold water over her face. It was as she grabbed a towel that she heard Nora's voice.

'Pearl, what matter?'

'It's nothing, just a bit of an upset stomach,' Pearl lied as Lucy returned.

'You look awful. Are you all right?' Lucy asked, eyeing her.

'I've been sick, but I'm fine now.'

'You must have eaten something that was a bit dodgy.'

'Yes, probably,' Pearl agreed. She didn't want to think about Bernie's remains again, to be sick again, and so asked, 'Lucy, how did it go with Eddie?'

'Thanks to your advice, we've made things up.'

Pearl tried to look pleased for her, but the weight of what she had just been told was heavy on her mind. 'That's good,' she managed to say, 'but I must open the shop now. We'll have to chat later.'

'Yes, all right,' Lucy called as Pearl hurried downstairs, but she didn't open the shop. Instead she dashed over to Derek's stall.

'Blimey, love, what's wrong?' he asked.

'Kevin just rang me. He ... he said they've

found Bernie's body.'

'It's about time. He must have been missing for what, about nine or ten weeks?'

Pearl felt her stomach lurch again, and found herself swallowing bile before she was able to say, 'They didn't find all of him. Just his ... his torso.'

'Bloody hell, that's awful! Pearl, you look a bit green. Are you all right?'

'I still feel a bit sick. I was hoping they'd find Bernie; that his funeral would help John, but not like this. Kevin said there won't be a funeral until he's been identified.'

'How are they going to identify Bernie if there's only a torso?'

'I don't know, but Derek, how am I going to explain that to John? I can't tell him the truth, that there's only a bit of Bernie left. Like me, he'll be horrified.'

'Between us we'll find a way, perhaps say that identification is going to take a bit of time because he's been in the water so long. John doesn't need to know the rest.'

'Yes, we'll tell him that,' Pearl said, feeling marginally better now. She could see a customer trying to get into the shop and though she wasn't looking forward to opening it, at least it would give her less time to think if she kept busy.

The shop had been quiet all day, but Pearl kept herself occupied by rearranging the displays. She waited until after dinner that evening before speaking to John and then said as gently as she could, 'John, your grandfather's body has been found.'

He paled, but then said, 'I ... I'm glad – sad, but glad. I hated the thought that they'd never find him. Did Kevin ring you? Is that how you found out?'

'Yes, he called me ... and John,' she said hesitantly, 'there's something else. Your grandfather's body was in the sea a long time, and I'm afraid it's caused a bit of a problem. You see, until he's identified, Kevin can't arrange the funeral, but hopefully it won't take too long.'

John lowered his head as he digested this and Pearl hoped he wasn't imagining what the sea and the creatures within it had done to his grandfather's body. He finally looked up as Ginger strolled haughtily into the room to rub against his legs. John bent to pick him up, stroking his head and then said, 'He's hungry. I'll feed him and then I ... I think I'll go to my room.'

Pearl could see that John was holding back tears and she wanted to go after him, but Derek laid a hand on her arm. 'Leave him, love. I reckon he needs a bit of time on his own.'

Though growing up fast, John would always be her baby and Pearl wanted to comfort him, but perhaps Derek was right – maybe he needed a bit of privacy to vent his feelings. But she found that the pull was too strong, and she shook her head as she rose to her feet and dashed from the room.

John took one look at her, fell into her arms, and Pearl found herself crying with him.

Chapter Forty-One

As the weeks continued to pass, Pearl saw that Tim's gift to John had been inspirational. It was now a Monday morning at the beginning of October, but John's interest in photography hadn't waned. He spent all the money he earned from his Saturday job with Derek on buying film and having it developed, along with a bit of additional pocket money she gave him when necessary.

Of course not all of John's efforts turned out well, but he had a unique way of taking photographs, sometimes just an arched window, or a lone tree that echoed his melancholy. He had a way of catching the light at the perfect moment too and for Pearl, some of her son's photographs were like works of art.

Pearl sat eating her breakfast on what should have been a special day, but it had soon become obvious that Derek had forgotten their wedding anniversary. She took her mind off it by looking at John's latest snaps and saw that he wasn't really interested in taking snaps of people. It was structures and architectural angles, along with the shape and form of trees, that fascinated him. It was then that Pearl had an idea and she said, 'John, we could get some of these enlarged and framed. If I put them on display in the shop and they sell, it would give you more money to spend on equipment.'

He looked pleased at her suggestion and said, 'If you think they're good enough, that'd be great, Mum.'

'Of course they are. When you come home from school we'll sort out the best ones,' she said, pleased to see his smile. There was still no news about the funeral and Dolly remained in hospital, but there were times like this when John could forget it for a while and for that Pearl was thankful.

In the cottage, Adrianna was growing restless. She wasn't a complete idiot and as it had been so long now without a single viewing, she guessed that Kevin hadn't put the house on the market. She didn't know what his game was and hadn't bothered to confront him. He'd only lie, and now, with him out at the shops, she was once again searching for his money.

Adrianna was sick of Kevin's promises that he'd be a rich man soon, and she wanted to move on, to get away, but to do that she had to find what was left of his stash. It might not get her far, but surely there'd be enough to pay for a ferry ticket to France?

In the spare room that John had once used, Adrianna pulled out the stiff bottom drawer of an old cupboard. There was nothing beneath it on the floor, but when she tried to replace the drawer, it kept getting stuck.

Impatiently Adrianna tugged it out again and upended it to check the sides, only to find a long, yellowing envelope stuck to the bottom. Her heart skipped a beat, but when she opened the flap, there were only a couple of sheets of paper inside. Adrianna felt like screaming with frustration as she jammed the drawer back in place.

What good is this, Adrianna thought as she took the document out of the envelope and flopped, defeated, onto the bed. It wasn't money and therefore useless to her. She began to read it, soon realising that it was the will that Kevin had been searching for.

Flaming hell, Adrianna thought as she continued to read, her eyes widening.

There was something about the expression on Pearl's face when he left to set up the stall that had been playing on Derek's mind. What had he seen? At last it clicked. Disappointment, that was it, and disappointment in him. He searched his memory, remembered the date and groaned.

He'd have to buy her some flowers, but as he hadn't given them to her before he left, it wouldn't be the same. It was then that he saw Lucy passing through the market on her way to the shop and with another idea, he hurried over to her. 'Lucy, can I ask you to do me a favour?'

'It depends on what it is,' she answered, though smiling.

'I know it's a bit last minute, but I've just remembered it's our anniversary and I want to take Pearl out tonight.'

'You've only just remembered? Oh dear, no wonder you look in a bit of a panic.'

'The thing is, you know she won't leave Nora and John alone in the flat. Is there any chance you could come round this evening to keep an

293

eye on them?'

'Yes, all right, but I'll have to bring Clive.'

'Of course you will. Though I'll make sure we aren't late, you could kip in your old room for the night if you like.'

'Yes, good idea.'

'Thanks, Lucy, and don't say anything to Pearl. I'll make it a bit of a surprise.'

'My lips are sealed,' she said before hurrying off.

Derek saw that Eddie White was watching Lucy's departing figure and grinned. The two were an established item now and he walked over to Eddie's stall.

'I hope I haven't spoiled your plans,' Derek said. 'I've just asked Lucy to baby-sit for me tonight.'

'Baby-sit! Surely your lad's old enough to look after himself?'

'He is, but you try telling Pearl that. It's not so much for John though, it's Nora.'

'It's no problem. We hadn't intended to see each other tonight.'

'That's all right then,' Derek said, going back to his stall. He'd take Pearl to a nice restaurant for a slap-up meal. They rarely had evenings out and it would make a nice change, one he hoped that, like him, Pearl would enjoy.

Lucy walked into the shop, and said brightly, 'Hello, Pearl.'

'Hello, there. You're not going to believe this, Lucy. For the first time ever, Derek has forgotten our wedding anniversary.'

Lucy didn't know what to say. She daren't give

the game away, instead suggesting, 'Maybe you should jog his memory.'

'No, he'll only be cross with himself for forgetting, and anyway it's not as if we're newlyweds. Talking of newlyweds, how are things going with Eddie?'

'I like him a lot, but I'm still not ready for marriage. Mind you, I must admit that he's at my place more than his own nowadays. At first I was worried about how Clive would react. It had been just the two of us for so long and I was expecting jealousy, but he's taken to Eddie and the two of them get on like a house on fire.'

'So you were worried for nothing,' Pearl commented.

Lucy nodded in agreement but as Nora was vying for her attention she took her upstairs. With Clive and John at school it was just the two of them, the morning a quiet one until Nora paused in her dusting.

'Bad man,' she said forcefully.

'What do you mean, Nora?'

'He coming!'

It was almost a replica of her warning about Kevin and Lucy wondered if she should mention it to Pearl. Yet surely Kevin wasn't coming here again? He was at his mother's cottage in Hampshire and there was now no need for any more of his cloak and dagger antics.

Yet if it wasn't Kevin, who was Nora talking about?

When Kevin returned to the cottage he found Adrianna fuming. Like a spitfire she threw something at him, yelling, 'Take a look at that! Huh, so much for you inheriting this place!'

He failed to catch it, but as he picked it up Kevin saw that it was his father's will. However, before he had a chance to look at it, Adrianna yelled again, 'Read it! Go on, read it!'

'Give me a chance,' Kevin snapped, and sitting down at the table he scanned the contents. He didn't want to believe it at first, but there it was in black and white, signed and witnessed. 'The bastard! He's left everything in trust to John. I'm getting nothing! Nothing!' Kevin yelled.

Consumed with rage, he upended the table, sending everything on it crashing to the floor. Still incensed, he picked up a kitchen chair, smashing it into the wall, then another, and another until all that remained were sticks of wood. Panting now, Kevin's shoulders heaved, and when he at last looked at the remains of the room, he also saw that there was no sign of Adrianna. It was then that he realised that she must have been terrified and he dashed upstairs to find her.

Contrary to what he'd expected, Kevin found Adrianna in the bedroom, her cat-like eyes staring coldly at him as she said, 'Have you finished having a tantrum now?'

'Yes, sorry.'

'Instead of doing your nut you should be thinking clearly. When you've worked it out you'll realise there's only one thing we can do.'

'Oh yeah, what's that?'

'Even when your father's body has been identified, the cottage isn't yours to sell now so there's no point in staying here. Hopefully though, the money you've got left from selling your car will be enough to get us to France at least, and that's a start.'

Kevin knew Adrianna was right. They had no choice and he nodded. 'I'll see if there's anything in this place worth flogging. It could raise a good few quid, and then we'll leave.'

'It might help if you don't smash up any more furniture.'

Kevin looked up, saw that she was smiling and the last of his anger drained away.

The restaurant was nice, Derek thought, a bit up-market with white tablecloths and napkins. Music played quietly in the background, the soft lighting intimate, and when Derek saw that Pearl had eaten everything on her plate they smiled at each other across the table.

'That was delicious,' she said.

'Do you want a pudding?' he asked, glad now that he had brought her here for their anniversary.

'I don't think I've got room for one ... but then again,' she said eyeing the dessert trolley, 'that chocolate gateau is very tempting.'

'Go on, have a piece,' Derek urged.

Pearl looked at it again, and smiling, she said, 'Yes, all right.'

Derek beckoned the waiter over, and along with Pearl's choice he ordered a slice of strawberry cheesecake for himself. It was nice to see Pearl looking relaxed and happy, if only for a short time. For so long she had seemed strained, worried about John, and even though he had a new hobby, the lad was still upset about his granddad's death and waiting for his funeral. John was concerned about his gran too, but there was no sign of Dolly being allowed home.

'Is it nice?' he asked, smiling as Pearl licked her spoon.

'It's fabulous,' she said.

'Mine's good too,' Derek said.

'Can I taste a bit?'

They exchanged samples, ate the rest and ordered coffee. 'I'm glad you forgot our anniversary,' Pearl said as she spooned in sugar. 'This has been much nicer than your usual card and flowers.'

'Who said I forgot? I could have been planning this for ages.'

'I don't think so,' she said with an amused smile.

'Yeah, you've got me,' Derek said holding his hands up, 'but maybe we should do this more often.'

'If we get the chance, I'd like that.'

All too soon the evening was over and they were on their way back to the High Street. They found Lucy absorbed in watching the television, but she smiled and said, 'Did you have a nice time?'

'Yes, lovely,' Pearl told her. 'If you ever need a baby-sitter too, Lucy, you only have to ask.'

'Funnily enough, Eddie's always saying that he'd like to take me out instead of sitting in every night.'

'In that case,' Derek said, 'I've got a suggestion. Why don't we make this a regular thing? You baby-sit for us once a week and we'll do the same for you.'

'Oh yes, that's sounds like a smashing idea.'

Derek was pleased with himself. When they had lived with Pearl's mother in Winchester, she had been a ready-made baby sitter and they'd enjoyed nights out. Since moving to Battersea they'd been mostly cooped up indoors night after night, but now that was all set to change.

What Derek couldn't have known was that dark forces were gathering – and that the changes on the horizon were going to bring horror and heartache.

Chapter Forty-Two

'When did you say that dealer is coming to take the rest of the furniture?' Adrianna asked Kevin on Tuesday evening.

'On Thursday.'

'Good, as soon as he's loaded it up, we can leave.'

'Yeah, but for now, give us a cuddle,' Kevin said, pulling her playfully onto the sofa.

She pushed him away, saying seriously, 'Kevin, don't you feel a bit bad about your mother coming back to an empty house?'

'Not really. She's completely lost it and I reckon it'll be ages before they let her out. Even then I doubt she'll be able to look after herself so I can't see her living here. Anyway, as you've found out, it isn't her place, or mine. It's John's, though he won't inherit it until he's eighteen.'

'Why haven't you told him?'

'He'll find out soon enough. My dad put his affairs in the hands of a solicitor and once they've identified his body, as far as I'm concerned, he can sort the will out. The funeral too.'

'Aren't you going to tell John that we're leaving?'

'No, I'm not. The fire service may have found remains at Vince's house, but like my dad's, I haven't heard if they've been identified. Until they are, we won't know whether Vince got out or not and I don't want to leave a trail that could lead him to us.'

'Yeah, good thinking,' Adrianna said.

Kevin continued, 'Now that the telephone has been cut off, John won't be able to ring me even if he wants to.'

'You don't seem a bit interested in your kid,' Adrianna mused.

'If I wasn't leaving the country I'd have made an effort to get to know him, but there's no point now,' he said as he crooked his finger. 'Now come here, you.'

Adrianna relented enough to allow Kevin a cuddle, but that was all and when he began to nibble her ear, she pulled away, saying sharply, 'I'm not in the mood.'

'Come on, Adrianna,' he said, his tone insistent.

Something snapped inside her and she sprang to her feet. 'I said no!' she yelled, then began to pace the floor. 'I'm sick of this. I can't stand any more.'

'Bloody hell, what's brought this on?'

'You're no better than Vince, treating me like your property and keeping me a virtual prisoner. I couldn't get away from him, and now I can't get away from you.'

'You're not a prisoner. If you want to leave, there's nothing to stop you.'

'You know I can't go anywhere without money, but as you're holding it all, you know I've got to stay,' she said angrily.

'It's my money, Adrianna.'

'Yes, go on, rub it in; let me know you've got the upper hand and that I've got to dance to your tune. What you don't seem to realise is that this relationship means nothing if I'm forced to stay with you.'

Kevin jumped to his feet and grabbing his jacket he pulled out a wallet from the inside pocket. 'Here, I won't hide it any more. If it means that much, you hold on to it. All I ask is that you don't go until we leave together.'

Unable to believe it, she took the wallet. 'I wouldn't leave without you,' she said, yet knew that if she wasn't still worried about Vince, she'd be off like a shot. For now though, Kevin offered a bit of protection, and anyway there would be a bit more cash coming in from the sale of his mother's furniture on Thursday.

In Battersea, Lucy was curled up beside Eddie on her sofa. He was pleased about the baby-sitting arrangements and was planning where to take her on their night out.

'How about the flicks?' he asked.

'I'm not sure there's anything showing that I

want to see.'

'Dancing.'

'No, thanks,' Lucy said. 'I haven't been for years and haven't a clue how to do the latest dances.'

'Me neither, though I can do a pretty good smooch.'

'Had a lot of practice, have you?'

'Jealous, are you?' he asked, grinning.

'No, I am not,' Lucy insisted.

'Well if you are, there's no need and I hope you realise that now.'

A small voice interrupted her reply. 'Mum, my head hurts.'

'Does it, darling? Come here and let me feel your forehead.'

Clive trotted over, but instead of remaining on his feet, he scrambled between them. When Lucy checked, he didn't feel hot. 'I don't think you've got a fever.'

'Can I stay up for a while?' Clive wheedled.

'Sweetheart, it's way past your bedtime.'

'Please, Mummy.'

'No, Clive, you've got school in the morning.'

'Come on, soldier,' Eddie said as he stood up. 'Let's get you off to bed and I'll read you a story.'

Clive trotted off without protest now, and Lucy had to smile. After his initial sulks and the endless vying for her attention, Clive now accepted Eddie and couldn't spend enough time with him. It made her realise how much her son must have missed having a man in his life, and Eddie was so good with him.

As for herself, she had never expected to find a man who could replace Paul, but her feelings for

Eddie were growing stronger and stronger. They were so different: Paul had been quiet, loving but introvert, whereas you could hardly say that about Eddie. Yes, he was loving, but he was mostly boisterous and joking, rather like a big happy kid most of the time. It was probably why Clive had grown so fond of him, the two of them romping around, or pretending to be cowboys with mock guns.

'He's gone out like a light,' Eddie said when he returned.

'He likes you.'

'He's a good kid and I like him too.'

'Eddie, you know I said I'd like a long engagement?'

'Yes, I remember.'

'Can a girl change her mind?'

His eyes popped with astonishment. 'What? You want to get married?'

'Not right now, but maybe next year, perhaps in the spring.'

'I don't know,' he said, straight-faced, as he stroked his chin in thought. 'This is rather sudden and I'll have to give your proposal some consideration.'

'Is that a fact?' Lucy said. 'Well don't take too long to think about it 'cos I might change my mind.'

'In that case, let me see. I suppose if you insist on making an honest man out of me, I can hardly say no.'

'You daft sod,' she said, smiling. 'Anyone would think I was twisting your arm.'

Eddie grinned as he held out his wrists. 'I'm

happy to put the shackles on, and next spring it is.'

Lucy was then pulled to her feet and into his arms which soon led to more. As Eddie swept her up to carry her into the bedroom, Lucy found that she was finally able to let go of Paul. She would always hold him in her heart, but this time when Eddie made love to her she was able to give herself to him completely. Their lovemaking took on a new dimension and when they finally reached a climax, there were tears in her eyes.

When Eddie saw them, he looked worried. 'Lucy, what is it? Are you all right?'

The words were whispered, but as she said them, Lucy knew with all her heart that they were true. 'I ... I love you, Eddie. Don't worry. They're just tears of happiness, that's all.'

She saw how his eyes lit up as he gathered her into his arms again. 'I love you too, Lucy. I always have and I always will.'

For a moment she felt a tremor of fear. Everything she had loved seemed to have been taken away from her. First her parents, then Paul, but no, she was being silly. She still had Clive, and now she had Eddie too.

It was going to be all right, of course it was. Sighing, Lucy relaxed into Eddie's arms.

Chapter Forty-Three

He preferred the darkness. No one could see his face in the dark. It was two o'clock in the early hours of Wednesday morning as he went over the plan in his mind again. There was only Derek Lewis to worry about, but as he hadn't been in a boxing ring for years, he was sure to have gone soft.

He nodded to the man by his side, and in minutes the rear door was efficiently and quietly forced open, both then pulling black balaclavas over their faces. His was too memorable to take risks.

He was the first to step inside and with stiff, gloved fingers he turned on a small torch that emitted a thin ray of light. There were no words exchanged, only their soft footfalls breaking the silence as they went upstairs to the bedroom where he knew they'd be sleeping. His informant had been a good one, and the layout of the flat was imprinted on his mind.

He paused with his hand on the doorknob to check that the other man was ready and receiving a nod he gently pushed it open to step inside. Even with the dim light of the torch it was swift, Derek subdued with a whack on his head before he even woke up. 'Good work,' the man told his accomplice and then ordered, 'Now tie him up.'

He switched on a bedside light, and exchanged

the small torch in his hand for a gun that had a silencer attached. Pearl Lewis's eyelids fluttered and he pointed the gun at her face. 'Wake up, sleepyhead.'

Her eyes suddenly opened, cloudy with confusion, but then they widened in fear. She opened her mouth to scream, but he clamped a hand over her lips, hissing menacingly, 'If you utter a sound, I'll kill you. Do you understand.'

She nodded, and as he removed his hand her head turned swiftly. She gasped, but as she was seeing her husband being trussed up like a chicken, he allowed that small sound. 'Don't worry. As long as you cooperate he'll be fine.'

'Wh ... what do you want?'

'Kevin Dolby.'

'He ... he isn't here.'

'I know that, but I think you know where I can find him,' he said, but then there was a loud thump.

'Shit! He came round a bit quick and I wasn't expecting that.'

He saw that Derek Lewis had somehow rolled onto the floor and anger surged. 'You idiot!' he shouted at the man who was with him. It was the first time he'd used this bloke and it would be the last. 'Put him out again!'

There was a satisfying crunch as the cosh landed, but with the sound Pearl Lewis screamed. She jumped out of bed, but the man grabbed her arm, digging his fingers cruelly into her flesh as he pressed the muzzle of the gun hard into her cheek. 'Now tell me where Kevin Dolby is or next time your old man will get a bullet.'

306

'He ... he's staying at his mother's house.'

'Is Adrianna still with him?'

'Ye ... yes, I think so.'

'Address,' he snapped and when there wasn't an immediate response he dragged her to the other side of the bed.

Derek Lewis was on the floor, out cold, and he pointed the gun at him. 'I'll give you to the count of three. One... Two...'

'No, no,' she cried. 'I'll tell you.'

He listened as she stuttered it out, making a mental calculation of how long it would take him to get there, but then out of the corner of his eye he saw a movement in the doorway. He swung round to see a young lad, eyes wide with shock, yet he was so like Kevin Dolby that his guts clenched with hate.

'Dolby's spawn,' he spat as he aimed the gun, about to pull the trigger when with a cry of anguish the woman swung round in front of him. As the bullet struck, her eyes rounded as though in disbelief, then she dropped to the floor.

'Silly cow,' he said; then issued instructions as the lad rushed towards his mother. 'Grab the boy and tie him up, the woman too if she ain't dead, and tape all their mouths. There's another one to put out of action, an idiot I'm told. I'll deal with her.'

Twenty minutes later, the car drove away and feeling stifled in the balaclava, Vincent Chase wrenched it off. Then he removed his gloves to reveal hideously scarred fingers and hands, which he knew matched his face. The doctors had offered plastic surgery, but Vince wasn't going

307

under the knife until he'd sorted out Dolby.

At first, when Adrianna had gone missing, he'd thought she had torched his place, but then one of his narks had told him that a bloke returning home after a burglary and watchful for other vehicles on the road, had seen her in a car with Kevin Dolby, heading out of London.

Vince'd been stuck in hospital, unable to do anything himself to find them, growing angrier by the day when his informants came up with nothing. It was only when his mind was clear of painkilling drugs that he'd remembered Kevin's ex-wife and son, and now they had proved as useful as he'd hoped.

'Head for Southsea,' Vince ordered. Now that he knew where Dolby and Adrianna were holed up, he intended to make sure the pair of them suffered the same fate. They would experience the same searing agony as he had when their flesh burned and melted – but unlike him, they wouldn't walk out of the flames alive.

Adrianna had been thrilled when she'd put Kevin's wallet into her handbag. The money had given her a strange sense of power that had been reflected in their lovemaking. Kevin had been surprised when she'd taken the initiative, straddling him, yet as it was the first time that she hadn't felt used, she'd found it liberating.

After a night of passion, they had fallen into an exhausted sleep, but Adrianna's was disturbed by a nightmare and she was groaning. The smell of smoke was choking her, the nightmare so real that she woke up in a panic. She sat bolt upright in bed, perspiration soaking her body, trying to shake off her feeling of terror, but then found herself in a waking nightmare. The smoke was real! The room was full of it. Panicking, she jumped out of bed to run to the bedroom door. She opened it, but to her horror saw a wall of fire that was almost upon them and quickly slammed it shut.

'Kevin! Kevin! Wake up.'

'Wh ... what?' he mumbled sleepily.

'Fire!' she screamed, and hearing the crackle of flames licking at the door she knew that the window was their only means of escape. She frantically grabbed her handbag and flung it open, shouting, 'Kevin! We've got to get out. The house is on fire!'

At last he responded, coughing as he dived out of bed to run to the door, unheeding as she yelled at him not to open it. As he flung it back the wall of flames burst into the room and engulfed Kevin in seconds, his whole body ablaze and his screams of agony horrific to hear.

In a blind panic, Adrianna scrambled onto the window ledge and jumped, landing with a jolt that knocked the breath out of her body. For a while she lay unmoving, sure she had broken something, but then as windows burst, showering glass, she managed to crawl away from danger.

Yet even then Adrianna didn't feel safe and her heart thumped with fear. She was sure it wasn't an accidental fire; that somehow Vince had survived, found them, and this was his revenge.

Vince wanted her dead, Kevin dead, and if he knew she had got out, he'd come after her.

Frantic, Adrianna hooked her handbag over her head and with it dangling in front of her she began to crawl again, passing rose bushes with thorns that tore at her skin and nightdress as she made for the shelter of the woods.

Only a small fence stood in her way now, and Adrianna scrambled over it, in the woods at last. Some way in, and behind a tree, she tentatively stood up. She was shivering with shock, sore, scratched and bruised, but otherwise unhurt. The horrific image of Kevin engulfed in flames flashed into her mind, and her stomach lurched. That had nearly been her – and she wasn't safe yet.

Fear drove Adrianna on and with bare feet she began to walk as fast as she could through the pitch-black woods, almost screaming out when a tree suddenly loomed up in front of her. Somehow she had to carry on, to stay out of sight and avoid any roads in case Vince saw her. All she had was her handbag, but with Kevin's wallet inside, there was money, enough to get her out of the country she hoped.

The soles of her feet were in agony, and almost at the end of her tether, it was only Adrianna's thoughts and plans that gave her the strength to carry on.

A new life beckoned, far away from Vince, and Adrianna stumbled towards it.

Chapter Forty-Four

Disorientated when he came round, Derek groaned against the agonising pain in his muscles. He tried to move, but his wrists were tied behind his back and his ankles were bound too. Something was stuck over his mouth and he worked his jaws futilely in an attempt to remove it.

He heard a strange noise, but when he lifted his head his eyes closed against the pain. That sound again – it was coming from behind him and with a supreme effort he rolled over.

Derek's mind screamed out against the sight that met his eyes. Pearl was on the floor, bound, and her nightdress was covered in blood, so much blood!

John was trussed up beside her and the strange noises were coming from him as he tried to talk through the tape over his mouth. The boy's eyes were rounded in panic, his face wet with tears as he began to fight unsuccessfully to free himself from the bindings. Derek tried too, but his frantic efforts were as useless as John's.

Derek rolled again and made it to Pearl's side, but seeing how deathly white she looked, a cry of sheer agony that couldn't find release through the tape over his mouth sounded like the bellow of a bull.

His head swam, he felt sick, dizzy, and moments later Derek returned to a dark void, unaware that

John was now gripped in the terror of claustrophobia. He'd been crying; his nose so stuffed up that he felt he couldn't breathe. He wanted to rip the tape from his mouth, but with his arms tied behind his back it was impossible and his eyes were wild with fear as he desperately sought air.

He was going to die – he knew he was going to die and seconds later, John fainted.

Nora had been terrified when she woke to find a man wearing something over his face roughly binding her wrists. She had thrashed, but he had hit her, telling her to lie still and to keep quiet. He'd taken his gloves off to pull a piece of stuff from a roll to stick over her mouth and she'd seen his hands. They looked funny, scary, and she'd cringed from them, but then he went away and she was so frightened that he'd come back if she wasn't a good girl, that she hadn't moved.

Nora didn't know when she fell asleep again, or what time it was when she woke up. For a moment she was confused to find that her arms had been pulled together in front of her and her wrists tied, but then she remembered. The bad man! The bad man had come!

She lay still, listening, but could hear only noises outside in the High Street. When she had fallen asleep it had been dark, but now it was light, so it must be morning. The bad man only came in the dark. He must have gone now and she dared to sit up.

Nora wanted to tell Pearl about the bad man, and though her wrists were bound she managed to pull off the nasty stuff over her mouth. Ouch, it hurt, and her cheek was sore where the bad man had hit her. 'Pearl ... Pearl!' she called.

Pearl didn't come so she tried again. 'Derek! John!'

Nobody came, so Nora bent forward and tried to untie her ankles. It was so hard and it took ages to loosen the knot, but at last she did it and stood up to stumble from the room.

'Pearl,' she whimpered, finding that nobody was up yet.

A familiar voice in her head said, *Go upstairs,* and Nora nodded at the command. She went into Pearl's room, her eyes rounding like saucers. Dead! Bad man had made Pearl dead!

John was making funny noises, blinking rapidly, and she bent down to pull the sticky stuff from over his mouth. 'Help ... get help...' he croaked.

She just stared at him, but then he said, 'Go, Nora ... run outside. Find someone.'

Eddie White was wondering why Derek hadn't turned up to open his stall. He was fussy about his display of china, taking great care to show it to the best effect, and was always one of the first to arrive. Eddie looked up at the flat above the shop, but the curtains were still drawn across all the windows.

When another half-hour had passed with no sign of Derek, Eddie walked across to Harry, but he couldn't offer any explanation, saying that Derek hadn't said anything to him about not opening up that day.

For some inexplicable reason Eddie had a bad feeling about it. Something was wrong – he was sure of it and he headed for the shop to see if he could rouse anyone.

Eddie wasn't aware that at the same time, Nora had run downstairs, or that she couldn't open the locked door. He thumped on it with his fist, then bent down to look through the letterbox, shouting, 'Pearl! Derek! Are you in there?'

A pair of eyes suddenly appeared to meet his and Nora cried, 'Help! Pearl dead!'

Eddie reeled back in shock, but then he swiftly recovered and urged, 'Let me in, Nora.'

'Can't. Door locked.'

'Where's Derek?'

'He on the floor,' Nora sobbed.

Eddie knew he had to get in, and quickly from the sound of it. 'All right, Nora. Stand back, there's a good girl.'

Eddie ran back, then forward to put his shoulder to the door. Nothing happened, so he tried again, this time it crashed open. 'Nora, where are they?'

'Uppastairs. Pearl's room.'

He ran past her, thumping up the stairs, and for a brief moment paused, shocked. Pearl was covered in blood but somehow Eddie held it together as he ran forward to crouch beside her, sure at first that she was dead until he found a faint pulse.

'Is she ... is she... ?' John cried.

'It's all right, she's alive,' Eddie broke in as he quickly checked John and then scrambled across to Derek. He was alive too, but barely conscious, and Eddie rose hurriedly to his feet. 'I'm going to call an ambulance,' he told John. 'I'll be back in a minute.'

The call made, Eddie turned to see Nora watching him, her face streaked with tears as she stuttered, 'P... Pearl... Pearl.'

'She's hurt, but she'll be fine,' he told her, hoping he was right.

Nora followed him up to the bedroom, watching ashen-faced as he again checked on Pearl before he untied them all. 'John, what happened?' he asked.

'Two men, they ... they must have broken in,' he said, his limbs shaking. 'Thirsty ... I ... I'm thirsty.'

'Nora, can you get John a glass of water?' Eddie asked.

'Yes,' she said, scuttling off.

John looked a little better after gulping it down, but he was frantic about Pearl, and Eddie willed the ambulance to arrive. If they didn't get here quickly, he feared she wouldn't make it.

'Is everything all right up there?' someone shouted and Eddie recognised Harry's voice.

He went out onto the landing, calling out, 'Pearl's been shot and Derek's unconscious. We're waiting for an ambulance. Can you keep an eye out for it?'

'Bloody hell! Yeah, all right.'

At last it arrived and they carried Pearl out first, followed by Derek. Though both John and Nora were able to walk, the paramedics said that they should be looked at too.

Eddie watched the ambulance drive away, and then did his best to secure the door while Harry and other costermongers plagued him with questions. One bloke who had a hardware stall offered him a padlock and between them they

315

managed to affix it to the door.

Left holding the key, Eddie didn't know what to do next. He knew that Lucy was going to be in a right old state when she found out, but better to tell her before she turned up for work.

Eddie asked Harry to keep an eye on his stall and then set off for Bullen Street, the image of Pearl looking so close to death remaining in his mind. He wasn't one for religion, but found himself inwardly praying that it wasn't too late for the doctors to save her.

Though concussed, Derek was desperate to find out how Pearl was, and struggled to sit up. 'I want to see my wife.'

'Mr Lewis, I've told you,' the nurse said, 'she's undergoing surgery and you won't be able to see her until she comes out of the operating theatre.'

Derek didn't know what had happened, why Pearl had been shot. His only memory was waking up to see her on the floor before he'd passed out again. The next thing he was vaguely aware of was being loaded into an ambulance. 'Where's my son? Is he all right?'

'He's fine and in the waiting room. If you behave yourself I'll fetch him in to see you.'

Derek scowled at being talked to as though he was a child, but the movement had made him feel nauseous again and he flopped back onto the pillows.

'Good,' the nurse said. When she went to the waiting room, Derek kept his eyes on the door until John appeared.

The lad looked awful, his face pale and eyes

red-rimmed, but seeing him he rushed up to the bed. 'Dad … Dad! Are you all right?'

'Yes, I'm fine, what about you?'

'I'm not hurt,' John said.

'Have you heard anything about your mother?'

'No, they … they won't tell me anything,' he said as fresh tears filled his eyes. 'All I know is they rushed her straight to the operating theatre and that was over an hour ago.'

'Come on, son, don't cry. She's in good hands,' Derek consoled, hoping against hope that he was right. 'John, what happened? Who shot your mother?'

'I … I don't know, only that he was a tall man wearing a balaclava. But … but he was aiming the gun at me, not Mum. She shielded me, put herself in front of the man and took the bullet. It's my fault, isn't it? My fault Mum was shot!'

'Of course it wasn't your fault. I don't know who that evil bastard was, but he was the one who pulled the trigger.'

John then put his head onto the bed, crying in earnest. Derek felt ineffectual as he stroked the lad's hair, while trying to work out why the man had broken into the flat. He had to wait some time before John pulled himself together and then said gently, 'John, the bloke who broke in. Do you know what he was after? Did he say anything?'

'There were two of them, and when the one with the gun pointed it at me, he said something about Dolby spawn.'

Derek frowned. 'Is that all?'

John thought for a moment, but then said, 'Af … after he shot Mum, he spoke to the other man,

317

said something about having to drive somewhere. He told him to tie us up, and then I think
he went to do the same to Nora.'

'Blimey, I'd forgotten Nora. Is she all right?'

'Yes and when she found us I told her to get
help. The police tried to talk to her, but you know
Nora and it was a waste of time. All she kept
going on about was a bad man with funny hands.
She isn't here now. Lucy turned up and took her
home.'

Derek tried to make sense of it all. Two men
had broken in, one it seemed intent on killing
John. He'd called the lad Dolby spawn and that
surely meant it had something to do with Kevin.
Who had Kevin upset enough to want a revenge
killing? The man had failed, he'd shot Pearl
instead, but would he try again? 'John, have the
police spoken to you?'

'Yes, and they want to talk to you too. The
doctor told them they'd have to wait.'

Derek didn't want them to wait any longer. The
sooner he told them about the danger John was
in, the better.

Chapter Forty-Five

Lucy had taken Nora back to her own flat and
was doing her best, but placating her was proving
almost impossible.

'Told you!' she cried. 'I told you bad man
coming.'

'I know you did, love, but I thought you meant Kevin.'

'No! It bad man!' she wailed, tears again filling her eyes. 'He made Pearl dead, Lucy.'

'No, no, Pearl isn't dead. She's in hospital, you know that. You went with her in the ambulance, and they're going to make her better,' Lucy said, hoping desperately that she was right.

'Not dead?'

'No, darling.'

'Go see her,' Nora appealed. 'Go see Pearl.'

'Not yet, love. She's having an operation.'

'I go now!' Nora insisted. 'I go see Pearl.'

'I told you, not yet, but maybe later.'

'Not later! Now!'

Nora was beginning to behave like a petulant child, but Lucy managed to remain calm. 'Darling, listen to me, we'll go to the hospital as soon as we can, but before that we have to make everything nice for when Pearl comes home. Would you like to go to the flat now and help me to clean it up?'

'Yes, yes, we do clean.'

'Come on then, let's go,' she said, relieved that Nora was quiet now.

'Is there any news?' Eddie asked, hurrying up to her when they approached his stall.

'I don't know. I haven't got a telephone, but I'll use Pearl's to ring the hospital.'

'Do you want a nice banana, Nora?' one of the costermongers called.

She trotted over to him, while Eddie said, 'You won't be allowed in Pearl's place yet. The police are in there, probably searching for fingerprints

319

or something.'

'I hadn't thought of that. What am I supposed to do with Nora? She won't settle at my place and I need to keep her occupied.'

'From what you've told me, if you give her your vacuum cleaner it'll keep her happy.'

'Yes, I suppose I can find some housework for her to do at my place, but she might play up when I try to take her back. Oh, Eddie, I just can't believe this has happened to Pearl and Derek.'

'None of us can.'

'Do ... do you think Pearl's going to make it?' Lucy asked.

'To be honest, love, I don't know. She looked really rough, but I did find a bit of a pulse so cling on to that. Where there's life, there's hope, Lucy.'

She nodded, but as Nora came back clutching her banana, Lucy was fighting tears. She had to remain strong for Nora's sake, but Pearl had come to mean so much to her and it was hard not to crack.

Derek was thankful that the two men from CID had taken him seriously. Without a description of the men, Derek doubted they'd be found, but as John had been the target they were going down to Dolly's cottage to interview Kevin.

In the meantime, Derek didn't want John to be left alone, and he would make sure he remained at the hospital until the police could arrange protection. Yet even if he'd been able to leave, Derek knew that John would refuse to go until they had news of Pearl's operation.

Another six hours of almost unbearable anxiety

passed before they were told that Pearl had survived the operation. The bullet aimed at John had been on a downward trajectory that missed her heart by a fraction, but this uplifting news had been tempered when the surgeon went on to explain his concerns about her spine. Pearl would remain in intensive care, immobilised and sedated, and at the moment they weren't allowed to see her.

They had both been so relieved that she'd survived, John crying again with emotion, and it was some time later before they considered the ramifications of the surgeon's words. John was the first to voice his thoughts. 'What did that surgeon mean about Mum's spine?' he asked.

'He said something about the bullet causing some sort of damage, but to be honest I was so over the moon to hear that she was all right that I hardly took it in.'

'Me neither.'

'I'm sure someone will come to talk to us again and then we'll ask more questions,' Derek said.

'Mr Lewis, this really can't go on, you know,' the ward sister complained as she came up to his bed. 'You are only supposed to have visitors during set hours. Your son will have to leave now.'

'He isn't going anywhere without me,' Derek said. 'John, find my clothes.'

'Dad, you've only got your pyjamas.'

'They'll have to do then.'

'Mr Lewis, you can't get up,' sister protested. 'You've had a severe blow to your head and you're concussed.'

'Try and stop me. In fact, I'm going to discharge myself.'

'I'll get the doctor,' she said, huffily bustling away.

Nothing was going to keep Derek in bed now and he wasn't worried about wearing pyjamas. They weren't going to leave the hospital yet so he'd hardly be an uncommon sight. He'd find the intensive care unit, and there was sure to be a waiting room where they could sit until allowed in to see Pearl.

At the moment Derek's head was pounding too much to think beyond that.

At five o'clock the same two men from CID, one called Riley, the other Shaw, found them in the waiting room.

Thanks to a sympathetic nurse Derek now had a hospital dressing gown over his pyjamas. She'd also lent him a few bob so they could go to the canteen for something to eat – the nurse was a proper angel in Derek's eyes. He'd pay her back as soon as he got hold of someone to fetch him some clothes and money, but he also intended to buy her the biggest box of chocolates he could find.

'Sorry, son, but would you mind waiting outside?' Riley said.

John didn't look happy, but he went off without argument. Both men sat down, but Derek was the first to speak. 'Well, did you talk to Kevin Dolby?'

Riley again did the talking. 'No, it wasn't possible. A fire gutted the cottage last night, and the fire brigade have found the remains of a body. I don't think there's any doubt that it was Dolby,

322

but positive identification hasn't proved possible yet. The brigade investigation team have indicated that the fire was set deliberately.'

'Do you think it was the same two blokes?'

'Yes, and this makes it a murder enquiry. We have little evidence to go on yet, but they're the focus of our enquiry.'

Derek frowned. 'They only found one body in the cottage?'

'Yes, sir.'

'But I'm sure I told you that Dolby had a young woman staying there with him.'

'You did, but there are indications that she escaped the fire. The local police had a report in the early hours of the morning about a young woman seen stealing garments from a clothes line. When it was daylight, they found a charred night-dress close by that she must have left behind.'

'Where is she now?'

'There haven't been any further sightings of her, so at the moment, we don't know,' Riley told him.

Derek found that his thinking was still a bit muzzy and it was hard to take it all in. Kevin had died in a fire, and though the police asked him questions about Adrianna, there was little he could tell them. He didn't know how John was going to react on hearing that Kevin was dead, but as the police were going to question him again too, there was little he could do to prevent him finding out.

John had been through so much lately and Derek feared the lad would fall apart. With Pearl in intensive care John would need him. Struck by a sudden thought, he rubbed a hand over his face. Had anyone been in touch with Emily? Did she know that Pearl was in hospital?

'I think that's all, sir. We'll talk to John now.'

'Not without me sitting in you won't, but do you know if anyone has been in touch with my wife's mother?'

'Not that we know of, sir.'

'Then before you talk to my son, I've got to make a phone call.'

Emily was called to the headmaster's office, and after listening to Derek on the telephone she was close to fainting. She found herself sitting on a chair and a glass of water had been put in her hands, then she became vaguely aware that Mr Chapworth was talking to Derek.

He replaced the receiver and came to speak to her. 'I've assured your son-in-law that you're all right. You are, aren't you?'

'I ... I think so. It was just such a shock.'

'Don't worry, I'll find someone to take over your class, but is there anyone I can call to take you home?'

'Home, I can't go home,' Emily cried. 'I've got to go to London.'

'Are you sure you feel able to drive?'

'Yes ... yes, I'm fine now,' she said, standing up. Though she felt unsteady, a sense of urgency kept her on her feet. 'I must go. I've got to go.'

Emily brushed aside Mr Chapworth's continued concern, her one thought to get to Pearl as she hurried as fast as she could from his office. She stopped only to get her handbag containing her car keys and then she was driving away from the school and towards London.

Pearl, my darling, her voice cried inwardly. *Please be all right. Please ... please be all right.'*

Chapter Forty-Six

Derek had been worried about going back to the flat, but with assurances that local day and night shift policemen would regularly check the perimeters of the premises, he had finally decided that with his protection too, John would be safe. The CID had tried to talk to Pearl, but she was heavily sedated and hardly able to tell them anything, other than that the two men had been looking for Kevin.

Thanks to Lucy who had taken on the job of cleaning up the blood, everything had looked normal, but Derek wondered if any of them would be able to forget that night. The door had been repaired, with new locks front and back, and Derek thanked Eddie White for all he had done.

He didn't want to leave John so hadn't set up his market stall and the shop remained closed, but money was the last thing on Derek's mind.

'Emily, are you ready?' he asked, noting that the strain of the last five days had aged her. Pearl was no better, and when they went to visit her she was still so sedated that she was hardly aware they were there.

'I'm ready,' she said, hooking her handbag over her arm.

'Me come too,' Nora said.

'Yes, Nora,' he said kindly, aware that without her getting loose and summoning help, Pearl might well have died.

'What about you, John? Are you ready?'

'Yes,' he said listlessly.

Derek knew that John was finding it hard to cope. Emily was doing her best to comfort him, but as he'd lost his grandfather and had seen his mother being shot, it was proving impossible. John asked if Dolly had been told, so Derek had rung the psychiatric unit. He had spoken to one of the doctors who was reluctant to discuss Dolly's condition, though he did say that she'd be informed when mentally able to cope.

What they needed was some good news and if Pearl showed any signs of recovery it would lift all their spirits. Hoping against hope, Derek drove them all to the hospital.

They returned disappointed. There was no change.

'Eddie, I've been thinking,' Lucy said that evening.

'Yeah, what about?'

'Derek isn't working on his stall and with the shop closed too, there's no money coming in.'

'Oh, right, I suppose that means you're worried about getting paid.'

'No, it isn't that. Derek won't let me down, but what I've been thinking about is offering to open the shop.'

'What about Nora?'

'Derek isn't working, John isn't at school, and at the moment Pearl's mum is there. They don't

326

really need me to look after Nora and I feel like I'm just getting under everyone's feet.'

'In that case, opening the shop makes sense to me,' Eddie said.

'I'll have a word with Derek tomorrow.'

'Yeah, you do that, but for now, how about giving me a cuddle?'

Lucy drew strength from being wrapped in Eddie's arms. She hoped Derek would let her open the shop, but knew she had another, unspoken reason for wanting to do it. Derek, John and Emily were so upset, Nora too, and it was awful to be upstairs in Pearl's flat when they were all there. She felt inadequate, unable to comfort them, but at least in the shop she'd be doing something useful.

At eight o'clock, Derek went downstairs when he heard a ring on the doorbell. It was the same two CID officers and Riley said, 'Sorry to call at this time, sir, but we have a lead. We need to have a word with Nora Dobbs.'

'Nora?' Derek said, puzzled. 'I don't see how she can help you.'

'It was something she said that we need to clarify.'

'You'd better come in then,' Derek invited.

'Before we speak to her, can you tell us if you've heard of a man called Vincent Chase?'

'Yes, he used to be notorious around here, but then he moved on to bigger things,' Derek said and then remembered something else. 'It was a while ago now, but someone told me that that Kevin Dolby was sniffing around for information

327

on Chase.'

Riley nodded sagely at his colleague. 'It looks like it's all coming together.'

'Yes, sir, it does,' Shaw agreed.

'What's coming together?' Derek asked.

Riley ignored his question, saying only, 'We'd like to talk to Nora Dobbs now.'

Derek led them upstairs, and though Emily and John left the room, Derek insisted on staying while they spoke to Nora.

When they all sat down, Riley said to Nora, 'Do you remember me?'

'Yes, I does.'

'That's good, and do you remember telling me about the bad man who had funny hands?'

'Yes, he bad man,' she said.

'Can you describe his hands for me – tell me what they looked like?'

She frowned then said, 'Nasty!'

Shaw took over and asked, 'In what way?'

'I not know.'

'Try to remember, Miss Dobbs.'

'Why I got rember Miss Dobbs? I know that me. I'se Nora Dobbs.'

Riley smiled and took over the questioning again. 'Yes, of course you are. Now shall we try again? Why did the man's hands look nasty?'

Nora looked down at her own and then said, 'Skin, it funny.'

'Burns, is that what you mean?'

'I not know what burn look like, but nasty, he had nasty hands,' Nora said.

As the penny dropped, Derek jumped to his feet. He couldn't believe how slow he'd been, how he'd only just made the connection. 'Vincent Chase! I thought the bloke who broke in here was after revenge and now it all makes sense. It must have been Kevin who torched his place and Chase was injured in the fire. Where is he? Where is the bastard who shot my wife?'

'Mr Lewis, we don't know, but we intend to find out.'

'How did you get on to him?'

'It was through the woman, Adrianna. When we spoke to John he said it wasn't her real name, though he couldn't remember what her true one was. The alias name, Adrianna, and John's description of her was circulated, and in a very short time another branch of the CID got in touch with us. They're involved in an ongoing enquiry regarding an arson attack on Vincent Chase's house in which two men died. Chase escaped, but it seems a woman who lived in the house with the name Adrianna, disappeared. She was one of his strippers, and from what you and your son were able to tell us, she then turned up at the cottage with Kevin Dolby. Added to that, we were also able to ascertain that during the fire at his property, Vincent Chase sustained burns to his face and *hands*. When we heard that, we remembered Miss Dobbs here telling us about the bad man with funny hands.'

'So what happens next?' Derek asked.

'When we find Vincent Chase, we'll pull him in for questioning.'

Derek thought about what they had on Vincent Chase and scowled. 'He's hardly going to own up to it. He must know that none of us saw his face, and I doubt Nora spotting the burns on his hands will be enough to convict him.'

'There's still Adrianna and she may know something,' Shaw said.

Derek shook his head. 'She's probably long gone.'

The men rose to their feet, Riley saying, 'We're doing our best to find her, but I don't think we need to ask Miss Dobbs any more questions.'

Derek walked them downstairs, and Shaw asked before they left, 'How is your wife, Mr Lewis?'

'There's no improvement,' he said, and noted that Shaw looked sympathetic before they said their goodbyes.

Derek closed the door behind them and locked up again, his thoughts turning. Vincent Chase had been the one who shot Pearl, but Kevin had been the catalyst that caused it. Derek would never say it in front of anyone, but he was glad the bastard was dead.

Chapter Forty-Seven

Emily thought it was a good idea to open the shop and supported Lucy in trying to persuade Derek.

'I don't know,' he said. 'I don't like the idea of Lucy being down there alone. Anyone could walk in.'

'Derek, now that the police have a lead and are looking for those men, I don't think we need to live in a fortress,' Emily said. 'I can't believe they'd dare to come back.'

'Who are they looking for?' Lucy asked.

'They're after Vincent Chase.'

'I'm sure I've heard about him, but it was years ago.'

'Yeah, he used to live in these parts.'

'And the police think he shot Pearl.'

'It looks likely,' Derek said. 'They think he's responsible for the fire at Dolly's cottage too, that it was retaliation because Kevin torched his place.'

'But why did Kevin do it?'

'I don't know, Lucy, but CID think it's got something to do with Adrianna, who apparently was one of Vincent Chase's strippers,' he said, going on to tell her everything that had come to light.

'Blimey, it sounds a bit complicated,' said Lucy. 'But as Kevin died in the fire the police will be after Chase for murder. I should think he's lying well low and as his face must be well known to a lot of people around here, he isn't going to show it. If you're still worried I could ask Eddie to spread the word amongst the other stallholders. They can keep a lookout for him and an eye on the shop too.'

'There you are, Derek,' Emily said. 'I think that sounds like a good idea.'

He still looked doubtful, but it was Lucy who pushed on. 'Pearl gets a lot of customers from the college and the night school art classes. If the shop doesn't open soon they might go elsewhere for their supplies and once they've gone, I doubt they'll come back.'

331

'Pearl wouldn't be happy about that,' Derek mused as he ran a hand around his chin. 'All right, Lucy, you can open the shop, but not until I've rigged up some sort of alarm you can press to alert me if there's any trouble.'

'Thanks, Derek,' Lucy said, looking delighted. 'And you don't have to worry. If you need me to keep an eye on Nora at any time, she'll be fine with me in the shop.'

With the decision made, Emily's thoughts turned back to her daughter. She had rung the headmaster to ask for extended leave and he had agreed to get a supply teacher in to cover her post; but even if he'd threatened to dismiss her, there was no way Emily was going to leave London until she knew that Pearl was on the road to recovery.

Tim had understood of course, said he'd drive down to see her on Saturday and she'd make up a bed on the sofa if he wanted to stay overnight. Emily hoped there'd be some positive news before then. It was dreadful to see Pearl lying immobile in intensive care. They had spoken to the surgeon and he told them that the bullet had lodged millimetres from her spine. It had been removed, but he told them that the needle tests he performed on Pearl indicated that at present she had no feelings in her legs.

On hearing that, Emily had broken down, but the surgeon told her not to give up hope. He said that Pearl's lack of feeling could be caused by swelling around the damaged area, a natural process of the body trying to heal itself. Emily now clung on to that, but as each day passed without any sign of recovery, she feared her daughter was going to be paralysed for the rest of her life.

Despite what he had just heard, John was unable to cry any more. He wasn't a child now, he shouldn't cry, but lately he'd been unable to stop. The terror he'd felt when that man had aimed a gun at him, the horror of seeing his mother shot, and the fear of suffocation, haunted him.

John wanted to escape the terrible memories of that night, but every time his eyes closed, he relived them. It didn't help that with the exception of when they went to the hospital, he had to stay in. He understood why his dad wanted to protect him, but the inactivity was driving him mad.

At times John felt that the walls were closing in on him, and he also resented not being told what was going on. It was for that reason that he had stood in the hall, listening to Lucy talking to his dad and gran.

He hadn't understood it all, but enough for him to work out that Kevin and Adrianna had played a part in what had happened. His mum had been shot because of Kevin, and John felt that he was living in a nightmare. So much had happened in such a short time and his mind struggled to grasp it all.

His grandfather had died but he still hadn't been buried, his gran taken into care and his mother had been shot. John then jumped when a hand touched his shoulder.

'What you doing, Johnny? Why you standing in the hall?' Nora asked.

'I'm not doing anything,' he snapped, 'and stop

calling me Johnny. It makes me sound like a baby. My name is John.'

'I'se sorry,' she said, her eyes welling with tears.

It wasn't much, but making Nora cry was the final straw for John. If it hadn't been for Nora, his mum might not have survived and now he'd upset her. He couldn't take any more, couldn't think any more. He ran to his room and flung himself onto his bed where he curled into a ball.

John closed his eyes, wanting escape from his tortured thoughts, and at last he fell asleep.

That afternoon, when Lucy asked him to put the word out, Eddie did just that, but it took him some time as every costermonger he spoke to barraged him with questions. He told them as much as he knew and they were united in wanting to help in any way they could. One bloke offered to get his son to run Derek's stall for a minimal wage.

Like Lucy, Eddie didn't think that Vincent Chase would show his face around there, especially in daylight, but Derek was sure to remain cautious at night.

Eddie thought it a wonder that newspaper reporters weren't sniffing around. Maybe they hadn't put it all together, but for how much longer? Vincent Chase's place had been torched, then the shooting, and somehow a stripper called Adrianna was involved. This was followed by Kevin Dolby's murder. It could have been headline news, but so far the story hadn't broken.

'Look at that copper,' Arthur said, a costermonger who had worked the market for over twenty years. 'He doesn't look old enough to be out of nappies. In the old days you never saw a plod around here. We used to take care of our own, and if anyone needed sorting out, we'd be the ones to do it.'

Eddie knew his father had been one of the lads too, but when ill health had forced him to retire far too early, he'd handed the stall over to him. His mother had always dreamed of living by the sea, and so they had moved to Brighton. Eddie hadn't been to see them for a while, but next time he took a trip he'd take Lucy and Clive along to meet them.

'John, wake up,' Emily said as she tried to rouse her grandson, surprised that the lad had managed to sleep for most of the day. 'We're going to see your mum soon.'

John rolled over to face the wall.

'Come on, John,' Emily urged.

'I'm not going,' John mumbled.

'Not going!' she parroted. 'Why not?'

John suddenly sat up and like a volcano erupting, he yelled, 'I can't stand this any more. I can't stand to see Mum like that. I've worked it out that she must have told that man where to find Kevin, but I don't care! I'm glad he's dead! This was all his fault and ... and I hate him!'

Emily saw that John was shaking with anger and sat on the bed, 'Darling, you've been through so much and no wonder you're upset.'

'Please, Gran, just leave me alone.'

'It might help if we talk about it.'

'No,' was the short reply.

'John, hate can eat you up inside. Don't let it do

that to you, darling. I know it isn't easy, but try instead to forgive.'

'Never! And what about my other gran? Her cottage is gone and when they let her out she'll have nowhere to live.'

'Oh, John...' Emily said sadly.

'I don't even know how she is!'

'Perhaps we can find out. I'll have a word with Derek,' she said, sadly leaving John's room, but as they weren't relatives she felt it would be impossible.

Derek was in the sitting room and when Emily walked in she said, 'John's in a dreadful state. He's been through so much and he's still worried about Dolly. He's finding it hard to see Pearl so badly injured and he doesn't want to visit her this time.'

'I'll try to find out how Dolly is,' Derek said, 'but John's coming with us to see Pearl whether he likes it or not.'

'I don't know, Derek, maybe it would be best to let him stay here.'

'I'm not leaving him on his own.'

'If he doesn't want to go, we can't drag him there. Look, you go to see Pearl. I'll stay with John.'

'No, Emily, that would mean leaving both of you unprotected.'

Derek went to the telephone and when he got through he spoke to someone for a long time, his expression sombre as he replaced the receiver. 'All they would tell me is that Dolly is unresponsive and unlikely to be released for some time yet.'

'Could we take John to see her?'

'They advised against it. Now I'll tell John what they said, and also that I want him up, dressed and ready to go to see his mother,' Derek said before he strode from the room.

Emily was worried about John's reaction, but only a short while later Derek returned to say, 'He's getting ready.'

'Is he all right?'

'He wasn't happy to hear that he can't visit Dolly, but there's nothing else I can do. I've told him he's got to come with us. I'm not letting him out of my sight until Vincent Chase is under lock and key.'

'Derek, are you sure you're not being overprotective?'

'I'm doing all I can to keep John safe. Chase tried to kill him and as he's Kevin's son, he might try again.'

Emily hung her head. Like Lucy, she felt that Vincent Chase was unlikely to show his face again around here, but Derek wasn't prepared to take that chance. She couldn't blame him, but when John came into the room Emily saw that he looked awful and she feared for his mental state.

Chapter Forty-Eight

Lucy opened the shop on Thursday morning, though it was hard to put on a cheerful face when she thought about Pearl. There were still no signs of improvement, and now John was in such poor shape that he was totally uncommunicative. She sensed that Derek was close to the end of his tether too, and poor Emily – lines had appeared on her face, and though she was already slim, the weight was dropping off her. Yet despite this Emily was happy to take on the washing, ironing and cooking now, relieved if anything to have something to keep her occupied when she wasn't at the hospital.

Lucy looked at the alarm button that Derek had installed close to the till. While she understood his caution, she felt it was unnecessary. Kevin Dolby was dead now and surely that meant Vincent Chase had the revenge he'd sought?

When a customer came in, Lucy painted a smile on her face, and by the time another two hours had passed, she was pleased with the takings.

'Nora's been cleaning like a beaver,' Emily said at midday. 'Now she wants to help you. Is that all right, Lucy?'

'Of course it is,' she agreed.

'It'll only be for an hour and then we'll be going to see Pearl.'

'Pearl get better now,' Nora said.

'Yes, I'm sure she will,' Lucy said reassuringly as she found a duster. It was awful to think that Pearl might never walk again, and it was hard to force brightness into her tone as she held out the cloth. 'Here you are, Nora. You can polish the counter.'

Emily went back upstairs, and soon after Nora was hard at work when the door burst open and Eddie dashed in. 'Where's Derek?'

'He's upstairs, but wait! What's going on?'

'I'll tell you later,' Eddie called as he ran past her.

Only minutes later, the sound of heavy feet clattered down the stairs, and with Derek just behind him, Eddie rushed out of the shop again.

'Now I wonder what all that's about,' Lucy said to Nora.

'I not know.'

'Me neither,' she said, but less than ten minutes later, Lucy found out.

Derek and Eddie pushed the thin, weedy-looking man ahead of them into the shop. 'Keep an eye on him while I ring CID.'

'Don't worry, Derek, he isn't going anywhere,' Eddie assured.

'What's going on?' Lucy asked.

'This bloke was showing a photograph of a woman around, and asking if anyone had seen her. When I looked at it, I saw it was a publicity shot of a stripper with the name Adrianna printed at the bottom.'

'CID's on their way,' Derek told the man.

'Let 'em come. I ain't done anything and you've got no right to keep me here.'

'I doubt they'll agree,' Derek said. 'The woman you're trying to find is part of a murder enquiry, and that makes you involved in it too.'

'Murder! I don't know nuffin' about that,' he said, looking panicky. 'I was just trying to earn a few bob, that's all. The word's been put out that Vince Chase is looking for that bird, and he's willing to pay good money for any info.'

'Where is he?'

'If you're talking about Vincent Chase, I ain't got a clue. As I said, the word was put out, it was passed on to me along with that photograph and that's all I know.'

'Why were you looking for Adrianna around here?'

'I heard that she was involved with Kevin Dolby, and he came from these parts, didn't he?'

'Yes, but it was a long time ago.'

'It was worth a shot,' the man said. 'Now I've told you all I know and I'm going.'

'No, you're not. CID will still want to talk to you,' Derek said. 'Whoever passed the word on to you might lead them back to Chase.'

'He was just a face and I don't know his name.'

'You're still going to talk to them,' Derek insisted.

When Riley and Shaw turned up Derek took them to one side and repeated what the man had told him. 'I hope it's a lead?' he added.

Riley walked over and gripped the man's arm, saying firmly, 'You're coming back to the station with us.'

'I know my rights. I don't have to come with you, and you can't hold me without charging me with something.'

'How about resisting arrest?'

'I'm not resisting.'

'So you say, but who's going to believe you?'

'Bastards,' the man murmured, but he went without further argument.

'Derek, do you think they'll get anything else out of him?' Eddie asked as the shop door closed.

'I don't know, but let's hope so. As long as Vincent Chase is on the loose, John's in danger.'

'I hope they find him, lock him up and throw away the key,' Lucy said.

'Yeah, me too,' Eddie agreed as he went over to give Lucy a swift kiss. 'I'd best get back to my stall, but I'll see you later.'

'Thanks, Eddie,' Derek said. 'I owe you one.'

'Don't be daft. Anyone would have done the same.'

As Eddie left, Derek's shoulders slumped. Even if Riley and Shaw managed to get any information that would lead them to Vincent Chase, he knew they had nothing to hold him on.

'Derek, are you all right?' Lucy asked.

'Yes, yes, I'm fine,' he lied. 'I'll go back upstairs now.'

As he tramped through to the back, Derek was thinking that their lives had been fine until Kevin Dolby had come back on the scene. Although he was dead now, Derek felt that everything was falling apart thanks to him. It may have been Vincent Chase's hand on the trigger of the gun that shot Pearl, but it might as well have been Kevin's.

Derek had heard something about not thinking ill of the dead, but when it came to Kevin Dolby he was finding it impossible. Now Bernie, he had thought well of him – still did – and maybe it was just as well that the poor sod hadn't lived to see the havoc his son had caused. Bernie had been very fond of Pearl and it would have broken his heart to see her lying unable to move her lower body, let alone witnessing the state John was in.

341

'You're better off out of it, Bernie,' Derek said, but then realised that if such a thing was possible, he was talking to a ghost.

Smiling wryly now, Derek climbed the stairs, but on the way up he found himself still talking to Bernie. 'I don't know where you are, mate, but if there's a heaven and you're in it, can you ask the governor to do something for Pearl?'

Chapter Forty-Nine

Tim arrived on Saturday morning and he was shocked to the core when he saw Emily. She looked dreadful and he took her into his arms, murmuring, 'Darling, you look so tired.'

She clung to him. 'I'm so worried about Pearl and I'm not sleeping very well. There's John too. He ... he hardly comes out of his room now.'

'That can't be good for him. If you ask me he needs something to take his mind off things for a while.'

'I don't think anything can do that. Too much has happened in too short a time and it isn't helping that he can't go out unless Derek is with him.'

'The poor lad must feel like a prisoner.'

'Hello, Tim,' Derek said as he came into the room.

'Hello, Derek, it's good to see you,' Tim replied.

'I'll make us all a drink,' Emily said and went to the kitchen.

Tim took a seat, wanting to help. He spoke to Derek. 'Emily has just told me about John and I wonder if you'd mind if I make a suggestion?'

'Go ahead.'

'I think it might help if I take the lad out, maybe to a park where he could take a few photographs. It might rekindle his interest and it would be something to occupy his mind.'

'I don't know, Tim. I'd have to come with you and I can't miss visiting hours at the hospital.'

'I'm sure we can work around that. Think about it, Derek – other than when John goes with you to see Pearl, he doesn't get out. He must feel dreadfully cooped up.'

Derek ran a hand over his face. 'Bloody hell, I've been so intent on keeping him safe that I haven't given his feelings a thought.'

'It's perfectly understandable. You're worried about Pearl and you're also trying to protect John. I can't imagine the strain you are under, but while I'm here, if there's anything I can do, please don't hesitate to ask.'

'You already have, Tim. You've woken me up to how John must be feeling... And yes, let's do something about it.'

They decided on Wimbledon Common, and though after visiting Pearl they all left the hospital decidedly subdued, John did begin to brighten when Tim gave him a few more tips on taking photographs.

'You were coming on so well, and I doubt I can teach you much, but here, try this larger zoom lens. I don't use it much so you can hang onto it.'

343

When John attached it to the camera and tried it out, he smiled. 'It's great. Thanks, Tim.'

From then on John became absorbed, and Nora was watching him, but Emily saw that Derek hadn't relaxed as his eyes constantly scanned for any sign of danger. She had noticed that when driving too, he was always looking in the rearview mirror. It affected her nerves, but as there were five of them she and Tim had followed in his car and she had been able to almost enjoy the drive.

The common seemed vast, and as Emily looked around there was hardly a soul to be seen. Now that it was mid-October, the trees in the distance were showing signs of turning and the landscape looked untouched. Emily felt a sudden longing for Winchester. She loved the autumnal colours of the countryside, walks in the woods with Tim, and though he was here now, she missed their shared breakfasts and evenings together.

'Are you all right, darling?' Tim asked as he came to her side. 'You look miles away.'

'I was just thinking about how much I miss you.'

'I miss you too.'

'Tim, I can't come back to Winchester until I know that Pearl is going to be all right.'

'I know, and I understand.'

Emily saw that the others were a little distance away.

She had been unable to voice her fears to any of them, but she felt she could confide in Tim. 'What if Pearl doesn't get better? What if she's never able to walk again?'

'Darling, she was badly injured and needs time

344

to heal. It's early days and I don't think you need to worry about that yet. For now, just take one day at a time and I'm sure there'll be better news soon.'

Emily clung to Tim's hand, drawing strength from his words. Pearl was going to get better. She *had* to believe that.

Derek was relieved that the trip to Wimbledon Common had done some good. When they returned to Battersea John didn't go to his room, remaining with them in the living room instead, and when Emily cooked dinner, he ate everything that was put in front of him.

The conversation was all about photography, and as most of it went over his head, Derek allowed his mind to drift. He would suggest a similar trip tomorrow, but he'd have to remain vigilant. He knew the others thought he was being overprotective, but if anything happened to John, Pearl would never forgive him. While he had been knocked unconscious and unable to do anything, she had risked her life to save her son.

Derek glanced at his watch. 'We should get ready to visit Pearl again.'

'Pearl get better,' Nora said.

'Yes, of course she will,' Emily assured. 'Now go and have a wash, there's a good girl.'

Derek wanted so much to believe that Emily was right about Pearl. It was all he had to cling to, but deep down he was beginning to fear the worst.

Pearl's condition remained unchanged and

though Derek woke up in a low mood the next morning, he did his best to hide it. Somehow, despite his doubts about Pearl's recovery, he had to present a strong front for John. It was a chilly but dry day, and he decided that they'd go out again after visiting Pearl, perhaps take a drive to the outskirts of London for a walk by the Thames.

They had just finished breakfast when there was a ring on the doorbell. It was Derek who went to answer it. 'Gran!' he exclaimed. 'What are you doing here?'

Connie Lewis was straight-faced, her answer clipped. 'You're all right then?'

'Yes, I'm fine.'

'I may be in a home, but most of the staff are locals and gossip still reaches me. It's just as well too, because you haven't bothered to visit me, or to let me know that you're all right.'

'John's in danger and I can't leave him on his own. I should have got a message to you, but with so much on my plate, I'm sorry, I didn't give it a thought.'

'Yeah, that's me. Out of sight and out of mind.'

'Gran, that isn't true. I'd have come when I could, but how did you get here?'

'As I can't walk far, how do you think? I got a taxi.'

Derek didn't know what to do. He didn't want his gran to say anything that might upset John, or Emily, but he could hardly leave her standing outside.

'Come in, but please be careful what you say. With Pearl in hospital both John and her mother are in a bit of a state.'

346

'I don't need you to tell me how to behave,' she snapped.

Derek didn't need this and agitatedly ran his fingers through his hair. Perhaps his gran saw something on his face, he didn't know, but her tone softened and she laid gnarled fingers on his arm. 'I only came to see you to put my mind at rest. I told the taxi to wait, and now I'll go back to the home.'

'Gran, there's no need to rush off. At least come upstairs and have a cup of tea or something.'

'No thanks.'

Derek tried again to persuade his gran to stay for a while, but she wouldn't have it, so he went outside to help her climb into the taxi. She managed it with difficulty and he was touched that she had come to see if he was all right.

However, as Derek watched the taxi drive away he was struck by a thought. His gran hadn't asked him how Pearl was.

Chapter Fifty

Riley and Shaw came back to see Derek the following week. When he opened the door to them early on Tuesday morning, both men were smiling.

'We've got him, Mr Lewis,' Riley said. 'We apprehended Vincent Chase in a private clinic where he was waiting to have plastic surgery. He's in custody, charged with murder and shooting with intent to kill.'

Derek didn't return their smiles. He knew it was pointless to build up his hopes and said, 'You might have him in custody, but for how long? None of us saw him, and without proof you won't be able to hold him.'

'You're wrong there, Mr Lewis. We have sufficient evidence to take the case to trial and until then he'll be remanded in custody without a hope in hell of getting bail.'

'I don't understand. What evidence?'

'That man you apprehended turned out to be very useful. What he was able to tell us led us to another man and a link in a chain that eventually led us to Vincent Chase's accomplice.'

'What, the one who was here with him?'

'Yes, Barry Rawlingstrum, a youngster who fortunately for us is new to the game. He's a small-timer who had only just started to work for Vincent Chase. When he thought he was going to cop the lot, to go down for murder, he soon gave us Vincent Chase.'

'What made him think that?'

'Let's just say he thought we had enough on him.'

'I see,' Derek murmured, still unable to believe that it was really over. 'Do you really think this Rawlingstrum will give evidence against Chase at the trial?'

'When we pulled Chase in, there was an unfortunate incident when the two passed each other in the corridor. Of course it shouldn't have happened, but when Rawlingstrum saw that Chase had spotted him, he soon worked out that it would be safer for him if his boss went down.'

'The incident sounds more fortunate than unfortunate to me and a clever tactic.'

'Tactic!' said Riley. 'I don't know what you mean, sir.'

Shaw was smiling faintly and Derek said, 'Look, as far as I'm concerned I'm just grateful that Chase is in custody. I can't thank you enough and at least my family can get back to some semblance of normality now.'

'How is your wife, sir?' Shaw asked.

'It's been two weeks, but there's still no change.'

'I'm sorry to hear that.'

'Yes, I am too,' Riley said, 'but it was a severe injury and I don't think you can expect a lot of improvement in two weeks. Don't give up hope, Mr Lewis. We'll leave you in peace now and though it may not be for some time yet, we'll let you know the date of the trial.'

'Thank you,' Derek said, surprised at this hard-faced man's sensitivity. He showed them out, and then went upstairs with a smile of relief on his face.

Emily was sitting at the dining table with John, spreading butter on her toast when Derek walked into the room.

'Who was that at the door?' she asked.

'It was those blokes from CID. They came to tell me that Vincent Chase is in custody.'

'Oh, that's wonderful,' Emily enthused.

'Yes, it is. John, do you realise what this means?'

'No, but I'm glad they've caught him.'

'It means that you're safe. You can go out when

you like now, and even go back to school.'

'I don't want to go back yet,' John protested, 'not till I know that Mum's going to be all right.'

'You can't stay off school indefinitely.'

'Just for the rest of this week then,' he said hopefully.

'John,' said Emily. 'Your education is important.'

'I wouldn't be able to concentrate on the lessons.'

'Nevertheless, you've already had about two weeks off and I think it's time you went back,' she insisted.

John turned away from her, appealing to Derek, 'Dad, can't it wait until Monday?'

'Yes, all right, but when Monday comes round I don't want any arguments. You're going back to school then and that's final.'

'Thanks, Dad.'

Emily didn't agree with Derek. She felt that returning to school would occupy John's mind and give him less time to fret about Pearl. However, not wanting to interfere, she said nothing.

'Lucy will be here soon,' Derek said. 'Once she's opened the shop I think I'll take a walk around the market to pass on the good news.'

'I'll take that roll of film I took on Sunday to be developed,' John said. 'It feels funny that I can just go out when I want to now.'

'Within reason,' Derek said. 'For instance, I want you here when it's time to visit your mother.'

John said he would be, while Emily was thinking how glad she was that Vincent Chase was now in custody. She hoped that more good news would follow – that Pearl would show some sign, however small, that she was going to recover.

John was the last one downstairs as they left to visit the hospital later that day. He was pleased that he could go out again, that he wasn't confined to the flat, but he wasn't looking forward to going back to school. He knew what it was like around here, how people gossiped, and everyone in his class would have heard what had happened.

They all said goodbye to Lucy and she called, 'Give my love to Pearl.'

When they got into the car, he sat in the back with Nora while his gran got into the front passenger seat. Nora said, 'Pearl get better, Johnny.'

'I hope so,' he replied.

When they arrived at the hospital and walked to the intensive care unit, the ward sister saw them and hurried out of her office, her face sombre. John's heart began to thump with fear and he felt his gran's trembling hand clutch his.

'I know I've always insisted on only two visitors at a time,' the sister said, 'but on this occasion I think you should all go in together.'

'Why? What's wrong?' Derek asked.

'Go in, Mr Lewis,' she said indicating the door into the unit. 'Your wife is waiting to see you. To see you all.'

With that she walked back into her office and sensing that the others were as worried as he was, John kept a tight hold of his gran's hand as they stepped inside.

Derek walked slowly up to Pearl's bed, fighting to hold himself together, then caught his breath when he noticed that she was sitting up.

'Hello, it's about time you all got here,' Pearl said, smiling.

'Pearl!' Emily cried joyfully. 'You look so much better.'

'I am, and look,' she said, pulling the covers to one side to reveal her toes.

Derek gasped when he saw Pearl wriggle them, and John dashed forward, crying, 'Mum! Oh, Mum!'

'Hello, darling,' she said, stretching up her arms to hug him.

'See, told you Pearl get better,' Nora said.

'Nora, you're amazing,' Emily said. 'We thought you were asking a question, not stating a fact. How did you know?'

Nora just shrugged, and went to stand at the foot of Pearl's bed, while Emily moved to the other side. When Pearl let John go, she took her daughter's hand. 'Oh, darling, this is wonderful.'

'John, can I get a look in now?' Derek asked.

'Yes, sorry, Dad,' he said, swopping places.

Derek leaned over Pearl and kissed her, so happy that he felt he was going to burst. 'I can't believe this. There wasn't any change when we came to see you yesterday. When did this happen?'

'I felt a tingly feeling not long after you left. The doctor came to examine me, and I felt it when he tested my legs with a needle again.'

'Why didn't you ring me?'

'I didn't want to build up your hopes, but when I woke up this morning more feeling had returned, so much so that I was taken off the medication. It's wonderful to be able to think clearly again, to move again,' she said, her eyes bright as her smile encompassed them all.

When Pearl went on to say the doctor had told her she would make a full recovery, the visit passed in a haze of happiness for Derek. He saw the joy on Emily's face echoed on John's, and Nora too seemed to be grinning the whole time. None of them spoke of what had happened that dreadful night when Pearl had been shot. It could wait for now, and when the ward sister appeared, Derek said dryly, 'That wasn't funny, Sister. You frightened the life out of us.'

'It wasn't my idea, Mr Lewis. Your wife wanted to surprise you.'

'But you looked so serious,' Emily said. 'As though something dreadful had happened.'

'Sorry, I didn't want to give the game away,' she said. 'Now I'm afraid visiting time is over.'

Derek found the time had passed so quickly, but they would return that evening. They all said their goodbyes, and for the first time left the ward with broad smiles on their faces.

Chapter Fifty-One

John's freedom turned out to be short-lived. It must have been Vincent Chase's arrest that triggered it, and the next morning the national newspapers broke the story. Suddenly there were reporters hanging around the shop, pouncing on them when they went outside.

Derek read the newspaper reports, finding that some were pretty accurate, but others sensationalised.

'Listen to this headline,' he said to Emily. '"Vincent Chase, a notorious nightclub owner, charged with murder." It goes on to say: "The revenge killing of Kevin Dolby, a man who had served thirteen years in prison for robbery with violence, involved an exotic dancer, known only by the name of Adrianna. In his attempt to find this woman, Vincent Chase questioned then shot Dolby's ex-wife, who remains in hospital, mortally wounded."'

'At least they've got some of their facts straight,' Emily commented. 'Though Pearl is going to be fine now.'

Derek picked up another paper. 'This one describes what happened here as a night of carnage. How did they get hold of this rubbish? It's nearly all pure fiction. I hate it that our names are all over the newspapers.'

'Someone from this area must have spoken to a reporter and what they didn't know, they invented. It'll pass, Derek. As soon as another story hits the headlines it'll be old news.'

'In the meantime they're after us as soon as we show our faces. Lucy has had to close the shop to keep the hacks at bay.'

'As long as we can get to the hospital to see Pearl, that's all that matters,' Emily said.

A thought struck Derek. 'Emily! What if Pearl gets hold of a newspaper? We haven't talked to

354

her about that night, or told her about Kevin's death.'

'Ring the ward sister. Ask her to keep them away from Pearl and warn her that reporters might try to get in to see her.'

'Yes, I'll do that now,' he said, hurrying to the telephone and hoping that he wasn't too late.

'Well, what did she say?' Emily asked as soon as he replaced the receiver.

'She said she'd do her best and that only relatives will be allowed in to see Pearl,' he said as he went to look out of the window. A few reporters were still hanging around, cameras at the ready. 'I'll be glad when they give up and our lives can get back to normal.'

Yet in truth, Derek wondered if their lives could ever be the same again.

Two other men and a woman, all in different locations, were reading the newspapers.

One man was partly relieved that Kevin was dead, yet sad too. Rupert laid down his paper and stood up to look out of the window of his hotel room in Cornwall. The sea view had been pleasant in the summer, but now looked grey and bleak, as bleak as his mood as he decided to pack. He could go home now, but the house would feel empty now. Kevin had used him, hurt him, made a fool of him, yet despite this, Rupert had loved him.

As he folded shirts to put into his case, Kevin's handsome face floated into his mind. The newspapers had written about a girl called Adrianna, and it was obvious that she was the reason for

Kevin's betrayal. She hadn't been found, but as far as he was concerned, ultimately she had caused Kevin's death. Rupert hoped that wherever she was, Adrianna wasn't happy, that she was suffering in some unspeakable way.

Stupid, you're so stupid, he told himself. Adrianna had been Vincent Chase's tart, then Kevin's, and Rupert suspected that girls like that would always fall on their feet.

As he left the hotel Rupert was unaware that in another place, distant from Cornwall, another man was in a state of shock as he read the newspapers, though he had no interest in Adrianna. His concerns lay elsewhere and regardless of the consequences he was packing hastily, desperate to pay his bill and leave.

Adrianna wasn't suffering. She had made it across to France, and thanks to a rather nice-looking and well-preserved older man on board who had a car on the ferry, she had been driven on an onward journey to Spain. The further away from England the better, she had thought, while sitting happily beside him in his leather-seated Jaguar. Obviously besotted, he had swallowed her story about having her luggage stolen and willingly forked out a nice bit of money before they left France on several lovely new outfits.

She had felt like a million dollars in her designer suits, and seen the desire in his eyes. However, on both occasions when they had stopped overnight, she had insisted on separate rooms.

Never again would a man use her; instead she'd use them, and as this one had told her that his

356

wife had died, before going on to brag about his villa overlooking the sea on the Costa Blanca, he would do until she had the means to ditch him.

For now though, she was sitting on the terrace of his luxurious villa. It was now October, but it was lovely and warm in Spain.

'Katerina, would you like to go out for lunch, my dear?' asked Laurence.

'That would be nice,' she purred, not quite used to the new name she had chosen. With her dark, exotic looks she was now a woman of Russian descent, and as Laurence had believed her story, she was sure that others would too.

Every time they went out, Adrianna, now Katerina, noted how Laurence took her arm to lead her into a restaurant as though his trophy. She was putting up with it for now, but all the time she was taking stock, constantly on the lookout for a club that might have an opening for an exotic dancer.

When her chance came she'd take it, but in the meantime it was nice to be pampered, to have this idiot under her control, one who jumped at her every wish. Laurence was a far cry from Vincent Chase, a weakling really, and of course he was an old fool who was nothing like Kevin.

The image of Kevin as he was engulfed by flames haunted her at times, but with eyes set on the future, she forced the horrific memory away. She wanted to own her own club, to be the boss, and as Laurence smiled at her, she decided there could be a short cut. Surely she could get him to bankroll her? He was soft, and daft enough to do it without any strings attached.

Connie Lewis was reading one of the newspapers that had sensationalised the story and she was shocked to the core. She'd heard through the gossip that someone had broken in and she had been to see Derek, but nobody told her it had been as bad as this. The report described horrific violence, torture, and near death.

Connie's mind was all over the place and she was barely aware of a nicely dressed young man until he paused to point at her newspaper. 'I've just been to see my gran and she was reading that too. It's shocking what happened to that family.'

'You don't know the half of it,' Connie said.

'My gran knows Derek Lewis.'

'Oh, you must be talking about Ann. Yes, she used to live in the same street as me. Derek's my grandson.'

'Is he? Gosh, it's awful what happened to him.'

'He was fine before he married Pearl. She's ruined his life.'

'Really?' he said, taking a seat opposite her.

Connie nodded and with the young man looking at her so sympathetically she poured it all out, starting with the day Derek had first brought Pearl home to meet her.

Later that day, Derek did his best to shield Emily, John and Nora as they dashed for his car. He ignored a couple of reporters, saying nothing when they called out questions, but a camera flashed and he wanted to rip it from the man's hands. At last they were safely inside and driving away.

When they arrived at the hospital, Derek and

Emily went in first to see Pearl. Having discussed when to tell her about Kevin, they'd decided to do it sooner rather than later. They didn't want Pearl to read or hear about it from anyone else now that newspapers had printed the story.

'Hello, gorgeous,' Derek said, kissing her and taking a seat by the bed.

'Hello to you too.'

Emily had gone to the other side of the bed, and she took Pearl's hand. 'How do you feel? You look even better today.'

'I'm fine. I've had another X-ray and I think the doctor is going to let me get up tomorrow.'

Emily beamed. 'Oh, that's wonderful.'

Derek took a deep breath before saying, 'John is itching to come in to see you, but before he does, there's something you need to know.'

Pearl seemed to tense and asked, 'Is it about that night?'

'Sort of, though it's really about what happened later.'

'I've been dreading this since I came off the medication. But go on,' Pearl said.

'The men who broke in left us tied up and then drove to Dolly's cottage. They set it on fire and Kevin didn't get out in time. He died in the flames, Pearl.'

'No! Oh no!' she cried. 'The man with the gun threatened to kill you if I didn't tell him where to find Kevin. He ... he was aiming it at you and so ... so I told him. It's my fault ... my fault that Kevin died.'

'No, Pearl, it isn't. That man was Vincent Chase and he gave you no choice. If it wasn't for what

359

Kevin had done to him, he wouldn't have broken into our flat and you wouldn't have been shot. Kevin had torched Chase's place and run off with his girlfriend. Chase was looking for him and his search led to us.'

'But John must blame me for Kevin's death.'

'No, darling, of course he doesn't,' Emily said. 'He holds Kevin responsible for what happened to you.'

'Mum, he's too young to cope with all this.'

'It's been hard for him, but given time I'm sure he'll be able to come to terms with it all. Now we know that you're going to fully recover, it gave us such a boost, and it's made a huge difference to John's state of mind.'

Pearl hung her head for a moment, but then said, 'It's been like reliving a nightmare, but I remember most of what happened now. That man was going to shoot John and I tried to stop him, but after that it's all a blank.'

'You took the bullet,' Derek said.

'Yes, I realise that now, but I was so frightened for John,' Pearl cried, obviously distressed by the memories.

Emily squeezed her hand. 'Of course you were, but I don't think it helps to dwell on what happened that night. It's over now. It's time for you all to put it behind you and look to the future. There's my wedding, don't forget, and the sooner you get out of here the better,' she said brightly. 'You've still got your outfit to buy, let alone your hat.'

'Oh, Mum, you and hats,' Pearl said, smiling at last.

Derek could have hugged Emily and he felt a surge of optimism. Emily was right. It was over now and with Vincent Chase behind bars, they could get on with their lives. They could look to the future and all he wanted was to make it a happy one for all of them. He stood up, leaned forward to kiss Pearl and said, 'I'll send John in.'

'I'll come with you. I think it would be nice for John to have his mother to himself for a while,' Emily said before kissing Pearl on the cheek.

The visit turned out to be a turning point for all of them. When John returned to the waiting room, Emily could see he'd been crying, but his eyes looked brighter. When Nora went in to see Pearl with Derek, Emily was left alone with John.

'Are you all right, darling?' she asked.

'I feel so much better, Gran. I had a long chat with Mum and we talked about Kevin. She said he wouldn't have wanted to put my life, or hers, in danger ... that he couldn't have foreseen his actions would rebound on us.'

After what Pearl had been through, she could have harboured hate and bitterness, but instead she had an innate wisdom, a forgiving heart and Emily felt a surge of love and pride.

'Yes, your mum's right. Sometimes we all do things without thinking about the consequences.'

'I know Kevin wasn't a good man, but as Mum said, he was still my father. She said with nobody else to do it, we should arrange his ... his funeral, and my granddad's too.'

'Yes, I think that's a nice idea,' Emily said, sure that, thanks to Pearl's guidance, John was now on the road to recovery.

When Nora returned, Emily went back in to see Pearl, but shortly after, visiting time was over and they all trooped back to Derek's car. Emily climbed in, smiling, once again feeling that the worst was over and soon she'd be able to return to Winchester.

None of them noticed the man standing in the shadows, watching them intently from under the brim of a trilby hat. He couldn't approach them yet, it was too risky. His nerves jangled at what he soon intended to do.

As the car drove away the man turned and walked through the doors into the hospital where he followed the signs until he reached the unit.

'Excuse me,' he said to a nurse coming out of the ward. 'Could you tell me if Mrs Pearl Lewis is still in intensive care, and if so, how she is?'

The ward sister approached them and said stiffly, 'I'll deal with this, Nurse Roberts.'

'Yes, Sister,' the nurse said, hurrying away.

The man turned to the rather stern-faced woman, and managed a pleasant smile. 'I'm sorry to trouble you. I'm making enquires about Mrs Pearl Lewis.'

'Are you a relative?'

'Err ... no.'

'Then who are you?'

'Just ... err ... a friend of the family.'

'Your name?'

'Why do you want to know?'

'If you're a friend of the family, Mr Lewis will be able to confirm that.'

362

'There's no need to bother him,' he said hurriedly.

'I thought so. You're a reporter and if you don't leave, I'll call security.'

'All right, I'm going,' the man said, defeated, as he headed for the exit.

Chapter Fifty-Two

Derek couldn't believe it. Yesterday he'd felt optimistic that the future was going to be brighter, but now he felt as though he'd been kicked in the guts.

'How could you?' he growled when he arrived at the nursing home before ten in the morning and slapped the local newspaper down in front of his gran. 'Don't you think Pearl's been through enough without you making her sound like a money-grabbing tart!'

'I didn't know he was a reporter! He lied to me, said he was visiting his grandmother and I fell for it. Anyway,' Connie bristled, 'I was only telling the truth.'

'This isn't the truth! It's garbage.'

'No it isn't, Derek. How many times have I tried to get it into your head that Pearl twisted you round her little finger? She had you waiting in the wings in case her scheme to get pregnant by Kevin Dolby didn't work.'

'Gran, it wasn't like that. When Pearl came to live in Battersea she was a lonely, innocent sixteen-year-old who had spent her childhood in an orphanage. She was scared of her own shadow and I took her under my wing, but Kevin Dolby saw her as easy prey and she didn't stand a chance. He was a good-looking bloke who had a way with women and she fell for it, for him, only to find herself used and pregnant.'

'Yes, *unmarried* and pregnant. That makes her a tart, just like your mother!'

Derek's eyes narrowed. 'So this is what it's all about. We're getting to the bottom of it now. My mother, *your* daughter, was unmarried and pregnant with me. You were ashamed of her, but she died before you could pour out all your vitriol. As she isn't here to suffer for it, you've been taking all your anger and bitterness out on Pearl.'

'That's rubbish,' Connie snapped. 'Pearl dropped you for Kevin, but when he went to prison for robbery she came after you again and like a mug you married her. She took you away from me and I was left on my own to end up in this dump.'

'Pearl didn't chase after me. I've told you before, I was the one doing the running and when she agreed to marry me I *chose* to live in Winchester, though I came to see you as often as I could. As for ending up here, you like it, but you'd twist anything to blame Pearl and to justify what you told that reporter.'

'I don't need to justify anything,' Connie spat. 'Pearl's no good, but you're too blind to see it.'

'I've had it, Gran. You've gone too far this time and don't expect to see me again,' Derek said before he turned and stormed away. He had put up with his gran's bigotry for years but this was the final straw.

After reading the local newspaper, Emily was reeling that morning too, unable to believe that Derek's gran had said such awful things about Pearl. It was grossly unfair, a dreadful misinterpretation of the truth, and she wished Derek hadn't stopped her from going with him when he went to see Connie Lewis. Emily was usually an even-tempered, mild woman, but now she was boiling with anger, frustrated that she couldn't give the woman a piece of her mind.

If Pearl read it she'd be so shocked and hurt that it could set back her recovery. Somehow they had to prevent that from happening and there was John too. He was still in bed and hadn't seen the paper, but the gossip would be rife and Emily dreaded what he would have to face in school on Monday. Unable to contain her frustration Emily poured her heart out to Lucy.

'I know,' Lucy said when Emily was spent. 'I feel the same as you. Pearl isn't anything like that and it's so unfair. You're right, everyone will be talking about her now, but don't you worry, if anyone says anything to me, I'll put them straight.'

'Put who straight?' Derek asked as he walked into the room.

'Anyone who says a word against Pearl,' Lucy told him.

'Derek, you're back,' Emily said. 'Did you speak to your grandmother?'

'Yes, but I was wasting my breath. She's a vindictive old woman who prefers her own

365

twisted version of events.'

'We could threaten legal action against the newspaper unless they print a retraction,' Emily suggested.

'I doubt that would work,' Derek said as he raked his fingers through his hair in agitation. 'The reporter will say he got the story from a legitimate source, a relative of the family, and anyway, it's too late now. The damage has already been done.'

'I'd best get on,' Lucy said abruptly and left the room with an intent look on her face that neither Emily nor Derek noticed.

Lucy spotted a reporter as soon as she stepped outside. 'Can I have a word?' she said, walking up to him.

He looked surprised, but there was avarice in his eyes too as he said, 'A word about what?'

'The story about Pearl Lewis; the one that appeared in the local paper this morning.'

'It's got nothing to do with me. I work for the nationals, not some local rag.'

'Good. There's a café just down the road, we can chat in there.'

Lucy refused to say anything until they arrived, but when they had cups of dark, strong tea in front of them, she finally spoke. 'That local paper has got it all wrong. I work for Pearl Lewis and I can tell you she's a lovely woman. I want to put the record straight and that's why I'm talking to you.'

The reporter shrugged. 'Sorry, I'm not interested. People want to read about sinners, not saints. Now take that Adrianna, what do you know about her?'

'Nothing. I never met her.'

'What about the Lewises? Someone in that family must know something about her and that's the angle I'm looking for.'

'They don't,' Lucy said quickly.

'I'm not so sure about that. The rest of the strippers at Chase's club won't open up until he's convicted, but in the meantime the story is still hot. If you can tell me anything about Adrianna, or point me in the direction of someone who can, I might be able to make it worth your while.'

'I can't, and I only spoke to you because I thought you'd be interested in the truth about Pearl Lewis.'

'Sorry, love, but she's old news now.'

Lucy left her tea untouched and the reporter sitting there, sad that she had failed as she returned to work. It was so unfair that Pearl had been torn to shreds by that wicked old lady, and she hoped that Connie Lewis would live to regret it.

'Emily, what do you think I should do?' Derek asked. 'John isn't interested in newspapers so I doubt he'll read the local, but the article is sure to arouse a lot of gossip and it might reach him.'

'I thought the same and it might be best to forewarn him.'

'He doesn't know what Pearl went through in the past. He knows about Kevin, of course, but she kept the rest away from him.'

'It would be better to hear it from us, before someone tells him your grandmother's version of

367

events,' Emily said, but then as though hearing someone coming, she put a finger over her lips.

She was too late. John walked into the room and asked, 'What are you talking about?'

'You're up then,' Derek said. 'It's about time.'

'I'll get you some breakfast,' Emily offered.

'It's all right. I can pour myself a bowl of cereal, but I heard a little of what you were saying, something about me hearing something. What's going on, Dad?'

'Get your breakfast first and then we'll talk,' Derek said, playing for time so he could work out what he was going to say. He turned to Emily as soon as John went to the kitchen. 'I'm not sure how Pearl is going to feel about this. Maybe it should come from her.'

'That would mean telling her about the story in the local paper, and I'm hoping we can keep it from her. I think Pearl's been through enough at the moment. She's sheltered from gossip while in hospital, and hopefully it will have died down by the time she comes home.'

They both stopped talking when John returned, and he said, 'I've just got a glass of juice for now.'

Derek tried to gather his thoughts, and then said, 'There have been things said about your mother, that aren't true and…'

'What things?' John broke in. 'And who's been saying them?'

'It would help if you didn't interrupt,' Derek said irritably.

'Sorry, Dad.'

John listened without interruption this time, wide-eyed as he took it all in. Derek told him the

368

truth, refuting all his gran had said, and ending with, 'Your mother didn't set out to trap Kevin. She was shocked when she found that she was pregnant. She hadn't wanted it to happen; in fact she was so innocent she didn't even *know* it would happen. She married Kevin, you came along and she was so happy, until well, the robbery. You know the rest, that they divorced, and eventually your mum married me.'

John was quiet for while but then said, 'I used to ask you about your gran, wondered why I'd never met her, but you always managed to make excuses, said she didn't like visitors or that she wasn't well. I gave up asking in the end, but now I know it wasn't for any of those reasons. It's because she hates my mum.'

'She has no reason to, but though I've tried, she won't see sense.'

'If you ask me, Derek, your grandmother is a jealous, bitter woman who didn't want you to leave home,' Emily said.

'You may be right, but I didn't think she'd go this far.'

'John, we've told you the truth to prepare you for any gossip,' Emily said, 'and we would rather keep this from your mother.'

'If anyone says anything nasty about my mum to me, I ... I'll knock their block off.'

'Fighting doesn't solve anything,' Emily warned.

'Just point them in my direction, son, and leave it to me to put them straight,' Derek said, feeling the same as John. He knew there were those still in the area who already knew the truth, and with any luck they'd put it around, but there would be others who'd be happy to dish the dirt. This was all down to his gran and his anger mounted again. From now on, she could stew in her own juice.

'It's no good crying now,' Ann told Connie without a trace of sympathy. 'You should have known better.'

'Derek said he ... he won't be coming to see me again.'

'What did you expect?'

'I only told the truth.'

'As you see it, but your version doesn't coincide with mine.'

'Huh,' Connie sniffed. 'You don't know anything about it.'

'You're forgetting that I lived in the same street as you, and at the same time. I met Pearl a couple of times and I liked her. I also saw and heard what happened to Pearl and like a lot of other people in the area, I felt sorry for her. If you ask me, that poor girl was more sinned against than a sinner.'

'Well, I didn't ask you.'

'No, you didn't, and you never listen either,' Anne said, 'yet I'm still going to say my piece. You saw from the start how happy Derek was when he married Pearl and could have welcomed her into your family. Instead you chose to ostracise her, and you did it again recently when she came here to see you.'

'How do you know about that?'

'I'm not deaf and overheard what you said to her.'

'You nosy cow. You had no right to listen in,'

Connie snapped.

'Well I did, and after that show you were lucky that Derek still came to visit you. Now though you've gone too far, spewed your guts out to the press and I'm not surprised he won't be coming again. It serves you right.'

'Bugger off.'

'Charming, but don't worry, I've said what I had to say and I'm going.'

Connie watched Ann struggling away on arthritic hips and the echo of her words remained in her mind. Pearl sinned against! What a load of tosh, yet deep down Connie knew it was true. She also knew that she had gone too far and now wished she could turn back the clock. It was too late though, she had driven Derek away, but surely there was some way she could make amends.'

She closed her eyes, trying to think of a way, but the events of the day had exhausted her and soon Connie fell asleep.

Chapter Fifty-Three

Contrary to Emily's expectations, when they left the flat to visit Pearl, a lot of stallholders spotted them and a small crowd gathered. Eddie White was the first to speak as he brandished the local paper. 'Don't worry, Derek, we know this is a load of rubbish. If you're going to see Pearl, give her my best.'

'Yeah,' said Harry. 'Mine too.'

The flower seller stuffed a bunch of chrysan-themums into Derek's hand. 'Tell Pearl these are from me and I wish her all the best too.'

'Thanks,' Derek said gruffly, looking over-whelmed, yet gratified.

They left with many more good wishes ringing in their ears, and Emily got into Derek's car feeling a lot calmer. 'Wasn't that nice?' she said.

'They're a great bunch,' Derek agreed, 'and I don't just mean the flowers.'

John looked happier too, and with Nora smiling as she hung onto the flowers, they arrived at the hospital.

'Mr Lewis, I had to get rid of a reporter yester-day,' the ward sister said when she saw them.

'He didn't get in to talk to Pearl, did he?'

'Definitely not. He said he was a friend of the family, but then refused to give me his name. He soon left when I threatened to call security.'

'Thanks, Sister.'

'There's no need to thank me. I won't have my patients upset and I also have some good news. Your wife saw the consultant this morning and he said she's well enough to leave intensive care.'

'Oh, that's wonderful,' Emily said.

'She'll be moved later today so when you come to see her this evening, you'll need to go up to the first floor. Ward Seven.'

'Thanks, Sister,' Derek said for the second time and taking the flowers from Nora they separated, Emily insisting that he and John go in first this time, while she led Nora to the waiting room.

Pearl greeted them with a smile of delight and

after being hugged and kissed she asked, 'Did Sister tell you I'm being moved?'

'Yes, and it's great news,' Derek said.

'Did she also tell you that I was able to stand up today, and with support I was allowed to take a few steps?'

'Fantastic, Mum,' John enthused.

'If I keep this up, I'll be home in no time.'

'It can't come soon enough for me,' Derek said, gripping her hand.

'Nor me,' John agreed.

Derek knew that Pearl wouldn't have been this happy if she'd seen the local paper, and felt a surge of relief. After a while he and John left her side to allow Emily and Nora in, and though Derek kept an eye out, he didn't see any sign of the reporter that the ward sister had mentioned. The bloke had been turned away yesterday, so perhaps he'd given up, but would the staff in the ward Pearl was being transferred to be so vigilant?

All too soon, after seeing Pearl again, it was time to leave and as they drove home, Emily said, 'I've had a lot of time off work, but now I know that Pearl is going to be all right I think I should return to Winchester. We spoke about it and Pearl understands.'

'Gran, do you have to go?' John asked.

'I'm afraid so, darling, but I'll come back every weekend.'

Derek knew that like John, he'd miss Emily, but he too understood that there was a limit to how much time she could take off. 'When are you leaving?'

'On Sunday morning.'

'So we've got to put up with you till then,' Derek complained.

'Yes, you jolly well have,' Emily said. 'Like it or lump it.'

'I'll like it,' he said, smiling, well aware that Emily knew he was only joking. He had longed to return to Battersea, had thought that Bessie's flat and shop had been a godsend. He had done all he could to persuade Pearl that it would be a good move and it had all started out so well. He had his stall, Pearl had refurbished the shop, and even John had eventually settled down.

Now, though, Derek wished he'd kept his mouth shut. The move to Battersea, far from a godsend, had turned into a curse. It had all gone wrong and now he wished they'd never left Winchester.

'I'm glad you all did that,' Lucy said when Eddie told her about the support they had tried to offer Derek earlier that day. It was after nine that evening and Clive was in bed, but as usual he'd demanded that Eddie tucked him in.

'Harry was the first to tell us the story was all rubbish, and a couple of the other old traders agreed with him,' Eddie said. 'It didn't take long for that to spread, and anyway, Derek's one of us so it was the least we could do. A good few of my customers, local gossips – were ready to believe it, but I gave them an earbashing.'

'They're used to your cheeky banter so I bet that gave them a shock,' Lucy said, smiling.

'Yeah, probably, and a couple of them went off in a huff. Never mind, I'll soon charm them back. After all, how can they resist this smile, and

374

who else is going to flatter them? Not their husbands, that's for sure.'

'You don't half love yourself.'

'Not true,' Eddie protested. 'It's you I love so come here and give me a kiss.'

She obliged, then said, 'Pearl's been moved from intensive care.'

'Has she? That's brilliant.'

'Yes, it is, but as I know Derek is worried about the gossip I spoke to one of those reporters today.'

'You did what?'

'All right, Eddie, don't get on your high horse. I just told him that Pearl isn't anything like that story in the local paper, but he wasn't interested. He said she's old news.'

'If that's the case, let's hope he buggers off now.'

'I don't think he will. He wants to find out about Adrianna, and though I told him that none of us knows anything about her, I don't think he believed me. He's still going to try to talk to Derek or John, even Emily.'

'He'll be wasting his time,' Eddie said. 'They won't talk to the press.'

'I know, and at least the other reporters have gone now. I'm going to ask Derek if I can open the shop again.'

'When Pearl comes home do you think she'll be up to running it?'

'She walked a few steps today, so I think so, though maybe not at first.'

'If you take it on, don't get too cosy,' Eddie said. 'When we're married you'll be giving up work, and it isn't that far off.'

'Hold on, who said I'm giving up work?'

'It stands to reason,' he said. 'You'll have me to look after you.'

'I can still work and with two lots of money coming in, we can make this place look like a palace.'

Eddie pursed his lips, but then said, 'Yeah, all right, but you'll have to give up work when a baby comes along.'

'What if I don't want any more kids?'

'Oh, Lucy, don't say that.'

'Don't look so horrified. I'm only joking and though a baby will have to wait until we're married, there's nothing to stop us getting in a bit of practice,' she said, playfully unbuttoning his shirt.

'Help! Somebody help me! This woman is trying to seduce me.'

'You daft sod,' Lucy said, but then it was Eddie who was doing the seducing and she was more than happy to let him.

The man Derek had looked out for was nowhere near the hospital. He'd taken a huge risk in going there the day before, and had scuttled back to the safety of his small room in a boarding house.

He too had read the local paper that morning and threw it aside in disgust. It told him nothing about the family now and only raked up the past – a past he was familiar with.

Unable to find out what he wanted to know, it was torture to wait, but the High Street with its market was a busy place and it wasn't the best time to make his move.

With heavy furniture and dark curtains, his

room felt oppressive and he decided to risk going for a walk. He could wander along by the Embankment, or maybe find an out-of-the-way pub.

With his mind made up, he pulled on his overcoat, the trilby hat and went downstairs. He was just about to open the street door when the landlady appeared, saying sternly, 'I see you're going out, but I must remind you that I lock up at eleven o'clock and not a minute later.'

'I know,' he said shortly and then opened the door to step out into the chilly, dark night. He wandered, barely taking in his surroundings as his mind dwelled on his problems.

Two hours later he returned, the landlady letting him in with barely a smile. He went up to his room, undressed, climbed into bed and pulled the blankets up to his chin.

He had at last come to a decision. He was going to wait until Sunday evening before making his move. There would be few people about, and with any luck he'd be able to get inside without being seen by prying eyes.

He closed his eyes, but sleep was a long time in coming. He had no idea what the consequences were going to be, prison probably, but he wasn't going to let the fear of that stop him from doing what he knew he had to do.

Chapter Fifty-Four

Saturday morning loomed cold and wet, but the weather wasn't going to stand in Connie Lewis's way. As always she had to put up with help to fasten her buttons, hating it that she was incapable now of dressing herself. She had her breakfast, porridge again, but at least it was something she could eat without aid. She could just about grip a spoon, whereas cutting up anything with a knife and fork was now beyond her.

The morning dragged, but at last she took out her hat and coat. Though the coat had larger buttons this time she still couldn't fasten them and had to resort to asking for help again.

'Mrs Lewis, you really can't go out again,' the young woman protested.

'This isn't a prison. I'll go out if I want to and you can call me a taxi.'

'You know we aren't supposed to let residents leave the premises unaccompanied. I'll get into trouble again.'

'I won't be alone. The taxi driver will be with me, and as before, I'll ask him to wait. This is an emergency. I have to visit a sick friend, but I shouldn't be more than an hour.'

'I'm not sure about this, Mrs Lewis. I should get permission from Mrs Oliver, but she isn't going to be here today.'

'Even if she was, she couldn't stop me. I'm

going out whether you like it or not. If you won't call me a taxi, I'll walk until I find one, however painful,' she said, stuffing her old-fashioned black hat onto her head.

'You can't walk in this weather. You'll be soaked in minutes.'

'Then call me a taxi.'

'All right,' she said at last, 'but it might cost me my job.'

'Not if you tell her that my grandson was with me,' Connie said slyly.

'Yes, yes, I'll do that,' she said, looking a little happier as she fastened the buttons on Connie's coat before at last going to arrange a taxi.

When they arrived at the hospital, Connie didn't ask the taxi driver to wait. It would cost the earth and she'd find another one to drive her back to the home. The building was large, and it took an effort just to walk to the enquiry desk. When told that Pearl was on the first floor, she looked around, glad to see a lift, and struggled towards it.

At last she found the ward, and though it was ten minutes before visiting hours, Connie managed to walk inside without being challenged. Pearl was in the second bed. Her joints screaming in pain now, Connie walked up to it. She was aware of the look of surprise on Pearl's face, but seeing a chair at an angle to the bed, Connie gratefully sat down.

'I'm surprised to see you here,' Pearl said, unsmiling.

'Yeah, no doubt, but I had to come. I owe you an apology, I know that now. If I could take back the things I said to that reporter, I would.'

379

Pearl frowned. 'I don't understand. What reporter?'

'Oh no! Don't tell me you haven't seen the local paper?'

'I haven't. Are you saying there's a story about me in it, one you gave them?'

'Yes,' Connie admitted, 'but I'm going to get hold of that reporter again, tell him I made it all up and they'll have to print that too.'

'There's Derek now – perhaps he'll have a copy,' Pearl said.

Connie tensed and her grandson's voice sounded harsh to her ears. 'Gran, what are you doing here?'

'I ... I came to apologise, to tell Pearl that I'm sorry about that story in the paper.'

'We've been trying to keep it from her, but now you've gone and blabbed.'

'I didn't know that,' Connie protested. 'I feel awful about it, but I'm going to try to put things right.'

'It's a bit late for that,' he snapped. 'Just get out of here, Gran.'

Connie nodded and struggled to her feet. As she did so, her eyes met those of the young lad standing beside Derek and she gasped. It was like seeing a ghost, but of course it wasn't Kevin Dolby. This must be his son.

The effort of getting here had taken its toll and Connie felt her knees giving way. The lad rushed to her side to help her, and gratefully she said, 'Thanks, love.'

'You shouldn't have said those things about my mum.'

380

'I know, and I'm sorry.'

Pearl said, 'Connie, sit down.'

'No, I want her out of here,' Derek said. 'If you'd read the paper, you would too.'

'Derek, I can guess what's in the paper and no doubt my name is mud, but nevertheless your gran looks awful. She needs to rest.'

'The mud hasn't stuck,' Derek said. 'Most people don't believe a word of it and those that do can take a jump.'

'After what we've been through, a bit of gossip is nothing. It won't bother me, and at the moment I'm more concerned about your gran,' Pearl said firmly. 'Now do sit down, Connie.'

'Th ... thanks, Pearl,' she said, unable to stay on her feet for a moment longer. She wanted to leave, hating the way Derek was looking at her, but doubted she'd make it to the end of the ward.

'Pearl, I'm going to the waiting room and out of my gran's way,' Derek said. 'I'll send your mum in.'

'I'll come with you,' John said, both leaving without sparing Connie another glance.

Connie's eyes flooded with tears and she tried to blink them away. She said nothing for a few minutes, thinking only that she had failed. She then spoke hesitantly to Pearl. 'I ... I hoped that if I came to see you first and we could make things up, that Derek would forgive me.'

'So it's Derek's forgiveness you're really seeking, not my daughter's,' came a sharp voice.

Connie looked up at the woman who had joined them. Pearl's mother was a frail woman, but there was steel in her eyes.

'Mum, please,' Pearl said, 'it doesn't matter. Whatever Connie's motives were, at least she's apologised. There's been enough unhappiness in our lives and with funerals to arrange when I come home, it isn't over yet.'

'All right, darling, against my better judgement I'll say no more,' Emily said, presenting her back to Connie as she took Pearl's hand. 'Now tell me, did you manage to walk a little further today?'

'Yes, to the end of the ward.'

'Well done! As you know, I'm going to Winchester in the morning, but I'll be back after work on Friday. Who knows, you may even be home by then.'

'That would be wonderful,' Pearl said, 'but we'll have to wait and see.'

'We feared you'd remain paralysed and I'm just overjoyed that you're able to walk again.'

Connie felt excluded from the conversation, but it began to dawn on her just how ill Pearl had been. She hadn't spared a thought to the fact that Pearl was still recovering in hospital when she had spat out her story to the reporter. 'Oh, God,' she whispered. 'I'm an awful, wicked, wicked woman.'

'Connie, what did you say?' Pearl asked.

'I said I'm a wicked old woman. I don't deserve your forgiveness, but I really am sorry, so very sorry. I ... I'll go now.'

Connie struggled to her feet, and though Pearl urged her to stay, she shook her head. It took some doing, but she managed to leave the ward and find the lift.

What Connie didn't know was that Emily had

hurried to find Derek, and that after telling him what had happened, he would come to find her. She got into the lift, her heart aching as it descended, but as she hobbled slowly across to the exit, a hand cupped her elbow.

'Come on, Gran, I'll give you a lift.'

'Derek!'

'It seems that both Pearl and my mother-in-law think I should forgive you. Now I might be prepared to argue with one woman, but not two.'

Connie looked up at her grandson. 'I really am sorry, Derek.'

'Gran, I'm not going to find it easy and it might take a bit of time, but as Pearl wants it, I'll do my best to put this all behind us. Now let's get you back to that home.'

Connie knew she didn't deserve it, but thanks to Pearl she had her grandson back. She would still tell that reporter that the story she'd told him was a load of codswallop and he'd better print it or he'd wonder what hit him.

Chapter Fifty-Five

'Don't look so nervous,' Eddie said as he drove Lucy to meet his parents on Sunday.

'You've hardly mentioned them. What are they like?' Lucy asked.

'My dad's a bit of a joker and my mum sometimes pretends to be posh, but she can't keep it up.'

'Have you told them about me – about Clive?'

'Yeah, and they're looking forward to meeting you both.'

'I'm still nervous,' Lucy said worriedly.

'Don't be, they'll love you,' Eddie assured. He'd rung to say they were coming, but they didn't yet know that he and Lucy were now engaged. The summer season was well over and Brighton was a bit bleak on this cold October day. His parents lived near Black Rock and he took a left turn into their street. 'Right, here we are. Come on, Clive, hop out.'

It was his dad who opened the door, smiling a welcome. 'Hello, sonny boy.'

'Dad, this is Lucy and her son, Clive.'

'Hello there, come on in,' he welcomed.

'It's nice to meet you, Mr White,' Lucy said shyly.

'George, call me George.'

When they walked into the living room, Eddie saw that his mother was dressed up to the nines, her dyed blonde hair pinned up on top of her head.

'Mum, this is Lucy, and her son, Clive.'

'How nice to meet you,' she said formally.

Eddie had to smile at his mum putting on the airs and graces. She was always the same, but now he knocked the wind from her sails.

'Mum, Dad, Lucy and me, we're getting married.'

'Well, stone the crows,' his mother blurted out, all traces of her posh accent instantly gone.

'Now, fancy dropping a bombshell like that without warning,' George said. 'Still, congratu-

384

lations to the pair of you. I reckon this calls for a toast, Peggy.'

'Yeah, it does, and what about you, love?' she asked Clive. 'Do you fancy a glass of lemonade?'

'Yes, please,' he said.

Eddie followed his mother into the kitchen where she said, 'Are you sure about this, Eddie? You're taking on another man's kid.'

'I'm sure, Mum. I love Lucy and Clive is part of the package. Not that I mind. He's a smashing lad.'

'When are you getting married?'

'Early next year,' he told her as they returned to the living room.

'Now then,' George said as he handed out small glasses. 'There's only a bottle of your mum's sherry but as you sprung this on us without warning, it'll have to do. Here's to the pair of you.'

Lucy began to relax when Peggy started to chat to her about the wedding, and finding a pack of cards, George played snap with Clive. It was a nice visit, and at four o'clock they left to drive back to London.

'Your mum's nice,' Lucy said. 'Your dad too.'

'They took to you and you're part of the family now.'

Lucy smiled happily and Eddie was content.

They had been to see Pearl earlier, and now Emily was going to drive back to Winchester. She came into the room, suitcase in hand, and he said, 'You're off then.'

'Yes,' she said, 'but I'll drive down again on Friday evening and stay for the weekend.'

'Did you hear that, John? We may have to put up with your gran again, but at least we'll still get our Sunday roast.'

'Very funny,' Emily said, 'but seriously, will you be able to cope with Nora?'

'Lucy's here for most of the day during the week, and that only leaves weekends when you'll be here again. We'll be fine, won't we, John?'

'Yes, I suppose so.'

'Right, then,' Emily said. 'I'll go and find Nora to say goodbye.'

'No doubt she'll be cleaning something somewhere.'

'I know, Derek. She's really is a treasure, isn't she?'

'I must admit I wasn't keen on taking her on, but I don't feel like that now. She's always going to be like a child, if a rather large one, but I've grown fond of her.'

'It's hard not to,' Emily said, then went to find Nora.

Derek sighed. 'Well, John, it's back to school for you in the morning.'

'I know.'

'Don't look so downhearted. I know your gran's leaving, but things are on the up now. Your mum's going to be fine and with any luck she'll be home soon.'

It wasn't long before Emily returned. 'I've said goodbye to Nora so would one of you carry that case to my car?'

'I'll do it,' John offered.

Derek walked across to enfold Emily in his arms. 'Bye, Emily, and all joking aside, I'm going

386

to miss you.'

As he let her go, Emily patted his cheek. 'It'll be Friday before you know it. Now come on, John,' she said brusquely, 'pick up that case and let's go.'

Derek wasn't fooled. He could tell that Emily was feeling a little emotional, so for her benefit he planted a smile on his face. 'See you soon,' he called and she managed a smile in return before leaving the room.

When John came back he too looked a bit upset, but Derek decided to snap him out of it by suggesting they go for a drive.

'I'll get my camera,' he said, perking up at the thought.

'While you do that, I'll chivy Nora into getting her coat on.'

They were soon on their way, and Derek decided to head for Epsom Downs. It wasn't too far to drive, and the area might interest John.

When they arrived on the Downs it was windy and cold, but it didn't seem to bother John as he snapped away. Nora romped around like a big kid, doing the occasional front tumble, and Derek had to smile at her antics.

He was glad he'd suggested this drive. It had lifted all their moods, and when they went to see Pearl again later, it would be with smiling faces. She was right – after all they'd been through, what his gran had done, though rotten, wouldn't ruin their lives. The gossip would soon die down and they would be able to get on with their lives.

Derek looked up at the sky, hoping that nothing else would go wrong – that nothing else would stand in the way of a brighter future.

Chapter Fifty-Six

The visit had been a good one, and though there should only have been two of them in the ward, none of the nurses had protested when all three of them went in together.

They had all driven home, happy but tired nonetheless. As John was going back to school in the morning, both he and Nora were in bed and asleep by ten.

Derek was still up, but by ten forty-five he was yawning. He decided to turn in, but then heard a short ring on the doorbell. He tensed, wondering who on earth would be calling at this time of night. Dreading more bad news he went downstairs.

When Derek cautiously opened the door, he peered into the gloom at the figure of a man. 'Yeah, what do you want?'

'It's me. Can I come in before somebody sees me?'

Derek reeled back in shock. He knew that voice, but it couldn't be him! It was impossible ... but even as the thought crossed his mind, the man stepped inside and swiftly closed the door.

'I read the newspapers and had to come.'

'B ... Bernie,' Derek gasped. 'You're not ... not dead.'

'No, though I made it look that way.'

'But they found your body!'

'As you can see, it couldn't have been mine.'

'Bloody hell, I can't believe this,' Derek said, still unable to believe that his eyes weren't deceiving him.

'I'm desperate to know how Pearl is,' Bernie said. 'I took a risk and went to the hospital, but a dragon of a nurse thought I was a reporter and threatened to call security. How is she, Derek?'

'Pearl had a rough time of it, but she's on the mend now,' Derek told him, though his mind was all over the place. This was like talking to a ghost, but Bernie was solid. Alive!

'I can't tell you how glad I am to hear that,' Bernie said, taking his hat off and running a hand over his face.

'Bernie, come upstairs. You've got a lot of explaining to do.'

Nothing was said then until they were in the living room, and after shutting the door Derek went to the sideboard. He took out a bottle of whisky, poured two glasses and downed his measure.

'I needed that,' he said, passing the other one to Bernie who did the same.

Derek then poured two more and they sat down.

'How is John?' Bernie asked.

'How do you think? He fell apart when he heard what happened to you. How could you do that to him, Bernie?'

'I just lost it, Derek. I couldn't take any more and was too wrapped up in myself to think about the consequences.'

'I don't get it? Take what?'

Bernie told Derek how he'd thought he was going senile until he'd found out that Dolly was slipping him her pills. He'd been sure too that Kevin was involved, that they were planning to get rid of him. He ended with how he had cut his hand to leave blood in the car, hoping it would be enough to convince the police that he was dead.

'Yeah, well, it worked,' Derek said dryly.

'I shouldn't have done it. I know that now. I should have gone to the police, told them what Dolly was up to.'

'She's lost her mind again,' Derek said. 'She had to be taken away.'

Bernie's eyebrows shot up, but then he said bluntly, 'Don't expect me to feel sorry for her.'

'I don't, but it was followed by what happened here – Pearl getting shot and Kevin dying in that fire at your cottage.'

'I should be mourning my son, but in all honesty I can't feel anything, just relief that he's not going to ruin any more lives. I don't know what sort of man that makes me, but Kevin meant everything to Dolly so it's no surprise she lost her mind.'

'As far as I know, she's hasn't been told that Kevin died. She lost it before then, and though I can't get much out of the psychiatrists, it seems she's in no fit state to be told.'

'I see,' Bernie mused, a thoughtful look in his eyes.

'What are you going to do now?' Derek asked.

'Now I know that Pearl's going to be all right, I'll disappear again.'

Derek felt a surge of anger. 'No, Bernie. I know you're alive now and I'm not prepared to keep up the pretence that you're dead. John thought the world of you and felt partly to blame when you supposedly took your own life. He needs to know you're alive, and though it'll be a shock, he'll be over the moon.'

Bernie hung his head for a moment, but then said, 'All right, Derek, for John's sake I'll stay, but I might end up in prison.'

'What do you mean?'

'I didn't have any life insurance policies, so fraud doesn't come into it, but I still faked my own death.'

'From what you've told me, you were in fear of your life. Dolly was giving you her drugs and no doubt they played with your mind. In the circumstances, I doubt it'll come to prison.'

'I hope you're right. I'll get some legal advice, but not until I've seen my grandson, and with your permission, Pearl too.'

'They're going to be as shocked as me and I think I'll have to prepare them first,' Derek told him. 'Can you come back tomorrow?'

'Yes, but if I'm spotted, someone might tell the police. I don't want to be arrested before I've seen them.'

'Bernie, you're hardly a criminal. All right, you faked your own death, but if anyone recognises you, I doubt it would occur to them to tell the police.'

'Maybe I am being overcautious, but as I said, I'm not ready to hand myself in yet.'

'If you're worried, make it after dark – around nine o'clock. By then I'll have told John and Pearl.'

'Yes, all right,' Bernie agreed.

'Where did you go after shoving your car over that cliff?'

'I went to Guernsey. I had money in a numbered account there and didn't really fancy going abroad.'

'I should think that's about the closest you could get to it,' Derek said.

'Maybe, but it's a lovely island.'

They spoke a little more and then Derek showed Bernie out. He went to bed, but found sleep impossible, his mind still unsettled.

At last Derek drifted off; his last thoughts as he did so that he'd tell Pearl about Bernie when he went to see her tomorrow lunchtime. He wouldn't say anything to John until he'd spoken to her.

Bernie slunk back to the boarding house, and after thinking deeply he woke the next morning with a sense of purpose. What Dolly had tried to do to him still played on his mind and now that he wasn't going to disappear again, he had to sort something out before handing himself in.

He'd hurt John badly, Bernie knew that, but now the boy's safety was paramount in his mind.

There had been a train journey first, then a taxi, but at last Bernie walked into the hospital and up to the reception desk. 'Good morning,' he said pleasantly. 'My name is Bernard Dolby and my wife is a patient here. I'd like to speak to her psychiatrist.'

'What is your wife's name?' the middle-aged woman asked.

'Dolores Dolby, but she's never used her full name. She's known as Dolly.'

'Please take a seat over there,' she pointed, 'while I find someone to talk to you.'

Bernie did as she asked and after watching her make an internal call, it wasn't long before a man appeared.

'Mr Dolby?'

'Yes, that's right.'

'My name is Doctor Alcott. You had better come to my office,' he said, leading Bernie down a corridor and into a room where he sat behind a desk, indicating a chair opposite. Without preamble, he then said, 'I was given to understand that Mrs Dolby's husband had died.'

'My wife was trying to kill me so I had to disappear, but as you can see, I'm very much alive.'

The doctor's eyes widened imperceptibly. He asked for some proof of identity, and then after opening a folder he scanned it before saying, 'Mrs Dolby was admitted after an assault on a bank manager, but since then she hasn't shown any signs of violence.'

'Yeah, well no doubt you've got her on medication again. She'd stopped taking any, and instead she was feeding her pills to me. She's a dangerous woman and shouldn't be released.'

'Mr Dolby, at the moment your wife isn't responding to treatment, nor is she cognitive. You should talk to the police, and I can assure you that if it's felt she's a danger to society, she won't be released.'

'I'll do that, but before I go, can I see her?'

'It would have to be under supervision.'

'I'd still like to see her.'

The man pursed his lips for a moment, but

then said, 'Very well, come with me.'

Once again Bernie was following the psychiatrist, this time to a large room where he saw patients sitting on chairs, some rocking back and forth, some mumbling, and others pacing. Surprised, Bernie said, 'Dolly's in here?'

'We felt that putting her amongst other patients might stimulate a response,' Doctor Alcott said.

Bernie scanned the room and his eyes came to rest on Dolly. She was another one sitting in a chair, but as he drew closer, he saw that her face was void of any animation and her eyes looked vacant.

'Mrs Dolby, Dolly, there's someone here to see you,' Doctor Alcott said.

Bernie crouched down in front of her, 'Hello, Dolly.'

Nothing, not a flicker of recognition, but then one of the other patients began to play up and a nurse called out to the doctor. 'I won't be a moment, Mr Dolby,' he said.

Bernie felt that he was probably wasting his time, but nevertheless he hoped that somehow his words would get through. 'Dolly,' he hissed as soon as the man was out of earshot, 'Kevin is dead. Did you hear me? Your precious son is dead!'

For a brief moment Bernie thought he saw something in Dolly's eyes, but then it was gone and there was no other response. Had she heard him? He hoped so. His knees ached from crouching, but before he left, Bernie had one last thing to say. 'I'm going now, and I won't be back. Goodbye, Dolly.'

With John at school, and Lucy keeping an eye on Nora, Derek was alone when he arrived at the hospital to see Pearl.

He found her sitting in a chair by the side of her bed, but she rose to her feet when she saw him, her eyes shining as she said, 'Guess what? I saw the consultant this morning and he said I can come home on Friday.'

'Pearl, that's great news,' he said, and fearful of hurting her back, his hug was gentle. 'Do you feel all right about coming back to the flat?'

'Surprisingly, yes, and anyway, I haven't got a lot of choice. We agreed to abide by Bessie's will, made it our home now and there's the shop. I've got to take it easy for a while, but Lucy can look after it for me, and I've also got to attend out-patients regularly.'

'I'll make sure you do, but sit down again, love. I've got a bit of news too.'

'Not bad, I hope.'

'No, but you're going to be shocked. I certainly was,' he said as he drew up another chair. 'I ... err ... I had a visitor late last night. You know we thought that Bernie took his own life? Well ... err ... he didn't. He's still alive.'

'What!' Pearl cried, her eyes rounding. 'Who told you? Are they sure?'

'Bernie was the visitor, love.'

'Oh my God,' Pearl gasped. 'But it was ages ago when he drove over that cliff. How on earth did he survive?'

'He wasn't in the car. He faked his death.'

'But why?' Pearl asked.

Derek repeated what Bernie had told him, and Pearl listened without interruption, finally saying, 'So the body they found, or part of one, wasn't his?'

'No, it must have been some other poor sod.'

'Derek, did John see Bernie?'

'No, he was in bed and asleep. I didn't tell him this morning, thought it best to speak to you first. I told Bernie not to come back until nine this evening. Now it's up to you, love. I can tell John when he comes home from school, or wait until we visit you and we can break it to him together.'

'I think we should do it together, but when he finds out why Bernie faked his own death, I don't know how he's going to feel about Dolly.'

'She has a lot to answer for. John doesn't know what she did to you either, but I think it's about time the whole truth came out.'

'No, Derek,' Pearl said firmly. 'That's all in the past and best left there. John's had enough to cope with, but at least he'll have his grandfather back in his life again and I think that's going to make him very happy.'

'Yes, I'm sure you're right, and he'll be even happier when he hears that you're coming home on Friday.'

When John came home from school, Derek saw the bruises and his torn school blazer.

'What happened to you,' he asked.

'I got into a fight. A couple of boys said some nasty things about my mum and I wasn't going to stand for that.'

'Fair enough, but try not to make a habit of it,'

Derek said. He'd have done the same and was inwardly proud of John.

'Is John naughty boy?' Nora asked.

'No, he's just normal.'

'I thought you'd go potty, Dad.'

'I'm in much too good a mood, son,' Derek said, smiling.

'Why?'

'You'll find out soon enough. For now, get cleaned up, and after dinner we're off to see your mum.'

'Me come too?'

'No, sorry, love, but I'll take you tomorrow. I'm going to drop you off at Lucy's and you can play with Clive,' Derek told her, glad that he'd had the forethought to arrange this with Lucy. He'd only told her that he and Pearl needed to talk to John alone, and thankfully she hadn't probed.

Later, when they dropped Nora off, she didn't complain, and soon they were at the hospital. They both hugged Pearl, and then Derek said, 'Well, what shall we tell John first?'

Pearl smiled. 'That I'm coming home on Friday.'

'You are? Mum, that's great,' John said beaming with delight.

'Now you know why I was in such a good mood,' Derek said as they both sat down.

'John, we have something else to tell you. It's good news too, though you'll be shocked at first. I certainly was,' Pearl said, but then hesitated as though to gather her thoughts. 'John, your dad had a visitor last night, and ... and well, I'll let him tell you who it was.'

Derek took over, relating the story as he had to

Pearl, and though initially stunned, by the time he came to an end, John was clutching Pearl's hand and blinking back tears.

'I can't believe it,' he gasped.

'It's come as a shock to all of us,' Pearl said, 'but don't you think it's a nice one?'

'Yes, yes, it's great ... but how could my gran do that to him?'

'Darling, you have to remember that she's mentally ill and unstable.'

John nodded, but then his eyes brightened as he looked at Derek. 'Where is my granddad? I want to see him.'

'You'll be doing that not long after we get home. I told him to come round at nine o'clock.'

John looked overjoyed at that, and Derek was looking forward to seeing their reunion. Bernie would still have a few problems to face, interviews with the police and so on, but at least John would have his grandfather back in his life again.

Pearl grinned at him and Derek leaned forward to kiss her. They may have been through hell, but they'd come out the other side able to smile again. 'I love you, Mrs Lewis.'

'And I love you,' she whispered back.

Derek squeezed her free hand, feeling as though a new chapter was beginning. Pearl would be home soon and they had the rest of their lives to look forward to – a life he hoped would be filled with love and laughter.

The publishers hope that this book has given you enjoyable reading. Large Print Books are especially designed to be as easy to see and hold as possible. If you wish a complete list of our books please ask at your local library or write directly to:

Magna Large Print Books
Magna House, Long Preston,
Skipton, North Yorkshire.
BD23 4ND

This Large Print Book for the partially sighted, who cannot read normal print, is published under the auspices of

THE ULVERSCROFT FOUNDATION